The author insists all the characters in *Orchid Territory* are purely imaginary except for Aunt Charlotte, who is based on Dame Judy Dench playing Queen Elizabeth the First and her grandmother playing herself.

"In that curious, semi-closed world of South Florida's orchid growers, passions run high, politics are to the death and nothing is more important than the prizes at the Miami Orchid Expo. With her perceptive eye and vivid pen, the English author creates a charming story full of humor and wicked comedy. In among the orchids and the long knives of a decades-long feud are the glorious anthropological insights into social interactions among the characters of the author's world. There is also romance to keep us in suspense till the last page."

— *The Orchid Review*

Orchid Territory

A Comic Novel

by

Mary Motes

With grateful thanks to
Jan, Janell and especially Jo-Anne

Orchid Territory

Book design by Jo-Anne Rosen
Wordrunner Publishing Services, Petaluma, California

Library of Congress Control Number: 2005906987

ISBN: 0-9674343-2-7

Published by Redland Press
25000 Farmlife Road
Redland, Florida 33031
PHONE: 305-247-4398 FAX: 305-248-0216
vandas@mindspring.com

For
Martin

and also Bart and Alice
who were never taken to
Disneyworld because
there was always too much
to do in the orchid house.

Contents

1

Fetching the Pig

The dead pig jiggled behind Mark, sliding lightheartedly to and fro on a piece of bloodstained cardboard. Carlos was driving the old Volvo station wagon fast along the side of a field, creating a tunnel of dust so dense he'd put the windscreen wipers on. "We're in the dry season now, dear boy!" Aunt Charlotte had announced. Mark could taste the grit in his mouth but with a dead pig just behind him, preferred the windows open.

Here the land was so flat the South Florida sky seemed to tower right over the windscreen. It made Mark feel, warm as he was, that in this part of the world when you really got down to it, when the gloves were off, whether you were a pig or not, nature was basically cold and implacable. He hadn't expected to watch a pig die on Christmas Eve. The man called Ricardo had shot it with a pistol and then dragged it over to a tub and slit its throat. Worse, he'd done it in front of the other pigs. Perched on a rail above the squealing, Carlos had been more interested in the double row of home-made benches across the yard. "Ricardo ... *fights the birds!*" He'd shaken his head and grinned: *"Cubanos!"*

Cockfighting. It was the most Carlos had said to Mark since he'd arrived. On the way home Mark wanted to ask him if Mexicans practiced cockfighting, too. "Do the people in your country also," he repeated carefully, '*fight the birds?*' "

Carlos, a Mexican from Texas, always put on his cowboy hat when he drove. He wore it low and straight across his forehead like a bullfighter and was now frowning hard under the brim. Maybe, thought Mark, it's my English accent. As for Spanish, he knew if he went on trying to find out whether Mexicans indulged in the illegal sport of cockfighting, the closest he'd come would probably be: "Do your people make war with chickens?"

Carlos was, in Aunt Charlotte's words, "Orchid Empire's general dogs-body." Every morning he watered the orchids, every few days he fertilized them and once a week sprayed them with a variety of chemicals and mixes from a cluster of canisters and containers at the back of the shed. He also kept an eye on Rosita who did the potting and tidying and, since Mark had arrived, paid attention to him when required with an unselfconscious, formal courtesy that Aunt Charlotte avowed had not been seen in the average British worker since the beginning of the First World War. He called on reliable family members at show and sale times for extra help and this afternoon had been in charge of going out to Ricardo's on the edge of the Everglades and choosing the Christmas Pig. And he did all this at two dollars over minimum wage. "If anyone tries to steal Carlos away," Charlotte declared, "I will kill them."

They were on the main road now, heading towards Homestead. On either side U Pick fields open to the road were festive with winter tomatoes, sweet peppers and strawberries. Some had rows of annuals, mostly snapdragons and asters. This was the old farming belt south of South Miami, 'the winter garden of the United States.' Wayside stands announced: MALANGA, CALABASA, CARAMBOLA, YUCCA, GUAVA, MAMEY, COCO FRIO, PAPAYA, COCONUS 4 SEL. Many of the 'S's' were written backwards which made Mark, fresh from teaching Remedial English in North London, feel right at home. There was Daisy's U Pick and Glad Farms and a majestic field bursting with golden sunflowers which, according to a modest sign at the front, was *Guarded by Smith and Wesson*. A little further on an acre of strawberries declared: THIS FIELD IS PROTECTED THREE NIGHTS A WEEK YOU GUESS WHICH THREE.

Aunt Charlotte had been in this part of Florida, south of South Miami, for the last twenty odd years. South Florida, she said, "would see her out." Now, just hitting eighty and judging by her nightly intake, ninety percent pickled in gin, this seemed more than likely especially since the fall that had put her in a wheel chair and Mark in South Florida.

"Your aunt really needs you," his mother had said, calling one morning just as he was off to North London's Totters Green Comprehensive in a chill December rain. "She's broken her leg at the worst possible time, apparently. It's coming up to show season in the orchid world."

It had been good timing for Mark. He was not only escaping the December Preliminary Assessment Grading Period Report and 'We Are One World,' the Totters Green annual Christmas pageant but was now basking in warm winter sunlight. So if only it weren't for the Spanish, the flat and colorless South Florida landscape that looked about as exotic as Norfolk in November, the bloodstained pig, Aunt Charlotte and the whole business of orchids, everything would have been fine.

2

Christmas Eve: Preparations for the Party

"**Y**ou forgot the gin!" Topped off with a baseball cap from Bill's Bait and Tackle, the bad leg sticking straight out and aimed dead at him, Aunt Charlotte was grinding over the gravel in her high tech wheel chair. Watching her advance with a menacing whine Mark found himself thinking of those old wartime newsreels: '*Germany Mobilizes!*'

"Well, no one else drinks the stuff. Just keep my bottle on the porch. Get me refills as we go, water *and* ice. Can't afford to get blotto too early!"

Sporting a leathery tan from so long in the hot bits of the former British Empire, Charlotte looked pretty good for eighty and all that gin. Mark had promised his mother at Heathrow he'd see Aunt Charlotte took her pills. But the labels all said *Warning: Avoid Alcohol.* Charlotte had lifted her chin and stared at him for what had seemed a very long time the first evening he got up enough courage, after a couple of beers, to point this out. Mark reminded his mother on the phone that if Charlotte had been an intimidating aunt when she was small, she should see her now, over fifty years later with a second large gin in her hand. In fact, Charlotte was not his aunt, but his mother's, which made her a Great Aunt and when Mark met her there was no doubt in his mind that was indeed what she was.

Carlos had laid planks across the porch steps creating a makeshift ramp so Charlotte's chair could get out of the house and round the corner to the two small orchid houses unaided. Half hidden in a welter of philodendrons, bamboo, bromeliads and cycads, the porch looked like an ideal place to squirrel away a quart of gin. The broken rail had been patched with a piece of chicken wire and the rest of the bale was still there, together with a spade, two worn down maize brooms, some curly lengths of dusty driftwood and a forty pound bag of dog chow. When Charlotte died, she said the old, one-storey wooden house would be put on the market as a 'Handyman Special.'

"Dade County pine, wood's so hard, bends nails. Built by the first settlers. Their kids are still alive! Roads round here named after their fathers! Now, of course, going to hell in a handbasket like everywhere else. Well, it'll see me out."

Orchid Empire was tucked into two and a half acres in Redland, "last bit of green south of South Miami," still dotted with mango and avocado groves. Creepers and vines thick as monkeys' tails were taking over Charlotte's trees. Young palms, 'volunteers,' grew up haphazardly through their branches and some were curtained in grey Spanish moss, like an old black and white film with swamps, convicts and alligators. Mark had come across the remains of a giant mango, felled in some long distant hurricane, wreathed in vegetation and hard to distinguish, like some sunken ocean liner on the sea floor. Under the mahogany tree facing the porch hung two stag-horn ferns big as chandeliers but there were no orchids in sight.

"The last thing I want to do at the end of the day" Charlotte said, "is look at a damn orchid."

Fresh from England, Mark was amazed that no-one considered the possibility that it might rain. All the preparations for the Christmas Eve party were going on out of doors. After breakfast he was helping Carlos set up sheets of plywood on saw horses in front of the orchid houses which were still dripping from the early watering. One of Carlos' many aunts had been up all night, holding vigil over the twenty-four hour roasting of the pig, Cuban style, in a pit behind the orchid houses. A dignified old lady in a large apron, she wore a faded black T-shirt that read RAGE AGAINST THE MACHINE. A find from the Florida City Swap Meet, Mark guessed, like Charlotte's second hand Extra Large mens' shirts. Two more aunts were coming along that evening with the food.

"It's something of a Christmas Eve tradition wondering what will turn up on their fronts. Over the years, judging from the T-shirts, a surprising number seem to have served in the Marines. I'm still hoping for one to beat two years ago: 'Coon Hunters for Christ!'"

Sitting on the porch with Charlotte after the trip to Ricardo's, Mark had muttered that the pig was *alive* when Carlos picked it out.

"I am reassured to hear this creature was trotting about till the very last minute, bright eyed and bushy tailed! In much of the world, my boy, blood on the stairs does *not* mean voodoo but old fashioned quality control!" Charlotte, squinting into the sun going down behind the mahogany tree, sounded wistful. Mark reflected there had to be a smart comment there somewhere: *one way of explaining a bloodstained British Empire—old-fashioned quality control!* but thought better of it.

"Now it's dismembered carcasses in the supermarket: '*USDA Fresh!*' What? United States Department of Agriculture! What? The *other* pigs? Well you ARE a namby pamby!"

It was at moments like these that Mark felt Charlotte, after just one week, was basically keeping him around because unlike Americans he knew how to make a strong cup of tea. As for him, it was only because the weather was so good and the alternative was teaching remedial English in north London in January, that he didn't pay the penalty on his British Air Super Saver three month excursion ticket and just clear off.

Mark told himself he should have known; he had grown up with stories of Aunt Charlotte. She was named after Charles Darwin, his mother said, "And everyone could see why." When small, he and his sister had played Tigers with the narrow old cheetah skin that had been "shot outside Charlotte's tent in Africa." Every Christmas and birthday there would be the postcards: on one side waterfalls, coconut palms and elephants, women with long necks ringed in metal collars, half naked men in canoes holding spears, tea plantations, bunches of bananas and later on, the occasional dam and on the other, in

Charlotte's commanding hand, injunctions to work harder at school and not worry his poor mother. Charlotte had not actually seen Mark since he was about two years old and running around beating his toy drum and the cat but Mark could tell as soon as he put down his bag on the porch, that she was already considering he had not made much of the intervening twenty odd years.

Carlos was taking Christmas off and then going back to Texas for New Year so with Carlos gone Charlotte would have to rely on Mark, whether she wanted to or not. He had been out at seven thirty every morning that week to see how Carlos did the watering. "The key to everything!" Charlotte had declared. "If your watering is wrong, might as well throw your orchids away! In fact, *you will* end up throwing your orchids away! They all march to a different drummer. Remember: If a *Cattleya* looks like it needs watering, water it *tomorrow*. If a *Vanda* looks like it needs watering, water it *today*. If a *Phalaenopsis* or a *Paphiopedilum* does, you should have watered it YESTERDAY."

Right! thought Mark. Of course, it did depend on whether you could recognize any of them in the first place. There were almost no orchids in Charlotte's two greenhouses that looked like anything he'd seen in Marks and Spencers or one of the garden shops and there were almost no flowers. Rows of plants of varying sizes and shapes, some just green or brown clumps, crowded on to the benches. They were stuck into the wire along the side walls, hanging overhead in baskets, sprouting from coconut shells, clinging on to twigs and pieces of wood or in little wire pots with tufts of stuffing coming out. Like an aviary, thought Mark; orchids perched everywhere like dust colored sparrows and little finches on twigs and baskets, with an odd, exotic bird here and there sporting a brilliant crest or bizarre plumage and sudden nests of tiny orchid flowers with wide open throats like the outstretched gullets of hungry fledglings.

Mark had not got off to a good start with his aunt or the orchids. On his second day, trying to be useful, he had done a little tidying up in one of the greenhouses. Charlotte, who maneuvered her wheelchair into any odd corner when it suited her, informed him with relish half an hour later that he'd just thrown away her entire collection of deciduous dendrobiums and catasetums. "These dendrobiums are the Himalayan species! They're *supposed* to 'look dead!' The only way to grow `em in South Florida is to *ignore* them for half the year—recreate their native environment—dry period before the monsoon! Now, what's 'snail bait' in Spanish?"

Having been told not to fiddle with anything in the orchid houses and make the "basic shambles" any worse, Mark had felt free to relax. There was the watering and the daily warning from Charlotte that she did not suffer fools gladly but apart from that, he had three months 'all found' as Charlotte put it, unlimited winter sun, someone else who didn't give a hoot about housework or a balanced diet and apparently a totally unlimited budget when it came to alcohol. As Ned, his Aussie mate, was to ask plaintively in his very first email: "Why you, you undeserving bastard?"

Mark had made a diagram of the bizarre irrigation system:("Turn on the left switch for the *other* house but make sure the valves are open on the right except the one in the middle. That's the one you need a wrench for.") And though he didn't hold out much hope for Charlotte's party, hardly the place to run across someone like the busty blonde at The Rat and Parrot, he had landed up during the South Florida winter season when Miami, Coconut Grove and South Beach were hot.

But on Christmas Eve morning, wrestling with the festive plywood table tops, Mark felt only dread. Overnight everything had changed. He and Charlotte had been enjoying one last drink on the porch as thousands of insects chirped around them in the velvety night when out of nowhere she suddenly declared: "God help us, you HAVE to be Orchid Empire's new orchid man! What? The Queen's sniffing blood in the water, that's what! Carlos can't cope with her or her hangers on especially if they cart me off to hospital again. Doesn't have the English for a start. But I'm damned if my *Bonatea speciosa's* going to fall into the wrong hands! Can't just get that kind of material anymore. Not much to look at but for those who know...*Most* African orchids rather pallid, dear boy, from 'The Dark Continent!' Problem is I've made an enemy or two." Mark could well believe it. "We'll start you off at the party. Just put on that schoolboy stammer you used to have and that vacant look. Hold her off…That's it! My brilliant, dotty nephew taking inventory! Looking to inherit the whole damn thing! We'll talk it up on Christmas Eve. Be all round the region by Boxing Day!"

It was impossible to argue with Charlotte in the evening after a drink or two, or actually, thought Mark, tossing and turning later on the lumpy bed in the spare room, in the morning either. He had no idea what was going on in the orchid world of South Florida and wondered how much of this Charlotte would remember in the clear light of day but was sure it would be more than enough to make his life miserable. It was two in the morning. The spare room, cluttered as it was with books and magazines, was certainly full of relevant material for a budding orchidist. Mark had turned on the light. There were stacks of old orchid journals everywhere and trade magazines like *Greenhouse Grower* and *Ornamental Outlook:* "'Floramite' Gives you Three More Weeks of Improved Mite Control." IRRIGATION OPTIONS—Was Carlos using the *Misty Mist Nozzles*, the *Pin-Perfect Nozzles* or the *Nifty Nozzles*? Try translating THAT into Spanish. If he said all that to Rosita she'd probably slap his face.

Mark had pulled out an old *American Orchid Society* magazine from a stack and opened at random: *CHONDRORHYNCHA Native habitat: Mexico, Central America and Tropical South America—tribe: Maxillarieae: Subtribe; Zygopetalinae. Typical confusion leads to the very same species being sold as both Chondrorhyncha AND Cochleanthes.*

Christ. Aunt Charlotte was right. She'd been saying orchid people were nuts and here she was, the nuttiest: *You are Orchid Empire's orchid man!* She'd already warned him that orchidists would hunt you down mercilessly over the simplest mistake, a wrong label, a missing 'varietal epithet,' whatever that was. Even the mother of all stammers couldn't get him round this. He'd need to be deaf and dumb. But he saw the eager, friendly orchidists approaching—"So sad! Brilliant but trapped in his silent world! Here! I have a pen and paper!" He'd have to be the brilliant deaf and dumb orchidist with crippling arthritis. No, they'd show him pictures: they wouldn't let him alone. They'd be out to get him. "If you think this is *Chondrorhyncha* not *Cochleanthes*—just nod!"

Christ. He'd been hoping the old bird would have forgotten about it all by morning. But bright and early on Christmas Eve as he made the tea Charlotte had reminded him he was now her resident orchid scholar. "Just lie low tonight and put on your stammer. Piece of cake for you! Most Yanks think even standard Brits are pretty feeble and neurotic, anyway. You'll be perfect, dear boy."

3

❀

The Party

Dusk had started to fall but it was still early. Rosita was unfolding twin size paisley sheets to cover the plywood tables which were labeled with a cryptic word or two: 'Lge Bdrm,' 'Kchen Mid,' 'Bth Rear.' "Hurricane shutters," Charlotte said. "Nailed up once or twice since Andrew but nothing's hit. Andrew was the big one, of course, in 'ninety-two; at least a four, maybe five bottle storm. Hurricanes were classified by booze before the Samper Simpson scale! Andrew came so fast, no time to stock up! Carlos and I managed to save the breeding collection, stuck 'em everywhere—on the floor, on the chairs. This old house went through `26 and `35 so I knew I was alright."

Mark was impressed. He remembered Hurricane Andrew had been called the greatest civilian disaster in US history. They'd heard nothing for days, thinking Charlotte had gone down with her orchids, like the three men with the dream boat they'd been building. "It was the most *expensive!*" Charlotte snorted. "If they'd brought over a bunch of Haitians they could have rebuilt Homestead in a week from what people dumped by the side of the road!"

Rosita was putting candles into little glass bowls and Mark lit them and helped her hang them from the branches on either side of the drive so they seemed to float among the leaves. Her beautiful eyes were cast down and she had pressed her silent lips tight together as though to stop from smiling. As with Carlos, Mark felt he was the young Lord of the Manor in some BBC Heritage production, more likely the young, unworthy brother. He'd be the one sleeping with the parlor maids and shipped off to Australia.

Charlotte had insisted on bringing out the old hurricane lamps. Carlos and Rosita had cleaned them up and trimmed the wicks. "People like them. They lend atmosphere." They would also help people see what they were doing. Charlotte refused to have lights around the house and along the path, the sort of illuminated area recommended by the Dade County Police Department and Florida Power and Light. "Andrew was good," she said. "Took out the power grid. I like to see the stars." Mark could tell Charlotte liked even more to see people trip and stumble about in the dark especially if they were what she called 'townies.' Townies were people who couldn't walk along a path by moonlight, breathe without air conditioning or face a bug in simple, unarmed combat, one on one. "—Who are scared of the *real* Florida!" Staying with Aunt Charlotte was the real Florida alright. There were oranges and bananas behind the house, scorpions in the wood pile and snakes in the potting shed. "I've finally convinced Carlos snakes *prefer* to clear off, *will* just clear off—if you're not pounding them into the ground with a *shovel!* Scorpions? I've long wanted to write a little article: 'Scorpions as an aid to housework' for *Home and Garden. Meticulous* scavengers and bug hunters, very good against the wily cockroach. And they use those tails for balance like squirrels. What? Well, shake your shoes out, dear."

At 6.30 Mark went to get ready. He reappeared in slacks and a long-sleeved, white cotton shirt, nothing formal, but this was Orchid Empire's annual event and he was related to the owner. "They'll all think you're the waiter!" Charlotte crowed. "Down here, in 'deep South Dade' as they call us, long sleeves are for bankers and high ups in the supermarkets." She thought a moment, "Ha! and poor souls picking limes. Those key limes are the devil for thorns."

The lights of Carlos' truck swung round past the porch. He had brought back another pair of Mexican aunts, both as broad, bronze and mellow as though they'd just flown in from Tahiti. The new aunts had brought large earthenware bowls heaped with black beans and rice and metal trays of fried plantains. "Cuban fare to go with the pork. Standard now in South Florida like your fish and chips. Or, now I hear, *curry* and chips! Right! Let's check the T-shirts!" Charlotte was disappointed: this Christmas the tally was one MIAMI-DADE PARKS DEPARTMENT and a fading TOMMY HILFIGER. Carlos, smart in Texan boots, black shirt and silver buckle on his belt, was ready behind the pig, its smoky snout facing the drinks table. Underneath the pig were the dogs, pretending they weren't there. Normally they sprawled dramatically across the gravel at dinner time enacting their evening tableau: *Dogs Die of Hunger as Owners Ignore Plight.* Charlotte had three: Tod, mostly Great Dane, Bella, a mix of Lab and "God knows what" and Nip, an obnoxious little black and orange stray. "Nip attacks anything but only when Tod's around as back up so Nip's not so stupid as he looks."

Charlotte was in a crisp white shirt herself, the sleeves rolled up. Another Men's Extra Large that might have cost all of a dollar at the swap meet, Mark guessed. With everything ready she buzzed her chair along the drive beside Mark, checking the candle lights among the leaves.

"Something smells really beautiful."

"*Brassavola cordata,* unobtrusive native. Put just a few in the trees around the porch, sweetly fragrant at night. Now here's the *Sapodilla* tree. Jamaicans call them *naseberry*—sounds old English to me. You could check that out. Before mangoes became common they say down here it was always just 'sours' and 'dillies'—key limes and *sapodillas.* Fruit grainy, like a pear. Sap yields chicle—used to be shipped out of Mexico and Central America to make chewing gum. Now that's something to tell your class! Here's a *loquat,* the 'Japanese plum.' See how close these two are to the house? Always the sign of an old South Florida home-site. Planted by the early settlers, hurricane resistant. There's an ackee tree out near the mangoes. You know Jamaicans: 'Ackee, salt fish and rice!' They were on the phone after Andrew; 'Charlotte! *What* about the ackee tree?' Shame there won't be any of my old Jamaican pals here for the party. This will be my last—say that every year!"

Mark was trying to think clearly. He needed Charlotte to talk about orchids and orchid people, not fruit and trees. "What? Oh, the same old crowd. Commercial growers will be at the New Year's Eve do. Run by the Queen. Now *there's* blood on the stairs for you! Not enough coming for a whole pig like the old days but it'll be good for Carlos and Rosita to take home afterwards. What? —You don't have to know a *thing,* dear boy! A lot of orchid judges haven't grown a damn orchid in years! All you need to remember for judging is that you've always seen a better one of whatever it is, last year or in another region."

Mark was thinking perhaps he could play the part of a brilliant, *alcoholic* orchid scholar. That would be easy enough. Get drunk as a stoat early on and wobble off ("Merry Chrishmash!") and slide down under the chewing gum tree. "Charlotte! *Listen!* Your wonderful new 'orchid man' can't recognize one damn plant in your greenhouses!"

"You would, dear boy, if the phalaenopsis were in bloom! Whites and pinks are common as muck now. Most of this lot coming wouldn't be seen dead with a standard phal! Just stand back and let them ramble on. What did you do when you were young? No more train-spotting? Well, anyway, think train-spotters and bird watchers or stamp collectors and—that's enough— there's your orchid nut. And you'll meet them tonight."

By now it was already seven forty. "Charlotte, looks like no one's coming." Mark wondered if he could be that lucky.

"Oh, the old timers will tell you: long before the Cubans there was always 'Miami time.'"

Sure enough, at that moment Tod, Bella and Nip scrambled out barking from under the table and they heard the first car coming up the drive. And with the suddenness of a Florida sunset, people were arriving, had arrived, and the party was on. Charlotte was right: there were no long sleeves, only T-shirts and jeans, slacks, shorts, Indian cotton skirts and a solid woman in a lime green halter top. The most formal attire on display was a whole archive of T-shirts on a variety of chests and the hilly terrain of aging bosoms, advertising various orchid societies and past shows fading away back ten years or more. All arrivals made a beeline for Charlotte's chair. This was the first time she had been seen since the accident; apparently she had told everyone firmly not to visit. "On the mend! On the mend! My fault. Tried to pollinate the damn thing myself. Should have waited for Rachel, I know, I know...ALL our ladders are wonky! And *then* the damn pod didn't take!"

Mark, bringing Charlotte her second gin and lime, reported he'd seen someone slipping into the orchid house behind the trestle tables.

"Tall and thin? Pony tail? Some daft T-shirt?"

"Yes, blood red. Said PACIFISTS FIGHT FOR PEACE."

"That's Cooper, our *Vanda* man. Into fragrance! Doing some interesting breeding, back to species."

"He hasn't come out."

"Oh he always slides round the tables and disappears. He's thin enough."

"But there's no light on."

"Oh, that's how Coop likes it. He has a hard job with people. I just tell him, Cooper, don't pee on anything."

"—*Brassavola cordata,* Charlotte, if I'm not mistaken!" A large man in boy scout shorts was advancing on Charlotte's chair.

"*Exactly* what you're smelling, Cliff! In the Everglades you have *Epidendrum nocturnum*, Mark, another fragrant white native. But, if you're talking breeding, you need the Jamaican, Cliff! Far superior— prettier, heartshaped lip, more flowers on the stem!" Mark moved away carefully, grateful for the hurricane lamps' gentle glow, no probing 100 watt bulbs overhead checking out his credentials.

"*Ah! You* are Charlotte's nephew!" A woman with straight, iron grey hair and brand new jeans stiff as a board. She was pulled down on the left side by a big black shoulder bag that matched her glasses. Mark had seen her bending over Charlotte's chair, holding the bag back with both hands so it wouldn't swing forward and knock her out cold. Now she had Mark cornered. He could feel the sharp edge of the plywood table under the paisley sheet as he tried to move back. She thrust out her hand, "*I'm* Marjorie!" Mark felt uneasy. The words were said with the air of "At *last* you can put a face to the name!" "Of *course!*" he exclaimed, with an air of finally being able to put a face to the name while a voice inside yelled *Stop! You'll get in deeper and deeper!* "Well, so what do you think?" demanded Marjorie.

God knows. She'd had a face lift? Decided on jeans after a lifetime in Indian cotton? "Aahh...Well...I think... first I need to get you a drink!"

"Charlotte *must* have told you *that's* where we part the ways!"

"Um. How wise! Ah…a juice…"

"Not after what happened in Panama!" Marjorie swung the bag away from her shoulder and into the backside of a passing orchidist.

"Marjorie! Glad you could make it." Charlotte had driven up. "So you've met my nephew."

"Well, yes. Charlotte—"

"You need a drink, dear girl! Nonsense! Carlos has made just the thing! It's a very light punch his grandmother used to make for the children!" It was rose pink and fragrant and laced with vodka. "Not *laced*, dear boy!" Charlotte had protested. "I merely wafted the bottle over it. We need something that gets under the radar." Mark thought she must have had Marjorie in mind.

"Charlotte, I've asked your nephew—"

"Oh, let him get settled first! No snap judgments!" Charlotte had obviously decided to come to Mark's aid. He could have leant forward like the others and kissed her too. "You know, Bert's been looking for you. He needs your advice, your wise counsel. Ah! There he is! Rescue him from the Johnsons, would you?"

"Who *is* she?" Mark muttered as Marjorie made off, steering her bag through the guests.

"Student judge, 'researching African species,' God help us. I think it's all in her handbag! Not going to do her any good in this region. She wants to organize my collection, what's left of it. Just tell her you're looking forward to a quiet afternoon with her and my *Bonatea speciosa.*" Charlotte wheeled away.

"Oh *my*, Charlotte's nephew!" Mark was grateful the way Americans said the word. It could never match the John Wayne tough *Son* or *Dad*—but at least in American English the whispy English *nefffew*, had a hardy sound: *nev-yew.* A spondee, if you wanted to get technical, like Amen. "I *love* your accent!" The lime green halter was in front. Very much in front. "London! You are *so* lucky! We were there— which year was that, Earl? Well, anyway, it was uniquely wonderful! Charlotte? You know one winter we went on safari. Fell in love with the whole scene and can you believe when we got back we found Charlotte in our own backyard!"

They were snow-birds from Chicago. Earl had a boat down in the Keys and they stayed for the winter. "You know we don't even buy orchids anymore but Charlotte doesn't mind. She's just darling!" It was true, Charlotte seemed more tolerant of the idea of visitors than locals. Earl and his wife had certainly brought themselves to a well-oiled, light brown sheen, probably like the woodwork on their boat. It was the local residents Charlotte called the townies or sometimes co-lonials she couldn't stand: those who had come from the chillier parts of the U S and brought their gray little worlds with them. They wore polyester and permanent scowls; not the result of facing into the sun, Charlotte declared, but figuring out how much their air conditioning was going to cost them next summer.

"Well, it must be hard, you know, here, in the summer when basically most people are living in concrete boxes," Mark said.

"Then they shouldn't build concrete boxes!" Charlotte had snapped.

It certainly wouldn't be hard to revert to a schoolboy stammer. Mark only had to be addressed as 'orchidist' and his throat tightened up straight away. But so far no one at the party appeared to be brooding about the treacherous similarities between *Chondrorhyncha* and *Cochleanthes*. And as Charlotte's nephew he could hold the conversation to legs, fractures, Charlotte's defective ladders (that damn swap meet! those frugal Brits!) the American medical system, (a nightmare but so-cialized medicine had ended Britain as a world power) and Charlotte's wonderful character. And then it was either time to take the guest back to Charlotte for an audience or another guest had arrived and he could excuse himself and begin all over again. Mark was starting to think he might survive the South Florida orchid scene after all.

Charlotte, holding forth hale and hearty, looked like she had an-other ten good years in her. There seemed no chance of her getting more tired than her guests as she was the only one sitting down. He went up to check one more time to see if she needed a refill and saw her suddenly look a little weary. "Oh, here comes Tilly," she mur-mured. A tiny woman of uncertain age, Tilly looked as though she was being overtaken by a pair of sharply pressed khaki shorts, that if she didn't fight back would not stop until they reached her armpits. "Charlotte! I know this isn't the moment but I do have to bring to your attention our old friend 1356. 1356 *should* have been the little white *Encyclia* Moby Dick, the *mariae* one I was *so* looking forward to blooming out and what do I get but a bright yellow mini-cat! That can *only* be *Laeliocattleya* Memoria Doris Lackley Smith! Labeling! Charlotte, labels! Numbers!"

"Bring it back, dear, bring it back, but Doris Lackley Smith is a *far* superior cross and would have cost you twice as much."

"Oh, this was at the Society. I got it in the raffle, so it's not that. It's just, Charlotte, it's your numbers. Far be it from me..."

"Have a drink, Tilly! Look, there's Bert, he'll get you something." In spite of Tilly it was all going very well. The vodka laced punch was doing its job among the teetotalers. Marjorie had put down her big black shoulder bag among the dogs under the pig table and was talking to Carlos through a large piece of crackling. There must have been about thirty guests. Bert, obviously an old friend, was maybe a well-preserved seventy. He called Charlotte Charley and whenever he encountered Mark commanded "You look after her!" He was sitting now on the low coral wall in front of the closest orchid house, Charlotte's chair alongside. They were talking hard, occasionally looking his way. A few minutes later they were joined by Chris, the large man dressed like a boy scout. Charlotte waved Mark over. "As Mark reminds me, Chris, my problem's always been so many of the African ones won't grow here. Wrong elevation! Now, Central and South America—there's your treasure trove! *Greatest diversification of orchid species anywhere!* In the old days, Mark, Bert will tell you, any *hobbyist* who spoke a little bad Spanish could go down to Guatemala, Peru, where-ever, round up a cab driver, show the village kids a plant, offer two cents each and come back next day to *mounds* of orchids by the road."

"Airline pilots,'said Bert. "If they had a two day lay over. Same thing."

"And thank goodness *that's* all a thing of the past!" Chris raised a fervent cardboard cup. "Here's to the Endangered Species Treaty!"

Charlotte looked up sharply. "Orchids, the largest family of flowering plants on earth and the whole damn *family* is on the list! It's as daft as putting a hold on all *Compositae. What?* Come on, now, Chris! The family of the common dandelion!" Mark thought it might be the moment to drift away into the buzz of orchidists, the sound of the tribe Anglo-Saxon; sub-division: North American, class: Middle, species: *miamiensis* and, according to Charlotte, subspecies: orchid nut.

"Seven years! *Seven* years, my *sanderiana* had never bloomed! I was more excited than when Katie was born!"

"The cat got into my *Cattleya skinneri autumnalis* again. I've told Phyllis it's me and my orchids or the cat."

"...There's Ontario in June, Pittsburgh in August, Okinawa in October—who's doing them all?"

"I could do Okinawa but Pittsburgh's out."

"Then who's coming to Ontario?"

Apart from the occasional lost tourist in The Rat and Parrot and an unnerving interlude in Spain with a student from California who sat up in the middle of the night apparently recording what they'd just done in her journal, the only time Mark had observed Americans up close was in the queue for tickets for the Royal Shakespeare Company in the West End. But Charlotte had said orchid people were hardly typical. "They say it's an addiction! You hear all the time: 'I got just one orchid and I was hooked.' And what do I say? I say, thank God you *did,* dear!" The passion devoted to what could be called a mere hobby gave the group a very English air; Mark could see that. Wasn't it an American who'd defined the English as a people only experiencing strong emotion for tiny, unimportant things? Though it would be a brave man who stood in the midst of this lot, Mark decided, and called the orchid an unimportant thing.

"Last judging I had the *perfect paph* and Tommy said he wasn't happy that the margins were rolled back! *The margins were perfect!*"

"Take it to Oklahoma!" Tilly had appeared. "They award anything in Oklahoma!"

The only young person at the party was a pimply lad who reminded Mark of the more earnest members in the science club at Totters Green. Good old Charlotte, he thought, encouraging the younger generation, however depressing that might be. For him, there was certainly no one to lust after so if he had to play the nervy orchid scholar it didn't look, so far, as though it would be much of a sacrifice. This was the kind of Englishman, Mark knew, Americans considered very likely gay though too timid to pursue it and that certainly would have its uses if it kept some of the more bizarre females at bay. Full of tasty, tender pork and Californian merlot, surrounded by warm night air and warm and friendly Americans, Mark's fears had just started to evaporate when Charlotte called him over to her group. "–Very shy! Modest to a fault! Not like me! Just don't get him started on dendrobiums and catasetums—at your peril! Yes, to help me sort out Orchid Empire's collection, luckily a photographic memory. A lot of very rare and precious things, indeed. Still a little hush hush. Enquiries from Kew, of course. Well, with all the rules and regulations now...and the wars in Africa— Yes, I have one of them. Only three in captivity, as it were. Indeed, worse than trying to save the gorillas! Exactly! Destruction of habitat! Well, the Masai are basically on the way out. Masai— No, they're not orchids, dear, they're people but same problem, same problem!"

Charlotte was finally doing what she said she would do, getting the word out to spread around the region. Her brilliant nephew was in town. The orchidist to reckon with. The man to take on Tilly and Marjorie and the others. And who ever was the Queen.

"Hi, I'm Ken. That's Larry." Ken's receding hairline made him look sensible. "We're Charlotte's favorite people," he added dryly. Larry, fair and handsome, was in a Hawaiian shirt that Mark could tell he'd worn as a joke. "*Where* is she? *Char*-lotte! You are looking *fabulous!*"

"I love those boys." Charlotte had said. "The Queen hates them, of course. One thing, they're impervious to her charms. Drives her mad. They used to have a flower shop, mostly weddings and funerals. Then Larry had his breakdown. There was the contract with that film star out on Key Biscayne, a weekly order from L.A. and everyone, they said, was either getting hitched or dropping like flies. They had to slow the pace. Now they do mainly office rentals, bromeliads and ferns."

"Did Charlotte tell you?" Ken again, still dry. "We're basically bromeliads and ferns now but she still loves us."

Larry was squatting down beside Charlotte's chair, deep in conversation. He patted her hand and stood up. "The message from Charlotte is… 'Get me a drink!'"

"You're looking after her, of course," Ken said to Mark.

"Not very well."

"Oh, come *on!*" Larry cried, "Don't be so *English!*"

"It's true. But I'm glad to see she has so many good friends."

"Only us, *really*," Larry said.

"And Rachel" Ken added. "Is she here yet?"

"I'm afraid I wouldn't know," said Mark.

"Oh, you'd know!" Larry laughed. "Charlotte says she doesn't think she's heard the news yet," he said, looking pensive.

"Trouble is Rachel is like Charlotte," Ken said. "Doesn't suffer fools gladly."

"She's got balls," Larry added.

"Oh, local stuff, Mark. They're trying to get Rachel out of the Miami Expo. The big show."

"Not a pretty story for Christmas! So we'll see you New Year?" Larry asked. "At the party? You *have* to go. No, not Charlotte. Not in a million years! She'll want you to report back, though, carry the flag for Orchid Empire."

Either out of deference to Charlotte's age and accident or the impending Christmas Day, by ten thirty guests were starting to sort out whose Honda Civic was blocking whose Toyota Camry down the drive. Charlotte was back in her spot by the coral rock wall with Bert and Mark felt the worst was over.

"I need you to look at my catasetums." It was the man in the PACIFISTS FOR PEACE T-shirt. With the departure of the last cars he had emerged from the orchid house, blinking a little in the light from the hurricane lamps. He spoke in a low, slow Southern voice. "I *know* two are mislabeled. You can't trust the Venezuelans."

"After the holidays, Cooper!" Charlotte called out. "After the holidays!"

Cooper raised his head obediently, nodded goodbye and started loping off down the drive. Carlos was packing up the rest of the pig, leaving the carcass with the bones and anatomical bits for the dogs. The three were sprawled out, too full even to chase Cooper's old Chevy pick up down to the road.

"—Charlotte's been telling me about you!" A tall man with thick glasses and a sharp frown appeared from nowhere, younger than most of the guests and a good deal testier. Mark had observed him from afar: he seemed to get very angry over orchid related themes and Mark had registered him early on as someone to be avoided. "England! With that climate you've got to be serious. It's too easy here. People stick an orchid on a tree with Liquid Nails and when it doesn't die they call themselves orchidists. Charlotte says you have interesting ideas about temperature tolerant breeding." Where do these people suddenly come from? Mark asked himself and, more importantly, how can I silence Charlotte?

"I'm Mike, OK? What will interest *you* is the *Vanda tricolo*r in the botanical garden at Ann Arbor. Blooms nearly non stop all year. *Michigan!* Here? Lucky if it's twice. Why? Grows up to seven thousand feet in Java, natural habitat! Cool conditions. *Elevation!* Well, I don't have to tell *you* that! We'll get together after the holidays. Oh, Merry Christmas!"

Rosita and the aunts had already left in a faded Toyota Corolla. Carlos was getting ready to leave when an old blue truck ground up almost to the tables, scattering the dogs. A girl with short, swinging ash blond hair jumped out. She was in T-shirt, shorts, and tennis shoes, tanned and glowing at ten forty pm. Mark thought this must be Rachel. Charlotte, talking about the local orchid scene had mused "You know, the only one to be serious about is Rachel." Mark found himself immediately feeling the same way. Rachel was one of those sun-kissed, leggy American beauties that Mark firmly believed, however much global warming took place, could not be duplicated in the United Kingdom. Impossible to know how old she was. Here, in the shadows she looked sixteen, over by the lamps maybe early twenties, waking up on the pillow next to his, who knew? "Oh, hi. Sorry I'm so late. You must be…"

"Mark."

"Mark! Yes— Charlotte's told me all about you!"

"In that case I might as well say goodnight right now."

"The English sense of humor! How is Charlotte *really* doing?" Rachel had lowered her voice. Charlotte was heading their way.

"Well, you know Charlotte. In some ways her own worst enemy, tries to do too much."

"Yes, she was like that when she was on her feet. I think she's incredible!"

"Yes, well, here she comes. Can I get you a drink?"

"No I'm fine. I just came over to say Merry Christmas. So what do you think of our local orchid scene?"

"Well, it's still all quite new to me."

"*Rachel!* Did you do anything with the pollen from that *merrillii* cross? Good girl. So this is my nephew. Here he is. Don't let him near your catasetums!" Charlotte cackled. "Mark, you've met your match with Rachel! She's extremely knowledgeable! Need to get you two brainstorming on some of the thornier problems of nomenclature and the rest of us will just stand back and watch you slug it out!" *Charlotte, you're an evil old woman!* For a moment Mark thought he'd said it aloud. Rachel smiled. If the busty blond at The Rat and Parrot had ever looked even half as good at that moment, Mark would never have left North London. Charlotte had said. "Rachel knows her orchids but it won't do her any good in this region. Why? She won't toe the line! She's got balls! Orchid politics, dear boy. She's the only one with balls!" Everyone, it seemed, talked about Rachel's balls. "Rachel stands up to the Queen! What? Oh, *she* wouldn't set foot on my property! I'd loose the dogs on her!" Good old Charlotte, full of the Christmas spirit. Bert was saying goodnight. Rachel gave him a kiss and a hug. What a waste! Mark howled to himself. Seeing Charlotte starting to fade, Rachel said goodnight too. Mark helped guide the chair up the ramp even as Charlotte growled, "I'll manage! I'll *manage!*"

Mark went back outside as soon as he could, hoping Rachel might have lingered but her truck was gone. She had offered to help tidy up but Rosita and Carlos had done too good a job; there were only a few scattered napkins and cardboard cups. Charlotte had given her an envelope she'd been sitting on: "That's for the flasking and something for Christmas."

"Come on, Charlotte! You've already promised me some flasks…"

"Of course! What am I going to do with all that material at my age?"

"Maybe Mark," Rachel had ventured and Charlotte snorted. Mark couldn't make out if Charlotte had told Rachel the truth or not. That he was not our man from Kew or anywhere else in the orchid world, just our man from Totter's Green Comprehensive: Remedial English and First Year Football, someone who had never even been good at Botany. He found himself hoping that Charlotte would be unable to resist telling Rachel the truth, so it would become their very own secret to share.

4

Christmas Day

Squelching back to the porch on Christmas morning after fighting the kinks in the hose and the leaking Nifty nozzles, Mark eased off his wet tennis shoes and sat in a patch of sunlight to dry. Charlotte was already in her favorite spot, chair braked next to a rickety little bamboo stand with its Beefeaters gin bottle and solid square glass. "Got to toast the Queen!" Charlotte always listened to the Queen's message on Christmas Day, tuning in to BBC World Service on her shortwave radio. Not that it made her nostalgic for Britain she insisted but for all those Commonwealth territories and imperial leftovers she had grown orchids in. "'—Where my caravan has rested' as old Colonel Fielding used to say. Now Dottie, his wife, was a great lady. Never intimidated by protocol. Well, certainly not after nine pm and a few gins."

Mark had never intentionally listened to the Queen's Christmas speech but as Big Ben struck and it all began: *This is the BBC World Service...*Or, perhaps, *This is the World Service of the BBC,* he was ready to sit up straight on the verandah, as Charlotte often called the little porch. He would narrow his eyes against the sun shining through the lush tropical leaves and raise a Johnnie Walker, no ice. It would be a James Bond moment in this outpost, Orchid Empire.

Charlotte must have heard the Queen's annual address in many places. She seemed to have been perpetually on the move, one step ahead of unsympathetic governments, insurgencies, independence or "too much damn interference," growing orchids anywhere English was spoken and it was hot. Her favorite spot was Kenya where she'd made some white farmer's collection of orchids ("And I say this with all due modesty") the best in East Africa. There had been South Africa, a brief spell in Singapore, a disastrous interlude in Malaya:("Let's just say I do not suffer fools gladly!") a pause in the Bahamas and a happy period in Jamaica. As a refugee from the shrinking British Empire and an orchidist Charlotte had always been chasing the dwindling world of warm climate, stable Anglo-Saxon government and cheap labor. "And God save South Dade, Florida," Charlotte had announced with a grin, raising a glass, "where we've still got all three!"

Carlos, rattling into Orchid Empire every morning with his new second-hand truck sporting the Mexican flag, had started off as very cheap labor. One of those short, dark-skinned young men walking to the launderette or standing round on street corners who made Homestead early on Sunday mornings look like a little Mexican garrison town full of conscripts far from home. His had been a typical migrant family, Charlotte said, following the seasons across the US: harvesting winter vegetables in Florida and as it grew too hot, by April up to the Carolinas, in the mid west for the summer and by September heading on back for the winter harvests again down in Florida. Charlotte was proud of the fact that Orchid Empire had interrupted the cycle. One summer for some reason the family had not gone north. Carlos had come to her for summer work off the books, just till the picking began and she had offered him a permanent job. "Best decision I ever made."

As Carlos was home with his family for Christmas it was Mark who had headed for the orchid houses early and switched on the pumps. Charlotte insisted on hand watering all the hanging orchids but the threads on Orchid Empire's Nifty nozzles were so worn and ill-fitting that a constant stream of water ran down the hose and into Mark's armpit. Today Mark didn't care. He was pleased, touched, that the strictest care in watering applied to the small clay pots full of baby seedling orchids, the 'compots,' from Bios Orchids, Rachel's lab. Twenty four hours earlier Bios Orchids had meant nothing; now Mark could hardly wait for New Year's Eve and the Miami Orchid Club's dinner and dance. Unlike Ned, Mark had always found it a little hard to launch right in on a first date, especially if it had the potential to become serious, not just flirting with the blonde at The Rat and Parrot. But New Year's Eve was New Year's Eve. Even the stiffest Brits had been known to grab hold of perfect strangers as the clock struck midnight.

Mark knew he was not in the same league as Rachel. He had brown hair, hazel eyes and "a *very* nice speaking voice," according to his dear mother. Much more relevant, of course, was his rating from Aussie Ned: "Not a poofter!" Also in the plus column the blonde at The Rat and Parrot had declared he was the best looking bloke in the place. Mark stifled the thought that usually the only other able-bodied men in The Rat and Parrot were from the betting shop next door or a few pasty-faced office workers sliding in for a quick one on their way home. There were more thoughts to be stifled: that Rachel already had a serious boy friend, that his bogus role as orchid expert was about to explode in his face while his aunt no doubt looked on and laughed. But the fact that he woke up every morning to South Florida sunlight and would not be reporting to Totter's Green at the start of January made everything, for the moment, bearable. The vibrant mix of the new Britain that would be welcomed by the monarch in her Christmas address was always well represented in remedial classes in Britain's comprehensives. And reflecting on some of the Queen's younger and more lively subjects awaiting him in the North London school system, Mark felt that even though it was a close call, he would, for the time being, stick with his aunt.

"No Majesty today!" The short wave radio could not be found. It seemed Rosita, well-meaningly, had sent it off to the hospital with Charlotte where it had disappeared. Good, thought Mark, I can talk about the party and lead up to Rachel. "Who was that man at the end, talking about mountains and ...Michigan?"

"Mike? He should still be in a cellar in Wisconsin or somewhere with his orchids, his lights and computer and Mother calling from the top of the stairs that his dinner's getting cold! Mike's another one who keeps out of the Miami Orchid Club because of the Queen. More people grow orchids here than anywhere else in the States and the Club keeps getting smaller! Well, I think I'll celebrate Christmas with a tangelo, dear boy!" According to Charlotte, the tangelo, a cross between a grapefruit and a tangerine, did better in South Florida than the orange. Oranges were like Brussel sprouts. " That's why the groves are much further north. They need cold to sweeten them up."

At least no one staying with Charlotte was in danger of getting scurvy. Orchid Empire was awash in vitamin C. Charlotte had two Key limes, a Persian lime, a big craggy fruit called a rough lemon, a sour orange ("for marmalade") three grapefruit and two tangelo trees. Mark took one of the old wicker baskets from the porch and went off round the back ducking under the sagging clothes line. With the sun on his face and the fruit warm and heavy in his hand, Mark started thinking of Rachel again. On the way back in he collected a couple of cold beers from the newer fridge in the potting shed which, unlike the one in the kitchen, had a door that actually closed all the way. It was empty except for little manila envelopes of orchid pollen and a large, saffron colored papaya that looked likely to disintegrate if moved and had probably been there since Charlotte broke her leg. In the kitchen Mark loaded a tray with Crawford crackers and a wedge of Stilton cheese, Charlotte's Christmas present, something he'd discovered strangely enough down in Homestead. He got a bowl for the tangelos and sliced a lime for Charlotte's gin and tonic, thinking it was a good job alcohol was cheap in the States otherwise Orchid Empire would have to be selling a lot more orchids. As Mark set the tray down on his own wobbly bamboo side table Charlotte asked, "So what do you think of our Rachel?"

"She seems very nice."

"So you want to get in her knickers?"

"She's certainly very beautiful."

"Same thing!"

So much for that. "Um, what about all the talk of shows and her being out—Rachel having problems…"

"It's a long and sad tale said the dormouse! Student orchid judges should keep their mouths shut no matter what and Rachel, like Mike, has a hard job with that. Most of the judges are intimidated by the fact she's come down here as a microbiologist, of course. Wonderful mind! Full of ideas on breeding, propagation. She'll make her mark. If she can stay afloat."

"So how long has she been here?"

"Mike prefers the north for orchids: candle power, *brain* power, earnest young men converting their basements. Couldn't do it here— no basements! We had a lad came to meetings always asking questions: hydroponics, candle power. Apparently got busted. An ounce of marijuana is worth more now than an awarded orchid. The *ganja* boys in Jamaica must be having a field day."

"—When did you first meet Rachel?"

"One year they discovered a cocaine lab down the road opposite the local elementary school! 'Enough ether to blow up a city block' the cops said. Or maybe several, I forget. But someone sniffed the beautiful South Florida air one morning—wind blowing the wrong way—and Bob's your uncle."

"So Rachel has her own lab?"

"Of course, no one knew a thing. Perfect neighbors! No loud music. No coming over for a cup of sugar! In the best English tradition: *they didn't like drawing attention to themselves!*"

"So, Charlotte, when *did* you meet Rachel?"

"What? Must have been about two years ago. Told her she could do some lab work for me and I'd spread the word. "*Micro-propagation!* How can you beat that!"

"Must be hard."

"No surprise she scored the highest of any student judge with her paper: 'Variation among clonal mutations: how they occur and how to judge them.'"

"So she's pretty serious—not much time for ...not much free time."

"Deep into species, such a purist. I told her, apart from the paph people who are total nuts, concentrate on breeding fancy catts. The Japs are paying unbelievable amounts for cattleyas. We need to get Rachel more commercial. Can't you just see her, blonde bombshell with rich Latin clients?" Unfortunately Mark could, only too clearly. "Well, she needs to get some decent income. The gal who's sharing the rent will be leaving, apparently. Too far south for her, she works down town."

There were all kinds of questions to be asked about Rachel. But Mark had the feeling that with Charlotte, if it wasn't to do with micro-propagation or orchid marketing any query would probably just lead back to knickers.

"And now Rachel has to contend with the Queen. We've certainly got her to blame for everything." Charlotte for a moment, sounded almost sympathetic. "Her real name? Regina! So we christened her 'The Queen.'

Christmas dinner evolved slowly throughout the afternoon. Not so different from home, Mark thought; Christmas Day being the one time a year when his mother drank, totaling up a good amount of sherry while she cooked. At Orchid Empire Christmas dinner started off as a very late lunch taken on the porch: roast pork and more tangelos, Californian merlot again, Taco chips and Crawford crackers, Stilton cheese and gin. Charlotte said the only Christmassy thing she usually did was buy a fruit cake and stick a sprig of Florida holly in it. "That's what they call the Brazilian pepper. Covered at Christmas, bright red berries. The American robins used to get drunk on them. Seem to have changed their migratory pattern. Used to be lined up on the telephone wires here in December, made us think of Christmas. Haven't seen any last few years. Few summers ago you couldn't say goodbye to someone at dusk outside for the mosquitoes. Now? Hardly notice them. And where are the wasps? They've got to be spraying. Where have all the wasps gone?"

Mark thought it highly appropriate that Charlotte should wax nostalgic not about the absence of butterflies but the absence of wasps. One migratory pattern hadn't changed: this Christmas day just before dusk they were visited suddenly by a swirl of turkey vultures, so big they cast their shadows over the gravel. "Coming in low, maybe some road kill, some carrion somewhere," Charlotte said. "Maybe someone ran over a possum last night leaving the party. Or a raccoon. Though that for them would be pretty fresh. Not African, dear boy, they're New World. Come all the way from *Ohio!* When the vultures return they have a festival but when they're back in the fall we just say 'Start of the tourist season!'"

How wonderful just to be a tourist, thought Mark wistfully. "Cooper wants us to get together," he told Charlotte, peeling another tangelo. "He wants me to check out some orchids. Said something about not being able to trust the Venezuelans."

"Oh, Cooper's a pussy cat! He's really into warm-loving species, Thailand, so you shouldn't have to know about them. Venezuelans? I've no idea, dear boy. He gets bees in his bonnet. They all do. Cooper's another bright soul maneuvered out of the orchid club by Regina. Why? Potential threat! Apparently knows a lot about her shady deals in Thailand. Has a computer buddy over there. Marvels of modern science, as we used to say. A defrocked Buddhist monk, or something. Cooper tries to be non-confrontational. Saw his T-shirt? Isn't that wonderful? Just about the most aggressive shirt I've ever seen. Asked him to get me one but he says they don't do Extra Large. These pacifists are all vegetarians. Says he learnt non-confrontation from the Thais. Drives me mad! I want him to take on the Queen. Of course, the last time he did that, that's when she got him out. Cooper's a hoot. Gets steamed up at the drop of a hat! That's why he tends to lurk on the fringe. Usually to be found in the bushes!"

Charlotte was almost nodding off, empty glass held firmly in her lap. Mark rocked on the porch, nursing his last beer, enjoying the delicate spicy fragrance of the *Brassovola cordata*. The orchid name he remembered, the only orchid allowed close to the house; *the lady of the night, our unobtrusive native of Jamaica with modest white flowers.* "Orchids that need *moths* for pollination are fragrant after dark and tend to be lighter in color— the white or yellows! There's the hallmark of your orchid—adaptation and intelligence!"

Mark went to feed the dogs, a mere formality as they were holding out for more disposable bits of pig. They each had their own old, inverted hubcap that skidded across the gravel as they ate. Charlotte said she'd always used a collection of worn out frying pans till a Haitian helping trim the trees one day had scrubbed them clean in his lunch break. He asked to take them home at the end of the day. "Cheap nonstick, the chemical innards starting to show. That's why they were chucked. Should've said no."

It was very quiet. There was no traffic on the road for Christmas Day: no giant temperature controlled trucks taking off from the local foliage nurseries with their rubber trees, bromeliads and ferns; all the ornamentals headed for the hotel lobbies and dentists' waiting rooms of North America. Mark could seen them at night at the end of the drive, trundling past Orchid Empire, tiny Christmas lights outlining the rigs, lit up like fairground rides in the dark. When Mark ventured out in the Volvo, ("Sometimes it just stops, dear. No, Carlos's Uncle Victor can't find anything wrong. It's just old age.") there always seemed to be one of those massive trucks behind him, turning with unarguable force out of narrow nursery gates. Now *orchids* were being grown by the truck load too in South Dade, Charlotte said. "After Andrew, huge investment in state of the art greenhouses—all that insurance money! Bert says in a way the small guys brought it on themselves; made so much money on their quick phal crops the big guys stepped in. Orchid production here now measured in acres. Bigger than Hawaii, Mike says. Well, my little hodge podge will see me out."

Mark sat there in the dark listening to the insects chirping and cheeping as loud as baby birds and the sound of the bamboo creaking as the breeze lifted and died. Charlotte was really asleep now, earlier than usual, snoring with an even rattle and snick like an old-fashioned lawnmower. Mark had learned not to pester her to go to bed. She would wake up in an hour or so and drive off. Sitting at the computer in the spare bedroom, he would hear the high tech whine of the latest in ultra light wheelchairs as Charlotte negotiated the Florida room or a crash as she caught the side of the bamboo stand. During the day Charlotte would command Mark to do nothing, whether it was to help move the chair or rescue something she'd dropped. After she'd fallen asleep he would go round picking up like the parent of a toddler. Slinging out the odd tortilla chip and crumbs of Stilton cheese over the porch railing in the general direction of the dogs on Christmas night, watching the small grey lizards running along the porch rail chasing each other, Mark wondered what kind of fight Charlotte had got into with the 'Queen,' wondered if she had made a will and pleaded with fate that like the old Volvo, Charlotte could scrape along for another two and a half months till it was time for him to leave.

5

New Year's Eve Party

"Hey! Mark! Over here!"

You had to hand it to Americans, Mark decided. He had met Ken and Larry only briefly on Christmas Eve and now they were welcoming him to their spot of polished party floor like, he had to say it, like old friends. Whereas in England at the most you'd get a bloke drifting over with an "Er, didn't I see you at that thing the other night? Ah…thought so…" and having got that straight he'd drift off.

"So what do you think?" Larry asked with a grin. Mark was wondering where Rachel was, whether she had come yet, when it would be OK to ask about her without giving rise among her friends to the more discreet version of Charlotte's "So you want to get in her knickers?"

The venue for the Miami Orchid Club's New Year's Eve party was a private residence but it was huge. Two towering palm trees appeared to have been planted just inside the front door. No lime green halter tops here or fading Orchid Adventure T-shirts. Larry wore a midnight blue silk shirt, his fair hair gleaming with elegant highlights. Ken was all in charcoal with a charcoal and gold tie, the bald half of his head polished and shining as Larry observed, in full party mode. Mark had partnered his wrinkle free, fifty percent polyester dark blue shirt, long sleeves and all, with his best pair of khaki slacks and the only tie he'd brought, a tasteful silk paisley, but here he wouldn't cut it even as a waiter. They were in tight black trousers and billowing white shirts. The dashing young man holding the tray of complimentary champagne and moving quickly out of reach, sleeves and all, was wearing white gloves.

"Mark!" said Larry, "we aren't in Kansas any more!"

Mark certainly felt a long way from Homestead. He'd been nursing the old Volvo north, along US1 in the slow lane for forty minutes while traffic streamed past, heading for a New Year's Eve in down town Miami perhaps or maybe even South Beach. But at least Charlotte's instructions had been crisp and clear once he'd persuaded her that "It's a piece of cake, my boy" was no substitute for the old left, right and left again of traditional directions. Mark just had to hold steady following the Christmas decorations and then turn where Charlotte told him. The local authorities or the chamber of commerce had chosen leaping plastic reindeers with twinkling crowns to grace alternate light poles along US1 while rather somber dark green wreaths hung on the ones between. Perhaps a holiday choice of the Florida Highway Patrol. Palm trees in occasional tufts and brief, postcard length rows made the brightly lit concrete look warm and sunny but a brisk wind was starting to blow, snapping the stars and stripes to attention over the car dealerships and cool enough to make Mark close the Volvo windows. Charlotte had said there was a cold front coming in for New Year. Mark had wondered if she would be warm enough on the porch.

"I'll move inside when I need! I'm not an invalid! We'll be alright unless it falls below fifty Fahrenheit, early on. Always watch out for winds out of the North North West, they mean trouble. Remember, however much of a tan you're getting, young man, from Orchid Empire north, it's one land mass all the way to Canada! When those winds get going in January that's the 'Siberian Express.' Just check the temperatures when you come home from the ball, Cinderella. In fact, about three in the morning will be perfect. And if in doubt—wake me up!"

Mark made his turn and suddenly was away from the Spa and Pool Supplies and Discount Mattresses into a tree lined, spacious, residential district glittering with Christmas lights. It was an instant, tree-filled suburbia of houses, gardens, dogs, bikes and then a large house with a circular drive and *Gone With the Wind* front rising above the parked cars. And, half a block and a few million dollars of private homes away, exactly as Charlotte had described, a discreet little parking lot, almost full by now, flanking a darkened tennis court. Mark locked the Volvo, still bemused that Charlotte had actually just told him where the place was, and the place to park the car; hadn't played with him, sending him on some futile odyssey into the dark American hinterland to strengthen his character and give her a good laugh.

"So what's Charlotte up to?" Ken was asking, pitching his voice against the band.

"The TV's on in her room but she may just stay on the porch."

"With the Beefeaters," contributed Larry.

"Yes, so following form, I don't think she's going to make it to New Year."

"But how sensible of her. We're stuck here in this *vault!*"

"You won't have to worry much about orchid talk here," Ken said. "Most of this lot are what Larry calls the buy and die crowd. They buy an orchid and they or the maid or the spouse lets it die."

"Sad, sad" said Larry, "but only if they don't come back and buy another one."

Mark was wondering why Ken had reassured him. Had Charlotte told? He knew she'd be enjoying this, his timid evaluation of every orchid related comment, however marginal. It was a reminder that in the orchid world of Miami, because of his aunt's little plan, he was not so much skating on thin ice as walking on water. Common sense, Mark knew, dictated he should just quietly tell everyone he'd come over from the UK to make the tea, get to the phone, help with watering and print out a few labels and that's it. And by the way, ignore anything his aunt said because she had become prey to irrational fears, crippling paranoia, creeping senility and was nuts. No, even without the threat of this Queen person, Mark couldn't quite see himself saying that. At least the music was loud enough to damp down most idle conversation. A *mariachi* band who might well have come up from Homestead themselves, was strolling around serenading the guests at close range. Under broad, gold trimmed sombreros and behind their bulky instruments, the players looked even shorter than Mexicans usually did, like serious children playing with grownup things. They didn't crack a smile even when they switched to Happy Birthday to You for a noisy bunch of Anglos. Mark was already into Dade County speak.

"Here *Anglos* are *Non-Hispanic Whites,*" Charlotte had explained briskly. "Doesn't that have a glorious ring to it! What could Shakespeare have done with those stirring words? Though interestingly enough," she mused, teacher again," Shakespeare's time saw the first great Spanish-Anglo rivalry. Walter Raleigh's still remembered in the Spanish Caribbean as the 'English pirate.'"

Sipping his one glass of free champagne slowly to make it last, Mark asked Larry if he spoke Spanish. "We have to. You go to Coral Gables: grandmother is in, she doesn't speak English. The maid doesn't, the gardener...well, we get by. I think our Spanish is so bad it's *simpatico*— we get a lot of laughs."

"And look at the guests. You've got to hand it to Regina," Ken commented. "She's getting the Latin community into the orchid scene."

"She's certainly made good use of her Latin boy friends," Larry said. "I wish I'd been so clever with mine."

There must have been at least two hundred people under the palms. It was certainly enough of a crowd that the white gloved waiters could easily back away and be swallowed up, tray and all, before guests could reach for champagne seconds. Mark asked Ken where the Tillys and Marjories of the Miami orchid world were. "Well, it's forty dollars a ticket even for members so a lot of the real orchid club people, like a Tilly, would rather stay home and bloom out three epicats instead."

"As for Mike or Coop," Larry snorted. "*that* I'd pay money to see."

"The money's supposed to go into publicity for the big spring show, the Expo" Ken added, "but we've never noticed it."

"Well, Regina's enterprise, Orchid Magic, jumps in every year to make this night *so* special. Observe—" Behind them on a white pedestal, a large plaster urn overflowed with a rather wispy explosion of ferns, orchids and sparkling scarlet ribbons. "Wholesale, two-fifty in ferns," Larry declaimed: "a couple of four dollar large dendrobium phals, three nameless oncidiums at two-fifty(wholesale) *and* one large plaster pot. No, let's be fair: *one imitation Grecian urn.* I would guess from the look of it, Fredz Kloze Outs, *maybe* six-fifty. But wait!

Wholesale discount! Looking around, appears Regina's done at least a *dozen* Grecian urns altogether, so strike six-fifty, at the most, *five*. Whole thing tied together with Glitter Glam ribbon, Dollar Stores and paid for at vast expense by the Orchid Club. And fading already! I bet they were rented out for Christmas. Regina is the original re-cy-cler, they should have her talk to the schools! It will be a miracle if that Oncidium in the front lasts as long as Charlotte tonight."

"Mark's not really interested," Ken said.

Larry ignored him, trying in vain to snag more champagne. "I'm getting tired pretending I've just arrived."

Ken said "Let's go wild and just *buy* a drink."

"Have you seen Regina's prices?" Larry protested. "It's worse than Miami airport." "Give it a rest," Ken said.

"You see?" Larry turned to Mark. "No-one faces up to her. No-one's got the balls."

Good, now we're back to Rachel, thought Mark. "So, Um. Anyone else from the party coming?"

"If it's like last year, very few. Look around, Ken! Less and less real orchid people. I don't even see many commercial growers. Oh, oh. Mark, here comes one: emphasis on the *commercial*."

"Hey, boys! Still keeping the dream alive?"

"No, but the nightmare continues. How was Christmas, Alvin?"

"Don't even mention it." Alvin was short and stout in a navy blue suit and red face. "That dumb Tex Mex got lost on Christmas Eve, drove the van right into Liberty City. If it's not cruising full of stolen TVs it'll be lawn maintenance by now."

"Sounds like a satisfactory outcome."

" Shut him up, Ken."

"What happened to your driver?"

"*Says* he was knocked on the head. Spent a day sitting in emergency, expecting me to pay. Probably sold the shit himself."

"What about the police?"

"*Please!* Said lucky me my driver wasn't dead and wished me a Merry Christmas! In Spanish." Alvin sniffed and swirled the Scotch round in his glass. "So this is Charlotte's family!" He looked up at

Mark. "I hear you've come to sort the old lady out. Been going down hill for a long time. They say it's a regular junk yard out there, some good stuff just dying off…Well, that's where you come in. Chip off the old block, what, what?" Alvin suddenly brayed. "So you're selling? What's the scoop? Taking over? Running the thing?"

"I don't even think Mark knows this," Larry lowered his voice so Alvin came closer. "Charlotte really wants to return her special orchids, her pets, *to the wild. We're going to cage them up and take them home and set them free!* —Where would it be Mark? South of Kilimanjaro?"

"Shut him up, Ken." Alvin made off back towards the bar.

With the drop in temperature and the air conditioning full blast, Mark was feeling cold. Charlotte had reluctantly vetoed his jacket, his Oxfam Harris Tweed with the faded leather patches on the elbows. Mark had worn it over on the plane, seeing himself going out to the Everglades in the dawn for a little bird watching or attending an evening talk at the local library: *New American Voices: Poetry in the Nineties* and drawing the attention of some sensitive young female South Floridian. But the only talk advertised at the little Homestead branch was: *Tax Tips: Hunting for the Refund.*

Larry, who had been off talking to a fair-haired man in a blazer was back. "Here's why Alvin's *really* pissed! Word is his shipment from Thailand got held up in Paris over Christmas. They've frozen half the plants, some major fuck up. Excuse me, Mark. Then USDA found some bug in one box and fumigated the whole lot. *And* it was Friday afternoon. They didn't release them till Monday. He'd imported mostly in spike for the Las Olas Show. What's not dead will need to be grown on for at least a year. It is SO perfect."

Ken explained Alvin knew nothing much about orchids but had a business partner with money and imported the cheapest stuff from Thailand and Hawaii to sell right away: "Before they kill it. They ship the plants out to florists and sometimes hire people to sell out of the back of vans along Old Cutler."

"Anyone want to buy me a drink?"

"*John!* How was Christmas?"

Tall and spare, slightly hunched over in an old black suit, John gave a general impression of honest cheekbones, knuckles and wrists, like an Abe Lincoln impersonator. "No walk in traffic. Only old ladies with four dollars and five hours to spend. Where's the blue rinse brigade?"

"John still dreams of Frank Sinatra on Miami Beach, gigantic cattleyas on magnificent bosoms," Larry said to Mark. "Or was it magnificent catts on gigantic bosoms? Well, John, now you've got South Beach."

"Lot of half-naked girls with their titties hanging out, on roller skates. I tried to get rid of my calanthes and *Rhyncostylis,* Ken but no-one was buying. I've always said Christmas is a tricky market."

"No one wants to commit till Christmas Eve," Larry said. "You can't wrap up a plant in November and put it in the closet."

"I used lights, Ken. You know those *labiata* hybrids? Tried running the lights on them. Timing was wrong. Now they're all going to pop after Las Olas and before Valentine's and the Expo."

"Try them on South Beach," suggested Larry. "Find out where those girls keep their money."

"Well, Alvin lost his van on Christmas Eve," Ken told John, "with everything in it."

"Oh, did he?" John cheered up immediately.

Alvin, Mark could see, was not a favorite. And he was learning that among the commercial orchid people, the simple question: How was Christmas? had nothing to do with the holiday, the turkey, or the family.

"Now Alvin's going to fire what's-is-name."

"Pedro? Pedro with the three kids?"

"No, not *Pedro.* Alvin's not stupid."

"Yes, but wasn't he the guy when the minium wage went up fifty cents an hour got rid of the old man who'd been working for him for years?"

"No, Larry," said John, "not even our Alvin would do that. It was that guy over on Palm Beach. Then let his whole collection die because he couldn't find anyone who knew orchids and would work for five bucks an hour. Well, time to move on. Keep the faith." John nodded to Mark, patted Ken on the arm and ambled off.

"When you think about it," Ken said, "Alvin's more out of date than John. He should be buying all his cheap commercial plants from the local big growers. They're shipping trailer trucks up north to New Jersey and he's fighting Air France and USDA."

"Well if he's lost the buds on this lot, he'll *have* to go local and broker in material," said Larry, "what with the Las Olas Show coming up in two weeks —Anyway, it all means we need a drink, whatever the cost, to toast Air France. *And* USDA."

Larry told Mark to stay put under Fredz Kloze Out Grecian urn. A minute later Ken, deeply apologetic, spotted someone in the crowd he had to see. Mark, finally alone, could just stand with his empty champagne glass and savor the fact that here he was in the capital of the Caribbean, Miami, gateway to Latin America, on New Year's Eve. He had got Charlotte and the orchids settled for the night, he had lined up the hubcaps and fed the dogs. Mark did, indeed, feel like Cinderella. He had escaped to the ball and, however hopeless the quest, was dreaming of somehow attracting the attention not of the Prince but the most beautiful non-Hispanic white in South Florida: Rachel. But why did she always have to be late? In the lab till the last minute. Why did she have to be so late? Mark felt an obsession coming on. There were dark, gorgeous girls all around; many it had to be noted, with dark, gorgeous escorts. Great local talent, sexy dancers, bilingual—they would rattle along from Spanish to English and back again so quickly he lost the idea of where they'd started—but none were as stunning as Rachel. If she didn't appear New Year's Eve would be ruined.

"That may be one of England's finest shirts but you look so damn cold!" It was Larry, holding out a large rum. "Drink up! The prices are not *that* bad. I just can't resist carping when it's the Queen. She's too good a target. Sometimes I think, as Ken says, if she didn't exist I'd have to invent her."

Warming up with the rum Mark said simply: "Larry, you are wonderful."

"English understatement!" Larry raised his glass. "It will have to do! So Ken abandoned you."

"Yes, it was rather nice. I mean, just to watch the crowd. Usually I like to listen, too..."

"Don't you *hate* it. Just as some juicy bit is coming up—why Maria is dumping Jose—everyone gets excited and roars off into Spanish and leaves you hanging. Eavesdropping in Miami, most of the time you might as well be in Madrid. Ah, Ken's back. And he must have run into the girls." Suddenly there was Rachel in a short black dress with tiny straps, hunching up bare, tanned shoulders. Her hair, tucked under one ear, swept over the other, shining almost white. She was wearing emerald eye shadow and long, extravagant earrings that swung and sparkled. Mark had to acknowledge no way did Rachel look like she needed any encouragement, helping hand or companion to make a transition from the isolation of the lab into the big world outside. "I'm *freezing!*"

Good! Mark nearly said it aloud. Shivering always provided the potential for closer contact especially on a New Year's Eve. Shame he didn't have his old Harris Tweed, something rough and manly to throw over those slender shoulders. But there had to be some strategy. Mark had to think ahead for the rest of the evening: how he must be at Rachel's side the moment the clock struck twelve. And then what? Mark told himself firmly he believed, like all English majors, in the magic of the moment. There were many examples in the world of literature, if not among his friends and acquaintances. Or in his own personal life.

"Hi, Larry!" Larry got a kiss. "Oh, hi Mark!" Rachel was a good four feet away. "This is Jen."

So she was the one who helped Rachel pay the rent: short brown hair tucked behind the ears, brown eyes, medium brown person. She was even in brown silky trousers and some kind of cosy, sensible top. No bare skin there, no collar bones or saucy knee caps. It might be New Year's Eve but Jen was obviously not putting much belief in the magic of any moment: she wanted to be warm. Mark felt a stab of admiration. He should have worn his Oxfam jacket and said to hell with the lot of you. Larry for one would have loved it.

"So how's downtown Miami?" Larry was asking Jen.

"Still downtown, unfortunately."

"We should have said 'How's the commute.'" Ken was sympathetic.

"The turnpike just gets worse, the toll plaza useless unless you get there before seven, backing up for miles. Sorry," Jen turned to Mark. "Very boring."

"No," said Larry firmly. "You need to vent. Come and vent over here," and he held his arms open wide.

"Actually," said Jen, "it's Rachel who needs to vent if it's true—about the Expo."

"*Is* it true?" asked Rachel. "I waited to ask you guys because I didn't believe it. I'm *out* of the Expo?"

"Well," said Ken reluctantly, "the final straw seems to be that you had old Mrs. Vanderpool in your booth. You know, sharing booth space is not allowed."

"But she's a *missionary,* for God's sake! Charlotte's friend! Sure, she sold a few plants but they were for that AIDS campaign in East Africa. And what about those Hawaiians selling out of Alvin's booth last year? Does our glorious President think *they're* part of his shitty business? And WHY am I being told only NOW when it's too late to challenge it?"

"Apparently it's all there in the bylaws, the fine print," Ken said cautiously.

"*That's* why the contracts were sent out late this year!"

"And there was the matter of you refusing to move the garden cart, apparently. And getting a little verbal."

"They'd given me the worst spot, the narrowest corner and I had to unload. This is all trivial shit from a year ago! Where *is* that woman?"

"Rachel! You'll only make it worse."

"Ken's right," Larry added. "Regina would love that. Make you explode, then, while asking you gently, 'What's wrong? What can *I* do?' she's already drafting the letter to have you thrown out of the Club for conduct unbecoming. You know that's what happened with Cooper."

A white gloved waiter was sliding by. Rachel flagged him down and swiped two glasses of champagne: "Jen!" She was obviously saying, Jen, get your own; these are for me.

"Who needs these shows, anyway?" Larry started, "renting the U haul—"

"I do" Rachel half yelled, pitching her voice against the band, "I need the exposure! You know I can't afford to do New York or Philadelphia."

Mark, running through a whole string of conversational options along the lines of humor, comfort, encouragement and or commiseration and having tried to think of something funny, comforting, encouraging or sympathetic to say, kept quiet. "Where *is* this woman?" Rachel, earrings flashing, blinked hard and Mark thought, she's getting angry so she won't cry. This is a really big deal. "I'm *OK*, Ken." She drained her first glass. "I have to find Tilly's old Mr. Steinberg, anyway. None of his epidendrums germinated. It must have been old seed."

Ken and Larry looked dubious, as though they wanted to frisk Rachel: go though her little black bag for a little black gun. Jen seemed unruffled. She had taken Rachel's empty glass away and, with no waiter in sight, was poking it down among the ferns in Fredz Kloze Out urn. Rachel said, "See you guys *later!*" and wheeled off holding her second glass of champagne as though she'd just arrived. Ken watched her go. "Well, I've been meaning to wander in that general direction." He headed after her at a discreet distance.

"She'll calm down," Jen said. "Just letting off steam."

Mark was planning to follow Ken, rescue Rachel from old Mr. Steinberg, buy her a real drink at the bar, expense no object, escort her to dinner and go from there. But just as he was about to make his excuses Larry beat him to it. Seeing Mark still sipping his rum and Jen with her champagne, he announced he had to do a little networking and he'd leave them go eat together. Mark protested that the next round was his.

Larry waved this off. "Just don't leave it too long to eat! Last year Rachel got into an argument with some Peruvians about masdavalias and by the time we all got to the buffet it was derelict: trampled broccoli and baked beans left over from Hurricane Andrew. Whenever I go to one of these functions I'm always reminded of Andrew; they're still using up the cans. Oh, and note whether they're having a Caesar salad or not," he instructed as he made off. "I have it on good authority that decisions on the salad for tonight could *not* be made because Regina was off in Thailand. Only Regina can make the call!"

"So how is Charlotte?" Jen asked as Larry moved away.

"Drinking too much," Mark said, surprised he should just have told the truth. "Me too," he added.

"Well, it's understandable, I mean for Charlotte," Jen said and then caught herself with a laugh. "Oh, I'm sure it is for you, too." There was a pause. The Mexican band had drifted up to a well-heeled group close by and started again. In spite of the relentless youth of their faces the group appeared to be the busty blondes of yesteryear who had snared a generation of promising young lawyers, doctors and dentists thirty or forty years ago and had been left *very comfortable* as his mother would say.

"So what's Jen short for?" Mark began at a near shout.

"Jennifer, of course. I always hated it, sounded so feeble."

"Like nephew."

"*What?*"

"*Oh, nothing!*" Mark prided himself as an Honors English graduate on being able to talk at great length, any time, anywhere, about basically nothing but he was cold and hungry and disappointed. Rachel had disappeared almost as soon as she had arrived and he wanted at least to make her the center of the conversation but realized, as his sister would say, in some dim recess of his doggy male brain that would not have gone down well with Jen, however sensible her clothes were. Jen seemed a little older than Rachel but Mark decided it was probably just the clothes and her attitude. Rachel should be about twenty three, graduated from college and according to Charlotte, been struggling in the orchid world for a year or two. "Are you hungry too?" he yelled. "Sorry, but I'm ravenous. I rushed off after feeding the dogs. Somehow I thought there'd be masses of food as one came in the door."

"It looks like that's not Regina's style."

Some part of Mark, no doubt the doggy male brain bit, would have liked to stay behind on that spot, thinking Rachel might come back but the other basic urges for food and warmth were stronger. In fact, Mark needed his own chivalrous male to wrap a dinner jacket round his shoulders. He'd nearly made a joke of that to Larry but thought Larry might take it a little too literally and go off and find him one. There was a flurry over towards the entrance, a ripple through the crowd. "Maybe it's Regina." said Jen.

"Either that," said Mark "or someone's fainted from cold and hunger and they're being carried off."

"Let's hope it's not Rachel," said Jen, "confronting the woman." They made their way towards the buzz and saw a striking figure in a long scarlet evening gown, with glossy black hair, bright red mouth, moving forward, arms stretching out to shake and hold hands. "Evita!" murmured Jen. Mark determined to be neutral and form his own opinion. He had seen Charlotte in action; he knew she had it in for Regina. So did Larry and Rachel. He had come in from outside, free of perceived or real slights; in fact, he might even effect something of a reconciliation. And if that were the case, he thought wildly, maybe even get Rachel back into the Expo. Mark reran the scene: from a few yards away, what appeared to be a beautiful woman in a striking scarlet dress, black hair, vivid smile, warm manner, walking among her subjects. No, cancel that last bit; that was Larry-speak. Regina, the President of the Miami Orchid Club swept closer, turning with a power-house smile to a tall, imposing man in an impeccable suit beside her and a dark young man one step behind: *Mr. Moneybags and boy toy.* Mark was channeling Larry again. How insidious gossip was, he told himself piously. But it was true that the handsome young man in the dinner jacket behind Regina looked a cross between a sultry waiter, a sulky boy friend and a rather lightweight bodyguard. Perhaps, in keeping with Regina's reputation for cost cutting and economy, all three.

"So that's her" said Jen. "No sign of Rachel. At least she hasn't assassinated her. Should we get in line?" The queue snaking away from the buffet table was already long. It looked as though memories were still fresh of the baked beans and dejected broccoli for those who'd been slow off the mark the year before. There didn't seem to be anyone around from Charlotte's Christmas party. Jen was saying she was sorry she missed it. "I had an *office* party, had to be there."

"Charlotte's certainly seemed a lot more orchid-y than this one," Mark said.

"Sure. Regina's more into the Miami business and social scene.

That's where the money is."

"Looks like we're into agonizing choices," Mark commented as they reached one of Fredz' urns at the edge of the buffet. "These plates aren't designed to hold more than two food groups. Maybe another of Regina's cost cutting measures." But Jen clapped three together and started piling up the triple strength paper plate with great precision: chicken, sweet corn, string beans, baked cauliflower with cheese, rice, a roll perched on top, a little green salad and even gravy. She caught sight of Mark watching fascinated. "See? As it buckles in the center it holds the gravy. Do you want me to do yours?"

"Yes, please."

"Hold mine. Any allergies?"

"In my family we weren't allowed allergies. Too many old relatives would bring up the war." Jen, Mark noted, was not ashamed to fill her plate, or plates. His mother would approve and from that deduce her character: 'Good in an emergency,' her highest praise for any girl.

Mark was wondering how Jen and Rachel had met. That's a legitimate question, he told himself: it shows as much interest in Jen as it does in Rachel.

"I was visiting an aunt in West Palm Beach and Rachel was running some errands for Larry and Ken. They'd had a big order for a dinner party and I helped her carry up the orchids from the car park. She bought me a coffee." Mark thought what a great way to meet Rachel. It would mean more than the total five minutes of conversation he'd managed to get with her. "We got talking. I had found a job here and needed somewhere to stay and Rachel needed a tenant. Only problem is, she's so far out because of the orchids and I have to go down town."

"So, what do you do?"

"I work in the budget office for one of the cruise lines. The dumb thing is I don't even like cruises. But it's my degree in economics and good money. So I hear you're a teacher and a real figure in the orchid world. I know nothing about plants."

"Oh, I teach English, actually."

"Man of many parts! Well, I still have to figure out what I really want to do. I don't have any great passion, not like Rachel. Or you." They found two chairs free at one of the small tables and no longer had to yell. The *mariachi* band had disappeared and been replaced by someone at the grand piano and a woman with long black hair and a cello. "So you're quite the orchid expert."

"Charlotte does tend to exaggerate."

"Rachel said she was bragging on you. So you should be flattered. You know Charlotte doesn't give praise lightly."

"Yes, but poor Rachel," said Mark. "Bad news for New Year. About this Expo. What will she do?"

"Nothing much she can do." Jen shrugged. "Trouble is that's the biggest show and Regina seems able to control it. I remember Charlotte telling Rachel; 'Don't get too excited if you do well there. It'll have to last you through the summer.' Everyone depends on it for cash flow. The orchid scene here pretty much closes down after. It's like your London season. After Wimbledon or something the Queen goes off to shoot things in Scotland and it's all over till the Fall." Jen had cleaned her three limp plates, solidly eaten everything, another plus with his mother, Mark noted, and wondered why his mother was creeping into this more and more. He decided it was because Jen was really not so bad, reasonably pleasant and sensible and next to Rachel, for him a non sexual object, like his mother and his sister. Not that his mother was very sensible, or for that matter, Mark thought, reflecting on old grudges, that his sister was always pleasant. Standing up, Jen announced she was off. Mark felt abandoned. For a moment he nearly said "Can I come too?" He was surprised that it should be Jen who was leaving him when he'd been thinking all the time how could he get away from her and now suddenly realizing how stupid: Jen, of course, was the key to getting back to Rachel.

The woman with the long black hair was playing something mournful on the lower register of the cello. Music To Make New Year's Resolutions By, Mark thought glumly: music to review the follies of the past year by and one's miserable short comings. Certainly temporary teaching at Totter's Green was his cruise line job. Never really got to know the kids for long even though with remedial work that was so important. Certainly no passion there. The passion was all in not committing, keeping aloof, in not being passionate so you could stay free, for what? For a different school, a new Totter's Green, next term.

Mark couldn't find Larry and it nagged at him. Like all Englishmen Mark came from the tradition of your round, my round. It might sound petty to Americans but keeping that kind of thing straight was the backbone of the English pub system and honorable relationships between males. Thinking Larry and Ken might be at the bar Mark made his way over, weighing up the straightness and brightness of US1 against the alcoholic content of American beer. Thank God for US1 and Christmas decorations. With them in his sights, he'd could follow the trail of the plastic reindeers almost all the way home. Waiting in line for his beer, Mark was reminded once more he was in Miami: he thought of the comment he'd read somewhere, that the sound of Spanish was like a stick drawn across a row of railings. The two young bar men and a lot of the customers were making English sound like that, too. "You won't hear good Spanish in Miami," Charlotte said. "Well, if you do, you're usually standing next to someone from Columbia or Bolivia. And sometimes the Latins with the perfect *English* are not locals either, especially the older ones. As kids they learnt English in Buenos Aires or somewhere, not grown up here with Spanglish."

Mark paid five dollars for a weak American beer in a freezing can and moved to the side to watch the dancing. No Rachel. Some gorgeous, dark-haired girls moving like silk, guys too, arms out, horizontal, and just somehow rippling from the waist down. Quite a few non-Hispanic whites bobbing about, and the Mexican band was back and no more waltzes but salsa and rhythms and dances Mark had never heard before. Mark was not much good at dancing. If he were out there he'd be one of the non-Hispanic whites ruining the view. He had almost stopped looking for Rachel or any of the others. John ambled up to say goodbye: he was off and give his best to Charlotte. "Tell her she's not missed much. Did the right thing to stay home."

Mark had seen what he thought was probably a vestige of the old Miami orchid world: one or two serene, elderly ladies in long pastel dresses with real orchid flowers pinned on to their soft, straw hats.

The music was getting hotter and faster but Mark was feeling colder as though someone had left a door open. Suddenly he saw Larry waving at him frantically from the fringe round the dancers. Bert was close by, talking hard. God, Mark thought, Rachel has done something. He made his way over.

"Mark! Mark! We've got to go! Cold front! The front has come in hard. Bert was just leaving early and there's ice on his windscreen!"

Some of the dancers were stopping. A burly man was striding through them tapping people on the shoulder, waving his arm. Suddenly the band died away and the music skidded to a halt. Another man in a dinner jacket took the microphone that for a moment squealed and then hummed. "We have just received word that the cold front has come in much faster and harder than predicted for. It's already down to thirty seven, Fahrenheit. Yes, folks, thirty seven. No, we don't know, either. I'm afraid everyone who doesn't have timers, well, yes, Terry even those—There may well be power outages due to increased demand. This is the big one, folks. This is it. I'm afraid unless you've got loved ones at home ready at the switch and *knowing* what's going on, you all are going to have to high tail it outta here. And so, Happy..."

The speaker's ironic concluding New Year's Eve greeting was drowned in the sudden rise of voices and commotion. As Ken was to describe it later, to announce 'Freeze!' in a place packed with orchid people was like shouting 'Fire!' in a theater. It was ten past ten on New Year's Eve and for every orchid grower in ear shot the party was over.

6

Cold Front

Outside it was pandemonium, people slamming into cars, grinding gears, reversing, swerving desperately round still empty vehicles. Someone trying to jump the queue backed into a flower border. Horns were sounding off in sharp, warning bursts and long lamenting wails. Men hunched over fumbling with car keys while girls and women in skimpy dresses clutched their forearms, shivering, scrunching their shoulders up to their ears. Mark, shaking in his polyester cotton shirt couldn't believe it. His own head was so cold it ached. But there it was glistening on the car roofs and windows: *Jack Frost!* Everyone was moving as though battling a savage wind, shoulders up and heads down, but the air in fact was quite still. That was the trouble. "When you're talking cold, my boy," Charlotte had said, "cloud cover and even wind are always better." The sky was so bright it glittered. "Radiant heat" Charlotte had called it, heat radiating up through clear, still night air. And down below, under those brilliant Good King Wenceslas stars, the whole damn scene was radiant. Strands of tiny Christmas lights twinkled along the tops of garden hedges, circled palm trees, looped radiantly under eaves and porches. This balmy piece of South Miami with its palms and jacaranda trees, bougainvillea and hibiscus had turned into a winter wonderland, a setting for Christmas carollers with hot punch at the end of it and everyone in mittens and mufflers. What the hell had happened?

Mark set off, head down, down the drive with a straggle of other guests making for the tennis courts, the group breaking to both sides as departing cars nosed through. Mark started fumbling for the key to the Volvo but his fingers were so cold he shoved it back in his pocket afraid he'd drop it. A BMW coming up behind him nudged the back of his knees, the driver yelling something in Spanish. As Mark moved out of the way, the man beside him laughed and shouted something back, apparently quite cheerful. Maybe an orchid spouse, thought Mark, hoping the cold would take out all the damn orchids at home once and for all, so there'd be time and space for something else, like golf or woodwork. Another car nudged past, heading home, hood steaming, windscreen wipers swinging from side to side. And in the one behind that, someone was winding down a window. As Mark was about to yell in English, and to hell with Spanish, "I'm getting out of the bloody way!" he saw it was Larry.

"Ken's going to pull out and wait for you on the side," Larry was yelling too into the freezing air. "Follow us! We'll go down Old Cutler. It's quicker from here than US1!"

Thank God for Ken and Larry, thought Mark, drawing a total blank on how to get back to the highway. He had no idea where Rachel or any of the others were. So much for New Year's Eve, the magic of the moment. Mark jabbed the key at the freezing door of the Volvo and slid in, shivering at the ice cold seat, his fingers numb. He backed straight out in front of an irate Mercedes which blasted its horn so hard all Mark could do was shout "Shut the fuck up!" three times to clear his head. He saw a car to the right, flashing its lights on the grass under the trees and there was Larry waving him over. Ken swerved into traffic, Mark tight behind him but the cars were hardly moving and Old Cutler was only a two lane road winding south, under a canopy of trees. He couldn't stop shivering, his nose was running but he'd clamped his hands to the steering wheel as though if he let go he might lose sight of Ken. Sniffing big, old-fashioned sniffs, like so many of the kids in remedial, Mark thought of the box of paper handkerchiefs he always kept on his desk: what was the good of saying, 'You should have brought something'?"

Mark knew the air could not really be colder than the stuff that surrounded an early morning North London bus stop in January but after nearly a month in South Florida sunshine Mark felt cold in a different way, as though he'd been picked out for punishment below the freezing stars. The old windscreen wipers scraped the glass, back and forth, scrape and clunk. Mark sniffed, ducking his head forward, wiping his nose on his sleeve, those long sleeves. As the air conditioning didn't work, condensation built up on the inside of the windows and he used his elbow and forearm to clear the glass—*finding uses for long sleeves in South Dade.* Mark thought of the calendar in the spare room:'South Florida Pioneer Days,'with its photographs of the first white inhabitants. There they were with their tin trunks and hatchets, their log cabins among the stumps of trees, the Dade County pine, and those high cotton necks and long sleeves even in summer; not turn of the century decorum but defense against mosquitoes. Hard to picture South Dade as a steamy malarial swamp, Mark thought grimly, teeth chattering. But reading about Miami, an Indian trading post just over a hundred years ago, with its malaria and mosquitoes, hostile natives and yellow fever, all sounded like tales of the British Empire. But more like steamy West Africa than Charlotte's beloved East, more like West Africa, the white man's grave.

The stream of cars had slowed so much Mark could have got out and walked home under the trees. He could hear some desperate driver honking away somewhere up the line, probably an orchidist. According to Charlotte a crisis like this was nothing new. "And each time the papers call them 'the once-in-five-hundred-years freeze.'" Carlos had already prepared Orchid Empire's two small greenhouses for winter. To Mark they already looked pretty flimsy even in the sun, with their plastic roofs and shade cloth round the sides. The 'winterizing' as Charlotte called it, consisted of Carlos furling curtains of no-tear transparent plastic in loops above the shade cloth, ready to be dropped when cold winds barreled down the peninsular. In fact, Mark, following Charlotte's instructions, *had* dropped the plastic about mid afternoon while the sun was still warm, long before he'd even fed the dogs but this cold would cut through any plastic. It would cut through a bloody brick wall. Think England. And it was Catch 22: wind was bad, blowing in the cold; no wind was bad, the still air letting the freeze settle in.

But Charlotte *had* said that Orchid Empire would be OK. They had their conference before he left. Shame, thought Mark, swiping the windscreen once more with his sleeve, there were no independent witnesses. With Charlotte you needed your defense rock solid and your case watertight. *"Off you go! Tonight we're in the clear!"* If Charlotte could not remember that line, delivered just before she launched into her Cinderella at the ball bit, then Mark knew his remaining weeks at Orchid Empire would not be happy ones.

The relentless icy sparkle of Christmas lights everywhere, blurring and spattering against the steamy glass, made the night seem even colder. Many were on Christmas trees placed out on the lawns in that generous American way, not just glimpsed inside through half closed curtains. There were no plastic reindeers under these trees and on these spacious lawns, not their natural habitat. Old Cutler was the historic route into Miami from South Dade, Redland. Everyone at Charlotte's party had told Mark that was the way to go: curving through the avenue of old trees, live oaks and tropical hardwoods, opening out further on to fifty year old mahoganies. But tonight Mark would have killed for the three bare, bright lanes of US1 heading south. The radio stations were interrupting their New Year programs: *"Now is the night for those sweaters Granny knitted for Christmas! But seriously, folks, bring in the pets and cold sensitive plants. So put down your drinks and funny hats and before you open the champagne just check everything is OK and the dogs are inside. Now let's go to Tom at our weather desk!"*

"Frigid air has blown into South Florida tonight and according to the weather center record lows are predicted, caused by the same arctic air mass which is blanketing the North-east with several feet of snow and blinding blizzards. This has happened much earlier and more savagely than predicted for, so please take all precautions necessary."

Orchid Empire, all Redland, counted as inland areas; twenty miles plus from the warming influence of the sea. At this rate those Himalayan dendrobiums on the north side might be all that was left; the ones that looked dead to begin with. What had Charlotte said? The dendrobiums *could* take a light frost. "Could even *enjoy* a light frost." That was a good word: 'enjoy.' Ken was finally moving faster and suddenly Mark thought, God, what if Charlotte had *not* nodded off, or, more likely, nodded off on the porch, then, Christ, the cold would have woken her up. Christ! What if she were out struggling to try, in her chair, to turn on the pumps and after several gin and limes. The whole thing was becoming more of a nightmare every minute. Mark could hear his mother: "Let me get this straight," she would start with that deceptively gentle, neutral tone. "You left Charlotte, your invalid Great Aunt, in her wheel chair on the coldest night of the year, *outside* on a porch, (Thank God, thought Mark, she doesn't know about the broken railings,) with a bottle of gin, and went off to a party. I see ...and this party was, how far away? About fifty minutes. Oh? For Americans that's '*not very far?*' So what happens when their elderly, sick family members are left alone...? And I thought it was your job to look after the orchids, too. Yes, Charlotte had a phone but her friends were at that party which was what? Almost an hour away? She had the numbers of doctors, did she? And the hospital? But you knew she'd never call there, you know Charlotte. So anyway, off you went to your party..."

Mark wondered how Bert was doing, Bert at seventy plus with his two workers both in Mexico. Another curve, past a cluster of shops, a gas station and Ken flashed his lights: he was slowing down, turning into a side road. Larry slid out and round to Mark's window, his midnight blue shirt flattening against him, billowing out at the back. Now the wind was picking up.

"Keep on following Old Cutler till you hit US1! Can't miss it! OK? Good Luck! Throw the water on!" Larry thumped the Volvo as though he were hitting a horse to make it go and yelled something into the wind but Mark didn't stop to hear. Another swooping curve, so unusual for American roads with their grid system, all numbers and right angles. What was that line? 'The rolling English drunkard made the rolling English road...' Kipling. No, not Kipling— Kiplingesque. It was Chesterton, of course, G. K. Chesterton! Popular in his day; considered pretty minor now. Due for re-evaluation. Probably had been, Mark thought, while I was in the pub. Christ, how pathetic. Whereas micro-biology, *bios*—life! *Microbiology: The study of microorganisms and their effects on other living organisms.* He wondered how Rachel could keep in such wonderful shape, hunched over in a lab most of the day. Mark took the next curve too fast and was nearly off the road. Old Cutler had been created by horses and carts. It was the old road into Miami, all the way to Coconut Grove and the sea, the way they'd brought everything up to Miami in the old days. Ruby, the elderly black woman who was coming in to help Charlotte, said her mother remembered the carts bringing up guavas and produce from Redland. She'd remembered the guavas. Maybe, Ruby said, because they had a real strong smell.

South on US1 there were still one or two old packing sheds alongside the Florida East Coast railway track and some odd square buildings with blind walls, granaries marking the railheads where the farmers brought their produce. And where *was* US1, Mark asked himself, taking curves one after the other in the dark, the only car now, no street lighting, hands freezing on the wheel, window open to de-fog all the glass. Maybe he'd missed a turn; maybe Larry had been shouting something about making a turn. At least the Volvo hadn't stalled at a light. Charlotte was in the right place, Mark thought. Right now, South Florida did not seem a pansy place. How recent it all was: Homestead, the calendar said, founded at the turn of the century, almost five hundred years after the first settlement in Virginia. Hadn't Virginia been founded by Walter Raleigh, 'the English pirate'? That first batch of settlers disappeared in the cold of one Virginia winter, apparently, no trace. Mark shivering in the dark of Old Cutler could well believe it. Naranja, with the big Kmart, had been named for the orange groves and Princeton, where the post office was, by a graduate who made a fortune with a saw mill, turning the virgin pine forest all around into planks. It hadn't been a few district officers in Miami waiting for orders from Whitehall or the Colonial Office but Americans getting down to it: cutting canals, draining the Everglades, drawing up the grid system for roads, felling the trees, the pines, laying the ground work for Kmart in Naranja.

Suddenly Mark was running through an area of small, one storey houses where fences were looking higher because the pavements and road were only a few feet away from the front doors. There were bikes on porches, cars up on blocks round the side. A group of black teenagers standing round a car in sweaters and wind-cheaters, knitted caps pulled down hard over their eyes and ears, shoulders hunched, hands tucked in, stared at the Volvo as it went by. A few strings of Christmas lights, a plastic Santa in a little front yard, a tiny white church, a chapel. This had to be where Ruby lived. Cars everywhere, almost dwarfing the small homes, nosing in round the fences, gathered for New Year. A football field. And the last stretch, a run down grocery, two old cars, two young and two old black men staring, and then the blinking orange light, the intersection, and there was US1. Across the road, into Redland: Hainlin Mill Drive, the saw mill for the pine, Silver Palm Drive, and Coconut Palm.

As Mark turned off US1 he was startled by a great slapping whoosh across his windscreen. Water. The road ahead was wet in shining arcs as the water was flung out across the fields. And there was a low humming and throbbing on all sides. Every farmer and nurseryman had the water on. All the way home to Orchid Empire the whole of Redland humming with water; a warm sixty-three degrees out of the ground. "They used to do what they called smudge pots," Charlotte said. "Burn old tires in the fields and round the plants to keep everything warm. First winter I was here, got talked into it. Black gunk all over the plants, the phals. Had an old guy working for me—real Florida cracker. Used to rub WD40 on his hands for arthritis. We're losing those old boys like we're losing the wasps and snakes."

The dogs came down the drive barking, the cold making them excited and hungry again. As Mark got out of the car he could hear the hum from all around, the irrigation systems pumping out the water and there was an ominous flap of plastic from the orchid houses. But first he had to check on Charlotte. Not, thank goodness, on the freezing porch. No lights in her bedroom, just in the Florida room. That one usually burned all night because Charlotte had a hard job reaching the switch. Mark went through the Florida room and turned down the tiny passage way to Charlotte's door. He knocked, knocked louder. Couldn't hear her snoring. Mark pushed open the door gently to check. No chair, the bed empty. Christ, *Christ!*

Mark hesitated for a moment. He wanted something warm to put on, his Harris Tweed but couldn't stop till he knew where Charlotte was. Outside he suddenly registered the sound that meant trouble: the loud 'wop, wop, wop!' which meant the plastic sheeting on the north side of the first house must have pulled free and was billowing up and slapping back, slamming in the cold air like bellows. Where was Charlotte? If she'd have got close, her chair would have been knocked over. *Christ!* Thank God, nothing round the side, no tipped over chair. Mark grabbed a two by six plank and shoved it against the side to keep some heat in for a little until he got the pumps on. In a moment the wind was under the plastic, billowing it up as it tossed the ten foot plank away into the bushes and suddenly Mark realized the pumps *were* on. Charlotte must have put them on, must be out there some-where. *Christ!* She was not inside the first house, not outside the sec-ond but there she was, just in the doorway of the potting shed, chair swivelled in against the bench, rummaging through the tools, shiver-ing and, worse, looked like she was soaking wet. She must have been caught by the water when she managed to turn it on. "Looking for the bloody stapler!" Charlotte shouted. "Where's the bloody stapler?"

The heavy hammer stapler was on the shelf above the bench and, thank God, the box of staples too. Without stopping to talk, Mark grabbed them and raced out. He shoved against the plastic at ground level with all his weight trying to smooth and hold it down. He could feel it lifting him away, the force so strong, and had to wait for a lull in the wind, between *wops*. It was like trying to furl bloody *sails* with a stapler. When it came to a hurricane, Charlotte said the last thing you did before the storm hit was cut the shade cloth free, like cutting the sails on a ship in a storm. "Always the hardest decision to make: that way you might save your greenhouse." The wind could race through the structure, like the wind through the bare masts of a ship. "My old Florida cracker warned me you always lose orchids *after* a hurricane. The weather's usually hot and bright, like after Andrew and with no leaves on the trees, no shade, the cloth blown away, the plants just burn to death in the sun."

Mark waited for a lull, slammed his shoulder against the wood strip and hammered just two staples in. He had only half a box left.

Inching down, Mark was about to hammer two more when the wind pulled the plastic free, the precious staples flying off past his face into the wind and then the plastic was slammed back against the side. He couldn't put a ladder up: the wind would hurl a ladder away like the plank. Mark rammed his shoulder again against the plastic, holding it down and hammered hard, then once more, further up before the wind ripped it away. This time the plastic held and before it could tug free, he edged up and slammed in a couple of staples at shoulder height and higher. Now he could get the ladder close for the top. More staples, fingers freezing. God, he was freezing and he wasn't even wet. Mark knew Charlotte wouldn't go inside till she saw the houses secured. Until then, any help she would toss off like the plank hurled away by the plastic.

The side was done and the wind for a moment died down a little. Mark walked round the outside of the orchid houses, checking, seeing, thank God, the water hitting against the plastic from the inside, the plastic warm but he went in and squelched through both houses, to check the sprinklers were all working and only then came back to Charlotte's chair. It was still by the potting bench, Charlotte's hands tight on its sides. For a moment Mark thought maybe she'd had a stroke. "Charlotte! Come on!" She shook herself, shaking her head at him. Then she turned the chair slowly, shaking off help. Mark walked slowly beside the chair and up the ramp. "Charlotte you need to get out of those wet things!" Mark shivering himself, called after her, across the Florida room.

"I'll manage. I'll manage," Charlotte's voice was faint. Mark followed her chair down the little passage. "Don't touch me! Charlotte commanded "I'll manage!" She rolled her chair deliberately into her room and nudged the wheels of the chair against the door to push it shut.

Mark knew Charlotte couldn't manage. He himself could hardly get out of his soaking clothes. Shivering and hopping about trying to get the damn wet trousers off Mark knew he had to call someone. But Ruby couldn't come out at this time of night even if he could reach her. He'd have to call Rachel. Rachel, Bert, Larry—they were all busy with their orchids, their livelihoods. Maybe Rachel would know someone who could come.

"Hi. You have reached Rachel Templeton of Bios Orchids and Jennifer Marshall. There is no one here right now to take your call but if you'd like to leave a message, wait for the beep: our fax number is... our e mail address is..." Christ, get on with it! Mark groaned even as he recognized Rachel's voice. He tried once more.

"—Hallo? Who's this?"

"Mark. ...Jen? Is Rachel there?"

"Yes but she's out with the orchids. We had a bit of a disaster with the plastic."

"Oh. Well, the problem is Charlotte. She won't let me touch her. She's soaking wet. I know she wouldn't mind Rachel...Do you think Rachel would know any other... anyone else...?" Mark's voice trailed away.

"Hang on." There was a pause. "Look, I could come over. Why don't I come over? Charlotte knows me. Take me about fifteen minutes plus. Rachel is just too preoccupied right now."

"That would be great. She won't let me touch her and I'm afraid..."

"I'll be there in fifteen."

"Thanks. Thank you."

"No problem."

7

New Year's Night

The dogs, always relishing the prospect of Orchid Empire coming under attack, scrambled up from under the house barking wildly when they heard Jen's car. Out on the porch it was not the cold that hit Mark as much as the brilliance: '*The moon doth shine as bright as day.*' He could have sat out there and read the weather report from the *Herald* by moonlight.

"Rachel says looks like a solid freeze." Jen came up the ramp, a canvas bag slung over her shoulder the size of a small hammock, her breath white in the cold air. Buried in a long woolly scarf and thick white sweater down to her knuckles, she looked ready to cheer on the Totters Green Cavaliers from the freezing sidelines. Weaving her way through the old rattan sofas and bamboo coffee tables in the Florida room Jen turned out of sight along the little passageway leading to Charlotte's room. Mark heard her knock on the door. "Hi, Charlotte!"

"Rachel?" Mark had to listen hard to hear Charlotte. That was something new.

"She's with the orchids. It's Jen. I'm here instead."

"I don't need anyone! Go away!" The weak, querulous note in Charlotte's voice was something else new.

"Charlotte, shut up." Just as Mark had been wondering what Jen would do. She said it briskly, going into Charlotte's room and closing the door. How right, thought Mark. No wheedling voice as though talking to a dog or a child, no *Let's all be good now!* Jen cut right through it: *Good in emergencies.* His mother would say she could have seen that right from the start, from the way she cleaned her plate. After about fifteen minutes Jen reappeared. "She's nice and warm, that is if

60

you don't need the little heater anywhere else? I found a pair of wonderful old flannel nightgowns in a bottom drawer, though don't ever mention it, she'll deny it. We'll have to hope for the best tomorrow. She's still shivery and got a temp. I gave her some aspirin and brandy. Doesn't want the doctor, of course, but maybe we could get Ruby. But what about you?"

"Well, if we miss out the nightie, I think I'm about due for the same: a brandy, maybe two, and I wouldn't mind an aspirin. Yes, I'll call Ruby as soon as possible in the morning." Ruby had been coming over to give Charlotte "a scrub down" on the days when she could get her old Cadillac to start. Charlotte apparently had gone through several 'health technicians' sent by the hospital and had finally been blacklisted. Ruby was a freelance and Ruby was it.

Jen sat her canvas bag down on one of the couches. She pulled out a large bottle of generic aspirin, a half bottle of brandy and a nest of paper cups. "I'm never quite sure what Charlotte's got," she said apologetically, setting two of the cups on a coffee table, "I've always got the feeling that she's still kind of camping out. Look, why don't I stay over. I can sleep here in the Florida room. It will be near Charlotte and there's certainly enough couches to choose from. That's one thing Charlotte's not short of."

"Well, I'm afraid it's going to be very cold."

"I need to stay a little longer anyway, see if Charlotte's really settled and if I'm going to have another drink too I'm not going to want to drive. It's turned into a pretty crazy New Year's Eve. Everyone racing off. We must have been one of the first cars out of there, you know Rachel. She's the one who flattened that bush on the edge of the lawn. Well, it certainly rained on Regina's parade. Charlotte will love that."

"What I can't understand," said Mark "is how everyone seems to have been caught off guard. Charlotte is always saying they watch the weather like hawks down here in the winter, at least all the farmers and nursery people. Like tracking hurricanes in the summer."

"Apparently the weather bureau people just screwed up. They've been cutting back, saving money. And most of the workers were off for New Year, a lot of them don't have phones. And as Rachel says, if it's really a hard freeze, tomorrow a lot of them won't have jobs."

"Well, the thermometer on the porch was already down to thirty-seven Fahrenheit when I got back. Charlotte says it drops two degrees an hour and the wind's died down and, what is it now? Already one o clock? If freezing is thirty-two degrees, then it's going to freeze. Sorry it's so cold in here. The Florida room's absolutely open, no glass, just screens. We'd be a lot warmer, if wetter, with the orchids. You know we could put up plastic here, cover the screens onto the porch."

Mark went out to get the stapler and hunt up some pieces of plastic. Orchid Empire's pumps, thank God, were still throbbing away. The plastic sides of the orchid houses were warm to the touch and, incredibly, the wind suddenly had died down; there was no tugging or tearing at the edges. The water that felt so pleasantly cool on those eighty degree days, now steaming as though it was coming out of the bowels of the earth. Mark stopped for a moment, his breath curling away in front of him. The moon still so bright he felt he was in the spotlight, on a stage. Not a leaf stirred. Instead of the light industrial, repetitive beeps and electronic chirps of the cicadas there was an old fashioned, solid throb coming from all across Redland; warm water being pumped out of the ground, on and on. But Orchid Empire didn't have a generator. "All we need now," Mark reflected, "is a power cut."

"You know, whenever Rachel and I come over we've always just sat on the porch. Charlotte hated to be inside." Jen's arms were folded across her chest, one hand holding the paper cup as carefully as though it were fine china. "I remember seeing that spear through the screens. I can just see Charlotte dragging it all the way from Africa. Doesn't look so sinister close up. No, I take that back, it looks like it's been used. A lot." There was a long spear hanging on the wall above one of the couches, its handle worn and sweaty like a an old cricket bat. Not from Kenya, Charlotte had said, an *assagai,* "Missile of the *South African* tribes."

Mark was measuring out pieces of plastic. "Could you hold it up on that side? I'm afraid it's black. That's all I could find." They were both speaking in low voices, reminding themselves that the real concern of the night had become Charlotte.

"I expect you know your bull-rushes need dusting." There was a clay water pot stuffed with plastic bull-rushes near the porch door, next to an old wicker basket full of flashlights that didn't work.

"Um, I'm afraid a lot of things..."

"Just *kidding!* I admire Charlotte. All those years she just did her thing. Way before it was easy for women or fashionable. Even now it can still be hard, you know, for women just to say 'So, my bull-rushes are dusty? So?' —You know, like Robert de Niro: 'You talking to *me?*' Oh, sorry. My end."

"Actually Charlotte says she leaves the screens dirty for the winter on purpose. The dust helps to keep the cold out." Mark didn't try and make it sound funny. On a night like this, he thought grimly, it wasn't. He was preoccupied trying to put the plastic up right the first time because there were very few staples left. He was surprised Jen had turned out to be so chatty. Mark put it down to the cold as much as the brandy and the late hour; everyone had been thrown a bit off center. The white sweater and scarf certainly made Jen look dark, more vivid. No obvious make up. She certainly hadn't dolled herself up for the party. Not that, Mark hastily told himself, he would consider Rachel's emerald eye-shadow *dolling up*. Mark winced as he whacked the hammer stapler against the wood, afraid of disturbing Charlotte, his fingers numb on the cold metal. "If it weren't for Charlotte we'd be better off making for a homeless shelter," he joked. "Sorry. It won't get much warmer but at least we've stopped the cold air coming in. We'd have to do a lot of heavy breathing to warm up this place."

Jen erupted into a laugh which she immediately squashed. She had a kind of burbling, unexpectedly subversive, sexy giggle.

"Did I say that?" Mark rolled his eyes. He'd been thinking of the Volvo, the steamy windows. "Let me get you a blanket and see if there's another pillow." One good thing about sleeping in the spare room, Mark reflected, you did know where all the stuff was. He couldn't hear any sound from Charlotte's room but Jen got up and checked for herself, padding along in her short white socks. She tucked herself into the corner of the couch facing his, across the coffee table and its big, square glass ash trays, knees under her chin, blanket round her shoulders.

"Charlotte says more people die of cold in South Florida than hurricanes," Mark said. "They drag barbecue grills inside and die of asphyxiation; they light up old kerosene stoves and burn their houses down. But if they live in houses like this, I'm not surprised." In addition to his Harris Tweed jacket, Mark had arrived in South Florida with a single one hundred percent Shetland wool sweater. Until now, he'd been embarrassed at the fact: that he was still deep into the old tribal ways that made it hard for the English to go anywhere in the winter or indeed the summer without at the last minute shoving at least one cosy woollen covering into their luggage. He offered the sweater to Jen and, still feeling cold, was glad when she said she'd be OK with the blanket. "Well, it seems a little unfair. I do have the jacket."

Jen smiled. "The English teacher."

"I'm afraid so."

"No, I didn't mean it like that, it's neat. Larry would love it. It's so English, so... *picturesque.* Is that the right word?"

"You mean like Anne Hathaway's cottage?"

"Come on! I'm an economist not an English major!" Jen's getting rather perky, Mark thought uneasily. He wasn't sure if she were feeling the effects of the brandy at nearly one in the morning, starting to flirt a little, or he was misreading the whole scene. Why should he have learned much about Americans, anyway, when he was spending all his time with an old English woman and two Mexicans? It was Uncle Frank who used to say weightily: "Because Americans speak the same language we forget they're foreigners." Though this apparently shrewd and fairly worldly comment was usually followed by his own personal opinion, never explained: "Mind you, if I had my way I'd drop a bomb on the lot of them." Jen certainly didn't seem very foreign, didn't even seem especially very American, just a low key, sensible presence. Unlike Rachel, thought Mark. You looked at Rachel and it put you on your toes. You wanted to write poems, make smart remarks and go forth, if not to fight for a better world at least to lift weights and buy better clothes.

"Even at this late hour, we need to toast the New Year," Mark said, preparing a retreat to the kitchen. "Let me get something to eat and real glasses; we can't clink paper! See, you've squashed your cup." God, he thought, now I'm being perky. The Miami Orchid Club dinner seemed so far away, the woman with the cello, the collapsible plates. Jen was probably as hungry as he was, and food would definitely warm them up. Mark had bought some smoked salmon as it was New Year's Eve but half past one in the morning didn't seem right for fish so it was back to the old chips and cheese. The elderly fridge in the kitchen with the door that didn't shut properly, had finally stopped throbbing. Exactly, thought Mark, the whole damn house is a fridge tonight. He got out the bamboo tray, seeing how grubby it looked and stained; all the woven strips havens for germs and stray crumbs. Hunting around in the kitchen drawer for something to cover it he found under a starched, embroidered table cloth, a whole treasure trove of mostly brand new tea towels. A few Charlotte had been using, obviously her favorites, faded and well worn: *English Wild Flowers, British Hedgerows, Save the Hedgehog, Hedgehog Habitats* and *Save the British Hedgehog!* Mark hadn't realized that in terms of the general public's affection, hedgehogs were right up there with the Queen Mother. There was a brand new *Tudor Kings and Queens* and *Birds of Britain*. Most of the unused ones were heritage or literary: *London Literary Landmarks— (Dickens, The Old Curiosity Shop: The Tower of London); Wordsworth's Lake District.* His mother must have sent one every Christmas: that was it; she always sent something light because of the postage. Mark settled on *Souvenir of Devon*: violets, a chunk of sea cliff, pot of cream, a thatched cottage. He wondered if this one could really date back to that holiday they'd had when he was what, fourteen? Mark got out the cheese, a knife, the chips, and the Scotch, and set down two square tumblers on the cliffs at Dawlish.

Jen, hands tucked in under her armpits, had got out of her blanket and was looking at the photographs. "Charlotte had quite a life. She's quite a lady." However full of herself she seemed to be now, Charlotte certainly hadn't hogged the camera in her early days. There was tea on the verandah, a group of young couples in what looked like forties clothes, the men with narrow shoulders and wide trousers; a slender blonde with a sunny smile perched on the front of a land-rover. Could that be her?

A large gent with RAF handlebar moustache beside a great clump of something—a massive orchid, Mark supposed. What had Charlotte said? "Some orchids you need a magnifying glass, others three men to carry them." There she was, older and obviously Charlotte, a sturdy trunk in evening dress, now lined up with dinner jackets and chiffon and taffeta, in a whole sequence of old glossy black and white prints. Always someone in the middle with a big grin, usually a man in a dinner jacket, sometimes a couple, holding a cup, a plaque, a rosette, a certificate, an orchid. These must have been the rich clients with the prizewinning orchids Charlotte had collected or bred for them. Odd, Mark couldn't imagine her playing second fiddle to anyone. Of course, that's why she didn't last long, why she kept moving. There was the inside of a greenhouse, two young Africans, perhaps, thin, young black men staring apprehensively at the camera while behind them stretched away benches of plants.

Mark poured out the Scotch: they were going to be hung over anyway, whether they mixed their drinks or not. The dogs suddenly started barking. They both listened a moment. The sound died away; only the pumps. "I heard a few shots coming over," remarked Jen. "Oh, no, just New Year. By the way, Happy New Year!" They stood side by side in front of the old black and white photos and clinked glasses in their socks. Being in socks made it oddly intimate. Mark had taken off his shoes too, and for the same reason, so he could push his feet together and try and get some animal warmth going between those two frozen parts. He wished there was a television in the Florida room to break the silence, or even a radio. There were more ash trays than anything else, at least two of those massive, glass squares to each coffee table. You could see the old linen runners under the glass, freckled with mildew and hand embroidered with faint blue forget-me-nots. Mark was sure they'd gone out with Charlotte when she left England. He could see her lecturing some African servant years ago when the blue thread was bright, on the seasons of the forget-me-not, its proper Latin name and usual habitat.

Jen had fallen silent. Mark rejected the idea that she was really starting to fancy him in his picturesque Oxfam Harris Tweed jacket and threadbare socks. After all, she hadn't come to sit around in her socks while he checked her out; she had come to help Charlotte whom she'd known a good sight longer than he had. Whereas I, on the other hand, Mark told himself, am the number one catch at the local Rat and Parrot! Not even historic, not even an authentic pub, never make it on to a tea towel. Jen was probably just between boyfriends, or about to be reunited for New Year with her high school sweetheart, a wholesome Mid-westerner. Held up by a snow storm, the blizzard conditions further north which were causing such havoc down here, he would suddenly appear, redirected by Rachel, ducking under the door-frame and giving him a real friendly grin with his great American teeth because he could see at a glance that Mark was no kind of competition.

It was all so traditionally English, here at one thirty am, in a nutty way, Mark thought. That was the cold. The fact that Jen's nose was such an authentic English red. That it was so bloody cold and cheerless. Like visits to relatives such as Uncle Frank who rejected the new Britain of central heating. Like student days, the second year when a group of them got a really great deal on renting a house because, as they discovered, there was absolutely no bloody heating and all the fireplaces had been blocked up. "I'm sorry, this can't be the New Year you'd expected." Mark broke the silence.

"Isn't this what we're supposed to be doing, staying up half the night and drinking too much?" Jen was back in her blanket, with a large Scotch and a plate piled with chips and chunks of New York Extra Sharp Cheddar.

"That's what I seem to be doing most of the year. It's a shame," Mark stopped himself. He'd been about to say it was a shame Rachel couldn't be there and that sounded odd. "A shame it's so cold."

"The main thing is if the *orchids* are going to be warm enough," Jen said. "You see? Rachel has got me trained."

"Do you think hers will be OK?"

"Well she managed to jerry-rig the plastic. You know Rachel, she'll probably just be out there with them till dawn." Mark could see Rachel, bent over the torn plastic in her low cut black dress, breasts surging forward, strands of ash blond hair whipping across her face. Jen was looking down at her Scotch, silent again. It was too late to resurrect New Year it seemed but too cold to sleep. Then Jen asked him how it had come about he was there, staying with Charlotte and Mark, reluctantly starting to talk, found it was quite easy. His mother was not Charlotte's sister but her niece and no, quite different. No, not that she was a great one for housework either, but the sort of woman you felt should be married, so more difficult for her when his father died. And that had been quite early on, he'd been twelve. And no, he didn't come from Devon or anywhere picturesque; his world would never be on a tea towel. "You know those old bits on TV with Benny Hill and Monty Python where the housewives and characters run up and down those tight little roads with all the hedges and front doors lined up? Well, that's about it."

Jen said well, *she* didn't really come from anywhere. She was an 'army brat.' Her father had been stationed all over, a career officer. They were in Japan when she was small, Germany and Georgia, no, not the UK: Mark was thinking more of air bases.

"Citizen of the world," Mark said, "I'm impressed."

"Citizen of an army base. I'd like to have come from somewhere. You know, like to be intense about something like Rachel. I'm not into orchids, of course. I've been helping some with sales and shows but basically I don't know one end of an orchid from the other."

Mark, groggy and off guard, just stopped himself saying, "Neither do I."

Jen fell silent. She had pursed her lips together almost like a Rosita, gazing across the Florida room, knees still up to her chin. The sound of the pumps came through the black plastic, Orchid Empire's, and all those beyond, across the fields and groves. Mark, sitting with his feet up on the couch opposite, was totally preoccupied putting one cold foot on top of the other. Get one warm somehow, that was the idea, and that warmed up the other. If it hadn't been for the feet he'd be starting to feel mellow, certainly fuzzy in the traditional New Year's way. *Hey, there was this crazy New Year's Eve, South Florida, shivering, freezing behind a curtain of black plastic garbage bags!* Ned would never believe him. Well, he would if Mark said there was a girl on the scene. "Hey, man, you gotta do what you gotta do."

"Let me check Charlotte one more time," Jen unwound herself from her blanket. Mark realized he'd fallen silent. If it weren't for his feet he'd definitely have nodded off. It seemed to be getting colder and colder. There was not even any warmth from the light bulbs. No bulb over forty watts, one of Charlotte's rules, just enough light so you didn't trip over the furniture; so sitting on the porch, nothing much disturbed the dark. Mark poured them both another Scotch.

"Charlotte's asleep. She seems OK." Jen was back, voice low. Mark handed her a glass.

"I know it's total overkill but so's the bloody cold." As Jen took a swallow Mark realized she'd got his glass—the wrong glass. "Sorry, that's mine."

"I don't think it matters too much," Jen laughed. "Got any terrible diseases?"

"Well, I haven't had to visit the clinic this month!" *Christ!* That was the sort of line he'd sling at Ned. The sort of thing Ned said at closing time to the blonde at The Rat and Parrot. Jen put her lips together, eyes down. Mark couldn't decide if she was doing a bit of a Rosita again or just trying not to laugh. "Should you go out and check the orchids one more time?"

For a moment Mark listened to the pumps, one more time. "Hell, no!" They could say it was thirty-two Fahrenheit and freezing, they could say it was colder than Minnesota. It didn't make any difference. Like almost everyone else in Redland, like all the "agricultural and horticultural interests of South Dade," of Florida, Mark had done all he could do. The plastic was tight, the water was on. Nature was on the rampage out there just taking her course, clumping down the peninsula: *Termi-nature!* And in an hour or two, with the dawn, they'd all see how merciless she'd been. "No," said Mark again. "To hell with the orchids!" He was thinking of the whole silly charade of being Charlotte's orchid man, the fact that everyone except Jen was into this whole orchid thing. "Happy New Year!" He looked down at Jen and added "*Jen*" to personalize the greeting, as they'd say. He thought of

Charlotte grumbling about the generic 'Happy Holidays' everywhere rather than Merry Christmas: "Christmas in a plain brown wrapper!" There was Jen, not so plain, but brown wrapped--Jenny Wren. She came up to his shoulder which was about right he thought. About right for what? There was a gun shot out in the dark "They're a bit late," Mark said.

"Maybe celebrating the start of the dawn— the actual New Year," Jen suggested. "Not long now."

Mark was reflecting if he couldn't get his feet warm he could at least show a little festive spirit. After all, it was New Year. Especially as he'd been a bit harsh about Jen earlier. And New Year's Eve *was* New Year's Eve. "Hey, Happy New Year, Jen." Mark started in with what he remembered began as a quite solemn, ordinary, chaste, in front of everyone kiss on the cheek, on one cold cheek that somehow slipped sideways. Or maybe Jen moved.

Later of course, that became one of the questions for the Commission of Enquiry: what motivated the subsequent course of action. Blaming the drink, the brandy and the Scotch, that was tried and true. They could both do that, going all the way back to the one small, stingy, introductory glass of champagne on offer at Regina's bash. It was, in fact, true that Mark been rapidly getting to the point where, if he'd been at The Rat and Parrot, they'd have taken the darts away from him, prized them out of his hand. But Mark blamed it on being in socks, having taken off their shoes. There was something about the socks. Also they were both shivering, and shivering was sexy. Mark found himself saying: "Look, if we moved the coffee table we could shove two couches together and ...get warmer." They didn't look each other in the eye. Mark went off to the spare room to get his blanket and his pillow.

"These are really long couches."

"Maybe like the beer—British imperial pints—the large imperial size. Maybe Charlotte shipped them in from Africa."

"You can really stretch out," Jen observed.

"We don't need to stretch out but huddle up," Mark said sternly. If this was the drink talking it was making him sound like a Totters

Green coach at soccer practice. He had taken his picturesque Harris Tweed jacket off and spreadeagled it over the middle of the blankets where it promptly slid off and fell to the floor. "Fuck Oxfam. You know how hard to it is to get feet warm? Let's *start* by getting our feet warm."

"Is that an English thing?" There was that subversive, sexy giggle burbling up. Illicit, thought Mark, that's another good word for it. Jen was burying her face in Mark's Shetland wool sweater.

"You know, if we really wanted to behave ourselves," Mark mumbled into her hair, "and by the way, your hair smells *excellent,* we would get the spear down and put it between us down the middle. And remain true to our vows."

"Do you have any vows right now?"

For a moment Mark thought of Rachel. "No vows," he said. "Just cold feet."

8

New Year's Day

"You don't have any coffee?"

"Only some old instant. Looks like it dates back to Hurricane Andrew. But I could knock a spoonful out. What about some tea? Nice and strong?"

"...OK."

" Have you heard anything from Charlotte's room?"

"She's still asleep." Jen was standing in the kitchen doorway, scarf wound round her neck like a massive bandage, eyes squinting in the sunlight.

"You know, we've probably got *frozen* orange juice out there. I don't know if we can rescue any of the citrus. When I went to get the paper even the clothes line, the row of pegs and the grass underneath, were white with frost. The orchids along the front of the greenhouses, the landscape orchids, their actual flowers were frozen under the sprinklers. Charlotte says a coating of ice protects; calls it 'relatively benign.'" Mark felt the need to keep talking. Jen was not looking at him. "You can hear the branches breaking where they've been running the water on the grove opposite, the ice has frozen in cascades on them. I'm wondering if the tamarind tree will die. Charlotte said it's from Thailand, *Tamarindus indica*. But it is close in by the shed."

"What about the *orchids?* The orchid houses?"

"The water's still running on them. Have to leave it on till the sun really warms up." The orchid houses were steaming in the early morning sun. That was another interesting thing to mention, but Jen had sat down at the kitchen table and picked up the *Herald*. "You finished with section A?"

72

"Yes."

"Do you need it for the weather?"

"That's Section B, thanks." They were acting like an old married couple except they were being much too polite. "Thank God, tonight's going to be warmer." *Tonight along the coast we'll see low to mid-fifties with lows in the low fifties in the inland and farming areas.* Mark just stopped himself from reading this out loud. He wanted to add: *Strawberries, beans, peppers, squash, tomatoes, all have been hard hit and if the cold repeats tonight the potato farmers warn of serious losses from water damage as the crop will rot in the fields. Spokesmen for the nurserymen also report heavy losses to ornamentals and exotics.* If he kept talking there wouldn't be space for questions or analysis. He certainly had the perfect excuse for sliding out of the imperial couches while Jen was still asleep; had to check the pumps. The pumps were on, throbbing away like his head.

"Have you called Ruby yet? Is it too early?"

Is Jen just playing it cool because she realizes I'm feeling cool or is she acting cool because she's really feeling cool or is she feeling cool because she sees me acting cool? Not that I'm acting cool, with my bloody weather reports. "I thought we'd better wait at least till eight thirty."

"OK. Do you know where I put the aspirin?"

"The Florida room, I think." Mark remembered the bottle sliding along the coffee table when they moved it. "Do you want something to eat?"

"Oh, boy. No."

"Um, do you take milk? Sugar?"

"No, nothing."

"Well, it's quite strong."

They were warming their hands on the mugs. Mark had refilled the kettle and was letting it boil so the steam would warm the air a little. The kitchen looked warm enough with sunlight streaming in though the window. "It's much warmer outside, now the sun's up."

"I'll be going when Ruby comes." Jen looked down at the *Herald.* It was comparing last night's New Year's Eve freeze to Hurricane Andrew: "Unexpected, swift and gone. In just one night, the landscape changed."

How true, thought Mark. How simple it all had been last night: Rachel is stunning, I am after Rachel. She has a friend; I am not interested in said friend. End of story. Ned, of course, would say it's always a good working strategy: if you can't get your first choice—A, then go for B, back up. And bingo! You got lucky, what's your problem? Trouble was Mark was sure Jen knew she was one of the B series. It had all been great and everything he could hear himself mumbling, but in the general scheme of things, as Ned defined events, last night was still a big whoopsie. And even Ned would have a bit of a problem with the ongoing scenario: B lives with A so there is no way to infiltrate A's life without coming into contact with B. Then if B tells A—Happy New Year! Jen's being good though, Mark told himself. She's not *Hey! Where do we go from here? Got season tickets to the big games?*

Mark called Ruby and then, grateful to be able to disappear, went to wait for her on the porch. Ruby was scared of the dogs. The second time she'd come she'd thrown chicken backs out of the car window to keep them at bay. The dogs, happy and excited at this unexpected turn of events in the middle of the day and with long memories when it came to food, had crowded round the old Cadillac the next time, pinning Ruby against the car door. From then on she honked the horn and Rosita would come out of the orchid house to escort her in while Ruby swung at the dogs' heads with her Blockbuster Video bag and Charlotte roared from the porch: "*Down* you dumb, damn dogs! *Down!*"

"My *Lord!*" Ruby would puff as she climbed up the makeshift ramp, "it's worse than Selma, Alabama!"

This morning she didn't honk the horn. "What she done to her self *now?*" Ruby was toiling up the ramp, bundled up against the cold. "If that woman is asleep that's all to the good."

It was ten past nine. Jen went with her to Charlotte's room. "I think Charlotte's going to be fine," Jen said when she came out. "She's weak but her temperature's down. She's just warned Ruby not to expect a deathbed conversion. I don't know what you think but I'd rather we didn't call the doctor. Because of the leg they'd probably take her in for 'observation.'"

"Well, Ruby said on the phone she could come in the mornings."

"That would probably be OK," Jen said slowly, looking at the floor. Again Mark was reminded of Rosita. Well, Jen wasn't a parlor maid but he was certainly not behaving like a gentleman. Due for Australia. That's where Ned got his genes from. "If you could keep an ear open at night," Jen was saying, "for a night or two, just in case. And Ruby's obviously just the right person for Charlotte." Ruby certainly had the same kind of killer look that made clear she did not suffer fools gladly. Hers was the spiritual version. When Ruby looked Mark up and down, he knew he should think twice about why he didn't go to church and put his faith in something stronger than Guinness and Johnnie Walker.

Mark was glad to escape. He went to turn off the water. Back in the house he had heard Ruby ask Jen where things were and they were rattling about together. This would have been the perfect morning to have spent an impressive amount of time yanking hoses about but as the water had been running non-stop since just before midnight Mark's main job was the other classic male role, not striding about earning a living for the women folk but keeping out of their way.

Charlotte's world, the world of last year, yesterday, right up to yesterday evening with the gin and chips on the porch, suddenly seemed so remote. Mark wondered if it would ever come back in all its ramshackle glory. Charlotte might have been a Great Aunt but her domestic life style was more like Ned's in Earls Court with his one fridge for beer, another (usually empty) for everything else and for whom house cleaning was a distant event that occurred after your lease expired or you'd been thrown out. A clean and tidy house for Charlotte had always indicated a shallow mind, though it would be a brave soul who'd try that one out on Ruby. Of course, if that were really the case, Mark reflected, that would make most of his male friends and his sister, very deep thinkers indeed, and Ned a total Einstein.

For the first time, walking into one of Charlotte's orchid houses felt like going into a heated green house in England, entering a warmer, steamier world than the one outside. The orchid leaves were still dripping. Mark couldn't see any cold burn on the leaves. Maybe with some species the damage showed up later. The birds were happy enough, gathered round the houses, singing, ruffling their feathers in the broad puddles underfoot. There were the blue jays Charlotte called welfare queens because they just hung around waiting to pinch the dog chow, doves and shiny black grackles taking over the scene like starlings and a flash of scarlet, an early cardinal.

Having come back tentatively to the house Mark avoided the kitchen and landed up in the pitch black, stone cold Florida room. He started to strip off the plastic from the screens. Charlotte's old South Dade home, designed to keep heat out not in, worked so well that Mark, having left his jacket on the sunny porch, went back out to put it on. When he ventured back into the kitchen Jen, talking to Ruby, already had her bag by her feet, long white woolly scarf folded on top. Mark was just about to tell her it was much warmer and quite pleasant on the porch but realized she was just waiting for him to come in so she could say goodbye.

"Has Orchid Empire survived?"

"Some of the damage may not show yet. I hope Rachel, Bios Orchids is OK. I hope Rachel didn't need you last night."

"That's OK. Don't worry." Jen got up. "Good bye Ruby, thanks a million." On the porch she said "Let me know how it goes. I'll be working tomorrow but I'll give a call."

"Right," Mark paused. "Well, thank-you so much."

It was Jen who said, chin up, looking over at her car. ""Hey, New Year's Eve, right? OK?" Jen letting him off the hook.

"Right. Look, thanks again." Mark thought what am I saying thank-you for? "I mean, all your help with Charlotte."

Jen slung the big canvas bag on her shoulder, walked down the ramp and opened the car door. "That's OK," she called, without turning round. "No problem."

Back in the kitchen Ruby said "I'll need some things from the store," handing Mark a piece of paper. Right at the top, in large, commanding letters, he saw 'Oven Cleaner.' Things in the kitchen were not so very dirty because they were never used but the oven, Mark knew, was crusty from pizza fall out. "Ruby, what do *you* like?" Mark was getting some housekeeping dollars out of the old ostrich egg, a South African souvenir from Cape Town, behind the tea caddy in the kitchen.

"I'll be going home before dark so don't you worry about me."

Mark wanted to ask Ruby how Charlotte paid her, and what extra would be needed but that would have to wait.

"If you could go now, "Ruby said, "that would be good. Find somewhere that's open."

Living within walking distance of the London underground and having so far avoided permanent employment, Mark did not own a car. So far, apart from the New Year's Eve adventure, he had only gingerly driven down what still seemed the wrong side of the road to Homestead where there was little danger of bumping into anything outside the big supermarkets because the car parks packed enough concrete to land corporate jets. You couldn't buy spirits with groceries, though, so for gin and whisky Mark had to find one of the small shops that thundered out the word LIQUOR over the windows, as though Ruby were in charge, like the tiny shacks with barred windows on US1 proclaiming ADULT VIDEOS and GUNS.

"People have been calling" Ruby reported when Mark got back. "But I don't mess with that thing when Charlotte's *well*." The answering machine. There was Larry and also Bert, asking about the orchids, not knowing Charlotte was now the concern. Then Jen, asking if Ruby had left, hoping Charlotte was OK, hoping she was asleep. Mark found himself saying thankyou again. He asked how Rachel was. She was sleeping. Mark realized Rachel would not call because Jen would have told her everything. Well, Mark hoped, not everything. Ruby had the old radio on in the kitchen and was listening to the noon news bulletin: "*...preliminary losses in the South Dade area alone. The Farm Bureau says they will be appealing for assistance and may well ask the governor to declare certain counties disaster areas. As more reports come in some spokesmen are even saying they will be appealing to the President to declare most of Southern Florida a federal disaster area. Now a report from Miami Beach where our winter visitors are once again out enjoying the sun.*"

"I've got a neighbor still picks beans," Ruby announced. "Picks beans and plays the lotto. *EV-ry* week: 'Ruby! I got me all but two numbers! All but two right!' I say pray to the Lord and put your money in your pocket but he's out there picking beans and off to Farm Stores handing over his money on Friday. Well, I guess he won't be there *this* Friday." Ruby turned back to the stove. "Now Charlotte may not want anything much today. She's sleeping and that's best." She was slicing carrots very thin and sliding them off the cutting board into the pot. "You got the chicken? Put it right there. And you can turn that thing off now. It's my station for Sundays. So the girl's gone?"

"Jen. She's sharing a house with Rachel."

"Ah," said Ruby. "Now she seems like she knows what she's about." Ruby might not have approved of Jen last night round about two thirty in the morning, Mark thought, but wait till she sees how she cleans her plate. He could see his mother being right at home with Ruby. "Now, *Rachel,*" Ruby shook her head. "She and Charlotte are a pair!" Mark was taken aback. He'd been expecting something more along the lines of: "Now *Rachel!* What a beauty! And so clever too!" And maybe a brief but telling anecdote or description of a moment which revealed nevertheless how sensitive and thoughtful she was to those around her, especially, a little grace note here, to 'people of color,' like Ruby herself. "Those two go at it!" Ruby elaborated. "I swear they could be talking Chinese! And I hear you're another one! Me? I like the flowers. Charlotte's good, sometimes when she has them spare she gives me some for my church."

There were two big, beautiful spikes of *Vanda* flowers in the second orchid house, waterlogged sprays that had snapped under the weight of the all night water. The flower stems stood almost as tall as delphiniums. They would have been perfect for an altar; the individual flowers as large and as velvety rich as pansies up and down the stem.("You won't see *these* in Marks and Spencers!" Charlotte had said. "Warm loving species. Used to ship 'em to Manhattan every week— paid the mortgage.") Mark would have liked to give them to Ruby but Charlotte might want the pollen out of them, or Cooper. Probably not Cooper. He was no longer interested in the standard blues, Charlotte said, now you could buy them in Home Depot.

With Ruby in charge, the kitchen had taken on an entirely different character. She sat down heavily, cloth in hand. "I think I'll have my tea now." The mysteries of an English cup of tea Ruby left to Mark. She had worked some magic on the old kettle, it almost shone. "All we need now is a jug of fresh flowers on the window sill," Mark joked. "Ruby, you're Snow White."

Ruby, tucking her chin in a little, gave him a look. It was the dignified, southern black woman's silent equivalent of an expression which Mark's old Uncle Frank had long employed when contemplating his nephew for any length of time. "Mark," he would announce, "I don't know where you get it from, but you're daft as a brush."

Ruby left about half past three. Charlotte was "sleeping it all off" she said. "You don't have to mess with her unless she calls. I don't think she wants you in there now." Mark was glad. Charlotte sick, unnerved him even more than Charlotte hale and hearty. He didn't want to hear that newly frail voice. The whole point of Charlotte, like Jen said, was that she was strong.

"Well, tell Charlotte I called. Tell her when she's got her make up back on we'll come and visit." It was Larry again. "No, seriously, she's OK? We called Rachel to check how *she* was doing and Jen told us what had been happening chez Orchid Empire. Well, I'm so relieved to hear it! Ruby we haven't met but she sounds a jewel. Us? Oh, we managed. Ken, thank God, was prepared. The boy scout in him saw us through. Yes, we have heaters so only a few problems round the edges. And we're already getting calls from people who fried or froze their plants and need refills and replacements— so it's an ill wind ... and *wasn't* it an ill wind!"

"Speaking of *which* you HAVE to hear what happened after we left the party! Apparently there was a 'surprise' presentation to the Queen, *EL Presidente! (Notice, Mr. English teacher! NO feminine ending!)* This, of course, in recognition of all her *tireless* work on behalf of the Miami Orchid Club. There was a photographer from *The Herald* and *Floral Monthly* and the *MOM (Miami Orchid Magazine*—the Queen's private organ!) And of *course* almost everyone who was the least bit into orchids had FLED because of the freeze! So that left just about the mariachi band, the waiters and that woman with the cello. Of course, the Queen didn't have to flee. She's got her Cinderellas back home stoking the boilers. Anyway, Bill—one of the loyal foot soldiers—was going to make the presentation but HE left because of his beloved phals, and they're digging round to find someone to make a little speech and tell the world how wonderful Regina, our *Presidente,* is and they land up with Charlie, still propping up the bar."

"Now this, in itself, is worth the price of admission. Our friend Frank says of course Charlie didn't have a speech. He starts rambling on, looking for a theme, decides to survey orchid clubs he has known, rating them on their refreshments: *whether the cookies are homemade!* Obviously plastered. Though I'm surprised anyone even got cheerful, the prices they were charging. Anyway, the Spanish speakers just started conversing among themselves and one or two old grannies apparently got quite loud, a little bit deaf or maybe had found more of the champagne than *we'd* ever managed. Maybe *all* the waiters were Cuban. ANYWAY, they were obviously talking about Havana before Castro and New Years in the good old days because some start to cry and someone starts singing the old Cuban national anthem and the band joined in and Regina is *stuck* there! And Frank says *just* as she's about to accept, ignoring the noise, some old Cuban yells 'Next year in Havana!' And they *all* cheer and start crying and Regina grabs hold of this plaque with a face like thunder and the *Herald* photographer zooms in and Regina rearranges her face and starts to graciously accept and the Cubans are rushing outside and firing off guns over the remaining cars and from then on it gets confused. Frank says apparently a Puerto Rican yelled *'Gusanos'*—What? 'Worms,'it's what Castro calls our Cubans here in Miami—or 'Up the Revolution!' and someone took a swing at him. Everyone getting frisky with the cold. And the waiters who were going off duty joined in. Did you notice? Some of them were quite *sturdy* and an old Cuban spat at some Columbians who were laughing and Oh, GOD, we should have *been* there! I'm desperate to tell Rachel but she's still asleep, poor thing, up all night. And now let's hope the *Herald* has the guts to publish some pictures.

But I doubt it."

"Um, so what do *you* think of Rachel?" Mark found himself asking.

"What do you mean?"

"Um. Oh, I don't know."

"...Oh... *Mark,*" said Larry after a moment, sympathetically and with a wealth of meaning.

"Rachel is so *focused*... There'd be a lot of heartache there...I could have introduced you to SO many...well, never mind! Well, you two certainly must have a lot in common. Ken and I don't go in for heavy orchid theory. If it sits on a woman's chest, it's a *Cattleya.* If you can tart it up, charge 25 and still make 20 it's a standard *Phalaenopsis,* low end of the market. That's about as far as we get. We leave it to Mike and Cooper to go up and down the mountains with them. And Rachel, well, don't cry into your pillow. Anyway, thank God you're *here,* that Charlotte's got *family. That's* the important thing. *"*

Mark fed the dogs as quietly as possible. He ladled out some of the thick, chicken broth Ruby had concocted, warming it up and eating it out of the milk saucepan, back in his Shetland sweater and Harris Tweed jacket. He suddenly felt like calling home but just as his mother said "...Hallo?" with that familiar, cautious note in her voice, Mark remembered not only that it must be eleven at night in England, but Christ! Charlotte was *sick.* Good job he'd not made the classic New Year resolution: Always Tell the Truth. "Oh, *Mark!* How's Charlotte?"

"Um. She's managing very well...Those ultra modern chairs are incredible...Gave her annual party for Christmas Eve. Certainly has a lot of very good friends. You don't have to worry about that."

"Well, I *was* wondering...We hadn't heard from you at all. Only that initial call and the card and you know I've always had a terrible job with your handwriting. Let me have a word with her."

"Well she's asleep right now. New Year's Eve! You know Charlotte!"

"Oh dear, I was hoping she'd slowed down a bit."

"I've called rather late, I know. We did call Christmas Day but couldn't get through. Orchid Empire's got a computer so you can always email."

"I'll leave that to your sister. So how are you, Mark? Having a good time? Seen anything of Miami? Met anyone interesting? I expect Charlotte's circle of friends maybe a little old for you though she was always known for running with a lively bunch."

"Actually, haven't seen much. The help is away right now. I like to be on hand for the business calls and you know distances over here... We're really rather far down. Everything's very spread out. It can be like going from London to Nottingham when you talk about an evening out. And Charlotte's Volvo is not very reliable."

"Well, I hope you're getting some sun and meeting some interesting people. Uncle Frank called. Sends his best. Thinks it's a really good opportunity for you to be over there. Why don't you have a word with your sister? We don't want to run up Charlotte's bill too much. Missed you for Christmas of course and...Happy New Year!"

"Y'right?"

"Alright. You got Orchid Empire's email address."

"Sorry! Well, nothing to report. New Year's at Nina's. Got smashed of course and someone broke a window."

"Don't tell me: Derek."

"Oh, that didn't work out."

"I thought he was OK."

"Nope. He was just better than Nige. So got up to South Beach yet? Snapped any thongs?"

"I was telling Mum. Everything's a long way away. South Beach would be almost like going up to Nottingham. And anyway, I am companion to my eighty year old aunt. Like something out of Jane Austen."

"Then you'll be OK. Haven't you seen the films? Some handsome, rich young lord will arrive and sweep you off, falling in love with all your wonderful, modest virtues."

"Yeah, right."

"No, really, lucky you. Tanned and sitting round under palms. You know what's the temperature right now?"

"Let me tell you, little sister, last night we had a freeze."

"Come on!"

"Oh, yeah. Frost this morning. Disaster for the farmers. Big story.

They should have a bit on ITN and BBC."

"—So what did you do?"

"Ran the water on the orchids and kept them warm."

"Oh."

"Did go to a party last night. Some gorgeous young Latin girls. Most with gorgeous young Latin males. Can't swing a cat without seeing one of Nina's To-die-for's."

"Maybe I'll come and look after Aunt Charlotte too."

"Well, keep an eye on the old parental unit. And send me an email."

Outside milky clouds swirled over head; the thermometer read 65 Fahrenheit, the ones in the greenhouses, sixty-nine. The insects were starting up again, having been shocked into silence. They were probably a better indication of the weather than the forecast, Mark thought. He checked the plastic was down tight all round the orchid houses, realizing, heart in mouth, he didn't have any more staples anyway. Tomorrow if they were lucky, it would be back to the old worry: "Hangers under the plastic getting too hot: plants up high starting to fry." Tomorrow, decisions on watering. Better leave them dry another day. Tomorrow buy staples. If there were any to be had. And don't even think of the whole A B business: Rachel and Jen. There was no light on in Charlotte's room, no sound. Mark stifled the thought she might have died. He was going to follow Ruby's instructions and not mess with her. Ruby would be coming tomorrow. Anyway, as Charlotte would doubtless say: "If I'm dead what good are *you* going to be?"

9

New Year's Week

Jen was still checking in regularly by phone, offering to come over if Ruby couldn't make it. Mark reported Charlotte's voice was getting stronger. By the end of the week, if he wanted to, he'd be able to decipher what she was saying to Ruby behind the bedroom door. Jen sounded cool, brisk but she was calling from work. She never mentioned New Year's Eve. *Hallo,* thought Mark one morning as he shaved: had he considered maybe *he* was one of the B series for *Jen* or, even worse, he was *now,* after New Year's night. Hardly optimum conditions, huddling behind black plastic in the freezing cold. Not so much a balmy, romantic interlude in South Florida as a fumbling night in a Moscow tenement. But at least Jen had said firmly, as Ned put it, she'd taken care of the business side of things. Her trademark, "It's OK. No problem."

Everyone was grumbling about the lack of warning, the inadequate forecasts on New Year's Eve, which meant that, as Mark put it, any cold damage at Orchid Empire could not be viewed by Charlotte as an exclusive Mark cock up. Much of the entire Redland looked blasted: the freeze had swept through like a forest fire. In the orchid world harrowing tales were still coming in of faulty heaters, torn plastic, clogged sprinkler heads; managers and owners left alone to struggle in the cold and dark, while their workers were seeing in the New Year in Texas taverns or with fireworks in Mexico. And now there were reports of blackened, burned leaves, blasted buds, and *botrytis,* brown spotting on the petals, with the first big show, Las Olas, up in Broward County, only just over two weeks away.

Carlos would not be back till the second week in January. With

Charlotte sick Mark was solely responsible for Orchid Empire. The days were sunny, the sky an innocent tourist blue, the night temperatures predicted "in the low fifties." How *reassuring* Mark would mutter with heavy sarcasm to the dogs as he unfurled the plastic round the houses mid afternoon. That had been the *very* same forecast for New Year's Eve. The only thing to do was to check the temperature drop each night. With the dry season, as Charlotte said, came the desert phenomenon: as soon as the sun set, the air grew cold. At six, with the temperature falling, Mark would get a cold beer from the potting shed and switch on the little TV in the kitchen for the local news. Deadly car crashes, murderous Latin lovers, corrupt Miami officials, smoking ruins of family homes where children just a few hours before had discovered the excitement of matches, nothing registered. Mark was waiting only for the weather chart to arrive: the high pressure, the low pressure, the cold fronts drawn across the map of the States like the loops of a necklace across the broad bosom, the ample chest of the lower forty eight. But more often than not, Mark waited for the weather segment so intently that when it was over, he couldn't remember a thing that had been said.

Maybe Charlotte had a stash of Krugerands somewhere or stocks and bonds but it seemed that everything of real value she owned was outside: that was the trouble. The tea towels, ash trays and plastic bull-rushes, the cumbersome couches and rickety little tables were inside, protected. The orchids, from the bread and butter ones to the unique, the treasured collection, Charlotte's specials, her odds and sods, were all laid out under the stars like the family silver on the back lawn, vulnerable below their thin layer of plastic, tender, open to abuse, to nature's whims. At night when Mark heard the wind getting up and the branches swaying hard outside the window, he would go to his weather station, the open patch of scorched grass by the clothesline. With the dogs surging round his legs in the dark, he would lick his finger like a boy scout, holding it up into the cooling night air, trying to work out which way the wind was blowing and what might be coming.

"If any night you're not sure," Charlotte had said "throw on the water just before dawn, that's the coldest time." But that was exactly the time when Mark, exhausted by his worries, finally fell asleep.

Rachel was calling, too. He would find her strong, clear voice on the answering machine when he came in from the morning watering: "Ask Charlotte is the pod parent of 'Blooming Fine' Philadelphia Crimson Glory'? Thanks, Bye." Mark would write the names down and Ruby would take the phone into Charlotte, frowning at the piece of paper which read like a betting slip. If Mark had been at The Rat and Parrot he'd have a hard job convincing the regulars that 'Wild Crimson Sun' or 'William's Yellow Fandango' were not tips for the three-thirty.

Same kind of world, Charlotte had said. "You've got your blood lines and your winners. Horses can have four words, orchids only three. Make a new cross, a hybrid, or win an award, you can put any name on it. Register with the Royal Horticultural Society and you're part of orchid history!" Mark had wondered why many of the orchid names, unlike the horses, were names of people. *Phalaenopsis* 'Iris Mary Potter,' hardly conjured up an image of natural beauty. "Orchids get named after people a lot: the old *In Memoria* and live people; in Regina's case, of course, a roster of those she needs to butter up. She had a whole lot of 'Leslie Huckenbacker III's.' And Regina wasn't the only one. There was a wave of orchid hybrids lumbered with the name. He was a classic orchid nut and a very rich man, rumored to be looking to place his fortune somewhere in the orchid world...And then the bugger upped and died. That's when they all discovered his first love was still model airplanes! But his widow to this day thinks he's the most beloved of all his fellow orchidists!"

With the questions and calls between Bios Orchids and Orchid Empire during the day, Mark began to see a possibility of meeting Rachel without the complication of Jen. Get Charlotte to invite her over to discuss the merits of crossing 'William's Yellow Fandango' to one of old Leslie B Huckenbacker's, or whatever. Then, as Rachel left Charlotte's bedroom, there would be the cold beer and chips waiting on the porch, the sun going down, the swift dark of a Florida sunset, the fragrant ladies of the night blooming in the branches. Perhaps not, after the freeze. But Rachel gleaming, that ash blond hair, lighting up the dark like the lady of the night herself. That same pale beauty attracting men like moths. Though the image of large moths frying themselves in the light fixtures, a nightly occurrence, was not quite what Mark intended.

However, Rachel said firmly, "Charlotte won't want to see *any* of us yet. Not till she's back on form." And Mark could not find an excuse to visit Bios Orchids. Not with Charlotte still in bed. He'd thought at one moment there would be an exciting dash over to the Bios lab with a bursting seed pod. But Rachel had misread the pollination date and Mark had to report that the seed pod in question was still green and not ready and *no luck* as he muttered to the dogs, milling round the bottom of the ramp.

So far the closest Mark had got to Rachel was the orchid screen saver on the computer. "Oh, the *Coryanthes*," Charlotte had said. "That's Rachel's little joke because of the piss ants. *Tiny* creatures, give you goose bumps at the kitchen table. Remember going hot and cold? Formic acid. They don't bite they *pee* on you! Well, when they're not running around the kitchen table they set up colonies in the roots of the *Coryanthes,* the bucket orchid. The formic acid stimulates the flowering and by the way, here's one of your classic stories of orchid pollination, dear boy! Lip like a bucket, flower fills up with water, the *Euglossine* bee falls in and, wings all wet, the only way out is up the spout where, of course, the pollinia stick to him. Attracted to another flower, and lucky for the *Coryanthes*, a slow learner, he stumbles through the whole process again, leaving the pollen on the *second* flower's stigma. Neat! Your botany people should be teaching this stuff: the fascinating and varied sexual habits of the orchid. Perfect topic for adolescent boys and between the sniggers they might learn something!"

Mark had thought for a fleeting moment that Charlotte might well meet her match at Totters Green but it was only for a moment.

Charlotte was getting so much stronger that Ruby called the physical therapist to restart her sessions but when she arrived Charlotte was asleep and Ruby decided best to leave her.

"OK," said the therapist, "I'll just visit for a while." Althea was named after the tennis star: "Althea Gibson, the first black woman to win your Wimbledon!" Mark had met her the day after he arrived. "So this is your nephew, Charlotte? Well, you ARE lucky. I wish *I* had such a handsome, nice young man to come look after ME."

They sat round the kitchen table and Ruby asked Mark to make his pot of English tea. Althea exclaimed how good and strong it was. "Not like American!"

"It's *Red Rose!* It *is* American tea! Problem is no-one here cares if the water is boiling and no-one *warms* the pot!" Mark stopped. He was resigned to Ruby considering him a total nitwit but was sure that after a minute or two of this Althea would be catching Ruby's eye and nodding slowly. Althea, like Ruby, had presence. She was poised, from the balls of her feet all the way up to her tight black hair. Mark knew if he'd possessed that air not just of health but physical certainty on the playing fields of Totters Green, first year football would not have been the shambles that it always was. Althea said she'd coached girls' high school basketball till an old knee injury got worse and now she was a physical therapist at the local hospital. She'd known Ruby since she was a girl. "Couldn't ever put anything past 'Miss Ruby,'" she said with a smile.

Ruby, fleetingly, looked very sad. Mark thought of the daughter on crack, the one who for a long time probably had seemed just like Althea, maybe was her friend.

The things on top of the chest of drawers in the spare room were Ruby's, Charlotte had declared, put there for safe keeping. Mark had wondered where the silver cup commemorating Second Place Dade County Road Runners Marathon, 1979, fitted into Charlotte's life and the photograph of a black policeman in a sterling silver frame. There was a cut glass jam dish and sugar bowl, full of brooches and bead necklaces, a bulging photograph album tied up with red ribbon and a framed photograph of a young black woman with bright eyes and a generous grin. Mark had thought maybe she was a young East African or Jamaican, destined, with Charlotte's help, for a place at a British university, a bright young botanist, perhaps.

When Ruby first came she used to stay to watch a video in Charlotte's room where the large television was. Mark, bringing in the tea, had found the choices puzzling: some domestic drama with Whoopi Goldberg, Eddie Murphy in *Dr. Doolittle*. It was hard to square his aunt's admiration for the Zulu's of the Cape or the Masai warriors of East Africa with the talents of Whoopi Goldberg and Eddie Murphy, magnificent as those talents might be. "Oh, they're not for *me,* dear boy!" Charlotte said. "I fall asleep once they start. Ruby can't watch at home. She doesn't have a video thing…. My dear, she has a daughter on crack. She doesn't have *anything* that's portable and worth a *dollar* in that house."

The phone rang while they were all having their strong English tea. Mark began "Good afternoon, this is Orchid Empire" but a voice cut in. "Charlotte sick *again!* And according to Marjorie nothing has been done to *help.*" Mark somehow knew immediately this was Regina, the President of the Miami Orchid Club. Mark must be the relative from England. Welcome! Now, Charlotte, such an *old* and valued member of the Club, had been worrying, in fact, *disturbing* the other members for a long time. She, Regina, knew there were treasures at Orchid Empire which, the Lord willing, had survived the freeze, it would be tragic to let fall prey to continued neglect. As President, a Christian and a friend it would only be doing the right thing as we're told in the Bible to send her manager over with the van.

"Um, how kind. But actually, I, I *am* looking after and Carlos will be back—" The President of the Miami Orchid Club was not listening. She must have turned away from the phone, conferring with her manager. "Ha—Hallo? I don't think Charlotte—" Mark saw Althea raising her eyebrows. "—I really think you should have a word with Charlotte's *care-giver,* Doctor Gibson." Althea, starting to grin, took the phone. "To whom am I speaking?... A*ha!* Well, as her primary care giver at this *time...* Total bed-rest means no upsets, no visitors. Well, I am sorry you feel that, I am sorry you feel that way. Well, I am the authority at this *time.*" Althea was having fun. "That would be a question for the patient in a few days. You would need authorization. I can't make that decision. I can tell you that her nephew from England is in charge, very *much* in charge. We will certainly let her know you called and your name is... Oh! She didn't say goodbye!" Althea put the phone down delicately on the table with the air of 'Did I do right?'

"Althea," said Mark, "you rule."

Ruby looked at him.

"Ha!" Althea sat down and thrust out a pink palm over the tea mugs. "Give me *five!*"

Ruby looked at Althea.

"You two," she said, "don't you go messing with stuff."

"Wow!" exclaimed Althea. "Your president wants what she wants when *she wants* it! Know what I'm saying? Is she a first class—" she glanced at Ruby— "*pain* ...or not?"

"Absolutely first class, apparently," said Mark.

With Carlos and Rosita back on Monday, Orchid Empire took on its natural rhythms again: fertilizing, spraying, the potting and tidying and in the benign presence of Carlos the worry about night temperatures shrank to a manageable size. ("Think we're OK tonight, Carlos?" "Hokay!")The porch was brighter; most of the lush foliage shading it had turned brown and withered away. But there'd been no repeat of the New Year's Eve freeze, no second killer cold front, not even a milder version coming in over the Gulf of Mexico. Mark's big worry now was customers, wholesale or retail, who might drift in and Charlotte's 'orchid nuts' who, if he weren't careful, could con him out of something precious. He had watched a trio of orchidists fork over a reverent five hundred dollars for a tray of desiccated odds and ends just before Christmas as Charlotte recounted historic plant expeditions across raging rivers and dusty plateaus. "We *are* Orchid *Empire,* dear boy," she'd observed in her swooping, upper class English accent that was dying out even among members of the Royal family. "That's what sells. Just don't let any of these types poke about on their own."

Charlotte had joked that if Mark could recognize an orchid, he could probably sell it. It would be one of her 'cash crop.' But now she was sick he couldn't just race up the ramp with a pot and ask "How much?" In fact, no one had come. No-one since Mark's first sale: half a dozen *Dendrobium phalaenopsis* to a desperate florist. She had needed six table centers in pink. Nothing obscure from the Congo with incredible price tag or from the banks of the Limpopo river, nothing those old native bearers would have dragged in, just something in pink. Charlotte had been right; Mark recognized the flowers, a little like large sweet peas or outsize violets. He'd seen them in pots and fancy baskets in florist shop windows at home.

"If she came here that means no-one else has got anything left."

"She said she's a regular customer."

"They all say that, dear boy."

Unfortunately for Mark the people who found their way to Orchid Empire in the first week of the New Year were serious collectors from the temperate zone spending their New Year holiday hunting orchids in the sub tropics of South Florida. The first pair, research chemists from Massachusetts, were eager for news of the *Taeniophyllum* and perhaps even an *Acampe,* the two African members of the sub-tribe *Aeridinae,* though as they themselves observed, most were, in fact, native to tropical Asia and Australasia. "Right," said Mark.

Charlotte was still as Althea put it in the 'bed rest' phase and anyway could not be expected to trundle down the ramp at short notice. But the pair were heading back that day for Miami International and home and Mark had felt for the first time in his life the special pang, the commercial tug at the heart: had he—*lost a sale?* The next afternoon a second couple arrived, unannounced, confessing their preoccupation with the vandaceous alliance. Alliance, that stirring phrase, so redolent of diplomacy, armed camps and war; how fitting for the orchid world, Mark thought. They had some interesting crosses they'd flowered out from vanda seedlings bought from Charlotte a few years ago.("Some of the buggers take so long to bloom," Charlotte had observed, "you forget what you *did* sell.") And they had many questions such as— "What about the influence of *cristata?*" What indeed, thought Mark. Their brand new Lexus with all leather interior was parked outside the potting shed, belying Charlotte's claim that most obsessive orchidists were retirees on fixed incomes or guilty housewives spending the grocery money. Again Mark felt a pang but Charlotte had contradictory stories of big spenders.

"There was this woman hunted Orchid Empire down from a florist on Miami Beach, a few years ago. Found an old tag on one of our plants, came with a chauffeured car and *her own pilot:* 'Do you know what they're selling your orchids for up there?' And I said 'None of my business!' She wanted to buy something wholesale—a trophy price to prove how damn clever she'd been. Now, one time at the big Miami Expo, Friday night, ten to ten and up comes, he must have been a security guard—custodian type—bit of a uniform, nothing new, no gun. Asked how much was the big blue *Vanda* standing at one end of the table. Well, I say, that's a hundred, I'm afraid. Pulled out a hundred dollar bill, this pretty woman, not young, on his arm. A very dark-skinned kid with them. And off they went arm in arm with this damn big plant. She was smiling up at him, like he'd just proposed."

Mark had no idea what Charlotte's finances were like. She told him to take 'pocket money' out of the ostrich egg behind the tea caddy which housed a roll of twenties and some fifties. As for orchid expenses, Orchid Empire had credit with the local suppliers: Homestead Plumbing and Irrigation, Beemer's Farm Supplies, East Coast Fertilizer, Sunshine Orchid Depot. The smaller trucks came up the drive, the large ones blared their horns till Carlos, knee deep in dogs, went down with the garden cart. Most of the drivers were Spanish speaking, their English often apparently non-existent, so Carlos, checking the stuff off with the clip board and having a chat, was better equipped to deal with them than Mark. There were small amounts of fungicides, fertilizer, insecticides and big buckets of industrial soap that made Orchid Empire smell, as Charlotte said, like a Chinese laundry. She had already ordered baskets, plastic pots, hooks and wires, getting in the last of her expenditures for the old business year. And there were always the irrigation parts, the Nifty Nozzles.

Charlotte still wrote the checks for Carlos, Rosita and to Mark for housekeeping and expenses, on Thursday for Friday in a large, slightly shaky hand. He wondered if, indeed, Charlotte should think about selling up. Any savings she had from where her caravan had previously rested must have gone in setting up Orchid Empire. Maybe she'd taken out a second mortgage. How did they work? You had to hand over the house by a certain date? That would explain why Charlotte drank so much. Maybe she had to die before she hit eighty-five in some macabre agreement cooked up by the bankers.

Mark, sitting on the porch a few afternoons later, could hear the voices coming from Charlotte's bedroom on the other side of the house, and Althea's sudden gusts of laughter. The phone had rung and Mark froze, thinking it might be Regina again, then hoping for Rachel but it was Jen calling from work asking one more time how Charlotte was doing. "She seems to be fine. Ruby says she'll be up and in the chair in a few days. Althea's arrived, the therapist. They're all in there, in Charlotte's bedroom, laughing and drinking tea."

"Well, it sounds like everything's OK."

"So how's Rachel? How's Bios doing?"

"OK. Well, I guess we can say Charlotte's out of the wood."

"Yes, thanks again for all your help. It's really thanks to you, Jen. Jen? We ...all ought to get together some time..." That 'all' was the killer. That was one of the least romantic sentences in the whole of the English language.

"Right," Jen had paused just a little. "The Las Olas show's coming up. We'll all be seeing each other then."

10

A Visit to Orchid Magic

"**D**on't let her anywhere *near* Orchid Empire!" It was Rachel on the phone.

"I don't think Charlotte's closed the gate in years. Orchid Empire doesn't even have a padlock. Gun? Christ, no! Well, she always talks about setting the dogs... Tod wouldn't. He only pees on wheels. Nip's too small. Carlos has a machete, of course. There's always the spear on the wall! No! I was *joking!*"

"Well you could go out and *buy* one." Mark had missed something, had Rachel said a padlock or a gun? He could see those green eyes darkening, darkening at the thought of the Queen, poor Charlotte and *someone*, a Mark who shall be nameless, as Larry would say, too English and namby pamby to hustle up a padlock, find a gun, toss a spear—do anything to keep evil at bay. Mark was wondering if this sort of thing was normal for the orchid world.

"This is *Miami,* dear boy!" Charlotte had said. "One year we had bullet proof vests and body-guards at the Spring Expo! Go to any orchid society in America and say you're from Miami and it's '*Aha! What's the latest?*'"

Well, thought Mark, maybe it *was* Miami. Just north on US1, wedged into a little weatherbeaten strip mall of tiny enterprises: Beauty Nails, TIRES, Tattoos, Guitars and two pawn shops (Gold and Guns!*)* was a Military Surplus store. Until Christmas an armored vehicle had sat outside complete with a blonde mannequin dressed in fatigues and sporting an eighteen inch waist and for New Year they'd towed in a tank, its gun turret trained on the Pelican Mall across the road.

"I'd hate to see Charlotte taken advantage of," Rachel sounded

94

weary, "her collection spirited away. Oh, yeah! Ask Bert what happened to the books in the orchid library! We could all take some plants for safe keeping but that's too upsetting at her age. I know she calls them her odds and sods but they're her treasures—and what else does she have? No real family. Well, sorry Mark but you know what I mean. No one close."

"Well, you, of course."

"You think so?" Rachel sounded surprised.

It was the afternoon and Mark was alone on the porch. One lasting result of Charlotte's New Year upset was that Ruby was coming in the mornings now and cooking a hot lunch. When she left, Charlotte was ready for a nap. Mark would take the phone and *The Miami Herald* out to the porch and settle himself in the cane rocking chair, his feet on the old wicker one with its faded paisley cushions. In deference to Ruby, he now put down the Business section or Automotive News under his heels. Rachel had agreed it was better not to mention Regina's call to Charlotte. Mark had wanted to ignore the phone for a while but thought if Regina got no answer she might just hop in the van with her manager, as God had instructed, and come on over. But as luck would have it when a second call came Althea was sitting in the kitchen just before going home, while Mark made the tea. As soon as Mark heard Regina's voice he handed the phone over.

Althea turned to Mark with her broad grin, saying "This *is* Doctor Gibson," and for about five minutes all Mark heard was "Aha, aha. Yeah, I hear what you're saying." And "No, no, I hear what you're saying." When Althea put down the phone she reported, "This woman is *so* concerned, know what I mean? Should take certain orchids away 'for safe keeping' then 'for a prospective buyer,' who 'needs quick decision—a wonderful opportunity that won't come again.' You know the scam: '*Offer expires while you wait!*' Seems to think maybe she'll get further talking to me than you—*Why's* she hustling you all along?"

As Ruby wasn't present, Mark was able to be more graphic. "According to Charlotte she's after her prize orchids. She's a real bitch, apparently. Hard to believe."

"Oh, I believe," said Althea. "I believe."

"'*Found a buyer!*'" Rachel cried down the phone. "Regina's cooking up something!"

"Well, Althea seems to think she's just making all that up."

"Althea doesn't know her."

"Althea seems to have a pretty good idea."

"I've got it! She wants to talk about prospective buyers for Orchid Empire? Tell her you can't *possibly* discuss this in front of Charlotte. She'll lap that up! Say *you'll go see her!* See whether she'll even let you in! I sent Jen along once and they stopped her at the gate. You could check out what Regina's bringing in for Las Olas! What she's *appropriating*. Hey! Industrial espionage! And *fun!*"

About many things Mark could keep an open mind and be willing to listen: for example, should the British film industry look to the government for financial support. But Mark had reached the age when he knew what his idea of fun was and, more importantly, what it definitely was not. "No, Rachel. Definitely not."

"Come *on!* You can run rings round her! Her 'greenhouses and farms' in Thailand! Her 'research facilities!' Her incredible number of crosses, *identical* to those made always *first* by the Thais!" So much energy was coming through the phone, Rachel must be fresh out of the lab, Mark thought, stripping off her latex gloves and straightening up. "At rock bottom she's incredibly ignorant with *no* intellectual interest in breeding. *Or* real solid knowledge of orchids or even any botanical training. When you think about it, it's incredible!"

"Hard to believe," Mark murmured faintly.

"She has this guy Antonio, Tony, the manager, who does it all and absolutely adores her. Suggest Monday. They're closed and he's off then. And she'll like that too. She can get you all to herself, unless she's swanning around with one of her boy toys. Maybe she was checking you out on New Year's Eve! Tell us whether she manages to seduce you! In her golf cart! And if she takes her gloves off! Remember, hold on to your virtue until the very last moment. Only give in if it will further the interests of Orchid Empire!" Rachel gave a snort. Mark wondered if Jen was there too, listening in on a Saturday afternoon, and how serious Rachel was after all. And wondered for a moment, if maybe Jen had ever said anything to her about New Year's Eve. And wondered if laughter had ever been involved.

Now in order to win Rachel's heart, even, he suspected, just to be invited over, he must face the evil Queen, Snow White's step mother, Joan Crawford, *Regina*. Someone, apparently, whose unbelievable ignorance in all major departments of orchid knowledge could only be equaled and, in fact, outdone by his own. And that was another problem.

"They say up to even twenty percent rate of infection in the lab bottles can be considered standard but I'm not happy with that," Rachel had commented on the phone one morning while waiting for Ruby to relay a message. "Charlotte says you're not doing any more flasking but I can still pick your brains."

So even as he was just keeping his head above water with all the orchid stuff, Mark realized Charlotte was pouring it on more and more. And the problem was the longer this went on the worse it got. Even if he confessed to Rachel now, Mark knew the damage was done. The whole orchid thing was Rachel's area of expertise, her pride and joy, her professional self. Mark felt more than a little uneasy at the prospect of a Rachel realizing a little late in the day she'd been made a fool of. And if pretending to be an orchid expert was a protection against Regina and the reactionary forces she controlled, Mark mused, then why hadn't Charlotte enlisted *Rachel's* formidable talents as an ally? Why had she treated her almost as though she were Regina herself? Not to be entrusted with the truth? What had Larry said on New Year's Eve? "We love Charlotte madly but I expect you've already found out she can be..." he'd grinned, "well, just totally... *Charlotte*." That is, *nuts*, thought Mark. But we can't say that, because of people like Alvin and the Queen.

Now Mark found himself driving up to South Miami on a beautiful Monday afternoon in early January, on his reluctant way to Orchid Magic. However much Rachel scoffed at Regina's lack of knowledge Mark knew it was enough to find him out, even if she were only half as cunning and devious as portrayed in local legend and song. He had made the call to Orchid Magic, clinging to the hope that entry would be denied: after all, he would remind Rachel, he was actually living in the enemy camp. Whatever else might be gossip or exaggeration, Orchid Empire and Orchid Magic were at daggers drawn and the hostility between Charlotte and Regina long predated Rachel's arrival on the scene. And if Jen, nice, normal Jen, with no claim to orchid knowledge or expertise, had been turned away from the gates, well, there was hope.

Regina herself had answered the phone. That was the first blow. No heavily accented secretary rattling along in Spanglish, no chance to get away with: "*Would* you believe! *Only* in Miami! I could have *sworn* she was telling me 'Monday, eleven forty-five' but apparently she was saying 'Wednesday at *ten!*'" Regina appeared to be expecting the call which made Mark even more uneasy. "It is *Mark* isn't it? Well, I was about to call *you!* I made enquiries at the hospital and they have never *heard* of a Dr Gibson!"

"—*Right.* Well, I think it's that old, ongoing rivalry between, between the medical profession, the establishment doctors, your Harvard and Yale and ... the natural, *healing* ones! Dr. Gibson is a ...natural healer and of course, Charlotte, ever since Africa, and well, one could say ever since *England.* My mother says she was one of the first I believe to chew grasses for rheumatism! Of course, that *was* during the war."

"This is *so* Charlotte! To have a kind of *witch* doctor in charge! Now Mark, Charlotte is a very special...very *special.* But we need to be perfectly frank about the whole situation at Orchid Empire. Luckily I am here for Charlotte not only as President but as a truly caring *friend* and a Christian. You don't need to go to church to have Christ in your heart! But you are right. We will discuss the whole thing *without* Charlotte. Monday would be best. I need to show you Orchid Magic and *someone* should start to pick your brains! You're a very dark horse! No one seems to know what your area of orchid expertise is!"

Ever since university Mark, in times of stress, had a recurring nightmare. It was the first day of Finals and suddenly he was realizing that for three whole years he'd done nothing much but lie about and drink beer. He could still wake up with a start and for a pounding moment relive the terror. Mark was feeling something similar now. Like university, there had been every opportunity to learn at Orchid

Empire, to get ready to be tested. Living with Charlotte was one endless tutorial and material for the diligent student was knee deep at every turn. Even in the kitchen *The Manual of Cultivated Orchid Species* and for some reason, *Orchids of Borneo,* sat on a shelf beside *The Joy of Cooking* together with *Meals in Minutes* and *Phylogeny and Classification of the Orchid Family.* He could have got one of them down while waiting for the kettle to boil.

In Mark's own room, the spare room, there was no need to access anything on the computer; *American Orchid Society Bulletins* were stacked up all round his bed. One could skip *Singapore to Host Orchid Congress* and no need to jump right into *Showy Miniatures from Venezuela* but there had to be lots of articles on Charlotte's stuff: *African Treasures I Have Known* perhaps, or *I Have Grown; Taeniophyllums in the Wild* or *In the Greenhouse* or *On My Windowsill; Acampes: The Inside Story; The Vandaceous Alliance: Whither?* And though he had to take the lamp shade off to get any kind of reading light, Mark certainly had the quiet and the time. But Mark had to admit the only thing he'd tackled on a regular daily basis with any consistency and sense of purpose was to teach Tod, by means of the Taco chips, to roll over and die for the Queen. And with a dog like Tod, it was hard to measure success.

With twenty-four hours to go, Mark asked Charlotte on Sunday night to fill him in on the real Regina. Confront your worst fears, you were told: reality is always so much less scary. Not in the case of the President of the Miami Orchid Club, Mark discovered. If only half of what Charlotte had said were true, Regina would eat him for breakfast. "How on earth did she get to be President and all the rest? Rachel says she doesn't really know much about orchids at all."

"Regina cuts through this genteel garden club world of amateur orchidists like a knife through butter! Started off as an air hostess we used to call them. Went after this older man collecting orchids in Central America. But she had a lover on the side. Juicy stuff! Planned to use orchids as a front for bringing in drugs so goes the story. That goes sour. Regina squeals to the cops, gets this lover put away. What? Oh, well over twenty years ago. Well before I got here. *Wait,* dear boy! *Then* persuades First Class sugar daddy to pour thousands into orchid houses and stock here, in South Dade. Then discovers, whoops! she doesn't love him after all. Poor man was on the fringe of the orchid world for years, wouldn't hear a word against her! That's a great skill: make someone as dust beneath your chariot wheels and have them choke up and say *Thank you!* You should hear Bert: 'Ignore her! Take it easy!' Bert sees himself as peace maker. I say 'Bert! Save your energy! I'll see that woman in hell first!' So there you are. In this region if you don't allow the Queen total control. If you don't tow the line..."

"If you have balls," Mark contributed.

"Yes! You're on the royal shit list as they say here. And now for some petty little rule the Queen and her loyal subjects will have Rachel, the 'troublemaker,' out of the spring Expo which until we get the guts to do something else is the only game in town."

Mark had told Charlotte he'd been invited to Orchid Magic. "Regina wants to check me out."

"Whoops! Watch out, innocent young school teacher!" Charlotte chortled. "I've heard some of *those* stories too! Of course, it's a waste *you* going; the *last* person to spot whether old Mrs. Trent's *Cattleya iricolor* has landed up on one of Regina's benches, tucked behind some little phals from Kmart."

"She's going to find out, isn't she?" Mark said. "That I don't know a *Vanda* from a hole in the ground, or at least a *Dendrobium*..."

"Well, you've learned *that* much, dear boy! Or you'd better, if you've been doing *my* watering!" Charlotte, Mark thought, was maybe a little mellower since New Year's Eve. "I don't know that any of it all really matters," she mused. "Regina would be sniffing around, out to get you, even if you were Curator of the Queen's herbarium. No! Correction! *Especially* if you were Curator of the Queen's herbarium!" She'd paused. "Does the Queen *have* a herbarium?"

Mark had noticed whenever the question of driving up from deep South Dade arose, the locals dropped whatever they were doing to review options and suggest modes of attack and operations with a high seriousness and concentration on possibilities, time assessments and constraints more suited to planning the invasion of Europe in

1944. There was the turnpike extension; there was the expressway, 876; there was stalwart old US1; for aesthetic consideration, there was winding Old Cutler; there were, for the adventurous ones, ready to give old Jerry a surprise, so to speak, daring cross country forays following the network of new arteries through the burgeoning western suburbs. All were designed to shave off a few minutes from whatever time had been established as the norm for the trip or the champion time to beat. Mark, far from wanting to beat some local record, always pleaded for good old cosy US1. But in keeping with the imperial aura of Regina, debate was a nonstarter. "You will take the turnpike extension, then 876" Regina announced on the phone. "Write it down." And there was no doubt in Mark's mind that if he had tried to sneak up Charlotte's favorite, Old Cutler, or his, US1, Regina, inspecting the tread of his tires or the kind of insects caught on his windshield, would have known right away.

Mark took the turnpike extension past the rural names posted over the concrete, Quail Roost Drive, Snapper Creek, turned off where Regina had instructed and there, soon enough, was an endless, straight, humorless road. A palm or two popped up behind evergreen shrubs and hedges. Low blocks of commercial greenery fronting low blocks of commerce were punctuated by glum apartment blocks in varying shades of East European brown. But just as Mark was reflecting on the meaningless sacrifice of the pioneers, the axes and ox carts, the mosquitoes and malaria, he made the turn as Regina commanded into a broad, tree-lined street with a delightful variety of gardens full of old fruit trees, mangos and avocados. The houses were all different vintages, with the occasional big, overgrown lot round a small utilitarian fifties house truculently occupying what had become a choice, expensive square. Charlotte had said Regina's Orchid Magic was once a five acre mango grove she had bulldozed out for her greenhouses. "And knocked down a lovely old coral rock house, Bert says, so she could put up some damn packing shed."

There was the name, Orchid Magic, stamped on a metal rectangle bolted onto the gate. Below the letters was the imprint of an upturned magician's top hat, an assortment of flowering orchids struggling over the brim. Two strands of barbed wire ran along the top of the six foot fence and over the gate. It was impossible to see what lay on the other side; swing open those gates and the US cavalry could come trotting through. Mark could hear no birds, no sound, just the distant drone of cars. There were no weeds at the base of the fence only a strip of yellowed vegetation. For a moment Mark, fresh from Orchid Empire, registered this as very accurate peeing, perhaps by a brace of Rotweilers, no doubt Regina's dog of choice, and then realized it was marking of territory by weed killer. The sun was hot against the wooden fence and the back of Mark's neck as he checked the sign on the right above a metal box and button: 'PRESS. Please State Business.' It was two-thirty in the afternoon. Grateful the gate was so definitively closed, Mark was marshaling his excuses for a quick getaway as he read the signs and notices: OPEN Tues thru Sun: 10-5; Please Keep Gate Closed At All Times; Do Not Obstruct Entrance; More Parking At Rear; Commercial Trucks And Vehicles To Back Entrance Turn Left; No Solicitations. It was only after reviewing possible excuses to present to Rachel and realizing none of them would work, that Mark pressed the bell and spoke into the metal box on the right. "Just state who you are!" Regina had commanded.

Silence. Great! Mark thought, I can sneak away: *Obviously wanted to get me on a wild goose chase. You're absolutely right. Woman's impossible! Never mind. We'll just keep our distance*—The high gate started moving slowly inward in front of Mark with a grinding, grudging sound but certainly swung back smoothly enough to shut hard behind him. No Dogs; No Food or Drink to be Consumed on Premises; No Smoking; Shirts and Shoes Must be Worn; Children Must be Supervised at All Times; Do Not Touch The Flowers; Do Not Handle Plants; Please Wait for Sales Staff; All Major Credit Cards Accepted. Not a soul, only a very thin old man in a straw hat, raking the gravel, the color of porridge. Two fairly large orchid houses sat side by side, between chunky date palms and landscaping, hotel style. Benches in front were flanked by large concrete litter bins, the tops of black plastic bags discreetly showing at their rim. The old man raking the gravel slowly and carefully, did not look up. There were two shuttered kiosks close to the entrance, a Kodak sign on one. More notices: Leave All Packages At The Office; Weddings Conducted; Permission Required To Take Pictures. "You know Parrot Jungle?" Larry said. "You pay to have your picture taken with a bird on your shoulder. At Regina's she's started this racket you can pay to have your picture taken with a *Phal* on your shoulder or a *Cattleya* on your front. And, maybe, a *Vanda* behind your ear or an *Oncidium* up your—OK, Ken!"

Here and there Mark recognized a familiar shape from the New Year's Eve party; Fredz Kloze Out Grecian urns, giant economy size, toughing it out in the sun and rain. And right in front, on its own little island above the gravel, hanging on the main branch under a gnarled old tree, a massive orchid in bloom, a cascading explosion of tiny golden flowers. How would you describe that, Mark wondered. Well, in practical, commercial terms, Mark knew what he'd call it; *variety: 'Too big to steal.'*

"So Rachel, first, there was this big yellow orchid hanging in front under a tree." That's a real botanical description, Mark told himself sarcastically. He'd been at Orchid Empire long enough to guess it was probably an *Oncidium.* But even if he got *Oncidium* right, that was only the beginning. Mark knew all flowers had their botanical name: any weed could be called something like *Tangularum visicatum* known to everyone as Creeping Granny's Nightshirt. But meadow flowers and weeds, God bless them, didn't get awards. You could say to a botanist, "Ah! Creeping Granny's Nightshirt just by your left foot, Tangularum visicatum I presume!" and it was "Jolly good show!" and on you went but when it came to orchids you'd hardly started. Begin breeding and the naming never stopped: "*Ah, Laeliocattleya* Pizza Princess! *Obviously Cattleya* Tomato Twinkle *crossed with Laelia* Pepperoni Pete!" Then you showed the best one, got an award and started all over again. And there you were: *Laeliocattleya* Pizza Princess var. 'Bert's Pizza.'

This massive yellow must be at least 'Regina's Big One' or 'Regina's Delight'; maybe one of the milestones in breeding everyone was supposed to know about, the living legends paraded out at the big events: "Ah, Regina's Big One! Once again in bloom for *Las Olas!*" And these produced so many winners that you were supposed to be able to recognize them and their genetic characteristics: "*Phalaenopsis* Flopsy's Folly, parent of all those pinks! And look at *Ascocenda* Billy Boy's trademark spots all over *Vanda* Edith Hackensack's lower sepals!" So what indeed could he tell Rachel?

"Up front Regina has this really big yellow *Oncidium*." *Maybe all* oncidiums *were yellow.* Maybe this wasn't a man made cross after all but an old jungle collected original? Or an early cross, a now out of date hybrid, breeding days over, turned out to graze, so to speak, living out its days hanging from the tree, wowing visitors with its size? Mark didn't even know what orchid facts it would be legitimate *not* to know. Stopped dead for minutes in front of the very first orchid he'd come to, Mark felt a nostalgic twinge for the minor problems of Totters Green: racial tension, unwanted pregnancies, accusations of shoplifting from the sweet shop on the corner, the standard punch up after Fulham beat Arsenal. Mark had to admit that the reason for all this orchid anxiety was more Rachel than Regina. Of course, he told himself, because he didn't care what Regina thought of him. As Charlotte would put it, he had no desire to get into Regina's knickers. On the other hand if Regina found him out first, who knew what stories she'd spread?

"She's a shrewd and brilliant liar," Charlotte had said. "Here's a for instance. Cooper writes a scholarly article or two for the *Awards Quarterly* and suddenly we're hearing from around the region: What a shame he should be into drugs and perhaps—just a hint—maybe *dealing.* Tailor-made for the parochial Anglo-Saxon mind with its suspicion of intellectual achievement: Coop a loner, no visible means of support, thin as a drainpipe, into eastern mumbo jumbo, goes to Thailand and just too clever by half. Cooper didn't care but I had people even like Tilly saying how sad it all was."

"How did you know it was Regina?"

"Trust me, dear boy! And then the cherry on the top. We heard Regina was trying to get Coop into a Christian group for support and counseling!"

And speaking of Regina, thought Mark, where was she? Or her workers? Between the two orchid houses was a little fountain with the grave, cool sound of running water and a greenish bronze figure of Pan playing his pipes, with pointed ears and a cunning smile. In the little pool underneath coins could be seen through the rippling water. There was a small sign in front: *The Silver Fountain*. Larry had said "Regina's starting The Legend of South Miami: mere pennies are bad luck. If it's not *silver* shining through the water Pan gets really pissed!" Still no one had appeared. Only the old man and the hiss of the rake over the gravel. But *someone* had opened the gate. Mark went round to one side, following the path left, wary about going into an orchid house alone. He had heard Charlotte on the phone: "Oh yes, they let him wander back there...Yes, pollen missing—the awarded one of course! Back in Taiwan no doubt, breeding with it even as we speak!" Apparently for industrial espionage among the orchids all that was needed was a toothpick to lift the pollen from the flower and sometimes not even the toothpick. "Some slow-witted orchid husband sitting in as Security at Las Olas last year, let a sweet lady who needed a flower for her hat, take 'just one' off the Best in Show, the final day, just before they closed. 'It matched her dress!' Oh yes! The wife of that little man who was starting up his orchid lab in the Bahamas!" An awarded orchid of course, was like a prize race horse. "But a damn sight easier to breed with!" Charlotte had chortled, "All you need is the toothpick!"

Maybe Regina was letting him wander about, Mark thought, to be tempted to try and pinch something. Maybe there was a hidden camera in one of Fredz Kloze Out urns, though according to Rachel, Orchid Magic had nothing worth stealing, "Unless it's something she's stolen first." Mark saw an open shed at the back, the packing house and made for it crunching firmly over the gravel to attract attention. There in the shade were three Rositas, short, dark, pretty girls with bright green rubber gloves on, standing with their hands over an open box, gazing at him. They looked like a group of surgeons: as though they'd opened up the box and were performing operations on its insides. Around them were more boxes and mounds of paper. Mark couldn't tell if they were packing or unpacking. The three Rositas looked him up and down and went back to the innards of their large cardboard box, lowering their voices.

"Mark! *Mark!* What are you doing snooping round *here?*" Regina had suddenly appeared, driving up in a golf cart. There were the gloves, short black ones, reminiscent of a serious French cyclist. Black designer glasses swept down almost to her nostrils but there was no mistaking the brilliant scarlet, broad smile and the inexorably black hair under the brim of her straw hat. "We must show you round!" Regina patted the seat. As the golf cart swerved off Mark was slapped into Regina's side engulfed in a perfume that hit the back of his throat like Ruby's oven cleaner. The cart stopped with a jolt in front of The Silver Fountain and Pan with his sly grin. Regina, Mark noted, had not explained the initial silence. "I was wondering for a while if I'd come on the wrong day."

Ignoring this, Regina announced: "Now I know we're in total agreement about Orchid Empire so first let me show you *our* operation. I hear you're something of an expert, but impossible to get anything out of you! English modesty! Hard to believe you're kin to Charlotte. A lot of people find that charming but *I* say we should be smoking you out and picking your brains!" Regina led the way into the first orchid house, removing her straw hat and shaking her coal black hair loose, relaxing now, not because she was out of the heat Mark sensed, but out of the sun. Set at a timeless thirty-one or two, this was a face like one of Mike's warm loving orchids in a northern cellar, more suited now to bloom under artificial light.

Two broad aisles stretched down the orchid house, broad enough for Regina's little golf cart between the ranks of *Phalaenopsis:* white, pinks, pinstriped and plain, some with scarlet lips and a phalanx of yellows. "We know Charlotte's little group like to sneer but this is the classic orchid everywhere now, weddings, graduation."

"Beautiful display," Mark murmured. The gravel was raked so clean, not a leaf, the display was perfect, the hum of fans low and efficient. "Seems you didn't suffer much in the freeze." In the corner, Mark saw a dark face with big black eyes staring out from behind the blooms; another Rosita, waiting for Regina to pass by. "Well, *I never* let my workers go home for Christmas and New Year. Too often prime time for bad weather! Now I know what *you'll* be looking for." Mark froze. "Not many stanhopeas or lycastes here! I know cymbidiums and paphs are big in England but here we mostly leave them to the West Coast. We should get you out there to speak! How long are you here for? We need to find out *what you know!*"

The words hung in the air. Mark stared over the gravel out into the sunshine. "Actually," he started slowly, "I hear from Dr. Gibson that you have been kind enough to explore the possibility of a buyer for Orchid Empire."

Regina turned her dark glasses on Mark. Her mouth suddenly looked quite small. "Where did you hear that? *I* never said that. Don't take information from that woman! Why would I discuss anything with *her?* I did emphasize though, the need for safe keeping. But why is this Gibson woman answering the phone! *In charge!*"

"Dr. Gibson *is* a little abrupt but *so* good. Brilliant, in fact, but certainly doesn't suffer fools gladly. Er— suffer *any* of us! Gladly or— (What the hell is the opposite of 'gladly'? Mark asked himself.) "But of course, anything to get Charlotte on her feet again!"

"And that brings up the big question," said Regina smoothly. "This latest *mishap* is by no means the only one. I will be presenting *my* thoughts to the committee. I may be President but I only have one vote! I think sometimes people forget that! A lot of us feel Miami gets a bad press—bad *orchid* press—and I'm afraid members like Charlotte, dear as they may be, do nothing for our image. I really feel there should be a policy, a limit, a moment when we can all agree—for the sake of the society and the individual—" What she was proposing, Mark realized, was Charlotte could be declared too *old* to partake in the Miami Orchid Expo and probably by extension, any of the South Florida shows. Mark could hear Charlotte: "You're next Bert! She's picking us off, one by one!"

"So erratic..." Of course, Regina would have to make it 'drunk and disorderly' in order to effect Charlotte's ouster. Too many long term old biddies in the society, according to Charlotte; a bit near the knuckle for Regina to play the age card alone. As with Charlotte though, Mark was learning when to keep quiet. He wondered whether Regina ever got drunk. Do her good. "Three score years and ten!

Mark! Three score years and ten!" Regina was walking Mark up to the far end of the house, past the *Phalaenopsis,* the *Dendrobium* phals, and the little lacy golden yellow oncidiums, maybe the offspring of Regina's Big One. On a lower level racks of paphs, with striped pockets and pouches came into view but then a whole range of stuff he had no idea; a lot of purples, pinks, tiny chocolate brown or lemony blooms on the end of long stems. Encyclias? oncidiums, encidiums? epidendrums? Hadn't Charlotte said that encyclias now were called encidiums or epidendrums? Or was it the other way round? Not content with having the largest group of flowering plants to play with, it seemed orchidists couldn't leave well alone. They were everlastingly taking an orchid out of one group and putting it in another or giving it its own group. "Why, dear boy? Your serious orchidists are always having second thoughts—about pollen and stigmas and root systems. Then they call up a taxonomist buddy in Zurich or New Haven and start wrangling."

Regina had asked Mark nothing about orchids so far; luckily she was preoccupied with Charlotte and Orchid Empire. "Now it's all preparation for the show. I've been telling our members they can look for good things from Orchid Empire especially as you say you suffered little damage in the freeze. We know Charlotte always has good things blooming for Las Olas."

"Yes, exactly. And that's the thing. I don't actually think Charlotte wants to give up Las Olas."

Regina stopped dead. "I have *told* them." Her tone was icy and final. "We had agreed. You gave me your word!" Mark opened his mouth and closed it. "*Well?*" She had turned and faced him, folding her arms across her crisp white shirt and somehow that big generous scarlet mouth had all but disappeared. "What am I going to tell my members? And then there's the Major." Regina was pulling her straw hat back on. "*Well?*"

For a moment Mark hung there, like a toad on the edge of a spade, then he rallied. *Wait a moment. What are we talking about here? First of all she's lying. And all over a few lousy plants.* And if it were a question of who could fluently tell the biggest whopper, then Eng. Lit. put one right ahead. "Of *course* Charlotte doesn't want to face facts. *This* has been her whole life! I'm sure you can well understand it's a terrible moment when you realize you're too old—" Mark skidded, braked and backed right off. "Um, impossible for you, of course, to understand the heartbreak. Dr. Gibson is worried; we *all* are. Charlotte is still a little fragile. She needs a little more time before we tell her Las Olas is out and though it's a *little* unfair to the *Las Olas* people, we need to keep them in the dark for a little longer." (Too many *littles!* Mark told himself.) "I had promised my mother—" he wondered if a little sniff might be too much. He could put in a gulp, more manly: "After all," swallow, "that's why I'm here."

Regina's mouth was returning to a generous width and by the time they had reached the other house, she seemed to have regained her good mood. Thank God, thought Mark, no wonder people just gave up and agreed with the woman. "I would be *more* than happy to show case any plants for Orchid Empire. It's not just one individual, Mark, it's all of us pulling together. Though some find it hard to work as a team. The show title is 'Orchid Treasures' this year and we know Charlotte certainly has *many* of those."

Regina's second orchid house seemed a little bare: none of Charlotte's steamy riotous mixes, no danger of any of these orchids dangling into someone's hair, trailing out of their baskets or tipping their pot sideways on the bench, as they grew. Charlotte's whole operation reminded Mark of the old fairground Haunted Houses. He was much taller than anyone else at Orchid Empire and everywhere he turned some strange looking plant with dangling roots or odd shaped leaves was bobbing or trailing against his face. Here, even the vandas were subdued, their long, fat roots docked like the tails of pedigree dogs. Now Regina had stopped between benches covered in squares of tiny pots with little plants, the flowers poking their heads, tongues, pouches, lips and whiskers above the leaves. The overall impression was of gravel, metal bars, potted pebbles, green plastic and wire mesh, labels and tags; regimented rows, many little snub nosed species up to their ears in special mixes, all strapped in tight with a variety of restraining devices. "We often find it useful to use spreader trays for the larger seedlings."

"Right!" What the hell were spreader trays?

"There's a lot we can learn from standard floral nurseries but of course we have to maintain the mystique of orchids and price is certainly a large part of that, though the days of backyard eccentrics in the orchid world are, as we see, definitely numbered. Now! Marjorie has been trying to see Charlotte's African orchids for at least a year. It worries us, thinking maybe they're in bad shape."

"No, I can assure you—"

"Good. Get me a list of the species, up to date. Orchid Empire we know has some unique material and as President I feel it is my duty to make sure nothing gets lost. I don't have to tell you that taeniophyllums and acampes, the African angraecums and Charlotte's special 'toys' from Madagascar, are not to be found in every collection. I've had quite a few enquiries. On Charlotte's behalf."

Mark was looking down at a pair of cattleyas in bloom, trying to decide whether they looked more like painted Pekineses or demented psychedelic daffodils. He was wondering why he couldn't come up with a more poetic appreciation of these gorgeous, fascinating flowers that held so many in thrall; the whole mysterious world of orchids with their long intricate names, their tribes and sub-tribes sweeping over continents and across mountain ranges like the troops of Ghengis Khan, their intricate mating rituals, their crafty deceptions with gullible insects. Perhaps because they were work now, to be tended like cows or pigs. "Hear them mooing out there!" Charlotte would joke. "Gotta get out and water the buggers!" But more than that it was because of the crazy position Charlotte had put him in: for Mark, the supposed orchid man, every orchid was a test, a problem, a hurdle, a potential catastrophe of discovery.

"Thailand is definitely not a third world country anymore," Regina was saying. "Hard to get good prices. Of course, I have my own people out there, my own growers." Mark remembered the stack of boxes he had seen in the packing shed, the piles of paper, those large, flat cardboard boxes the size of children's coffins: KEEP FROM COLD AND HEAT RUSH–RUSH. They probably weren't packing but unpacking, getting ready for the Las Olas Show.

At the end of the orchid house beyond the cattleyas and other mixed genera, set back a little behind a metal lattice screen was a small Buddha seated in the lotus position, smiling his almost Mona Lisa smile through closing lids. Mark was drawn to the figure. A spider had woven a web between the elbow and folds of the Buddha's robe over the thigh. Mark wondered how long that spider would be allowed to exist, undisturbed. "Mark, I shouldn't tell you but I see you have a feel for these things...Indeed I know you'll respect the confidence." Regina lowered her voice: "Actually, this one is real."

"'Real'?"

"One gets to know people, how these things work. As you know, our great country has provided *such* a safe haven for these kinds of treasures. I think of it as performing a public service. We *are* blessed as a nation; in this crazy world a tranquil land!" Certainly the police siren was quite a distance away and the only noise intruding was the *ding ding* from the packing shed where a truck must have been backing up. There was no bird song but then it wasn't really the right time of day. "Didn't you see a sign," Larry was to joke later, "'*No Birds?*'"

"We'll go to my office where it will be quiet. And I do have to check in as it's Monday. Get in!" Mark wondered how Regina kept such a neat figure and whether she ever walked at all. The cart with its whine reminiscent of Charlotte's chair, wheeled out between the benches, the cattleyas with their fat, frilly pug faces watching it go.

Inside the office it was ice cold. No wonder Regina just sat down in her cart when the Florida sun hit her. The walls were covered in American Orchid Society certificates and trophy ribbons; First Place, Award of Merit, Highly Commended, Best in Show and group photos, every one framed. There was the full complement of Orchid Magic, Regina in the center, lesser souls kneeling on either side: Regina with winning exhibit, Regina with winning cup, Regina holding a certificate aloft. For a moment there was silence then Mark realized he needed to drop his contribution into the silence: "Very impressive!"

"Oh, just a few here!" Regina was free to proceed. "Next time you have to come to the house. We have a whole room there, the whole history of Orchid Magic!"

Charlotte had a whole mess of show ribbons too: First Place, Grand Trophy, over twenty years' worth of faded reds, blues and whites, greens and gold all over the potting shed. They were hooked up on the corners of the peg board by Carlos or Rosita, tangled up with old dog collars, chains and a plastic fly swat and shoved into an old string bag full of reusable tags which had hung around so long they were illegible. "Ribbon judging" Charlotte had said, "that's just local, 'Biggest Turnip in the Village' stuff. Now American Orchid Society judging, *that's* what goes in the record books and so that's what's bad with someone like Regina."

Regina had sat down behind her desk, squeezing a pencil in both hands, lips pursed, dark glasses turned on Mark. "Regina has to have *control.*" That was Rachel's take. Mark could believe it. Anyone who could have a desk top that size, uncluttered, on a Monday afternoon, was definitely in control. "It is certainly a shame Charlotte has not thought of donating her orchids to the Miami Orchid Club permanent collection. We keep them here. We have the facilities. Since Andrew hit I think I can safely say Orchid Magic has become the largest and most important of the local, traditional orchid establishments."

"One of her favorite sayings is the Lord helps those who help themselves," Larry explained. "She certainly helped herself to old Mrs. Armstrong's collection for 'Safe keeping.' Mike says a lot of plants reportedly 'died off.' Right! Several rare ones were apparently born again in the greenhouses of a rich customer in California."

There was a knock on the door and the girl from the outside office, having waited discreetly for a '*Yes!*' brought in the coffee. "Cuban! I hope that's all right? With sugar? No cream? So, Mark! I'll rely on you to get me the list of Charlotte's material for Las Olas. And who knows? If some of it never made its way back, well it would be one less burden for her."

"Well, I don't think—" Mark stopped. He breathed his all purpose, "Right!" He was in so deep now, he was starting to feel light headed. Rachel and Charlotte would have to fight it out with Regina. After all, that's what they seemed to relish. He'd just stand back and hold their coats, as they said at The Rat and Parrot. At least he'd been spared the test of orchid knowledge; a few more sips of coffee and he could say goodbye.

"Now! I need to get your opinion! Come with me!" Once more into the cart and back to the species area, the special collection, to one side of Buddha. Mark was in the place he dreaded where every pot and clump or tuft was a stubbornly different orchid; special, complicated, no doubt with an intricately long last name, Regina's treasures. But, he suddenly realized, in a burst of relief, this was not Charlotte's world, her apparently anonymous odds and sods, her toys that didn't need names because she knew them all. Or, with no padlock on a gate that didn't close anyway, were not labeled because"Why sign post the good stuff? Don't have to point it out to any Tom, Dick or Harry who wanders in." With Regina every plant was labeled, down to the most wizened little thing poking through the heavy gravel or pebbled pot. He could just pick up each one and study the tag as though checking if it were correct and there would be the name! Exhale a few "Ah! *interesting!*" and "Glad to see how well these thrive here." Throw in a few "God! What you can do when you have proper organization, climate *and control.*" And he could be on the other side of the stockade, breathing hard and all set to pick up the milk at Farm Stores and home for tea.

Mark squinted down at a cluster of pots. "*Zyg.*" Fuck! Of *course,* they were all abbreviated. What the hell was 'Perr.'? Regina was called away by one of the Rositas but the respite didn't help. The names leapt up at Mark: *Zyg.* again, *Lc., Pot., Rntda.,* and *Vasco., Hok., Obst.,* like a row of bloody German dwarfs. How could he finish even one name? Much more of this and he'd be sinking to his knees on the gravel, whimpering.

"I knew that one would interest you." Regina had returned while he stood there paralyzed by the little wisp he had picked up at random. "Do you think it's rather large for its type?"

"Of course, under optimum conditions..." *We could reunify the Korean peninsular, end world hunger.* Maybe, Mark thought, maybe he could wander off into a weather forecast. '*We do find when the Westerlies take hold in June...*' He could here the sound of raking in the distance.

The old man hadn't stopped. Was he scared of Regina, too? Of course! There was that police car again— *They're coming to take you away!* And then an odd little noise started coming from close to Regina's private parts. A little tinkly noise like a distant ice cream van. Of course, a cell phone. It was playing the first two lines *of My Funny Valentine,* over and over. For a moment Regina let it ring. She's definitely on to me, Mark thought. She's letting me and my optimum conditions just hang there and then curiosity and the tensions of Monday without Antonio saved him. Regina pulled her cell phone up out of its holster, looking hard at Mark from behind the dark glasses. She tossed her hair free and slid the phone under. Mark, eager to give her the courtesy of space for a private conversation put down the tiny pot slowly and deliberately and walked quickly away, Regina's voice traveling effortlessly across the gravel:"You can't come to me on a Monday with that kind of problem. No! *No!* That's *your* problem. This is not a charity! What you heard and what I said are two different things." The *ding ding* from beside the packing shed had started again and there was the sound of raised voices. Someone shouted. Regina, still fuming, turned her head quick as a whippet.

Mark said "I can see you're very busy. It *is* Monday! Thank you so much for showing me everything. You have a very impressive operation." Regina looked Mark up and down. She was no fool. But Tony was off, truckers were to be dealt with and there was a dangerous atmosphere of unsupervised lives in the air. "Get in! Mark! We *will* get everything resolved. We will discuss this over dinner. Do you like Thai? Mexican?"

"At the moment, of course, I don't feel like leaving Charlotte for too long..."

"Where's your car?"

"I parked outside."

"Another time, come *inside.* Oh, and by the way," Regina called from the opened gate as Mark got in the Volvo and wound down the window to say goodbye. The old man with the rake had reached the Silver Fountain, all the way over to the orchid houses. "*Do* give my best to Rachel. I think you'll be seeing her? Tell her how *sorry* I am Bios

Orchids won't be in the Expo but rules are rules. I tried my best to make her case. You know, that's my responsibility. But unfortunately the show committee's very firm on this."

Well, there's always next year," said Mark.

"Oh, I'm afraid not," sighed Regina, lowering her glasses again so Mark could see how genuine her sympathy was. "We have *such* a waiting list. That was something the committee decided upon as only fair, at the last meeting. Any one vendor or business which drops out or is rendered illegible for whatever reason is *out*. Rachel is a big girl, she knows that's life in the big city! We had tried to give her a few warning signals. No, once you lose your spot!" The gate swung shut and Mark heard the whine of the golf cart and the crunch of the gravel growing fainter as Regina buzzed away.

11

Las Olas Show: Preparation

"I'm giving Orchid Empire's spot in the Las Olas show to Rachel," Charlotte announced. "I take it that's alright with you."
Mark could hardly believe it. Just as he was losing hope suddenly Rachel was being offered to him on a plate. Larry had said everyone complained about the Las Olas show: the long ride up to the hall, north of north Miami, first to put in the exhibit, then back and forth again, for three whole long days stretching into evening, vendors crammed into a tiny booth space hours on end. As for putting in the exhibit, according to Larry exhibitors stayed up till all hours, some all night, sending out for pizza, someone bringing in a six pack. In terms of getting up close and personal it would be even better than a New Year's Eve. And it would be the perfect way to get back on a social footing with Jen. She'd arrive after work, if she came at all and there he would be: Orchid Empire partnering Bios Orchids, late into the night or whatever. Not his choice—just the rules of the game.

"So what have you been cooking up with Regina behind my back? She's just called to tell me she's a very Christian woman. Always a signal for the rest of us to take to the hills!"

Charlotte far from being upset was, in fact, relishing the accounts trickling in of Mark's visit to Orchid Magic. "Regina crushed you like a grape, didn't she? You're getting her a list of my treasures, are you? Destined to enhance the Miami Orchid Club exhibit at Las Olas but just *accidentally* sidetracked into Orchid Magic. That woman has crust! And by the way, ever heard of a 'Dr. Gibson'? My own special *'keeper'*? I swear Regina's got to the point she believes her own fabrications."

"What did you say?"

"Take what ever you want! I exist to serve you!" For a moment Mark was startled. Then the classic cackle emerged. "I had great pleasure in informing the woman that Rachel is undertaking the Las Olas show for Orchid Empire and Bios Orchids, a joint venture, showcasing her considerable talents, prior to lodging a complaint with the Miami Orchid Club Show Committee *re* her expulsion. By the way, don't say anything to Rachel about *permanent* expulsion. She has enough to deal with at the moment. Well Regina's certainly got it in for you now. Better make yourself scarce at the show."

Like Charlotte, Rachel was obviously enjoying the prospect of a confrontation. Thank God she was, thought Mark. Rachel was exactly the sort of person you needed when you'd got on the wrong side of someone like Regina. In fact, she was exactly the sort of person you would leave to confront a Regina, while you tiptoed away, planning to hide in the mens' lavatories. Though with these women Mark didn't think you'd be safe even there.

The Las Olas orchid show, up in Broward County, was at least an hour and a half away.

"Long haul there and back, I'm afraid," Charlotte said. "No problem!" Mark declared. Long journeys, just the two of them, both caught in rush hour traffic, transfixed, stopped in time. Rachel with her pensive profile and gleaming hair; the two of them close and enclosed in that tiny world. Of course, with the Volvo and no air conditioning, they'd need the windows open. But it would all be quality time, time alone, elbow to elbow; the world firmly outside, music optional.

And Mark would bring the odds and sods, whatever of Charlotte's toys and treasures were in bloom and then any commercial stuff to help fill out the exhibit and fill up the booth to sell. And they would put in this great little exhibit together, he kneeling with Rachel on the moss among the orchids and ferns late into the night, parking his cold beer beside hers, the night blooming orchids exuding their fragrance. There would be, finally, the fellowship and warmth that only working on a project together gave you, then the long ride back, in the dark. The first blow came when Charlotte said, "Rachel is borrowing a van. You'll take the Volvo. Orchid Empire's putting in 200 square feet."

The next morning after watering Charlotte had Mark go round with her, clip board and legal pad in hand, listing potential plants for the show. "Always a litany of disaster!" she announced cheerfully. "Cold damage, bud drop from high temps, flowers fading, flowers not open—It's show time!" In spite of all this they were assembling quite a collection of possibles for the exhibit. Not only the prize plants in bloom from Charlotte's old collections but a good number of commercial orchids presentable enough to help fill up space, as they hadn't had any sales: ("Regina's no doubt told everyone I'm dead!") Mark, following Charlotte's chair, holding the clipboard and ducking under orchid roots, was mourning the end of the dream of romantic journeys with Rachel, to and from the show. But at least he would be taking round plants for the exhibit to Bios Orchids and see where Rachel and Jen, lived. Mark needed to see not so much where Rachel lived, as how she lived: what she put on the walls, what books she read. And apart from all that, Mark wanted any excuse to get off the porch.

Someone had called one afternoon to see how Charlotte was, surprised Mark was still there. "Earl would have taken you out on the boat!" She was the snowbird from Chicago in the lime green halter top at the Christmas party. She wanted his impressions of Coconut Grove and South Beach, the Everglades and the Keys. "And don't forget Orlando and Disney world! That was the *one* place the Emperor of Japan wanted to go see!"

"Really?" said Mark. "Charlotte's been a little under the weather over New Year." He felt he shouldn't go off during business hours and at the weekends he was in charge of watering and that was prime time for retail. Not that anyone had come but that made him feel he should hang around even more. As for the evenings, Mark decided maybe the problem was he needed twilight, that long grey period in the temperate zone when you could mill around making decisions, checking the oil in the car, the times of movies, making a phone call. Night fell so abruptly at Orchid Empire that Mark often fed the dogs by moonlight. By that time he'd be on his second beer, facing the prospect of driving Charlotte's 'moody' Volvo off in the dark on the wrong side of the road, just to make it to the lights of US1. He would land up retiring with his third beer to the computer in the spare room and emailing someone else with nothing better to do, like Ned.

"No, actually, I haven't really seen much."

"Oh, orchids will do that to you!" the snowbird said. "You don't have a life! I found I would be going out to the plants *apologizing!* 'Mommy's leaving you for a few hours!' Worse than animals! That's why we had to give them up."

Having checked for possible exhibit plants just before the weekend, Mark and Charlotte had checked again Monday. "As I thought," Charlotte said, "the *other Angrecum* is fading. My special white *Phalaenopsis* has *botrytis*. One show, Bert says, an exhibitor spray painted his white phals white. Makes me think of the tale your Uncle Frank tells, when he was in the army and the Queen came and they painted all the coal black."

Mark had been waiting for Tuesday, the day he would deliver the plants, the day he would finally visit Rachel. And with Jen off at work, there could be no A and B complications. Rachel called: it was stressful and unnecessary for the exhibition plants to be handled so much. "I'll just come over and get them with the van." So there they were, the three of them, back on the porch. At least Rachel had come late enough in the afternoon to stop and have a beer. She was wearing a skinny T-shirt and short shorts, her hair drawn back, straight and shining, tied with what looked like half a bootlace.

"What's the theme?" Charlotte asked, fresh from her afternoon nap. "'Orchid Treasures!' Not again! How original. How do they think these things up? I thought Bert said 'Orchid *Paradise*' or was it 'Paradise of Orchids,' or 'Orchids from Paradise'? Doesn't make any difference. Could be 'Orchids from Hell,' you put in what you've got."

"Remember that time they had *Precious* Treasures?" said Rachel. "Old Lloyd parked a Ferrari among his ferns, and Roberto had a shrine with a weeping Madonna and candles and someone piled up plastic gems and beads like New Orleans Mardi Gras."

"I think they all dream of becoming window dressers at Bloomingdales."

"Chelsea's the same now," Mark said." What I've seen of it on TV: fountains and miniature waterfalls and grottoes."

"It's not even window dressers they need now, tarting it all up," Charlotte muttered, "it's plumbers. Well, it all helps to fill up space. Old John used to shove in something that looked like a kiddies' Hindu temple. God knows where he got it from. Didn't matter what the theme was. He always said 'I paid good money for that thing!' Could have been 'Orchid Treasures of New Hampshire,' it would still have gone in. Alvin always does his garden shed."

"Not garden shed, Charlotte!" Rachel protested, "*Gazebo!*"

"Who has that god-awful cardboard wall with the painted bricks? Not even strong enough to lean plants against! A pair of iron garden chairs will take you through most shows. And if you have a bird bath, well so much the better. Of course the best story ever about filling up space at a show was the tale of the mannequin at Miami! Small firm one year, no decent orchids to speak of, desperate to fill up space laid out a full size plastic mannequin on some kind of lounger right in the middle of their exhibit. Two piece swim suit, sun glasses, taking up more space than my *Cattleya guatemalensis*. Comes the premier party, Thursday night. This was before Regina's reign, plenty of free booze and it all got pretty lively, student judges at the end taking turns waltzing the mannequin round the room. All well and good! The older, staider members toddling off in a soft haze! Comes Friday morning ready to open to the public and the mannequin is back spreadeagled on her lounger with one plastic hand slid inside the bottom half of her swim suit! I don't think to this *day* anyone has owned up. She was discovered before they opened the doors which rather spoils the fun. Anyway, stern letters were sent! Everyone had to grovel. *That's* when there was some young blood and spunk in the Miami Orchid Club."

"Are you taking along anything just to fill up space?" Mark asked Rachel.

"I don't want to waste space in the *van,* that's the problem," Rachel said, "and I can't get excited about all the props. Some exhibitors, like Robby, actually rent things from a theatrical place. If he could, he'd rent Adam and Eve. And the snake."

"Well, he could certainly get some plastic apples, or go for the real thing," said Charlotte. "Buy a pound of Red Delicious, pick out the biggest one and Bob's your uncle."

"I wonder if Regina will take her Buddha along," said Mark. "Probably not. It's too precious."

"Precious? From Fredz Kloze-Outs?" Rachel cried, "I don't *think* so!"

"No, Rachel, apparently this is a real one, she said. I suppose she means from a temple. Obviously smuggled in—Couldn't resist telling me, rather proud of it, I think."

"Well," said Charlotte, "if that's correct, that's interesting. I wonder if Cooper knows about this."

Rachel had taken the clip board and started to make notes. "In spite of all your grumbles Charlotte, you always have really good material. You can bring the *Rhyncostylis gigantea,* Mark, those two albas and the red. And, unbelievably, my *Phalaenopsis amabilis,* the white, and *aphrodite* are going to be fine."

"Some of my African angraecums will make it." Charlotte said. "No bulbophyllums but there's the *Cattleya trianaei,* and what about Coop? He'll find you a 'real' *Vanda,* or two, not a hybrid, or at least a primary cross. What plants will fit in the Volvo, is the question. Plants for sale Mark can bring up Friday. Thank God Bert's bringing up the ferns. And don't forget the crates!

In Miami, Mark, they give out sand but at Las Olas *nothing* so the milk crate has always been the building block of the orchid displays. But the daftest thing was they *all* belonged to the dairies! The most respectable people used to snitch them from behind Farm Stores. It was always easier this end of the county; farm workers brought them into the fields to sit on while picking beans and when everyone piled into the buses they got left behind. But if the cops had raided the Las Olas show and taken back all those crates the orchid show would literally have collapsed."

"When I'm an accredited judge," Rachel declared, "I'm going to put in an exhibit and leave it bare, a few petrified and charred branches: title: '21st Century: Destruction of Habitat.'"

"Well, Rachel, you're young enough to live to see the day," said

Charlotte. "Of course, the *Stanhopea* is fading, Sod's law again. And Carlos managed to snap the prize *Vanda* spike when he tried to stake it. You can't yank a flower stem up if it's not been caught in time. It's like lifting a drunk man under the armpits, the head is still going to droop, however young the guy is. We staked too late. Nothing's presenting itself properly. Orchid Empire's letting you down, Rachel. It will be up to your ingenuity and Mark here, to make something of it! Can't see anything up for individuals. What? Entering an individual plant for ribbon or the AOS, young man, American Orchid Society judging. Well, neither of us are interested in ribbon judging. Is it Las Olas which has the tacky trophies? For years old Professor Hamburg was in charge. Gave out ashtrays every year, lovely lead crystal mind you, gives a great ping when you tap them."

So that's where those come from in the Florida room, Mark thought. Not some tobacco stained colonial outpost.

"What about Larry and Ken?"

"They've got this banquet coming up at the weekend," Rachel said. "I don't want to bother them."

"Nonsense! They'll be hurt not to be asked. They've got their giant *Vanda lamellata boxallii*. They'd love to show it off again—might even get an award this time or at least a show trophy ribbon and that baby takes up a lot of space! Remember I borrowed it last year? I think Ken said it could be sold out of the exhibit but he'd need 500. And if you can't use it I know Bert will."

"What about Regina?" Mark asked "Does she get her own way at this show?"

"No! At Las Olas people can actually compete for the show trophy and awards. Though they do that at Miami, silly buggers, even though they won't get anywhere with Regina running everything. But she doesn't rule the roost over the county line, not yet. The Major's pretty friendly to her, though."

"But he's a stickler for the rules." Rachel said.

"I get on fine with the Major," said Charlotte. "He's ex-military, covert operations, I think: Central America, the dirty wars of the seventies or eighties. Bert always says 'How do you know?' But you'll see; mention Guatemala, El Salvador, Nicaragua and he'll always say darkly: *'We did what had to be done.'*"

"No, what's crazy, Mark," Rachel said, "is the fact that the Major loves strong women."

Were there any other sort in South Florida? Mark asked himself.

"—So he can't help admiring Regina. *But,* of course, then there's Charlotte."

"Yes, indeed," said Mark.

"Actually it's not just Charlotte. It's Margaret Thatcher. The Major sees Charlotte as another Maggie Thatcher; he thinks the Falklands campaign the most brilliant military operation this century!"

"Certainly the nuttiest," remarked Charlotte. "He loved it, of course, putting the Argies, the Latins, in their place. Running out of steam a bit too, now. But I only have to say 'Didn't we show the Argies?' And he perks right up."

Mark wondered, not for the first time, why all these strong-minded people were in orchids of all things, intricate, delicate flowers rather than gun running or off shore drilling.

"Well of course, the Major got into orchids when he was down there in the jungle, lying in wait for guerillas," Rachel said. "What would you be doing?"

"Lying in wait for guerillas? Shaking like a leaf," Mark said.

"No! Checking out the wonderful stuff blooming out above your head in the forest canopy! God, they've got the rain forests there, the highlands. Talk about military terrain, it's *orchid* terrain!"

"You could argue orchids should be of great interest to the military mind," Charlotte observed. "Devious, clever, conduct covert operations—"

"Camouflage!" added Rachel. "They stalk their prey, their pollinators, without moving! Pseudo-copulation, pollination by deceit, pseudo-antagonism! They *anticipate* what an insect will do!"

"You can never get bored with the orchid. Highly evolved, Mark, highly evolved! Makes standard military intelligence look about as sharp as mud."

"You don't have to be an orchid to prove that point!" Rachel added.

"And they all gave a merry laugh!" Charlotte said with a cackle. She was definitely back on form and looking much better; Mark had driven her to the hairdressers, "To my little girl from Peru." Charlotte's 'little girl from Peru' worked at a hair salon in another tiny strip mall, Sunburst Plaza, south on US1. It was a one-storey row of individual enterprises each with a door and a big shop window and two parking spaces in front, looking about as solid as something hammered together out of scrap wood after the last hurricane. Mark thought maybe that was why so much of South Florida appeared so temporary, even ramshackle. Fear of hurricanes made much of the local landscape look like a hurricane had just swept through: no charming southern porches, no lacy wooden balustrades, no magnificent old trees outside bedroom windows. So many narrow windows or none at all, stores like concrete bunkers—architecture by insurance companies. And so few buildings more than one storey high, down here, south of Miami, it looked as though a hurricane had sheared everything at about twelve feet.

"Of course, Andrew took it all down!" Charlotte had said. "Driving along the streets was like Berlin in `45. Ruined houses piled up ten feet on either side. Not a tree standing, not a pole. And not a leaf! Not a leaf for miles. All grey. At night you could see the car headlights on US1 from here."

Sunburst Plaza boasted a tiny butchers, the daily specials written all over the window in Spanish except for one line in English, probably left over from Christmas, a faint *Order your "Pig" now!* Next door was another pawn shop: GOLD, GUNS, ROLEX WATCHES, TV; a lawyer for Immigration and Taxation sharing space with a Bail Bondsman, then two blank windows covered in old taped up newspapers and sun bleached posters for Mexican Day of the Republic, 1994 and a notice about signing up for the Guatemalan Soccer Club and then 'MARIA'S SALON HAIR NAILS WALK INS WELCOME.'

Mark had gone to sit in the Volvo and wait, watching the traffic on US1, cars with the sun roofs open, power boats being towed down to the Keys. The bus bench opposite, baking in the sun, announced BANKRUPTCIES across the back and gave a local number to call. Standing beside the bench was a thin black woman, ram rod straight under a black umbrella, gazing north, towards Miami. US1 was so bare here, there was nowhere for Mark to put the Volvo in the shade. He could hardly believe that there used to be an old look out tower, Charlotte said, like they had in forests to watch for fire among the pines, somewhere just here beside US1.

"Andrew ended most of what little Dade County pine was left; *we* had nineteen. That damn beetle and the woodpeckers! Tapping everywhere, all those dying trees after Andrew, like damn undertakers. Terrible to lose trees. People need trees more than birds do! You've seen the *Ficus religiosa,* at the turn for Silver Palm Drive?" Thick plaits of roots hung down all round the trunk, broad enough to take a park bench in its shade, broad enough for half a dozen Volvos. "'The tree under which Buddha discovered the seven fold path,' Coop says. Bert will tell you they used to be all along US1, arching over the whole road all the way through South Miami and right up to the Rickenbacker causeway." Mark, starting to sweat, was just wondering how long the woman under the umbrella would have to wait for a bus when there was a burst of squeals as two women suddenly rushed out from inside Maria's and pulled at the Volvo's door handle. "Come! Come!"

Inside Charlotte was repeating firmly, "*Nephew!* Not 'son,' *nephew!*"

Charlotte's 'little girl from Peru' turned out to be a small, thin woman with black eyes who looked as though she had indeed been earning her living since she was a little girl. She, with the other two assistants, had surrounded Charlotte, clucking at her leg, her chair and above all her hair, peeling off Bill's Bait and Tackle cap, shaking their heads while the two other customers, heads jammed under dryers, sat and watched. And now Charlotte was indeed looking smart and up together again, with cherubic, white curls all over her baby pink scalp. She wanted to hear how Mark had liked the little salon. "Did you hear? They're sweet gals but what really tickles me is that they always call me *Harlot!*"

Charlotte looked so up together and 'on top of her game' as she called it, Rachel was asking her whether she wanted to do Las Olas herself, after all. "No, No! Just take along the boy here and do the best you can! And sell enough so you won't want for meat on Sunday as they used to say."

Rachel was cracking open two more beers but Mark wanted to keep a clear head till he was sure he knew how to find his way to wherever the Las Olas show was going to be. The big Veterans of Foreign Wars Post, Rachel said. How appropriate, reflected Mark, thinking of the Major, the Queen, past skirmishes, ongoing battles and upcoming campaigns; so while Charlotte was telling him it was a piece of cake he had Rachel draw him a map.

12

Las Olas: Putting in the Show

Rachel had said don't try and beat the rush hour so by the time Mark pulled into the Veterans of Foreign Wars parking lot the sun was already hot and the early arrivals had taken the best spots: their vehicles nosed under trees, sidling along the hedge, hunting for shade like cattle in a summer field. Mark squeezed in next to Eileen's Orchids with its spray of pink *Phalaenopsis* painted across the side panels. Not wanting to leave the Volvo far from the entrance and full of orchids, its windows wide open, Mark grabbed two baker's trays of Charlotte's special 'tiddlers' and raced like a delivery boy between the vehicles. Most, like Eileen, had opted just for the classic spray of *Phalaenopsis* to advertise their wares but Orlando Orchids and Orchids From Denise laid it all out: address, telephone, fax, hours open and on the driver's door, email address and web site. One handsome, dark green van with gold trim belonged to Bagley and West Orchids, which sounded like an old law firm from a country town. (Maybe like Bert, thought Mark, they'd dreamed of retiring into orchids and did.) He caught sight of Bert's old van with trailer and right in front, overshadowing the disabled spots, two large white vehicles, the size of ambulances, with the black top hat and ORCHID MAGIC on the sides.

Standing for a moment in the entrance, sunlight streaming in behind him, Mark saw everything indistinct and hazy as though someone had just stirred up the dust. High overhead pipes and girders cris

127

crossed in the gloom above naked light bulbs. Down below the Las Olas Orchid Show was, so far, just a big bare space, with everything laid out on the floor. It looked like a third world market where the peasants were too poor to rent tables and stood with whatever they had to sell at their feet. Orchids were everywhere, flooding round clusters of ice chests, ferns, pots, potted palms, chairs, boxes, bags of mulch, wood chips, brushes and brooms, buckets, pipes, pieces of trellis, plastic trays, the precious milk crates and some unidentifiable objects that might be raw material for the 'Orchid Treasures' theme. Everything was being unwrapped and unpacked creating explosions of tissue paper, brown paper and plastic wrappings. Someone had opened the wrong end of a box and was wailing as Styrofoam beads rolled and spun away. All these out of town and out of state people, thought Mark, all reduced to just standing there, their stuff on the floor. And in the distance a stage where people with clip boards clustered around a table.

Mark passed a pile of boxes on a garden cart: Orchids by Ed, Orchids by Ed, Orchids by Ed, a standard spray of white *Phalaenopsis* printed on each one, simple boxes repeated like a greengrocer's trays of peaches or lettuce. A reminder that the orchid business could be just that, a business, not a clash of warring factions or a wild swirl of competing personalities; just people like Ed, lining up plants on their shelves to sell and just closing up at the end of the day, wanting nothing more dramatic than, once a year, the Las Olas show.

It was important to find Rachel fast, set down his tray of orchids and race back to unload the rest. Mark was deadly afraid the ones left in the open Volvo would either fade, fry, or be stolen. That approach, racing in, head down, not talking, was perfect. Mark wished he could do it all day. Charlotte had said most of the hard core Miami and South Dade orchidists would be at Las Olas and she seemed a little wistful not to be there to see how Mark handled them. He had the feeling now Charlotte was better she was viewing him as entertainment: Charlotte's little practical joke at the local orchid world's expense.(*"I always said you could get away with blind ignorance in this business! There's no mystery to orchids! Any fool can find their way around. Look at my nephew!"*) Certainly he'd got away with it so far. Mark suspected it might be that his jumpy, slightly furtive manner was considered pretty standard for the more eccentric and dedicated orchid scholar, the sort who spent their time wrangling about what group to put an orchid in. After all, it wasn't Mark who made a habit of lurking in the shrubbery, though for a wild moment Mark thought maybe that was because Cooper didn't know anything either.

Of course nothing, Mark knew, could save him from Regina. Regina who had been gracious enough to offer to take him to dinner. Regina who had not been informed that Charlotte was doing Las Olas after all. And the real truth for Regina was even worse: that Rachel would be doing the show instead of Charlotte, and he would be helping. Rachel, who could drag on an old T-shirt and yank her hair up with half a bootlace and still dazzle the back row, and, unkindest cut of all, hardly notice. Luckily Regina would never put in an appearance early, Rachel had said, creasing the crease in those slacks amidst the cypress mulch, down and dirty with the ordinary folk.

Mark, searching for Orchid Empire's spot and Rachel, caught sight of Bert who nodded over to a garden cart stacked with large cardboard boxes covered in red and white tape that read up and down: 'Level Nine.' On the other side of the 'Level Nine' barricade Mark saw Rachel, ash blonde hair shining in the gloom. Engulfed in baggy khaki pants that looked themselves like veterans of foreign wars, weighed down with pockets of varying sizes sagging with clippers, wire cutters and anything of any possible use swept off the orchid bench, Rachel was wearing a shapeless, sludge colored T-shirt that growled 'I am not female, not *anything* today! I am *concentrating!*' Mark realized even if they had spent the long ride up together, in terms of magic moments he probably hadn't missed much. Rachel was standing in the middle of a whole treasure trove of milk crates, some stacked up, some piled high with moss or holding orchids. "Hi! Mark!" She hardly looked at him, frowning at a group of orchid plants by her feet. "If you could just bring everything in. Sorry we don't have a cart. And *look* where they've put us!"

Orchid Empire's selling booth was going to be yards away, not across from their exhibit but past the 'Level Nine' Californians and the Hawaiians. Charlotte had explained how vital it was to have your exhibit close by, when you were selling mostly un-flowered plants and seedlings. "Regina of course, did it to me last year at Miami. I can still recite word for word what I was saying for three days: '*Yes, these seedlings should be a brilliant yellow. Go past this exhibit, then the next two, yes, up to the one with the balloons and then turn left at the Ladies and you'll see a bright yellow Cattleya in the right hand corner of that exhibit, in front. Yes, the one that's opposite the rest rooms, that's the one with the garden chairs and there's a Mexican hat? No, that's the other way. Well, that beautiful yellow Cattleya is one of the parents of this seedling which we're offering at only 15 dollars!*' And off they lurch, looking totally bemused and you never see them again."

Orchid Empire's exhibit space, two hundred square feet, was chalked out on the floor. There it was. On the other side of the chalk, garden carts like flat porters' trolleys came trundling through, pushed by Anglo Saxons with pink faces. Mark realized how after a month in Miami-Dade, ranks of Anglo-Saxons with pink faces, especially pushing things around, had become something unexpected, not the norm. The norm was Gerry, the black-browed UPS man, Carlos and Rosita and the aunts in charge of the pig. The air was getting heady not with any fragrance but the dense, layered smell of so many petals and leaves, warm and damp, taking over the dusty floor. There was the occasional yell and sound of a hammer and the constant friendly buzz of talk, everyone greeting everyone else.

"Vans blocking the entrance must be removed." The PA system suddenly came on loud and strong. "Any van blocking the entrance must be moved. Yes, Alvin, that means you."

A plump black man with name tag strolled by, jingling his keys, nodding in amusement at all the activity. Small palms were being trundled in with large ferns, plastic pots of philodendrons and any and all examples of the booming foliage industry of South Dade. Rachel saw Mark taking it all in. "What did Larry call the Expo last year at Miami?' The ultimate hotel lobby!'"

"So, lose anything in the freeze?" A nondescript man had stopped, addressing Rachel from round the side of a large potted plant he was clasping. *Nondescript* was good, thought Mark. What did the police say? 'No special characteristics.' Nothing personal, mate, just am happy to report no special characteristics like *tall, dark and handsome.*

"Hey Rachel, how's it going?" Another really nondescript male carrying some large piece of foliage. Mark was starting to feel better. Now the rush to unload the actual orchids had abated, it seemed everyone passing by, carrying in everything left, had time to stop and greet. Like the ants, thought Mark, on their way to and from the sugar bowl, pausing with a nod and bump of antenna and on they went.

"How's it going, Rachel? Where's Charlotte?"

"Hey Rachel, how's the lab doing?"

"Hey Rachel, how did the freeze treat you guys?"

Mark made his way out into the sun, eyes down, for the last trip. He wondered what he could say now, now everything was inside. *Can't stop! Got to put in an exhibit!* A woman this time, with a clipboard and forearms like a Sumo wrestler, glasses pushed up on her forehead was talking with Rachel when he got back. "Always takes time. My God, when Elliot broke *his* leg, tripped over the dog! Oh! And this is Charlotte's nephew? Great! And an orchid person too! Rachel, I brought my peanut butter cookies. You look like you haven't eaten since last year. Now, when you've decided the title of your exhibit let me know."

From a far corner of the hall came shrieks of laughter, a shout and a crash. "Las Olas, that society has the best time," Rachel said. "Remember Hank? He came by a few minutes ago? He's in charge." She had called out, "Going for the trophy, Hank?"

Hank in shorts and sandals, magnificently bald, his head shining in the gloom, had raised his arms high: "It's ours this year! Geoff's laelias are at their peak and we've got all Mary-lou's blue *Doritis* and my yellow phals are *killer!*" Hank was about the only one who had not grabbed Rachel, Mark realized. She must have been hugged twenty times already and mostly by males. Why hadn't he just come in and hugged her this morning? *"Hi, Rachel! How's it going?"*

For all the dire talk of the freeze there were flowering orchids everywhere. Mark even recognized some as he made the circuit, ostensibly going for coffee but making sure he knew where the lavatories were, in case Regina put in an early appearance. When he had asked Charlotte what might be in the show, she had smiled. "Well, let's start with the A's, dear boy. You've got my Africans, the angraecums: *eburnum, leonis, magdalenae, scottianum, sesquipedale* and *superbum.* You've got *Aeranthes, Aerangis* and *Ancistrochilus* and then there's aeridovandas and our old friend *Ascocenda.* This time of the year you can expect to see brassavolas and therefore Brassocattleyas, and BLCs, -Brassolaeliocattleyas, *Broughtonia* and its hybrids, lots of *Bulbophyllum,* and then jumping over to your C series, *Calanthe, Catasetum, Cattleya, Coryanthes, Cycnoches, Cymbidium.* Shall I go on?"

Most exhibits were still basic greenery: palms and ferns and winding paths of bright brown mulch between hillocks of sphagnum moss, tiny landscaped worlds where anything might appear: toy trains, puffing round a milk crate high mountain, or plastic soldiers trapped in a mossy canyon, re-enacting the carnage of the Revolutionary or American civil wars. Mark caught sight of Bert standing in the middle of a bank of white and pale pink *Phalaenopsis,* reminding him fleetingly of the old apple tree in the back garden at home, the daffodils and narcissus blooming under it.

"So what do you think?" asked Rachel, taking her coffee. "How does it compare with London?" Mark said cautiously it was certainly nice to have the doors open and sunlight pouring in, in January. Rachel grinned, shaking her head. "You are *so* diplomatic. I always leap in, running my mouth off. Even Charlotte says I'm much too critical."

"You should be at your age," Mark winced as he heard himself. "I mean, it's good to have high standards." Actually, he thought, looking down at Rachel's orchids, about all they did have to offer were high standards. After the flamboyant brilliance of so many show orchids everywhere on the floor, it was hard to see with these orchids whether some even had flowers at all. They appeared to be in the strict survival mode: their intelligence and energies running more to merging with their surroundings than setting out to catch the judges' eye.

"I know no-one's really interested in Papau New Guinea bulbophyllums or even the Indonesian ones. *Or* my Australian dendrobiums. The list goes on! And only Mike's going to get excited about my pleurathallids. You'll tell me I shouldn't risk it with pleurathallids here. And you're right. These *are* from the mountains, Costa Rica and the Andes, but not from high up, so don't give me a hard time! They're not *impossible* to grow in low land Florida."

"Right!"

Rachel started laying on the strips of sphagnum moss, making their milk crate mountains.

"Charlotte was saying you don't have a greenhouse anymore. That must be tough. I mean, *England.* I mean even with cool growing species."

"Well, hard to devote enough time when you're teaching. And then there's football practice, endless essays to mark. You know, orchids take time."

"Essays in botany? Wow."

"Um. Darwin still casts a long shadow. So how long do we have? When does the hall close?"

"It doesn't. Bert says one of the old late and great orchidists was met wandering out of the hall one year at eight in the morning, just as the judges were coming in for coffee and doughnuts. He turned right round and came back in with them. He was a judge too. Been up all night with his exhibit. 'Finishing touches!' he said, 'finishing touches!' I'm just off for a moment, Mark. Make sure no one grabs our crates."

Mark, only two years out from student life, didn't have to be an exhibitor at Las Olas to appreciate milk crates but it was the first time he realized they must *all* be stolen or appropriated and was curious as to how serious pinching one really was. One side of the crate referred him to sections 565 and 566 of the Penal Code: "For unauthorized possession or use of this case or obliteration or destruction of this case" he was subject to a thousand dollar fine or imprisonment or both. If the laws governing British crates were as harsh Mark could see the ever resourceful Ned incorporating the whole text into a new line: "Hey, doll, see right here? Who's risking jail time so you can sit down!"

Two thin men in jeans and white shirts had appeared on the other side of the chalk line. They had to be 'Level Nine Orchids' from California. Rachel was sure their name referred to levels of consciousness;

Mark suggested seismic levels of earthquakes. But the truth they'd never know: the pair refused even to acknowledge their presence. They were now cutting open large flat boxes and pulling out white plastic folding tables. Pretty soon they were set up and covered with black and red cloths, smart and shiny, some kind of sateen. And all this they'd flown in from California: Mark was impressed. As the sun warmed up streaming into the hall through the broad entrance and as more orchids were unwrapped, the vendors spraying their prize exhibits, the smell of wet flowers mixing with wet cardboard and concrete reminded Mark of the heady days in elementary school of May Day and Harvest Festival.

"Some people are already on their knees!" Rachel was back. It was well after eleven.

"Sinking to your knees in front of your exhibit usually comes much later! By the end of tonight I guess we'll all be on the floor. You'll be surprised how long this shit takes."

Even for two hundred square feet, Mark said, there seemed far too many plants.

"You always need more stuff than you'll actually use. See? Cooper's *merrillii* cross is already drooping. Did you bring the little sprayer? Oh. We'll have to borrow Bert's." Rachel heaved a deep sigh and wiped her nose with the back of her hand. Mark told himself this was it: he was alone with Rachel. "OK, Mark! Let's go!" They spent ten minutes trying to get Charlotte's *Cattleya lueddemanniana* to sit on a moss-covered milk-crate hummock. Every time they turned round the whole lilac mass was tipping gently forward. Rachel was starting with the *lueddemanniana* because it was the most important piece. Then why wasn't it sitting in the chair? thought Mark. Was that being reserved for one of the insignificant Australian dendrobiums in a calculated gesture of defiance? They were trying to perch it fairly high, a little to the right of the chairs, and the lesser specimens would reach up towards it and away down the slope on the other side.

"Leave it for now," suggested Mark. "Why don't we just place plants where we think they're going to go? Let's get the colors straight." Rachel had said there were strict rules for color: one color had to flow into another, no jarring contrasts or sudden clashes.

"There's another already fading!" Rachel was standing in their island of misfits, drooping ready-for-prime-time-last-week blooms, and the tiny, hard to register, species. The despised, last ditch resort, cheap commercial phals stood crisp and fresh on the side lines. Charlotte had sent half a dozen in with Mark. "Charlotte says she knows you don't want to use them but just in case and they can always go into the booth to be sold." They looked artificial: each pure white flower exhibiting the cool perfection of a starched dress shirt. Nothing else Mark had brought from Orchid Empire looked like much, even Cooper's blue vandas, blue so tricky in artificial light. They were always called blue though almost all were purple, lilac or violet. But whatever color, Rachel was right. They needed a spotlight, not this vague, warehouse wattage drifting down from the overhead pipes and girders.

They worked for an hour just trying to create a kind of mini mountain for the *lueddemanniana* just off center stage, with lesser peaks waiting to be crowned by prize orchids. Straightening up yet one more time from fighting the sliding sphagnum moss, Mark saw Rachel suddenly lifted into the air by a very large, very black man. He spun her round twice, plonked her back down with a classic Old Man River rumbling laugh.

"Archie! You doing a cut flower exhibit? You heard about Charlotte? Do you have time to come down? Oh, Doris and the kids are here. Yes, they want to go shopping. The price you pay! Tell Doris I said Hi. Archie, this is Mark. Charlotte's nephew, from the old country! Mark, this is Archie. From Jamaica."

"Well, you chose a *real* special person to be your aunt! And a tough one!" Archie put out a big hand and gave a massive laugh. "You see that *Broughtonia sanguinea?* That's the north coast type, see the deep red purple color and that *bright* yellow center! Bet that's from that big Guango tree Charlotte got me to climb must have been *thirty* years ago! And paid me pennies! Old days then." Archie was chuckling again. "Lon-don, eh? Now *you* would see the funny side a this. Ask Charlotte if she remembers. Friend a mine, band leader, played years ago for Princess Margaret when she came down one time. She ask him to stay late till about three in the mornin,' they call him ovah and with a great flourish she tips him... half a crown!" Archie exploded into laughter and shook his head. "OK, OK. Back to work! You think it'll be a good show? Oh! *Tilly, my love!* Where you bin?"

Tilly had come up behind them and Archie swept her off her feet, too, clipboard and all. Tilly loved it. Good for you, Archie, Mark thought. "Archie, anything for individuals?" Tilly asked as Archie set her and her shorts back down. Tilly was another one who really concentrated. "Yes, are you doing your own exhibit or for the society?" Rachel asked.

"Oh this time it's all Jamai-cah, my love!" Archie boomed and went off with Tilly to check in at the table with the women and the cookies and the clipboards.

"See? Florida-Caribbean *has* to be the *best* judging region!" Rachel was glowing. "Shame no one's here from Puerto Rico. Those guys are so great." Rachel was luminous enough when switched off, thought Mark. When she was happy with the orchid scene she was almost translucent. "OK! Where are we with this mess?"

"You said we were going to do the classic little path leading nowhere," Mark said. "And our focal point is two old iron garden chairs contemplating a bird bath and that's it. You need to take a turn round the hall. Check out no, not just the cardboard wall but there's some kind of aluminum wrap waterfall going up, there's at least one alligator looking like it's made out of old tires though actually, that's very clever, very life-like. There's a half dozen plastic pink flamingos, I can't decide if they're serious or not and, is it Bagley and West who've got one of those tiny bird baths with a naked little cherub? I think he's supposed to be filling up the bath by peeing, like the statue in Belgium, is it? But there's no water so it looks more like he's fiddling with himself."

"Well, I never wanted to do a standard exhibit, anyway. OK Let's put the important ones in and anything with height. Oncidiums, epidendrums. Could you hand me the *splendidum*?"

"Ah... Right."

"No! By the ferns! The *splendidum*."

"Um...Right."

"I'm like Charlotte." Rachel was apologetic. "I get tired of all the *business.* We need Larry and Ken. Last year Charlotte and I were tearing our hair out at eight at night and they came in and redid it all in half an hour. I'm just a bit stressed out doing the whole thing on my own. Well, I mean with you."

"So where's the old lady? She's got you doing it all?" Alvin was just beyond the chalk line, holding a styrofoam cup of coffee and grinning.

"She's graciously helping me get my student judge points. What's your excuse, Alvin?"

"Same old same old. So, got your boy friend helping?"

"Hi." said Mark.

"I thought I saw you trundling in palms," Rachel said, "What happened to the good old gazebo?"

"They backed the *U haul* into the damn thing. Yes, have a good laugh!"

"Well I heard you got rid of Pedro. He was good at this stuff."

"No, he's still here. It was Miguel. He's working for Steve over at OK Orchids now. I see you got your 'now you see me now you don't' tiny bits of shit orchids again."

"We're not all empty flash, Alvin. You got *miltonias* again this year?"

"Go get your hair done!"

"Fuck *off!*"

Alvin did move off, still grinning. Rachel laughed. "Alvin's obnoxious right up front. You know where you are with him." The boys from California were finally looking their way. "Hi!" Rachel called out demurely. "But still, *miltonias!* In South Florida!" she shook her head. "And the public saying 'Wow! Something different!' That's the trouble with Alvin. Absolutely no conscience." *Miltonias, miltonias?* Mark was treading water. "Of course UK's something else. Can't grow them here on a bet!"

"Right! I thought Larry said Alvin was a spear carrier for Regina?"

"Larry gets a bit paranoid. Of course, on a bad day you just get the feeling Regina poisons everything. Alvin just likes to take on everybody."

The Hawaiians were bent double on slopes of white and pink, the apple blossom colors of the standard phals. Next door the boys from California had disappeared. They'd been unwrapping tall, rushy plants with impressively large flower spikes of subdued mushroom, dusty pink and lemon. Mark remembered Charlotte describing them in detail, insisting he must have seen those orchids in England. Cymbidiums! Mark was so proud of remembering this he wanted to work it into the conversation: "Ah, I see they've brought cymbidiums!" One of the C series. Or "Well, cymbidiums again! Same old, same old!"

"Decided on anything for individuals?" Tilly was back. "It's Mark isn't it? How are you enjoying one of our shows? Has Rachel got anything for individuals? She usually gets us unusual species, something to wake us up to the possibilities, get us out of the rut!"

"She's gone to get the sprayer from Bert."

"And how is Charlotte? That awful freeze! She looked so good at Christmas. Tell her we miss her trenchant style! I believe Rachel is clerking tomorrow for the judges. That's good. She's so knowledgeable. Though between you and me that's not always too popular." Mark was warming to Tilly. "Tilly asked if you had anything for individuals," said Mark when Rachel came back.

"They aren't really interested in my stuff."

"You won't know unless you try. You know Charlotte says: 'Educate your masters!' How is anyone going to learn anything new unless you enter these plants for judging? And you can't tell me there aren't classifications for every last one." Mark had seen some scrap paper Charlotte was using for phone messages, the back of an old judging sheet. For just the *Oncidium* Alliance alone there were twenty classes: *Oncidium equitant hybrids, pink and lavender predominating*, then *yellow, orange, red predominating*, then '*other colors.*' Then, after having covered more variations than anyone in his right mind could even think or imagine, the list ended with: *Oncidium genera, species and hybrids—"other than above."*

"Just a medium sized genus before the taxonomists started to carve it up," Charlotte had said. "But the real problem *is,* when someone's got a plant, a pet they want to exhibit and there's not a division for it to be entered, they'll scream bloody murder."

"Let me get you something to eat," Mark said. "It's half past one and you haven't even touched your peanut butter cookie."

"Have you seen what Regina's lot are doing?" It was Mike suddenly appearing, over six foot two of jeans, black T-shirt and orchid knowledge behind those heavy glasses. "She's shoved in so many palms and foliage to fill up space it looks like *Apocalypse Now*. The Major may get flashbacks. Alvin's tacky as usual but at least no miltonias this time. That pair of Cubans have got a plastic angel shedding chicken feather wings all over their phals from Kmart, I kid you not! As usual everyone's knee deep in phals. Thank God for you Rachel! Some integrity! Educate the mob! Oh, hi, Mark. How's it going?"

"Talking of mobs," said Rachel, "do you remember what attendance was last year, Mike? Let's hope they've advertised the show enough."

"The Major is good, he doesn't cheat on ads," Mike said. "Have you seen him yet?"

"He's not been this way."

"I think there was trouble with parking and they probably called him to sort it out. *OK!* Here he comes."

A tall, spare man in an olive green tailored suit with a bright blue shirt had appeared, pausing to greet the Hawaiians standing knee deep in their phals. He strode on, past the Californian tables and stopped. His face was the mix of pink and pale that Mark come to recognize as belonging to red heads in the South Florida climate. "Ah, Rachel! Where's Charlotte? Heard she's out of it for a bit. What's the story?"

"Going to be fine, Major—just sent me along to fill in for her this time."

"And who's the young man with Mike?"

"This is Mark, Charlotte's nephew from England. I thought he might be allowed to observe the judging tomorrow."

"Welcome. I'm afraid can't have you take part unless you're an accredited AOS judge, but certainly very welcome as Charlotte's guest."

"So, Mark," said Mike, when the Major had passed, "how does this stack up against the London Show?"

"Well, of course, same problem there," Mark started cautiously. "Phals, of course... cymbidiums. Same as here, Mike, too many phals."

"I need to get over one year. Want to check out the lycastes and stanhopeas. Carry on to Russia, now that would be a deal." Mark was thinking the orchid societies of Omsk and Novi Sibirsk should certainly give Mike a break from *Phalaenopsis*. "Mike, I was just going to get something to eat."

"Not for me. I'm on my way to see how Bert's doing."

When Mark came back he persuaded Rachel to stop. He put a can of diet Coke and ham and cheese sandwich on an upturned bucket and brought over the remaining crate.

"Sitting on this crate, the whole thing looks like *shit*," Rachel announced. "If that *lueddemanniana* tips over one more time! And the Californians have got extra lights and those other people from the west coast are blowing up balloons. All we need are Macy's Christmas elves. And I'm landing up using those phals."

"Yes, but phals look woodsy enough among the ferns. Pretend they're cow parsley or daisies just peering out."

"Botanically it's totally incorrect!"

"So in nature your little beauties always cluster in sphagnum moss round the legs of iron garden chairs? Have you thought about the name for the exhibit? Everyone keeps asking."

"The name of this mess? It was *intended* to be all species and primary hybrids. In which case, Mike was daring me to call it 'Pearls before Swine.'"

"'Orchid Treasures,' 'Orchid Treasures,'" Mark was musing. He should be able to dredge up some quote or felicitous title: Precious Something, the kind of bland and luscious phrase found on the lid of a box of chocolates. Nature's Beauties sounded like a nude review.

"Mike had a good one for Regina's: 'Stolen Beauty!'"

Most exhibitors had slowed to a stop and, like Rachel, were sitting dejectedly on the indispensable crates. The ones on their feet were deep into what Mark was privately labeling the exhibition dance. Repetitive and automatic as the fox trot, with certain individuals it was as savage and plunging as the tango. Feet together, a plant was chosen, the exhibitor moving forward intently into the intricacies of the exhibit, among the sphagnum hillocks and fern covered hill sides, plant weighed in the right hand at that moment more like a slow bowler, then with a swift sometimes passionate swoop forward the plant was placed in the display. The individual then drew back as though stung, stopped dead, straightened up, eyes fixed on the plant and reversed, retreating slowly, two, three steps, a little wobbly, but eyes forward, stepping back, slowly, slowly, reaching the bare floor, took the whole scene in and almost every time, plunged back in, stepping high and took the orchid out again. Even the Californians were at it, back from lunch, moving backwards and forwards among their slender tables.

Strips of moss were starting to peel off the baskets and crates again. After a while, still hearing hammering, Mark wondered whether people were in desperation starting to *hammer* the moss back on to the sides of their crates. Rachel, reluctantly, was starting to place Charlotte's *Phalaenopsis* behind her small botanicals; they were so sturdy, unbelievably white and useful.

"You have to check these guys to the left, past the Hawaiians," Rachel said. "Last year they were ahead of us by hours. When Jen came in late to help they were already putting in their last plants. And as soon as they'd put in the last orchid they started to mess with the exhibit. We left after ten in the evening and I swear, they were stepping back, having pulled everything out again, surveying the space and starting all over."

The hall was cooling off. Outside it was getting dark very quickly in the South Florida way. Looking at what they'd accomplished Mark could not believe it had taken so long. Half the orchids were just perching or sliding down hillocks, just placed roughly where they should be; no names written out, the *lueddemanniana* once more falling on its face. Rachel, yawning, eyes closed, was saying wearily "Five thirty. I'd give anything for a beer but I daren't."

"We came as soon as we could!" It was Larry. He didn't hug anyone. He stood in front of the exhibit and took a step back. "Nice, nice. Nothing overstated. A gentle drift from the angraecums, a *hint* of phals, classy! Well, we've brought along a few things. Ken is out there finding somewhere to park."

When Ken appeared, he was half hidden behind a great clump of an orchid, like a father bringing home the Christmas tree. "The *lamellata,* oh, you guys!" Rachel was ecstatic. "*Vanda lamellata boxallii!* Mark, we've got our center! Our focal point. And no way is this baby sliding anywhere."

"Charlotte suggested it," Ken said. "It's become such a fixture by the pool we weren't sure we could move it."

"She said you might even sell it? "Rachel asked doubtfully.

"No! Be like selling the family dog!"

A single spray of the *lamellata* flowers, small and white with brownish markings, would have been lost among the ferns but there were nine flower spikes and three blooming 'keikies, ("Hawaiian for the orchid's *offspring,*" as Charlotte put it.) The resulting cloud of flowers on twenty five spikes "just blows you away" as Larry said. Ken disappeared to get the rest of the plants. "Some *Doritis,* a really lovely harlequin phal. You need some emphatic full stops," Larry insisted. "We know you, Rachel, with your understated botanicals. You're supposed to leave all that good taste to the English, right, Mark?" They maneuvered the massive *lamellata* on to the right hand chair, where it took command of the whole scene like Queen Victoria. "So have you seen what Regina's doing?" Larry asked, backing out of the exhibit. "She's got her large burial mounds and wall to mop up some of the five hundred feet with cheap phals round the edge. Have to admit they look good and some very good plants, mostly from orchid societies, I bet and loyal customers. Now! We've brought some pate, crackers and brie and Beaujolais—something light! Sit down!" He unfolded a tea towel. "I told Mike to get Bert."

"We've used all the crates in the exhibit," said Rachel. "We've nowhere to sit."

"There are chairs provided, you know that!" Larry went next door to the Californians who seemed to have acquired four. "Move those two over, OK? Don't let those Californian queers steal everything."

"I can't believe you said that!" Rachel exclaimed.

"Well, neither can I," said Larry. "But it's been a long day and I don't like their attitude."

Rachel laughed. "But they're not even here!"

"You can tell from the exhibit," Larry said dryly. "What were they thinking of?"

"Let's all have a beer," Ken said. "Where's Jen?"

"Caught in traffic, probably," said Rachel.

So Jen *was* coming. Well, here they were all together, Mark told himself. Hadn't he said, "Let's all get together sometime?" And Jen had said, totally cool, yes, there would be the Las Olas Show. Letting him off the hook.

"How's it going?" Mark heard the standard greeting for the hundredth time. It was Jen in a pretty, peach-colored suit, Jen dressed up for down town, cruise ships, the world outside, the real world. "Rachel," she said, "it's looking pretty good."

"I wish."

"Jen's right," said Mark. "Hi, Jen."

"Hi!" Jen glanced at him and then slowly down at Larry's makeshift picnic. "Looks like I arrived at the right moment."

"A little crowded," Larry observed, gazing at the upturned bucket. "What we *should* do is move everything over next door." He nodded to the Californian display. "Are they serving *dinner?* What's with the *table cloths*?" Having repossessed Orchid Empire's two chairs, Larry added on Level Nine's and two from the Hawaiians who were going off for pizza. He sat everyone down, Mark next to Jen. Mark realized that with all the myriad smells, all the orchid flowers, Jen was smelling nicest of all. Mark found himself saying "You smell nice."

Jen opened her mouth and paused. "This is great," she said to Larry. Keeping her eyes down she muttered, "Don't sound so surprised."

By now it was quite dark outside. Rachel, following her beer with a glass of Beaujolais, was unwinding. "Larry, Ken, you guys are the best."

"Hey. we promised Charlotte," Ken said. "How's she doing, Mark?"

"She seems fine now. It's really thanks to Jen."

"That was some New Year's night," said Larry, "wasn't it?"

They'd finished eating by the time Mike reappeared. "Bert's got to take his guys home and he's pretty tired. I just helped them tidy up." He took over Mark's chair, Jen showing him the list of plants in the exhibit. Behind them all the *lueddemanniana* was tipping forward again. Larry told Rachel to stop shoving it. "Let's check the basic engineering." He and Ken stepped into the exhibit and firmed the drifting clump in one movement.

"Mark, we should just have waited till they arrived," Rachel said.

"OK, what's next?" Larry asked.

"Jen's writing names,"Rachel said. "Guys, I think we may be getting somewhere." Mike was cutting extra pieces of the hard black board for Jen, grinding away with a pair of kitchen scissors. Jen was bent over the clipboard. "Rachel, you've got a whole pile of names here. What's actually *in* the exhibit?"

"Watch out for the pens with that suit," Larry handed Jen a clean napkin.

"Yeah," Rachel said, "why all dressed up? Had something on at the office?"

"If you ask me," Mike raised his head, "the only way to get these shows into orchid territory is ban *Phalaenopsis* entirely. Then let's see what people have really got."

"Problem *is*," Ken said, "*Phalaenopsis* are great in an exhibit. The standard *Cattleya,* it's bright, big and frilly but too short on the stalk."

"Are we discussing some of the lady orchid judges?" asked Mike.

"Of course, in the old days these shows were *all* designed as *Cattleya* shows," Ken went on. "It's unbelievable how *Phalaenopsis* have taken over."

"Charlotte always compares *Phalaenopsis* to chicken," Mark said. "Says back in the day roast chicken was grand enough for Christmas dinner. Before battery hens and factory farms."

"It's not just mass produced phals out there now but people are still paying Christmas dinner prices for supermarket chicken!" Larry protested. "You see the rich and famous with their Italian marble fireplaces and early Jackson Pollocks, being interviewed with a standard ten dollar white phal beside them! Would they be seen dead with a cheap print of Van Gogh's Sunflowers over their marble fireplaces? I think not!"

"This from the man who feeds his cats salmon" Ken commented dryly, "on what he makes with his cheap phals."

"Trouble *is*" Larry ignored him, "phals are just perfect for shows and everything else: they flow, they sweep, they cascade. They just look damn pretty. And they last. They're tough. And they're cheap. By the way, Mark, have *you* checked the show? Go have a look. Take a break."

Mark found himself wanting to take Jen with him, to talk and explain, but explain what? What could he say? *You're really looking good and being cool and smelling nice but look at Rachel; every moment she turns, every angle, every movement, grungy T-shirt and all. Don't you see?* Ned who'd given him pointers in the past, would have kept Jen as reserve; kept his seat by the bucket, appropriated the scissors from Mike and warmed Jen up again, letting it all simmer along. "First rule: show the Sheilas there's always competition."

The aisles were still blocked by cardboard boxes and packing cases being used as miniature dumpsters. Humble plastic spray bottles, watering cans, brooms and even feather dusters were everywhere underfoot, together with spectacular orchids just waiting on the dusty floor, on the edge of exhibits, like stars in the wings. Mark found Archie's exhibit from Jamaica. It was sensibly small scale: there was a bottle of rum half buried in a drift of sand, a cutlass and a coconut but the cut orchid blooms were drooping already. No prizes for Archie and Jamaica but at least Doris would get in her shopping. There was another small scale, cut flower display next door; brightly colored orchids scattered between wooden lamas, brilliant shawls and bowler hats. Peru! Charlotte had said Peru was the ultimate orchid experience: *"Incredible* diversity of species due to the rapid rise of the Andes. Each group isolated in their own valley as thoroughly as if it were one of Darwin's Galapagos islands. Over every ridge line a new species! Survey and clear for a new road and they've got to bring in the taxonomists!" But whoever was in charge of the Peruvian exhibit had managed to keep their excitement in check: it was the shawls and bowler hats that really drew the eye.

Having raised his eyes from struggling with Orchid Empire's small patch, Mark was seeing how the dusty, barren hall had been transformed; the ferny glades and tiny mountain sides, river banks and garden nooks hosting the largest family of flowering plants, every sort of orchid settling in and taking off in all directions. Down in the front of exhibits sat flowers like tiny wheels and stars, further back up the milk crate hills others clustered like miniature weeping willows or trailing comets. Some sprays perched like rows of dragon flies alighting along their own stems, others like swallows high on a wire. The Miami Beach cattleyas, reminders of big bands and swizzle sticks, exploded in ruffles everywhere. The deep vermilions and maroons made Mark think of *Gone With The Wind;* velvet flowers made out of curtains. And for some reason something about them gave off a definite impression of the Household cavalry. Majestic old warhorses had been trundled out like Larry and Ken's *Vanda lamellata* var. *boxallii*, and tiny things were alighting on the hummocks of sphagnum like nervous butterflies. Charlotte's favorite blue vandas were rising above the fray with their elegant patterning of blue veins on white. "They'll ask for a 'plaid orchid' or a 'gingham' one," she said, "that's what they call the tessellated *coerulea* type! Last year's show, one young woman wanted the one 'like my kitchen table cloth!'"

So many orchid flowers were spotted, striped, splotched, blotched or splashed with a second or third brilliant color, even the *Phalaenopsis,* the Ph series. "Their breeding's really taken off; look out for scarlets and vermillion, really hot orange, spots, leading edge, Mark," Ken said. "You'll see a lot of 'novelties' too," Charlotte had instructed, "bronze and ice blues, burgundy and acid yellows. They're all going wild." As though, with orchids, nature hadn't done enough, Mark thought. It would be quite a change, not to say a rest, to go back to his mother's herbaceous border, with the straggly annuals along the front re-seeding themselves, the soggy clumps of delphiniums and Michaelmas daises.

The two Californians were back, stuffing their packing paper, boxes and styro beads into a large plastic bin. Behind them a series of picture frames perched atop the folding tables, each one framing a *Phalaenopsis* and ranged behind the tables they'd put a row of the large cymbidiums, an orchid hedge. "See what you can get away with when you're out of state," Rachel muttered.

Jen was asking, "Is Cooper coming in?" She and Mike were lining up gold printed name tags on the upturned bucket.

"Coop's got to be skulking round somewhere," said Ken. "For the big shows he usually emerges. He can't resist and there's enough greenery for cover."

"The *lamellata* is perfect!" Rachel was hopping happily into the exhibit with tags." Coop will love it!"

"Where are the South Americans this year?" Ken asked.

"There's that big show right now in Caracas," said Mike. "And isn't Puerto Rico having theirs next week?"

"No, just after the *Expo*, which is good. They come to buy plants." Rachel was walking away as far as she could, till she was almost bumped Level Nine's tables. She studied Orchid Empire's exhibit, half closing her eyes. "It's about as good as it's going to get."

"And you know," Mark contributed, "Charlotte won't care."

"Charlotte pretends not to care," Rachel said, "but she's very competitive."

Jen had been busy, very busy with tags. She had been too busy to talk. But not too busy, Mark noted, to talk to Mike; well, OK, she was working with Mike. But also to Ken. And Larry. It was eight o clock and pitch black outside and he had still not come up with any reasonable topic of conversation to interrupt the busyness. Pretty soon it would be *Well, good night, Jen and thank-you*. And it would be another heartfelt thank-you; thank-you for having such great handwriting that you are always the pick to 'do tags' and team up with Mike. All day Mark had been dreading the moment when Rachel would ask him, the orchidist from England, home of the Royal Horticultural Society and the official *Sanders List of Orchid Hybrids*, to write the tags and check the names.

The atmosphere in the hall was at once more mellow, end of the day, but also more desperate. The pair who had ripped everything out to start again were just sitting on their two chairs surrounded by plants, staring into space. Mark felt like telling them what the lime green halter had told him: "Sometimes you've just got to get away, away from your orchids. So don't apologize, just go."

"Aha! Here comes Regina!" Larry exclaimed. Regina appeared to be circling the hall and the exhibits with something of an entourage. There was the tall, older man in the perfectly cut suit Mark recognized from the New Year's party, and a short, dark, younger man, probably Tony, the manager of Orchid Magic and there was the waiter guy behind, and the Major. Regina was in the middle, her hat and dark glasses gone, the hair still that uncompromising jet black, still the khaki slacks with a lethal knife edge and this time, an emerald green silk shirt. "So horticultural!" murmured Larry. And here we all are, Mark thought, caught in the headlights, the gallant little band, the motley crew, with Cooper lurking somewhere. The Californians had gone home, the Hawaiians too. It was too late for him to try and disappear; the mens' lavatories were far away. Mark could feel Larry hoping for some kind of incident, something juicy for recounting to Charlotte. Here was a magic moment all right, summed up neatly in the literary world: Hell hath no fury like a woman scorned. Especially a woman of a certain age. And how Rachel rubbed that in; her hair just dragged back this time not with a bootlace but a scrap of material that looked like something teased out from Nip's jaws.

It was Rachel who spoke first. "Hi, Major! How's it going?"

"Fine, fine! Regina, you must meet young Mark here! Did you know he was Charlotte's nephew? All the way from England! And quite the orchidist too, I take it! A pleasure to have him join us!"

"We have met," said Regina. There she was and there he was but what did she expect? How could he not be loyal to Charlotte? The idea was ridiculous and then Mark realized of course, that was the whole problem. For Regina it was opposition itself, any whatsoever, that was ridiculous, unreasonable, absurd. She was approaching Orchid Empire's exhibit, picking her way through the huddle of drooping and discarded plants, the grocery bag from Larry and Ken's picnic, the upturned bucket, the empty bottle of Beaujolais and six beer bottles Jen had put on one side to take home for recyclables. "So, Mark," Regina raised her eyes. "So we are doing the show after all." Mark knew Larry, behind him, was trying not to laugh. "Our members were waiting for Charlotte's orchids. If Marjorie had not told us what was happening they could *still* be waiting."

The other faces round Regina were a blur. "You didn't get the message?" Mark started. "Oh, my apologies! Charlotte rallied so well that Dr. Gibson and, and the staff, decided this was just the tonic she needed. But how unfortunate you never got the message!" To Mark's surprise, Regina said no more. She smiled, that broad expanse of scarlet which Mark found more unsettling than a frown. "I see." There was a pause. "Well, *good luck.*"

The group moved on, the Major focusing beyond the Hawaiian exhibit to the next vendors, still struggling with their exhibit, kneeling once more, as Rachel had forecast, before their once again bare, sandy space.

"Are *you for* it!" said Larry with relish. "Oh! Just wait till Miami!"

"You are loving this, aren't you?" Mark said.

"Is it my fault if our *Presidente* grows tired of young Latin lads and decides to go for the shy, Anglo Saxon literary type?"

"Did you see that?" demanded Rachel. "The arrogance of the woman passes belief, parading round with the Major like she's the queen or something, like it's her show."

Ken asked mildly, "How far are we from wrapping this up?"

"Jen's finishing tags," said Mark. He'd asked, "Can I help?" from time to time but more for something to say. "I'm fine," Jen had replied, each time. "No problem."

"OK, so we're off," announced Ken." Where's Cooper? Still outside in the car park?"

"I saw him earlier," Mike said, "but there were too many people around. He'll surface in the early hours. Probably help that pair who dragged everything out again."

"What time is it, Ken?" Rachel asked. "Ten forty! And they're starting from scratch!"

"Is this a record? What was it last year?"

"We should have got up a pool."

"Coop will help them," said Larry. "He *is* a Buddhist. It will drive out bad karma or whatever, all the negative feelings he has about Regina. As for the rest of us we'll just bottle them up, let them age and enjoy." They all said farewells in the car park. A shame, thought Mark, these great spaces and distances. Everyone always said Americans were so friendly; good job they were with all these miles. Ken and Larry had come together but Jen and Rachel had to take off in different vehicles, Rachel in the borrowed van with the shag carpeting. "So stupid! Carpeting a *cargo van!*"

Mark had been the first to go. They all cheered the Volvo when it started. Charlotte had announced in her breezy fashion she'd be surprised if the old thing would make it all the way up to Fort Lauderdale and back. Jen and Rachel were going to 'ride convoy': see the Volvo almost home, just in case. So there they were in their three metal boxes. Mark wondered what music Jen and Rachel would be listening to. It was a long enough trip south to sample every station on the dial. Most of the AM stations were rattling away in Spanish. But between the commercials on FM there was mellow rock, mournful jazz, the golden oldies, country and western, the music of the seventies, Spanish rock, Christian rock, salsa, hip hop, the University of Miami station coming in as Mark got further south and then the Mexican waltzes from Homestead and something formatted for Mark's easy listening from the Keys. The windows were open under the velvety blue sky, a tray of rejects and a bundle of bamboo stakes behind Mark. The *Vanda merrillii* was beside him on the seat, fading but still fragrant and tucked under its basket Rachel's instructions: how to get home, both I-95 and, just in case, if he lost them both and missed the turn, down I-75 and then 836, in her firm, clear hand.

13

Selling at the Las Olas Show

"I'm *so* glad it's *you!*" Mark, lugging in a tray of Charlotte's specials, wondered whether he'd heard right: Rachel, in scarlet T-shirt and indigo blue jeans, bubbling over with delight that he had appeared. He was just on the edge of a magic moment when she groaned, "*Last* year we had *Marjorie* in the booth three days straight." So, nothing had changed; no recognition of intrinsic merit, shy charm, let alone animal attraction: he was merely a less irritating presence than Marjorie. And having met Marjorie Mark knew that tied him in solidly with ninety-nine percent of the human race. "There'll be just the two of us. Jen said we wouldn't need her. Though she knows it's always good to have more people at the weekend." Rachel sounded puzzled. "Said she had a lot to do."

The Las Olas show opened promptly at nine with a flurry of orchidists bursting through the doors, many hardly glancing at the exhibits in all their hard won glory but making for the sales booths, where they milled around like visitors to the National Gallery shop, undeterred by the magnificence behind them and intent on the postcards and pencil sharpeners.

"Orchid Society members come on Friday morning," Rachel said. "You have been warned." And sure enough five minutes after opening she was out of the booth, engulfed by a circle questioning her on compots, bottles and species, tugged to and fro thought Mark, like a piece of bread tossed into a pond full of fish. And then Rachel herself was off. "The guy from Georgia has a *Vanda helvola* for Cooper. It's one from Java he's been trying to get a hold of. Coop called me last night. I should only be gone for ten. This crowd know what they're looking

151

for. But watch out for the 'Friends of Charlotte' brigade. Just act dumb, like you don't know anything. And don't forget whatever they say, if they're Florida residents they pay sales tax! OK, I'm outta here."

Rachel may have grumbled about the lack of good light overhead but Mark felt lit up in front of the black curtain at the back of the booth like some overgrown puppet in a Punch and Judy show. He kept his eyes down, the buzz of the crowd in his ears, busying himself; lining up the calculator, two sharp pencils, tags, pens, not wanting to look up and catch anyone's eye, not wanting to sell anything. Just to be allowed quietly to go home.

"Hey! Where's Charlotte? Hold up, Ethel! I need to read this tag! I need something special. Doesn't have to be in flower. Charlotte always finds me something. We go way back."

"Don't you have a tray under the table? Under the bench? Are you sure? Look at the back. No, behind the curtain. That's where Charlotte used to put the good stuff. I'm a very old friend."

"*HA*-llo! Oh, boy, Charlotte never charged these kind of prices! And *tax!* I'm a *friend!*"

Mark could see what Rachel meant: Charlotte had a lot of friends.

The weather was not too hot, the forecast good. There was an ad in the *Herald* and *The Sun Sentinel*, the Broward daily, where the Major and the Las Olas Society had done the vendors proud: springing for two colors, an eighth of a page, and in Section A. *The annual Las Olas Orchid Show: 'Orchid Treasures' Beautiful Exhibits, Lectures, Thousands of orchids at affordable prices!* And the spot was good; situated right opposite *People and Places*. In the *Herald* it was marooned under *Mid-East Talks Resume*.

Mark managed to sell a bare root *Cattleya* seedling for fifteen dollars plus tax, deflected a customer to Rachel as she returned, over a question on compots, directed someone to the toilets and said Hi to a pretty young thing who was on her third circuit round the hall. Suddenly there was a lull. "What was the judging like yesterday?" Mark asked. "Sorry I overslept." No way would he have exposed himself to the judging, even as a mere spectator.

"Orchid Magic got First Place, best exhibit 500 square feet open class, the Show Theme Trophy, she *stole* it from Hank and the Las Olas guys, *and* the AOS Show trophy. She's swept the board again. Bert got a blue ribbon, Best *Oncidium*. Alvin managed to pick up a Second place, three hundred square feet, God knows how. Regina grabbed Best *Vanda*, Best *Cattleya* species, Best *Oncidium* Alliance Species, Best Miniature Orchid, the list goes on! She's not content with owning Miami Expo, she's got to have it *all*."

The Californians seemed to be doing slow but steady sales over at Level Nine. The Hawaiians had at least four vendors in their booth, empty boxes piling up on the side, RUSH, RUSH, KEEP FROM HEAT AND COLD. "The Hawaiians take no prisoners," Charlotte said. "It hurts people like Bert with his standard stuff."

"We'll discount the flowering material, the commercial plants, on Sunday," Rachel was looking at the crowd round the Hawaiians, "but the seedlings and flasks I'll just take back. There's a frenzy Sunday afternoon but you've got to hit it right. Charlotte was always good at that. Knew the moment to start to bring prices down."

Mark, to his surprise, found he could survive. With Rachel in the booth it only made sense to deflect questions to her. He knew enough from living with Charlotte to be able to state a few general rules: for example, treat *Phalaenopsis* like an African violet, great for beginners or those with *low light*; but you can't flower a *Vanda* just on a window sill even in South Florida. "Tell them what Coop says," Rachel instructed: "'Vandas need the spread of light that nature provides, the sun moving across the sky!'" And Mark had decided his answer to being told that there had been *much* better orchids in Home Depot last week for half the price would be "In *that* case I hope you bought one!"

Questions were coming thick and fast as the general public, the non-orchidists, started to circle the hall. How fresh is this flower? Will it get bigger? Will it have babies? Where will it have babies? I heard orchids have babies from the stem, from the top, from the bottom. There seemed a lot of interest in the reproductive life of the orchid, Mark noted, thinking of the orchid magazines in the spare room: all those dry, scholarly descriptions of its sexy behavior, *manipulative, deceiving, promiscuous*. "Orchids hybridize so freely," Charlotte had commented, "and of course, the word itself comes from the Greek, *orkhis,* testicle, from the shape of the tubers. Had a sweet old lady telling everyone at one of my parties she was suffering from orchitis, couldn't resist adding orchids to her collection. Had to tell her well, dear, are you sure? Orchitis is inflammation of the testicles! And you know I don't think she really knew what 'testicles' meant, either."

"Of course, what Rachel hates to admit, it's the great unwashed public who put food on the table," Charlotte had declared. "If the commercial people depended on orchid societies we'd all starve." Mark, wary of anyone with orchid knowledge, was warming to anyone who knew nothing at all, like the thin young woman brushing a strand of hair away from her eyes over and over again who asked shyly to see "that blue one." Mark brought the *Vanda* forward. "A beautiful blue and still three buds," he said. "I'm surprised it hasn't sold."

"I'm lucky!" the young woman stated with a beautiful, sudden smile. And Mark wished for a moment with all his heart that the flower would never fade. How wonderful there were such nice, uncomplicated people in the world, he was to think as the day wore on: *I like it and I'll buy it.* None of this—"What's wrong with that leaf? Where could I put it if I bought it? Tell me where could I *put* it?" Some woman kept asking this and Mark vowed if she didn't stop soon he'd be tempted to tell her. But there was a glorious moment in mid morning when an elegant woman in a long scarlet dress and soft straw hat chose to stop in front of Orchid Empire. It was clear, as Charlotte would say, she knew as much about orchids as a pig knew Sunday. "I'll take that purple one, yes, seventy-five is fine, the other purple, the white and this little yellow one. And why is that tall pink one a hundred? Oh. Well, I like it. Yes, add it on."

"And she wasn't even reacting to your cute accent!" Rachel marveled, a little out of breath because she had to dart off through the crowd to use Bert's credit card machine. Mark had perfected a streamlined answer to all cute-accent enquiries: "North London, actually, and that will be eighteen dollars plus tax." "Um, not Australia—England, and no, these only once a year." "London actually, and just before the second exit, on your left."

"Shame there aren't more men buying orchids," Mark commented to Rachel. "You'd be drawing them like flies." *Great! Right! How to Chat Up the Girl of Your Dreams.*

But it was true almost all the public were female, of all shapes and sizes: Latins and Anglos, straw hats and sun-dresses, old jeans and scuffed tennis shoes, tight polyester in plastic colors, Indian prints and African braids. There were fierce perms, perfect casual cuts, and wild and free: mad Miss Haversham, Lady Macbeth and Ophelia, Juliet and Miss Piggy. All finding his accent cute, his bashful manner based as it was on ignorance and fear of being found out, playing, as Charlotte predicted, as shy English charm that seemed to melt all but the most fanatic orchid heart. But Mark would have traded the whole mass of them for one Rachel, for one beautiful personal smile from Rachel, for any evidence of some spark between them.

But at least, here he was, Mark told himself, with Rachel, alone. That is, if you discounted a milling throng asking questions, demanding answers, wanting attention. It was like being in a room full of other peoples' toddlers. Just as he got talking to Rachel some creature was pulling at his sleeve, and tugging at her: 'When will this bloom?' 'What color will this be?'

"—*Will it do well on my windowsill, under my tree, by my pool, in the patio, by the front door, with an eastern exposure, for my mother in Boston, my father in Tucson, my landlady in Tampa?*"

"*How much light does this plant need? How much water, fertilizer, attention does this need? How much attention do I need? Well, thanks for explaining but maybe I should have told you I have a cat, dogs, ferrets, chickens, live in Nebraska, in a condo, under a bridge in a cardboard box so...goodbye!*"

"*Tell* me how you *grow* them!" *What, all of them?*

"Tell me how they grow!" and the woman having listened to Rachel, the expert, at great length, came over to Mark, and after a moment "Well, tell me how they *grow!*" Mark had yet to learn how to tow these people to one side.

"This is why you have culture sheets," Bert had said gently.

"This is why gin comes in quarts," Charlotte declared.

Mark had offered to get coffee Saturday morning, going the long way round. He was starting to enjoy himself, enjoying seeing the action, one of the players and he had proof: the coveted ribbon pinned on his shirt, the red one, Exhibitor, even better than the blue one, Vendor, that rather solemn Latin word. "Reminder to all vendors: do not remove orchids from your exhibit till the show closes Sunday at six!' "Vendors, please remove all vehicles from the entrance." Mark had always thought of 'vendors,' as one step above peddlers. He'd only heard the word in 'street vendors:' hot dogs, ice cream, selling fruit off a barrow. Charlotte had been joking that's what Rachel should do, if Regina kept her out of the Expo: "Take out a street vendor's licence with the City of Miami and set yourself up outside the hall!" Rachel had been living with the news of being banished from the Miami Expo ever since New Year's Eve. Maybe that was why he hadn't seen one of her dazzling smiles since. But Archie from Jamaica had got a smile and the *lamellata* Ken had hoisted into the exhibit. Bert seemed to be doing OK. He actually had a line of people holding plants and waiting to pay. No sign of Mike. Rachel said Mike was helping Bert. Maybe that's why there was such a long line. Maybe Mike, instead of helping out at the front, was round the side lecturing a hapless orchidist.

In spite of Regina apparently winning everything, there still seemed a good number of certificates, trophies and ribbons nestling in front of exhibits among the moss and mulch. So many classes and categories, it was like the Special Olympics; everyone got a prize. There were the names beside each orchid, along the mossy overhangs and winding paths, in gold or silver on the black poster board. Mark thought of Jen, concentrating, keeping the letters straight, using the gold pen, clipboard on her knee. That pretty peach color she was wearing, those long orchid names; the smaller the orchid, it seemed, the longer the name. Jen, tongue between her teeth, slow and steady. Her hair never fell forward; she clipped it back somehow. But it always smelled good. It had smelled so nice on New Year's Eve. Mark found himself feeling sorry, not relieved, that Jen hadn't come to help. He could see himself confessing his ignorance to Jen. And she'd say, *That's OK. No problem.* But it was because of him, obviously, Jen *hadn't* come. And that meant

Rachel was alone in the booth on a Saturday morning. Mark started to speed up, sliding through the crowds with Rachel's coffee.

Mark suddenly saw a cache of trophies, a magpie collection of bowls, ribbons and rosettes: Orchid Magic First place 500 square feet exhibit; AOS Trophy Best in Show; Best *Vanda*; Best *Cattleya* Seedling Blooming For The First Time. Best this and Best that, blocking the pathway, the ribbons streaming out like the fleet was in. And there was Regina's great big golden one, pulled into yeoman service once again, set a little further back, not quite up to the spotlight anymore as it was grown outside: the big yellow *Oncidium*. And Mark felt suddenly part of the show and the local orchid scene, an Exhibitor and Vendor and definitely, as Rachel called them, an inside dopester. He could hardly see Orchid Magic's booth for all the people milling round. All those people, even though everyone had been saying how outrageous her prices were. A whole lot of helpers too, at least a whole lot of people with Orchid Magic T-shirts, the top hat and orchids across chests and bosoms and stamped on baseball caps. People were strolling off with large bags declaring: *Orchid Magic says Thank-you! Thank-you from Orchid Magic!* and Mark saw a tiny bag: a little girl swinging one to and fro: *Growing Up with Orchid Magic!* God, Regina was the McDonalds of the orchid world. How could anyone compete?

Holding her coffee, Rachel said, "Mark, are you OK here for a bit? I need to chase up the Orlando guys. They owe me for some flasks and show time is good they can't say they don't have *any* money."

"Young man, if this is Orchid Empire where is Charlotte?" Just as Rachel had disappeared: an imposing black woman under a straw hat with a lilt in her voice like a native of Wales who'd grown up in India. It was the sound of the islands, as they said in South Florida, the Caribbean. Probably Jamaica as she knew Charlotte. "I am afraid she isn't here in person this year. Can I help you?"

"But she's here in spirit. Is that it?" A formidable mix of Ruby and Charlotte, she looked him up and down for a moment. "Tell her we *miss* her!" Mark realized this must be a connection going way back. Back to when Archie was a boy. "Such a scrawny little barefoot lad with a great big grin!" Charlotte had remembered. "Sharp though!

Always had to pay him twice as much as any of the others! But he got the plants; he knew where the good stuff was."

Archie and the Princess Margaret story: back when London was the capital of the English-speaking Caribbean. Now they said it was Miami. Mark who had picketed a McDonalds for a whole afternoon once, knew all empires were evil, even Anglo-Saxon ones. But without the British one he could not have been such a hit with the two stunning young black women from Trinidad. As Rachel stood there, looking puzzled, totally out of it, they were cracking up over something, something quite trivial, all three inside dopesters from the old Empire. Hearing he was a teacher they had sighed for the discipline of the British system. And Mark, recalling Totters Green, decided either American education must be much worse than he thought, or maybe it was true that old traditions hung on longest in the farthest, dusty outposts of empire. Maybe they were still standing up in Trinidad when a teacher came in the room, and maybe in some village school there was still the sharp, bendy little switch across the palm for minor transgressions.

"Orchid Empire wasn't supposed to *be* here!" Mark, straightening up with a fresh tray of seedlings from under the table, found himself face to face with Marjorie. There were the industrial strength black glasses and the big black bag. She was also carrying three more bags, all, Mark noted, with Orchid Magic writ large on the side. Marjorie managed to fix Mark with an unwavering stare as she checked the booth, assessing whether there was anything worthy of buying, anything left from the early morning scavenge. She pursed her lips. "Last year *I* was in the booth for the whole three days. Did you sell any of the African species?"

"Rachel sold some angraecums this morning."

"Which ones?"

"Hi, Marj!" Rachel was back. "Mark! Isn't there another tray of the 1113's under the table? Let's get them out. I see you managed to move those ascocendas." Marjorie was marginalized. Rachel and Mark were into the high seriousness of being vendors. Thank God for *vending,* thought Mark.

"If you had told me you needed to leave the booth—"

"No! No! Go enjoy the show! You deserve it! Last year you were tied down here!" Rachel turned away, busy, busy *vending*. "Was she bugging you?" asked Rachel as Marjorie left. "She's really a nuisance. Oh, not just the whole African thing. She's always snooping around. You see where she's buying? I think she's one of them."

The Californians were tidying up, the Hawaiians unpacking yet more boxes, getting ready for a dynamite Sunday. The security man ambled by, the standard, solid African American with his name tag and half smile; getting ready to make sure security was in place, nothing would get pinched. Like the Greek chorus, the commentator, that detached and mellow smile: *'Lord, what fools these mortals be!'* Mark thought of Althea, Althea rescuing him from Regina with that same amused smile.

Sunday morning was flat. "Bert says it's always slow till everyone's out of church but I don't think it's that any more. There's just so much going on in Miami now."

"You know Charlotte won't care. She doesn't seem too bothered about raking in the dollars."

"Yes and she's way too generous with me," Rachel said. "I owe her so much."

"She's very lucky she's got you," Mark said firmly. It seemed so often with Rachel he was adopting the tone of the wise and comforting old codger. Not quite the image he was after; as his sister used to say, hardly likely to further his cause. She used to lean over the banisters when he'd come home from a date and whisper, "Well, did you *further your cause?*" If he came in very late, she would announce the next morning: "You must have *furthered your cause!*"

"Well, who else would be carrying on those lines of breeding?" Mark asked. "Those African tiddlers, as Charlotte calls them."

"Yes, two eccentric female orchidists." Rachel sat down with a thump but immediately got up. "Yes? Can I help you? Oh, these will be very pretty and fragrant too! One of the parents is in the exhibit. No, right there, past Level Nine and the Hawaiians."

"Paid for your booth rental yet?" Alvin had wandered by with a coffee. "So how's your boyfriend doing?" Mark noted how irritated Rachel was at the word *boyfriend. Alvin,* he pleaded silently, *you are not furthering my cause!* But later on, early in the evening as she tidied up the seedling trays, Rachel suddenly said, "Listen, it's all been a bit crazy with the freeze, Charlotte sick, all the crap with Regina and the Expo, then Jen deciding to leave but you got to come and check out Bios. A meal, no less, and *I* will cook!" And there was Rachel's smile. Afterwards Mark calculated that it's message of unspoken possibilities, the optimistic spin it put on everything, lasted all of twenty minutes. It was round about the twenty-first, that a miserable, snotty nosed, cocky little Botany star had drifted up on his way out. Waiting for his parents, he had time to kill. Instead of being pegged out on a mountain side at an early age and left to die, he had grown up stuffed full of botanical knowledge which, standing in front of Orchid Empire's booth, he was cunningly turning into a stream of questions. They would have been elementary for a real orchidist, Mark knew, or even a low grade botanist and that was the problem. In a sickening moment Mark realized all this time he had been worrying about the wrong things: Charlotte's African orchids, how to classify something like Regina's Big Golden One, Mike and all his talk on temperature tolerance and elevation. None of that mattered.

What mattered was that Mark must know that *Orchidaceae* belonged to the order of *Monocotyledonae* and what made an orchid different from other flowering plants: the relationships of anther to stigma, apparently. And Mark was hesitating in front of this preteen when the reflex of long familiarity should have been there, when the botanical terms were so basic, so clear, so unambiguous and at that moment so damn unavoidable. It was all nodules, nodes and pseudobulbs, stomata and caudicles, words that Mark, had he been paying attention, could have registered on the blackboards of Totters Green during Advanced or even Basic Botany, together with the occasional saucy diagram of pistils and stamens.

The crowd had thinned; no lady customer to fuss over, rearranging her purchases, no talk of cute accents and places of birth, no grumpy buyer wondering about roots. Rachel had nothing to distract her. Mark felt her eyes on him and the boy and was overwhelmed by the desire to reach over the plants and whack the kid and his relentless, botanical inquisition so soundly he wouldn't stop till he landed in the pile of boxes behind the Hawaiians. And as the smug little bastard wandered off Rachel looked at Mark across the booth for a long moment and pronounced slowly and distantly the words he had been dreading to hear:

"You don't know the first *thing* about orchids, do you?"

14

Visiting Rachel and Jen

When first dreaming of an invitation to Bios Orchids, Mark had always planned to come as early as possible and stay late, very late. But now, instead of persuading himself that 'afternoon' could mean anytime after one thirty, Mark had put off his arrival as long as he could. Climbing into the old Volvo with a basket of citrus, a bottle of wine, a wedge of Stilton and a sinking heart, Mark thought if he left it much later, he might just as well stay in the car and watch the Florida sun go down. He had left the leaves on Charlotte's tangelos to show they were not 'store bought' as Americans said. They were the last of the citrus from the tree that had somehow escaped the freeze on New Year's night. And thinking of New Year's night and Jen, that was the other mess. As for Rachel, she had become so distant and frosty that by the time they were trudging to and fro removing plants and dismantling the exhibit on Sunday evening, Mark felt as flimsy and ludicrously out of place in the orchid world of South Florida as the wobbly cardboard wall being carted out with its badly painted bricks.

Bios Orchids was west, "cheap and deep" Charlotte said, prone to flooding when the summer rains came. It was beyond the true Redland area, out towards Ricardo's pig country, which was edging out towards the Everglades. No wonder Jen had found commuting down town a strain. Following directions, Mark found himself finally bumping over an unmade road to a sudden short row of fairly new, nondescript houses that just petered out next to a field of tomatoes. It reminded Mark of what Charlotte said about the local farmers. "They're getting rich now, planting houses." Unlike Orchid Magic there was no name on the gate. As a destination Bios Orchids existed for now, as a web

162

site. And if you're in the lab, Rachel said, and the bell rings, what you going to do?

It was gone half past four when Mark rang the bell. After a moment the gate swung open by itself like the stockade gates of Orchid Magic. There was Rachel's old blue pick up and Jen's small, green car in front of a garage door. To the left a racing bike with a flat tire leant against the fence. To the right, the gravel path skirted a frayed palm and a few bushes and landed up at an abrupt little front door porch harboring a pair of worn down, plastic flip flops and a bin half full of recyclables. Most were empty yoghurt containers, Mark noted, but there were two large, pale green wine bottles and a good number of beer cans though they all said *Lite*. This, Mark realized, was more revealing than a book shelf. Here in the bin there was nothing for show; this was the unvarnished truth. Mark was twisting his head sideways, trying to read the label on a large can with a picture of a sombrero on it when the door opened. "Don't let the cat in!" It was Jen.

"Don't let the cat in!" Rachel's voice came from inside.

"Trouble is she jumps up on the bottles," Jen said. A ginger cat was hard behind Mark's heels. "Quick!" Jen shut the door behind him. "It's a shame but when the orchid bottles get jiggled it messes up the medium and they're more likely to get infected. *So"* she stopped, looking up at him: "You finally got here."

Hardly a welcome, thought Mark, and hardly surprising. From just inside the door Mark could see across the living room and onto a screened in patio that led into a small orchid house, all bathed in late afternoon sunlight. And everywhere were the orchid bottles and flasks, each with bright foil wrappings over the stoppers in various colors. Charlotte had said Rachel was bottle central, while many of the breeding plants and larger seedlings were at Cooper's. "Rachel would *have* to work closely with someone, she just doesn't have the space. She's lucky it's Cooper."

"Thanks," Jen took the bottle of wine. "Ah! And Stilton! Rachel! Mark found some Stilton!" Jen raised her voice.

"Great." A flat voice, barely audible, from the kitchen. There was a lot of noise. A large television was on showing a row of men sitting behind a table talking at the top of their voices. Then came a roar and a football scene. "Super Bowl Sunday," Jen said. "Let me turn it down." She sank into one of the two old wicker armchairs. The other was so obviously Rachel's that Mark chose the frugal little couch between the two, piled with cushions. The narrow seat met the back at a puritanical right angle that made Mark sit like a maiden aunt who, as his sister would say, had never done it.

"So it seems we don't have to give you the grand orchid tour," Jen said, looking at the screen. Mark, sitting bolt upright on his rattan pew, couldn't think of anything suitable to say except "No." But he could do something on cats and orchids. "Charlotte says cats were useful. The rule was always: 'You need a cat in South Florida to grow *catts.* They should be able to walk along a bench without knocking the plants over. *Then* you have them spaced properly.'" Jen turned to look at him. "Um, she says that's what they always used to say here. You know, till the seventies orchids here always meant cattleyas." That's it, said Mark to himself, that's my hard won bit of orchid lore.

Jen chin up, turned back to the football with a faint, polite "Oh." Well, after all, Mark told himself, this *had* been an invitation from Rachel. He had to admit though, Jen, in a sleeveless navy top and grey cotton pants, brown feet tucked up, was looking pretty good. After a while she finally said, "Can I get you something to drink?" Mark would die rather than admit it but he would have loved a cup of strong English tea. "Time for afternoon tea, right?" Jen asked, "or I could make some limeade with Charlotte's limes."

"Limeade sounds good."

At first glance there seemed to be no books in the room at all, just the square-shouldered, old-fashioned milk bottles with varying growths of orchid plants inside. Some were still just a covering of emerald green on the nearly black medium along the bottom of the bottles, others looked like the standard slice of turf or a sprinkling of actual miniature orchids, tiny plants, on the other side of the glass. There was a computer on the table by the window surrounded by papers and folders and a grey filing cabinet to the side. Bottles with their different levels of green lay on window sills, in racks, and along the top of a small book case. Half the top row was crammed with folders but Mark also saw a chemical handbook, *Roadside Geology of Arizona* and *Small Business Manual*. Mark was adept at reading spines of books sideways across a room. One he was having real difficulty with: a long title, maybe a novel, dark green spine, gold lettering. He finally deciphered it: *Managing Your Golf Swing.*

"Sorry," Jen was relenting. "It's still just all the lead in." She turned the volume down on her way to the kitchen. "The Super Bowl *is* the Super Bowl; you have to have it on."

"Have you learned anything about American football?" Jen asked when she re-appeared, clearing newspapers to one side on the coffee table and putting down the lime juice. Mark was grateful to be allowed to make light, Sunday afternoon conversation. He wondered whether Rachel would even make an appearance at all. "It seems mostly very large black men with immense necks, pounding the shit out of each other. Then they point one out and say he's a junior in hospitality management."

"Maybe defensive ends but you've got to be confusing the NFL, the pros, with university college football. They're just students. Florida's got some great teams."

"I have a hard time picturing any of them cramming themselves into desks taking notes."

"Just don't talk about them all being large black men," said Jen. "It's not true. And you're being very politically incorrect."

"I've already been warned. That's what Althea says."

"Charlotte's therapist?" Jen was puzzled.

'We'd been joking around. I was saying I really liked her but obviously held back by age old prejudice: that if I were a bigger man in every way I would walk down the street with her without shame or embarrassment. And then, of course, I say, 'The problem is you're *taller* than me.'"

Jen, watching the screen, said "I don't get it."

"It's not that Althea is *black* it's that she's *taller,* a societal prejudice much deeper and more heartbreaking for a male... never mind." Mark trailed off. "Anyway," he began again, "Althea finally lets out this great Deep in the Heart of Africa laugh, that shakes the place."

"And you mentioned that too?" Jen asked, incredulous.

"Um, yes."

"You're a brave man."

"That's what Althea said."

"So you like Althea?" Rachel had come out of the kitchen. She was in a tight, honey colored T-shirt and skimpy white shorts. Honey colored thighs, honey colored arms.

"Um. No! Yes! I mean, she's fun. Fun to talk to. I mean, especially when the alternatives are Charlotte and Ruby. She's a whole lot younger for a start."

Rachel said sharply, "Charlotte's fun to talk to."

"Um, it's really not that important. Jen and I were talking about football players."

"Oh. How did the cat get back in?" Rachel demanded. She dropped the cat outside and shut the front door hard. Plopping down into the other arm chair opposite Jen's, Rachel gazed firmly at the screen. At least with the clips of old Super Bowls, interviews with mothers, managers, players old and new, experts and coaches interspersed with yelling throngs and high powered commercials, there was no danger of a miserable silence developing. In front of a large TV screen on Super Bowl Sunday who would notice Rachel wasn't talking to him Mark told himself but he felt he should make an effort.

"You know, with the really spectacular sunsets here, I've never actually seen anyone look up. One reason, I suppose is everyone's in a car so just as well there's no sunset-gazing. Especially with Miami driving. Otherwise the traffic reports would be starting: '*Another massive pile up on the Palmetto Expressway during this evening's spectacular sunset that caught even long term residents by surprise.*'" Mark had polished that one up on the way over but there were no takers. Jen smiled briefly and politely and said nothing. Rachel didn't turn her head, apparently absorbed by the sequence of ads for beer, pizza, cars and lap top computers. As the panel of broad shouldered men re-appeared, she said, "I guess I was going to give you the grand tour but it seems pretty useless now."

Jen turned the TV volume down. In the silence helmeted men with bulging forearms dressed in Christmas colors of gold and silver, scarlet and emerald, were pushing each other first one way then the other. Jen said coolly, "Mark's been living long enough with Charlotte and orchids to appreciate a tour, Rachel. And if you're going to make a big deal of this then if anyone ought to be grumbled at, it's Charlotte. What was she playing at, getting Mark to pretend he was the great orchid guru?"

"That was always the problem," Mark began, grateful for the chance to explain himself.

"We shouldn't blame Charlotte," Rachel said firmly. Right, well we all know who that leaves, Mark said to himself. She's not giving an inch. Rachel had her shining hair swept back and caught up by a tortoiseshell clip with big teeth. It was the sort of casual, sexy thing girls seemed to do: a few strands fell below, defining the nape of the neck while a shining tendril or two was about to slip out of the tortoiseshell jaws. It was all dramatic movement caught, suspended. You could watch the back of Rachel's neck all day, waiting for another tendril to slip away and fall.

Jen looked from one to the other of them. "O.K. In one minute I'm going back to the Super-bowl." Mark studied the pips in his lemonade glass and the faded rag mat under his feet. The wooden floor was stained a bizarre and unnecessary mustard yellow. He struggled to think of something to say. "Well, you've certainly got yourself well-established here with the lab."

"It's totally inadequate," said Rachel flatly "but it was all I could afford. It's close to the orchid growing area and the house has a lot of light. The orchids in flask seem to like it." Staring ahead, she started to chew one of her nails.

Mark was thinking how he had told Rachel she was family, the closest to family Charlotte had in America, which meant if Charlotte saw Rachel as *family*, well, she was notoriously hard on family, look how she treated him. And that meant Rachel should not feel hurt because of Charlotte's cavalier treatment, keeping her in the dark about his, Mark's, lack of credentials. If you could see it that way, then it really was a compliment, he would say, a heart warming development. Looking at Rachel chewing on her nails, Mark thought perhaps she was not ready for that little insight yet.

"When it comes to finding a place round here, there are no romantic, roomy little corners left," Jen was saying, "unless you have a romantic little quarter of a million. And God knows what I'll find further north. This is going to be the moment to stand back and make big decisions about the job, everything."

"Me too," said Rachel. "I'll have to look for someone else who'll put up with all this. I need a real orchid junkie."

Jen laughed. "There seem to be enough of those around."

"OK," Rachel stood up. "*I* am cooking. You two watch the game."

"Um, really, don't bother, I mean, just for me," Mark murmured trailing after her to the kitchen door. Rachel already had her back to him. She was studying a thick book open on a stand last used at Las Olas for *Native Orchids of South Florida and the Caribbean.* A variety of bowls, whisks and small pots were set out on the table in front of her, surrounding a heap of flour and some eggs. The small kitchen, dominated by a tall, avocado green fridge, was a depressing space: it said I am rented, not owned, let alone loved. There was a quantity of sturdy pottery everywhere, bowls of varying sizes for oatmeal and granola and large, heavy plates, all in the drab colors of earnest amateur potters, the earth tones of craft fairs. Beside the back door hung a large calendar from some chemical suppliers, with tiny notes beside the big figures in Rachel's neat hand. The screen door led out to a little passageway flanked by racks of orchid bottles and beyond that was the screen of the orchid house and the green of the plants, the orchids Mark had lost the right to see.

Mark, halted in the kitchen doorway, was repeating, "Please don't do anything special on my account." Rachel pretended not to hear. One hand raised with a whisk, she was looking at the printed page, her almost too slender back hunched a little forward, a tea towel wound round her hips. Was it Larry had said Rachel was from the Midwest? Not much left of the corn fed farm girl, Mark thought. He backed off, back to the living room. At least, this time, he bypassed the virginal rattan pew and sunk into the other arm chair, detecting no warmth from the recent presence of Rachel's frosty backside. The Super Bowl preview was still in full swing. Jen had put up the volume and tucked her self deeper into her chair. "Rachel has to concentrate," she said, without taking her eyes off the screen, raising her voice a little to combat the noise. "She tackles cooking like lab work. Precision. Down to millimeters. That's why she hardly every does it."

"What, what's she doing?"

"Some kind of souffle and something from last week's paper, Indonesian, I think."

"So Larry says Rachel's from the Midwest. Have you ever been to the Homestead Rodeo? Apparently it's 'the southernmost stop on the US rodeo circuit.'" The candidates for Rodeo Queen were pinned up in the local agricultural suppliers, local banks, cafes and car dealerships, grainy grey and white photos of young women like Wanted posters. "Florida's big cattle country up state, Charlotte says. Apparently there are a lot of cowboys in Florida."

"Really?" Jen had not even turned her head. Mark went back to studying the pips in his glass. Charlotte said pips meant the limes were real Key limes. "And that means you're in South Florida, unless you're in Mexico where they become the 'Mexican lime!'" Right. And all of this was Charlotte's fault, Mark reflected. He could have done with a Scotch, a beer, anything alcoholic but didn't want to draw attention to himself, certainly didn't want to go into the kitchen. The cat was outside looking in the window, a sweet, large ginger cat with a very pink nose, pink as the underside of Althea's hands, her palms. That was very endearing. No doubt another politically incorrect thought. From the TV screen came another roar as a different set of bodies briefly hurtled to and fro. Holding his empty glass of pips Mark stared at the screen, wondering if he could tiptoe out and just go home, without letting in the cat.

"They're going through old Super Bowl great moments." Jen appeared to be relenting a little, turning the volume down again. "There's a lot of fill before the actual game but the commercials are the best at Super Bowl time. Sometimes the commercials are the best part of the whole thing. People often watch just for them."

"The pick of English graduates they used to say went into advertising," Mark commented.

"Here it's the visuals," Jen said "but when you think about it, even with the best commercials what you remember are often the words."

" One of my professors used to joke the only reason to write your first novel was either to break out of advertising or to break in."

"Did *you* ever dream of writing commercials?"

"Oh, all English graduates do. I've composed the perfect ad for beer so many times but I've always been too drunk to write it down." It was a nice feeling to hear Jen laugh. Mark remembered it from New Year's; burbling, insubordinate, unexpected. It was always easy to make Jen laugh. He hadn't had any success with Rachel but then he couldn't seem to say anything funny to her. Jen had been so good not making a big deal of New Year's night. Maybe for her it had not been such a big deal. Mark, looking at a tanned, pretty Jen curled up in her chair, no socks, bare brown feet, wondered again whether he might be on *Jen's* B list.

"You know, I'd show you the yard but there's nothing much. The orchid house takes up most space and I take it you don't need to see the orchid house?"

"Not if I have to go past Rachel."

"Then let's not and say we did. I've got to ask you, why on earth did you go along with this crazy scheme to be the orchid man?"

"You know Charlotte. And somehow at the time, at the start, there seemed a point. She was basically worried about the leg, about losing control. I was never quite sure how serious she was. I know she's worried about the future of Orchid Empire."

"She and Rachel should really get together. I'm not even talking like the economist now. It would make business sense and emotional sense too. It's so obvious but they're both pretty stubborn and independent. I don't think they see it. On the other hand," Jen mused, "maybe they are *too* alike." Mark wondered where he'd heard something like that before. Ruby, Ruby on New Year's Day. "Strong characters! Look at this whole thing Charlotte got you into! Look at me. Look how Rachel has got *me* living!" Jen nodded at all the bottles. "It suited me at the time. I didn't want to think for myself too much."

There was a sudden call from Rachel in the kitchen. "Um, is this the moment we ask if we can help?" Mark asked. "Well, in that case, could I put in a plea for a beer, a wine, anything alcoholic?"

"All of the above," said Jen and unwound herself from the couch, uncurling her feet, bare and brown. Mark told himself, you've already noted that. Are you getting a thing about feet? He could hear a tense murmur of voices in the kitchen. Probably Jen was trying to persuade Rachel that will power alone could not cause a souffle to rise or an Indonesian recipe to yield up its secrets first try. Just put the Stilton on one of those mud colored plates, Mark pleaded silently, rip open the chips and come out and watch the game. Or at least enjoy the commercials. Jen brought him a beer and shook her head. That was it, no Rachel. "Sorry it's *Lite*. So did you play football? With you it's soccer, right?"

"Yes, and there's rugby. You run with the ball but no helmets, no face guards. If you see a guy with a broken nose in a pub, especially a middle class type, you always think he's a rugby player."

"Never just got into a fight?"

"Well, basically the same thing."

"We always hear soccer's a lot more violent than our football."

"That's the crowds. My uncle wouldn't take me on the terraces when I was a boy, too tough; all the men swearing and peeing into beer bottles."

"So when your father died Uncle Frank was your father figure?"

This was where we got close to whatever I said too much of, on New Year's Eve, thought Mark. How did she know his Uncle Frank was called Uncle Frank? "Uncle Frank? Father figure? God, no! But he'd appear from time to time. I think his main function was to stop me feeling sorry for myself; that there was something to be said for *not* having a father figure."

Just as Jen was putting up the volume again, there came a squeal from the kitchen and after a moment Rachel appeared, holding her wrist, flour down her front. She had burnt herself somehow and Jen went to get some ice and a towel. Rachel sniffed, looking very young. "Indonesia sucks!" she said, laying her head on Jen's shoulder.

"Come on! We should be eating pizza anyway! It's Super Bowl!"

Seeing the two together, brown and blonde, that closeness, Mark felt everything suddenly was falling into place. Of course! There he was, congratulating himself; *no sign of visible boy friends around the gorgeous Rachel, no male admirers, a chance for me!* What a fool he'd been. This frostiness was not just about Charlotte, this was not Rachel distancing herself just because of Charlotte's prank. There'd always been that distance, that coolness. And here he was being so grateful to Jen for not pursuing him, for letting the whole thing rest. Well, Of *course!* On the other hand Ned would be impressed. The ultimate challenge.

"I don't know how she puts up with it," Charlotte had said of Jen's daily, long commute. And why was Rachel pissed off now? Jen moving out, a lovers' tiff! Something soured in the relationship, Jen, getting drunk on New Year's night; he so worried he was being a shit, keeping her at a distance. How glad she must have been! What a fool *he'd* been! *A lot of heart ache there.* That was Larry. "Rachel is so *focused.*" Well, that was one word for it. Mark put down his beer and stood up.

"Um, look, it's been great. Thanks so much for inviting me but as we all know now I'm not really the orchid guy and with due respect, Rachel, you're not really a cook. Let's just cut our losses and call it a day. Don't worry about dinner! As they say, it's the thought. Great you invited me and I know you're very busy. Sorry about letting the cat in. Great to see your place, all the work you're doing. And I can see you're, well, you're..." Mark trailed off again. There was a silence. Rachel in the silence slowly raised her head, studying Mark, eyes narrowing.

"So, if you'll just point me in the direction of Charlotte's garden chairs..."

"You can see we're *what?*"

"Um, not, not really up to, not in the mood for company right now..."

"That's not what you meant at all," Rachel announced loudly.

Jen suddenly started her burbling giggle, pulling away from Rachel as though stung. "*Oh!* So Jen and I are," Rachel started, slowly and clearly, "—how would you put it, Mark, a pair, an *item?*" A voice behind her on the screen doggedly insisted it was the OH-fence not the DEE-fence. "This is such typical, arrogant, male *bull*-shit! How does it go? If we don't fall for you, if we're not all over you, we must be all over each other! This is *so* sophomoric!"

Mark had arrived thinking that things could hardly get worse with Rachel but he'd obviously been wrong.

"Whoa! Let's get this straight. Is this conclusion arrived at because, let's see! *One*, we're living together! *Two*, we both have *fairly* short hair; *could that be a clue? Three*, we aren't married and *Four* find most men not worth the effort? Take your pick, America!"

"OK! Come on, Rachel! Poor guy! First Charlotte, then Regina and now us!"

"So you want us to show you pix of boy friends, get out our diaries? The flings we have had?" Rachel was unrelenting. "You don't think we've had *offers?*"

Jen didn't catch his eye. She said, "Leave the poor guy alone! *I'm* going to watch the start of the game. You want to go on with this you two, go out in the kitchen! And speaking of which, Rachel, why don't we just order pizza and let Mark pay! Be macho man!"

"I need a real drink," Mark said firmly. "And if you don't have anything stronger than *Lite* I'm going off to get some. And by the way, which of you bought that *golf* book into the house?" The question stopped both of them in their tracks. Rachel frowned, Jen looked puzzled. Mark realized he was in the world of the non-readers. "Maybe it was here when we arrived," mused Jen. "So you don't play golf? Neither of you? Well, that's *some* comfort!" Mark declared this with a random ferocity that surprised even him. Jen was getting glasses. "Time to put the cucumber sandwiches away and bring out the sherry, right?" Americans seemed to love this kind of thing, thought Mark, celebrating Old England, those British Heritage hedgehogs. Meanwhile little English suburban man had his dusty videos of *High Noon* and *The Godfather*.

"OK.," Rachel conceded. "Order pizza but it will take forever unless we go pick it up because it's Super Bowl Sunday. Meanwhile I'm going to make *the* perfect parfait, frozen bananas from the lab and strawberries." She went back into the kitchen.

"You know," Jen said, "Rachel was really hurt Charlotte didn't let her in on your plot."

"I knew that would happen."

"And now *we* are an item! I would have thought—" Jen pursed her lips and stopped.

Mark looked at the floor. He wanted to say, Jen, isn't there a pub round here? Let's find a pub. How would that sound, right now? *Well, as you're not a lesbian after all, as I was thinking a moment ago, we'll let bygones be bygones and I'll buy you a pint!* "Do you have something stronger than *Lite*?"

"Sure," said Jen not moving. "You know, at one point I was waiting to cry on your shoulder about all the lousy men in my life."

"Why would you attract lousy men?" asked Mark in genuine surprise.

"I make a great effort to be normal and balanced and sane," said Jen "and you should see what turns up."

"Like me. On New Year's Eve."

"No, no! That was different. *You're* not married?"

"Christ, no."

With the television turned down low they could hear the cat crying to be let in. "When I go, I'll probably take the cat with me. Of course, with a condo you have to smuggle them in."

"What's his name?" asked Mark.

"I just say Kitty, so as not to build up her hopes, I suppose. She adopted us and I feed her." Mark found himself wanting to ask Jen about all these rotten males, or, at the moment, the absence of them. She seemed so mellow and well adjusted. That was another incorrect thought. "So you and Ned think we're all ragingly neurotic without a man?" his sister had demanded. "We need a male to make our lives complete? Without sex we're useless?"

Well, men didn't feel degraded to say that. Men had been saying that for years, for centuries, millennia. Look at poetry. Take all that out of Eng.Lit and you could graduate in six months. But now in a daft moment he'd called Jen a lesbian. In a way she should be flattered, Mark decided. He was saying: Be anything you want! Be all that you can be! No, that was the army. But the fact that he saw lesbians as attractive, normal people, not necessarily riding motor bikes and shaped like bread bins—An inner voice said "I don't care what anyone's shape is, I just want a drink."

Jen and Mark finally persuaded Rachel to come and sit down. In spite of all the talk of sherry, Jen brought out good solid glasses and a brand new bottle of Jack Daniels. Over the second Jack Daniels they decided they would reverse dinner. They would have the parfait and then Mark would go down to Homestead and get Mexican take out. That way they'd only miss maybe the first quarter of the Super Bowl. Rachel brought in glasses of mashed strawberries and half frozen bananas in some kind of blue colored cream. It was declared wonderfully refreshing and totally different and a perfect accompaniment to Jack Daniels.

"Do you think he should drive?" asked Jen.

"But we will go too" Rachel announced. "We are *the natives.*"

"No worries, then!" Jen said. "*We'll* be in the back seat. Back seat drivers!" They went off in the Volvo down into Homestead, Mark driving, Rachel and Jen in the back, giggling.

"*Girls,*" said Jen, "just want to have fun, dear boy! Just girls togethah! Carry *on!* What Ho!"

"Don't worry!" Rachel snorted. "We're not hup to any *fink* back `ere!"

"Do whatever you want," pleaded Mark. "Just don't do any more English accents."

15

Preparations for the Orchid Talk

"Better to hustle him in late."

"Oh, I don't know," said Charlotte. "Mark can waffle on quite well. Let him in early so he can chat and charm in a low level, bashful way."

"Like Prince Charles!" Larry said.

"Exactly!"

Americans didn't know what a calculated insult that was, Mark thought. Though he had met someone who had met someone who said Charles was charming and earnest and a lot of other good things. But that would never have been Charlotte.

"One problem might be that they often ask the speaker to introduce and comment on the plants brought in for display by society members," Ken suggested.

"All Mark would have to say is 'Supah! Supah!'" countered Larry, "'but won't grow in the UK!'"

"What about hot houses, Larry?" Rachel demanded.

"Mark says but not seen in *abundance;* not something generally collected. Mark won't necessarily be called on. And if he is, that's where his Brit modesty charms: *'Couldn't possibly comment! Defer to those whose knowledge of these far exceeds mine!'* And who's going to really have cold loving plants on a South Florida plant table? After all, they're bringing in their stuff that's in bloom to show off. And that's what they're interested in."

But that didn't seem to stop people like Rachel or Mike, thought Mark. Too many orchidists were liable to be nuts on all orchids, switching happily from discussing the mating habits of a certain species halfway up the Andes to recalling some clever little orchid that by the way of a scarlet throat, wobbly hinged lip or special smell was seducing insects throughout the central highlands of Cambodia. It wasn't like academia. Mark had a professor who'd lectured on Shakespeare's Early History Plays and that was it. They'd had the Early History Plays for half the bloody year and no one would have dreamed of mentioning one of the comedies or tragedies, or, on a typical bleak Monday, even one of the *later* histories. As for real history, a historian would state: "My field is late twelfth century agrarian revolts in East Anglia" and pity the poor fool who approached with a question concerning agricultural reform in the early thirteenth.

They were gathered in the Florida room: Charlotte, Larry, Ken, Mike and Rachel. Bert couldn't come, though Charlotte said she suspected he 'sniffed conspiracy' so stayed away. "He knows we're trying to cook up something and he's such a stickler for behaving himself." With Cooper, Mark knew, you didn't ask where he was. Maybe he was outside somewhere, in one of the greenhouses, maybe not. If so, he hadn't set the dogs barking.

It was Rachel who'd called the meeting. Mark had not seen Rachel since Super Bowl Sunday. She hadn't mentioned it; hadn't been particularly warm this evening, but hadn't been icy either. In fact she was only just rejoining the discussion. One of her economies was to forgo a daily paper so when she arrived at friends she was liable to hunt up the day's *Herald* and duck out of the conversation for a while. Now she was leaning forward, twisting her fingers together, elbows on her knees, in a tight little cotton cardigan top, the buttons hypnotizing in their placement: one button more, undone, would be too revealing: this button kept buttoned up, too demure. Mark remembered Jen on the same couch, knees up to her chin in the cold. Charlotte had said "I particularly made a point of inviting Jen over, too. She's been so good, calling and checking in with Ruby, ever since New Year."

Jen was in the kitchen, having offered to get the drinks. She knew where things were. In fact, Jen probably knew better than Charlotte, Mark reflected, who he was sure hadn't looked in some of those bottom drawers for years. "No, stay with the others," Jen had told Mark when he joined her. "See what they're cooking up."

The group had got together as a war party, devising a strategy, how to counter attack now that Regina had made her move. About a week after the Las Olas Show, Orchid Empire got a call from the President of the Sun Corner Orchid Society, North Miami. They needed a speaker for their monthly meeting in February. Geoff of Purely Paphs had to pull out at the last moment as his mother in law had a stroke. But by chance, he, the President, had mentioned that to Regina, the President of the Miami Orchid Club when she'd called to line up volunteers for the Miami Expo and Regina had suggested Mark fill in. *A great chance to hear one of the leading orchidists of the British Isles. Of course, he hadn't even known Mark was in town, such luck! But that was typical of Regina; always eager to help, and always knowing what was going on. And of course, Orchid Empire could provide a plant table for the raffle and Mark could pick up the speaker's fee. It was too late to put his bio in the monthly news letter, but they would get the word out.*

And Charlotte, instead of declining with regrets, instead of saying how wonderful it would have been if only Mark wasn't camping in the Everglades that night, attending a symposium on sympodial orchids in Chicago, or just sitting with a sick cat, Charlotte had said

"Splendid! How *thoughtful* of Regina to have thought of *Mark!*"

It had been Rachel who persuaded Charlotte they must somehow prepare Mark, not let him go down in flames: that Regina could not be allowed to win, to make a laughing stock of them all, to mock Orchid Empire and Bios Orchids. "Mark knows *nothing!* And Regina's setting him up! My *God!* He doesn't seem to know what a *sepal* is! Where do we *start?*"

"Even so he seems to have made a good impression on everyone," Larry offered. "Even orchidists. Of course, Ken and I had our suspicions; thought he was a little odd when it came to orchids but then look at Mike and Cooper."

Mark felt as though he might as well not be there or rather as though he were on the operating table with a ring of doctors high above discussing his condition over his prone front. He could be under anaesthesia for all the notice they took of him.

"You know, Rachel," Larry was saying, "we start from the fact that no one would even dream that Mark didn't know what a sepal was or any other intimate part of an orchid. No, listen! The orchid society hears from Regina, no less, that Mark's an expert and there you are! Ninety percent is just believing! Like those men who practice as doctors, even surgeons sometimes, for years and then it's found out they never even finished high school but their patients love them anyway and crowd the courtroom to say they have such confidence in the man!"

"Yes, let them make the running," Ken added. "A lot of the members are going to want to show off their knowledge, anyway. After all that's why they're in a society."

"You know Charlotte, you should really come," Rachel said

"Why me?" Well, for a start, Mark reflected, it's because of you that I'm in this mess to begin with.

"Charlotte, of course!" Rachel was insisting. "They ll want Mark to talk about British orchids! Stanhopea, lycastes, odontoglossums! Or whatever they've got at Kew. You can keep interrupting and answering for him." She'll be good at that, thought Mark.

"Well, don't look at me. I've been out of the bloody country for fifty years! God! almost sixty! No, Mike's your man. I never grew orchids in UK. Just dreamed of when I'd be able to get out and grow them somewhere else in sunshine and warm weather."

"Couldn't we present Mark in that same light?" suggested Ken.

"The dreamer, that sounds about right!" Charlotte cackled.

"He's got to know *something.*"

"Come on, Rachel. Some of these members don't know much more than the *Golden Book of Orchids,* if that," Mike spoke up for the first time. "They give that to student judges, for God's sake!"

Rachel looked glum. "Regina's going to be there. She may be pretty ignorant herself but she'll be the first to ferret out Mark's *total* lack of knowledge and make a big deal out of it."

"I think she has. Hence the invitation. Well, does it even matter any more?"

"Charlotte, we're not going to give her the satisfaction!" Rachel declared fiercely. She had parked herself, appropriately enough, on the couch under the spear. Mark registered for the first time its faded flower pattern, large blousy begonias, lolling over the seat and back. One white blonde strand of hair, that orchidists would call *alba,* an almost green white, kept falling forward as Rachel spoke and she kept pushing it back, behind her ear. An *alba* blonde, thought Mark: elusive, mythic, out of reach, like the mysterious orchids ordinary, non-orchid people would call about: *Where is the black orchid? The pure white Vanda? Have you heard of the ghost orchid?*

"Trouble is," Charlotte mused, "Mark's learned something about orchids here but they're mostly all the warm-loving ones we grow."

"Well, have him as the learner," Ken suggested. "It will make all the members feel good. They have enough of speakers who drone on about how special and rare *their* orchids are and create a lot of mystery, you know the routine."

"Culture class in reverse!" Larry cried. "Mark will ask *them*!"

"Just like when he was selling at Las Olas," Rachel said. "I thought it was clever British salesmanship. I didn't realize it was sheer ignorance."

"They'll love it." Mike turned from studying Charlotte's old photographs on the wall and looked down at everyone. "They can all be ignorant together."

Mark could see some merit in that. Put everyone on the same level. Like class discussion for paragraph writing. Ask some wary Pakistani or Sikh pupil what was the significance of something they knew. *Hassan, you explain Ramadan to us and Trev here, can stop gnawing on his knuckles and do Easter, or OK, Trev, so long as you keep it cool, the Rastafarians.*

"Everyone knows a little of *something*," Larry elaborated, "and we all pitch in together."

"Will you make a circle and hold hands?" Charlotte asked.

"If you're going to be a naysayer," said Larry, "then stay home!"

"Oh," said Charlotte, "I've decided I wouldn't miss this for the world!" That was what Mark was afraid of.

"Don't these societies always have an endless agenda, anyway?" Ken asked. "Rachel was complaining, remember, Rachel? They got you all the way up to Central Florida to talk micro-propagation and then what with the minutes and the discussions and the treasurer's report you had about twenty minutes at the end."

"Exactly!" said Charlotte. "I went up to Atlanta in Bert's van one year with my dog and pony show and it takes a wet week just to get out of Florida. Rare orchids of Kenya and the East African plains. Took stuff to sell as well as the plant table, after all, *Atlanta!* Capital of Georgia! There were about twenty-five people wrangling half the night about who was supposed to bring the refreshments. Like Rachel, about twenty minutes at the end and they introduced me saying, 'We have to be out of here soon so don't forget to put your chairs up on the tables!'"

"You never know," Ken said. "We've been in so many different societies and it can vary from year to year. Like teaching, Mark, you get the chemistry of a good group and then they pass on."

Charlotte snorted. "They do indeed pass on!"

"It's like everything else," Ken said, "the retirees are the ones with the time and the energy."

"Not necessarily!" Mike turned round again. "You should see the average age in orchid societies up north, a lot of males and much younger!"

"Mike, stop me if I'm wrong," said Larry. "But this is not the first time we've heard about these young males. Have I been missing something here?"

"Speaking of *which*," said Ken. *"Magic Springs!"*

"*Yes!*" cried Larry. "Of *course!* That might be the answer!"

"What Mark needs is something like they had in Magic Springs, Central Florida or was it the Florida North Central region? Anyway, an orchid society constitutional crisis erupting at the monthly meeting. This was killer: should two males living together be able to take out a joint subscription just like a law abiding *married couple.* They wrestled with it all night! Shut up, Larry."

"Those good old, God-fearing Christians," Larry elaborated. "I love my fellow man as Jesus taught me but may those fags and queers burn in hell!"

"Tough for the President," explained Ken. "Half the members were the old guard; up there a lot of retired military and ladies in hats and the other half were mostly florists and fancy men. And in come some militants out of the closet; guys marching in behind their orchids."

"It was San Francisco meets Yahoo Junction."

"No, meets Sun Golf Retirement Community."

"So what happened?" Mark asked.

"Oh, they let them in! They wanted the subscriptions. And some members under sixty."

"And they know those swishy types do such wonderful snacks!" Larry purred.

"Well, that's what you want," Ken said, "a crisis. Debate went on for hours. Took over the whole evening! And the societies always meet in these places like American Legion Halls or Community Centers where they have to be out by ten. So if you run out the clock you're home and dry. Don't look at us, though," he added. "Rachel, do NOT start persuading Larry."

"Even without that, there's the whole procedural fandango," Charlotte repeated.

"There's welcoming new members and visitors! We need to start the clapping!" Larry exclaimed. "Clap for each one and then there's sympathy for those in hospital and those among us who have died since the last meeting."

"There's Old Business and Reading the Minutes."

"Do we know anyone in that society?" mused Charlotte. "Someone who could really stir things up or a really cantankerous one we could get going."

"We need a Marjorie," Rachel said. No we don't! Mark cried silently.

"Yes, we need to plant someone, someone who's obsessed with some point of order or some problem. Got an eternal grumble about something."

"No need to plant someone," said Ken dryly, "there's always one of those. *Sun Corner,* it's a small society but it's that time of year. The winter folk, the snow birds, will still be here and they'll all be fired up with the big Expo up coming. Got to expect at least thirty, Mark."

"How long do we have?" asked Rachel. "I mean till he has to appear. They meet when is it? The first Thursday?"

"No, Wednesday."

"*OK,*" Rachel said. "Mark's got to be able to say *something.*"

"Apart from condolences to those in hospital and how great the cookies are," added Larry.

"He should just stand up and say 'Go on tacking plants onto trees and draping them round your pool and don't bother about names. They're not going to mean much to you anyway. Just don't call yourselves orchidists!'" Mike who was already standing, headed for the kitchen. "I'm hungry."

"You know, forget the young males," Larry said, lowering his voice, "*I* think our Mike likes Jen."

"As well he should," said Charlotte.

But Mike's odd, Mark thought. And Jen's so normal. But then when you got past the oddness he was certainly tall. And broad-shouldered. There's your Mid-westerner. And a deep voice. Taller than me and broader, Mark reflected and felt aggrieved.

"If each of us took a subject and coached Mark a bit then he'd at least have a chance to sound as though he knew something about *something"* Rachel was persisting, "and not make a total—" she turned to Mark, starting again. "And not be a *total* victim of the Queen." This was certainly what Mark had dreamed of: having Rachel pay attention to him. Total attention to him. As though nothing else mattered. It just wasn't quite as he imagined.

"Come on! Cooper's tropical, vandaceous, *history of,* plus cutting edge breeding. Mike, cool growing and the weird and wonderful; Charlotte, obviously her collection, especially African, East and South and some of the South American, the Caribbean. What about Mexico-Central America?"

Mark couldn't help noting that Rachel had not included herself in his list of tutors. No evenings with Rachel, then.

"Come on, Rachel, you and Charlotte know more than enough about everything!" Ken was protesting.

"We'll run interference, be sabotage," said Larry. "We start the clapping, bring up points of order and when Mark hits a rough spot spill coffee and create disturbances in the back row!"

Mike appeared, carrying the old tray with the beers and cheese, this time Vermont White, Extra Sharp Cheddar. As Mike set the tray down Mark saw Jen had spread one of the unused tea towels on it: *Literary Landmarks of London*. She was bringing in the wine and more glasses. "It doesn't sound like you're helping Mark at all," she commented. "We're just making him feel worse about the whole thing. And if you're just going to go and laugh then it would be a really friendly thing to stay away. Otherwise, I know you all, you'll be dining out on Mark's Terrible Orchid Night for ever."

"But he won't be around for too long to have to listen!" Larry protested.

"Right," said Jen, "that's true."

Mike had moved the ashtrays to one side and put down the tray. Jen set down the wine and glasses, eyes down, too. Mark was thinking how they'd moved the couches together on New Year's night, stacked the heavy ashtrays up out of the way.

"Rachel, stop worrying! The big thing now for *everyone* is getting ready for the Miami Expo! Every society now, it's all talk of the Expo and who's going to do what; are they putting in an exhibit and who did all the work last year and who lost a plant and was it a genuine mishap or was it stolen and how old Joe never gets an award even though his prize what's-his-face always blooms at this time and is the best anyone's ever seen—" Larry stopped for breath.

"Larry's right. Don't worry. It's back to sweet inarticulateness for our boy, Rachel," Charlotte announced magisterially. "You can't force feed all this stuff over night. And if Regina's there, well, she has a nose for un-authenticity. Takes one to know one! She's the expert."

"So then why should Mark be there at all?" Mike asked.

"He's there because he's Charlotte's family," said Jen and Larry together.

"Let that be it," Ken added. "He shakes hands, kisses some babies and sits down. Why be asked to speak? Misrepresented as something he's not?"

"That's Regina's whole *point,*" Rachel said.

"Yes, I started that, Ken," Charlotte admitted, "so that won't fly."

"Yes, it could," Mark spoke up. "I bet all the locals know that's just the sort of thing you *would* do. You are what is politely referred to as a character."

Larry grinned and looked at Charlotte. She studied Mark for a moment, tucking her chin down a little like Ruby, but didn't say anything. Mark could tell she liked it when he took her on.

Jen was cutting up the Vermont cheddar into squares and handing out plates. She and Ruby had found a nice set of Doulton botanical prints and Ruby had started using them. She brought them out when Althea came.

What had been resolved? Mark knew he was going to play ignorant; in fact, just *not* play. He *was* ignorant. He would be himself. Back to the first suggestion: he would simply share the travails of the orchid beginner in South Florida. "My esteemed Aunt taught me everything I know: the importance of watering, the problems with temperature, the nightmare of cold fronts." He caught Jen's eye who gave a quick smile.

"Brilliant!" Larry anointed the idea. "And you can still basically be the man from Kew. But fascinated by the South Florida scene: learning, learning! Problems and triumphs!"

"What triumphs?" asked Charlotte, innocently.

"And you'll say you'd *love* to return and do the whole Kew orchids bit for them but by then you'll be on the big silver bird."

"Mark will just be quiet and genuine and it will be fine," Jen said firmly. "Don't let this bunch throw you, you'll be fine," she repeated, "and I should know. I'm your ordinary non-orchid person."

"Ah, there's the fatal flaw!" Charlotte cackled. "These aren't ordinary people. They're *orchidists!*"

"And there's still the question of Regina," Rachel insisted. "You know she's going to be there."

"And they'll expect slides, anyway." Mike warned, gloomily. "They can't do without their pictures."

"But Jen thinks Mark's modest charm will somehow save the day," stated Charlotte as Rachel sat back, under the spear, biting into the Vermont Extra Sharp, and gazing sombrely across the cut glass ash trays on the coffee table to the dusty bull-rushes beyond.

"I don't see why not," Jen repeated, a little defensively as everyone looked at her.

"Well," said Charlotte, "we'll soon find out."

16

Orchid Talk: Part 1

A darkened sign on the outer edge of the car park announced: Smokeless Bingo Tuesdays. "Oh, darn!" hissed Larry in a loud stage whisper as he came in the door, "It's Wednesday!" "Now behave yourself," said Ken.

Larry patted Mark on the back as he passed along the last row with Ken, scanning the room, checking deployment of orchid society forces, maybe checking for emergency exits, Mark thought. They were both looking South Florida formal, in short sleeved shirts and light colored slacks. Mike was in jeans and a navy T-shirt; Rachel, a caramel colored T-shirt dress that just skimmed her knees and everywhere else. She and Mike had their backs to the room, checking out the evening's plant table display. People were carrying in boxes and plants. At the back two cheery women with shiny white hair were setting up a coffee machine and a third had started to wander the room with a clipboard and a pen and the plaintive cry: "Come on! We don't have anyone for next month!"

Mark inevitably had been unnerved at the very start. Introduced as Charlotte's nephew and the evening's speaker to an outburst of "Oh My's!" and "How lucky for us!" he had excused himself from the group round Charlotte and tried to lose himself among the chairs at the back. But only one old couple were sitting down and he had no folder or notes with him, no material to bury his face in. It was as hard to know what to do with himself as it used to be at school dances and just like those merciless evenings, with this kind of lighting there was no place to hide.

Mark was about to stand up and stride off purposefully towards the lavatories when Jen appeared and came over. Gazing ahead sombrely

187

at the rows of empty metal chairs, he was now seemingly engaged in serious conversation with a fellow orchidist brave enough to steal a private audience with the night's distinguished speaker. "So how are you feeling?" Jen asked in a low voice.

"Awful. This whole thing is so ridiculous."

"I thought you'd decided on some way out."

"In the cold light of day it all seemed totally inadequate."

"Oh." Jen lowered her voice even more. "Did you ever plot another strategy?"

"The trouble is Charlotte decides on a scheme but she gets bored quickly. That means if she thinks it might work and be too easy an option she comes up with something else." There was no need to whisper; no orchid members were near by except the elderly pair who appeared to have already nodded off. "First Charlotte decided we'd say I'd be talking about orchids in the UK but we would bring the wrong slides: *African Species, Madagascar: Habits and Habitat* and then Charlotte could wheel forward and say 'How fortunate *I* am here! And in her words,'Bob's your uncle!'"

"So what happened?"

"Well after a few hours she got bored with this apparently fool proof scenario and cooked up something else."

"Such as?"

"Now I have no bloody idea. Just before we left it was 'Scrap the slides, dear boy! Say we forgot them and you will just talk off the cuff!' *But* then she trundles in here with slides on her lap. If she weren't so sharp I'd say Charlotte was getting senile."

"Talking without slides sounds less technical, you know, more chatty."

"Chatting about *what?* And Charlotte just says breezily as she trundles in, 'Don't worry, dear boy! I'll fill in when things get sticky.' And that worries me even more."

"Oh," Jen paused. "You'll be fine. And remember you've got Larry here. And, well, it doesn't look like many people have come."

Not counting the ladies in the kitchen and Charlotte, Ken, Larry, Mike, Rachel and Jen, 'the Friends of St. Marks,' as Larry had dubbed them, there couldn't have been more than fifteen and most of those were clustered round Charlotte. She was in her chair for tonight but Althea was starting to get her moving and just the day before she had hopped and swivelled her way through the Florida room to the porch, with the aid of a formidable walking stick, a craggy black thing with a knobbly top like a miniature skull. Mark couldn't see Bert anymore. After parking the van he'd been cornered as he set foot in the door by one of the sterling orchid society ladies with impressive forearms and a clip board and for the moment had disappeared.

The hard, unsparing lights made Mark think of Totters Green. Fix a well worn blackboard behind the table at the end of the room and the venue for Tuesday's Smokeless Bingo could have been Monday to Friday's Totters Green Annexe. Larry, arms folded, was whispering something to Ken as he gazed benignly at the mostly large and gentle orchid society members moving to and fro. He caught Mark's eye and pursed his lips signaling I will be good, then suddenly shook his head with a horrendous wink, remembering, Mark realized, tonight he was supposed to 'run interference'; be bad. Ken was grinning now as Larry leant over and said something.

Neither of them looked worried. Mark, once again, found himself thinking that Jen, beyond the reach of the orchid world, was the only one he could really relate to, the only other person who realized what was about to happen. All Mark had in his head was one line, and then nothing. *Thank-you so much for inviting me here tonight.* Mark noted he was not stammering. He felt he would never stammer again, that he was on the verge of so many disasters he could hardly line them up clearly to worry about any one of them. Regina had set this whole thing up. Regina who was yet to appear. There was The Talk; at this time it was not even clear what the subject would be, only that whatever it was, he would know nothing about it. And before that came the flattering tradition of inviting the guest speaker to conduct the plant table, the show and tell, to identify and assess the orchids brought in by members. Mark had seen the plant table. It stretched all down one side of the room and there was an orchid every foot of the way, more than half of them, at a cursory glance, Mark was sure he'd never even seen before.

Rachel and Mike were still pouring over the plants. Another blow. They were not impressed by easy orchids. Mark could see one or two phals, a yellow *Oncidium*. Next to that had to be a *Cattleya*, pushing out its big frilly purple lips to kiss God knows what insect and then a wholesome little *Paphiopedilum* with green and white pigtails like something out of *The Sound of Music*. But Rachel and Mike preferred the rare and strange and there they were: everything from tiny, enigmatic clumps perched on twigs and bark to some orchid, visible from the back row with its brilliant flowers, clawing on to a piece of wood like a cagy old parrot. It got worse. Mark, with nothing else to do, had been observing their progression down the row. Mike and Rachel were now pausing even longer before orchids that looked fairly ordinary and those were the most treacherous of all, the orchid with a totally obscure reason for being special: *'It's the breadth of the side lobes!' 'It's the fact that this is a pink one and coming from the south side of those mountains in East Java that species should be yellow!'*

Mark wondered if it would help if he went up to Mike and Rachel, getting names and making notes. But Rachel had done no more than say hallo which had seemed strange after her fierce attempt to render Mark viable in the orchid world. More likely, he thought, Charlotte had told her everything was fine and they had it all well in hand. And, of course, if it were a question of vying for Rachel's attention when an orchid, let alone a whole table full, was in front of her, then that, as they said, was a no-brainer. Mike, he sensed, had no interest in saving him from ridicule and disgrace; might, in fact, rather enjoy it. Mark was at a loss to explain this till he remembered Larry's comment: Mike was sweet on Jen and Jen was now sitting next to Mark. In that case, tonight Mark was ready to hand her over in a desperate trade. "Take her, Mike! She's yours! Just give me names! Facts! Save me!"

"I don't see Cooper," Jen was checking the room. "Though, of course—" That didn't mean he wasn't there. Or necessarily alone out there in the dark. Larry said he saw a full social life emerging for Cooper. "This whole anti-smoking thing is going to transform Coop's life. On any given evening now, there are so many eligible young women and especially the foxes, outside, puffing away in the dark. Coop says it's starting to get so crowded out there he may be forced to come inside."

Mark thought if there were any foxy ladies anywhere in this society tonight then they must be outside with Cooper. There was a flurry at the entrance and raised voices. Mark kept his head down. "Who's arrived?" he asked. "Not Regina?"

"No. Some more women with boxes...I can't see... either orchids, I suppose or refreshments." They were silent. Someone had scratched 'Exit' on the back of the chair in front of Mark and next to it, drawn a palm tree. It was a palm tree that was on the state seal of Florida, *not* an orchid, Mark told himself desperately. A palm tree was a classic doodle, something you could always draw, right back to elementary school, like a Christmas tree. Though most of the artists working on the chairs at Totters Green spent more time carving out their choice of four letter words.

"So how long have you got here now?" Jen was asking. "With all this happening, you must be thinking longingly of going home."

"No," Mark paused. "You know, nuts as it all is, I don't feel like going home at all."

"Oh."

"Well, I've always loved the sun too but of course Charlotte won't need me much longer. And anyway my ticket will soon run out."

"You can get an extension for about a hundred bucks," Jen said. "It's no big deal."

The room was starting, if not to fill up, at least to lose its empty look. Here and there people were in clusters. Some had actually sat down. Larry had stood up and was talking to one of the mellow ladies in charge. Maybe asking her what they'd done with poor Bert. Even if he had wanted to check, Mark would not have been able to see the plant table any more; a row of members' backsides now blocked the view.

Here I am in South Florida with my mad aunt, the orchidist, Mark told himself. Ten years from now tonight will be another funny story, a traveler's tale, filled with flamboyant, brilliantly colored personalities who have become more flamboyant and showy with every telling. He watched one of the orchid society ladies arranging home-made biscuits, *cookies,* on a plastic plate. It was easy to tell the cookies were homemade Mark decided, because they, like their creators, generously overflowed their margins. In ten years he would have forgotten about the homemade cookies. Mark reflected how much travelers' tales were part of the South Florida scene, sometimes it seemed they *were* the scene. All the talk about tropical, lush, crazy South Florida; in practical terms, on a daily basis, what it really seemed to boil down to was a lot of mostly large, older, white people able to amble about in shorts in the dead of winter.

"Would you like a slice of marble cake, a cookie, coffee, cranberry apple juice? They're the choices," Jen announced. "I checked them out."

"I'd say coffee but I think I'm wired enough."

"It's a very friendly crowd and they're more interested in their own plants and just getting together. Just make them laugh. I've seen that with Rachel. If she ever lightens up and makes a joke in the middle of all the propagation and micro media info, they're eating out of her hand or at least keeping alert. Do the Prince Charles bit, like Larry says."

"I don't see any babies to kiss. Though the couple asleep over there look like they might qualify for the Queen's telegram."

"What's that?"

"If you live to be a hundred in England, that's what you get."

"Is that all?"

"I think they find that when you hit a hundred you're not too interested in being given a lot of stuff."

"Looks like Charlotte is having a good time." The group round Charlotte's chair had grown, they were all laughing now. "Probably cooking up a whole new scenario," Mark muttered. "Is it only seven twenty? God, you must be hungry." Jen, crisp in white slacks and olive green silk T-shirt, serious leather bag at her feet, looked as though she'd come, as usual, straight from work.

"Thanks for coming. Some societies have a real spread, right? Probably the ones where the ladies with the clip boards are most energetic but here it's pretty minimal. Anyway, thanks for keeping me company, Jen."

"So *you* are our speaker! You should have made yourself known! So glad you could be with us!" A short, fat man in a faded orchid show T-shirt had pushed his way through the metal chairs behind an impressive stomach. He was glowing with the warm, robust American energy that Mark was now taking so much for granted it would be a shock to hear that first tepid "Oh, you back then?" in the Totter's Green staff room. That is, if he were reassigned to Totter's Green.

"Charlotte's telling us *all* about you! Except *what's* your subject?"

"Didn't Charlotte say? I'm afraid she's in charge of the agenda."

"She said you were going to surprise everybody! And I guess she's right!"

"Oh, ask Charlotte really sweetly, she'll tell, I'm sure. And then," Mark added half to himself, "come back and tell me." Still beaming, the Sun Corner member moved off, shaking his head at the English sense of humor. "You and Charlotte, howzabout that?"

Mark thought how relaxed and happy almost everyone looked, milling about, chatting. And they were still coming in. God, Regina had really spread the word. *Thank-you all so much for inviting me here tonight.* A young Asian couple making for the row in front, turned to Mark and Jen as they sat down; "We are late!" they announced, beaming. If only that were true, thought Mark. It was still only twenty-three minutes past seven. Mark couldn't believe it. It had been five minutes after seven about an hour ago. When did the chairs have to go on the tables? Larry had said probably not before ten. Mark could see Larry, ready to help him in his hour of need, starting to stack chairs any time he gave the signal, with a high seriousness, like a ball boy at Wimbledon.

"OK, folks! Let's get this going!" The President had shaken Mark by the hand when he'd first arrived. *Thank-you so much for inviting me here tonight.* He was a tall, wiry man with a brisk, dry manner, another blow. Unlike many officials of amateur societies, he had obviously been elected because he was competent. What Mark needed was some gentle soul with about as much control of the proceedings as a fresh young graduate filling in for the Art teacher on a Friday afternoon. Suddenly members who'd been drifting to the back past Mark and Jen to the refreshments were starting to filter into the rows, with a drink, a cookie, a slice of cake and finding their own spot among the chairs to sit down.

"Let's call this meeting to order, folks! Running late again!" It was getting worse and worse. Mark had been counting on a good British tea break: half an hour at least, a leisurely break with an extra five or ten to make sure all the old ladies had time to go and have a pee and here, even in their leisure time and their retirement, these orchid society members were being productive, being time conscious, good Americans.

Charlotte was shooing off the people round her and steering herself to the side, to park by Larry and Ken at the end of the row. Rachel and Mike were still standing, still close to the plant table. Mike was staring at him, Mark noted, relishing his imminent downfall but then realized Mike was looking at Jen, who was, he had to admit, still right beside him. Too much going on, thought Mark. *Thank-you so much for inviting me here to be your speaker tonight.* It was not enough that Regina wanted to destroy him or at the very least see him bite the dust. Now Mike, and because of *Jen* of all people. Jen who was his haven from all this. Why wasn't Mike after Rachel? Rachel who was as nuts about orchids as he was. Rachel who, faced with a table crammed with orchids, just turned her back on him, left him to his fate. For a moment Mark forgot about the talk, the whole looming crisis. What was he thinking? What was happening? *Too much going on.* And in the middle of it all one thing had suddenly become clear and as Mark realized it, he realized how his dream of Rachel, the distant *alba* blonde, was fading and about to die.

"Now, tonight we must welcome..." the President of Sun Corner Orchid Society was waiting no longer for the last stray orchidist to sit down. Mark's heart started to thump. *Thank-you so much for inviting me here tonight.* "...must welcome our guests, visitors Truman and Cherry."

Someone started clapping hard, and another pair of hands joined in. The president had to pause. Good old Larry and Ken. Jen, smiling at Mark, started clapping too. Mark couldn't help noting that Rachel had her hands thrust in her pockets, looking glum while Mike just seemed irritated at the interruption. Thanks a lot, Mike! said Mark to himself.

"And Earl and Betty." The President was looking a little surprised at this outburst of goodwill and had said the next two names cautiously but as Larry started clapping again located the source and said, "Larry! Gotta dampen your enthusiasm—we have a lot of business tonight. Okay. So, yes, these are our guests tonight and welcome! And new members Kim Park, where are you, Kim? And Eric Hoftstadler, *yes*! Welcome, Eric. Harry tells me you're the man for Laeliocatts and have brought all your expertise into this region. From where?...*Virginia!* How about that! And Louise has brought along her niece—Hi there!"

The President was speeding up a little. Larry had caused the President to speed *up*. Mark felt a great lethargy come over him. It was the lethargy of pure fear. Tap him on the shoulder, present him with one more critical moment and he would fall into a dead faint, like a Victorian heroine.

"And we have many distinguished guests tonight! Larry has already introduced himself," the President said dryly. "Larry and Ken of No Limit Orchids, and in addition Rachel of Bios Orchids and Mike who knows more than most of us! All familiar faces and, of course, Orchid Empire's one and only Charlotte who we are so glad to see in such high spirits after her accident and mending well. *And* who has brought along our speaker for tonight, her nephew Mark from England! Yes, Mark, stand up!"

Hereupon Larry started clapping vigorously till gradually everyone joined in, turning to look at Mark until the President brought things to a close with: "And a generous plant table for our raffle. Oh yes, Arthur at the back has the raffle tickets and come on, buy, buy, buy! Maybe the last chance to get some of Charlotte's intriguing specials. And glad *we've* got such a good plant table with all these heavy hitters here tonight. Congratulations, everyone. Now some of you may already know that our President of the Miami Orchid Club, Regina herself, is coming tonight also and just called to let us know she's on her way so Pat, hold some of those chocolate chip cookies! Traffic's very heavy she says but she should be here in time for our speaker. So this is a very special evening and glad you all could make it. And no, Rosemary, I don't know the subject of tonight's talk! Well, it's a last minute deal. Charlotte's helping us out and we're all waiting for Mark to surprise us."

There was a ripple of laughter, some murmurings over which could be heard Charlotte's voice: "Oh, yes, dear, *oh, wonderful* speaker, well, his grandfather, you know…"

"Now, do we need to read the minutes of the last meeting? Lester, you going to propose we take them as read?" *No!* pleaded Mark silently, *Read the minutes! Americans are supposed to be legalistic to the core—Germanic! Everything solemnly spelled out and written down! Read the bloody minutes!* "So, all say Ay? Nay? *OK!* We'll take the minutes as read. Now, the treasurer's report. Maureen, can you come forward?" A tiny man in large horn rims stood up. "Oh, sorry, Ted, I keep forgetting Maureen passed the torch to you."

"So, how is Maureen doing? What do we hear of her?" Larry called out.

"Oh, helping her in-laws moving up to Sarasota," said the President.

"Wrong time of year to move north!" exclaimed Larry. Some members laughed and there was a murmur of agreement.

A male voice growled, "The time's always right to move north, now! Anywhere outta Miami!"

"Right on!"

Mark noted there didn't seem to be any obviously *non* Non-His-panic-whites present. Though as Charlotte said how could you know? "Alvin was grumbling away to this quiet, All-American boy at some show, about the lousy, loud Cubans; clean cut kid from South West High, been helping Bert and then this little old lady arrives and he slides into Spanish and off they go, the perfect Cuban grandson! It was a classic Miami moment. Shut Alvin up for a while."

Good old Arthur, though, getting an ethnic grumble going, all non-Hispanic whites together. "Hey! Whoa! On we go!" the President was saying firmly in a loud voice. It was clear there were going to be no ethnic grumbles on his watch. "OK. Ted, Treasurer's report!" Maybe the

Treasurer's Report was even better, thought Mark: raffles, expenses, car-washes, bake sales, trips, this could go on for hours and, at least in school circles, usually did. And no way could you ever abbreviate the treasurer's report. Out in the open! Nothing shady! Other peoples' money.

But Ted was having none of it. Maureen had left things muddled at the end of the year. No one had given in their petty cash receipts. Subscriptions were a mess and as for the annual auction, he wasn't sure what she'd been thinking of. It would all have to wait another month.

"Well, moving right along," the President was not happy but philosophical. "One thing, Ted, I think we can safely say the Christmas party was definitely a financial as well as a social success." Larry started clapping but with no support, had to slow down and stop.

"No! There was a major problem!" Some angular woman in the front, long hair, long dress. Fierce shoulder blades. Mark clung on to the hope that someone had embezzled something; took the raffle or the refreshments money and ran. "The only choice was beef or chicken!"

The President for a moment was lost. "Well, ah, strictly this belongs with *old* Old Business. Arizona, you weren't at the January meeting? Jean, would you like to say something?"

One of the women spoke up from behind the refreshment table. "Some members, unfortunately, didn't make their preference clear before hand."

"'*Beef or chicken?*' There *was* no choice for many of us! *No*, Arthur! A slice of stale cheddar does not an entree make! And Madison's whole family is Vegan!"

Jean from the back expressed the exact mix of sympathy, resolution to do better and weary reminders that if people didn't attend meetings and bring things forward then, then people couldn't be expected to be able to respond in a timely manner.

"You know if you can't persuade members, the society, to go Vegan or at least Veggie next Christmas, try for the annual picnic!" It was Larry. "The weather's warmer then, too. And there is this wonderful place on South Beach which caters or just does individuals. They have an incredible tofu quiche. Arthur? Arthur, *Listen!* You have to *try* it."

"He's godda be kidding!" *Come on, Arthur!* Mark prayed.

"OK!" said Larry. "But who's the one here with a triple bypass?"

"Whoa!" The President raised his voice for the second time. "Arizona, sorry about that. We will revisit this whole question of menus well before the picnic. Right. On we go. And Larry, don't forget we do have a suggestion box."

"One more thing! Re the party! Hang on, Leonard. I heard the music was *so* good. That group, can anyone tell me the name? OK. Was that with two 'm's? Do they only play country? And how would we get in touch with them?"

"Larry. Let me turn you over to Arlene, in the third row. Arlene can answer all your questions." Even with Larry the clock was only edging up to ten before eight.

"Well, of course, the big news since last month was the *Las Olas* Show! I know we all had a great time as always and congratulations to all the ribbon winners. Larry! Not now! We won't stop to mention you now but you'll all be there in the news-letter. And once again you helped Regina and Orchid Magic to their success with the Miami Orchid Club and I know Regina is very grateful and in fact will be here to thank you in person tonight."

"Leonard, I just need to mention—"

" Larry, I'm going to have to stop you right there. Time is running out." If only that were true, thought Mark. "Folks need us to move on." This was a president exhibiting disturbing dictatorial traits and tendencies, Mark decided, willing to ride rough shod over democracy. This was a president who knew everyone had to be out by ten.

"I don't have to tell you all, this is the last meeting before the Miami Expo and we want this to be the best Expo ever so I'm going to turn this over to Harry who's volunteered to coordinate everything for the show."

Jen turned to Mark and nudged him, triumphantly. She was right! Mark exulted. If they were getting into all the details of the Expo, the biggest show of the year, he was home and dry because the plant table would take forever too. As they'd all been commenting, it was a big one and Charlotte said no way could you ever cut the plant table proceedings short:"Hell hath no fury like an orchidist whose plant is ignored."

Harry turned out to be the short man with the expansive front who'd come up to Mark before the meeting. "Well, folks, you all know what's looming on the horizon. So all the usual warnings and then some! Gotta get those prize orchids on track for Miami: watch out for cold nights, we all know what happened New Year's Eve and we aren't out of the wood yet. There's *Thrips* to watch out for, all the usual suspects and don't leave grooming and staking till the last minute! You've got to get that orchid plant to put its best face forward for the judges and the public, to *present* itself and that ain't done the night before! Now, Regina is looking for volunteers and plants for the big show. You know she's always been there for us in the past and I know it's long hours, but this is the big one. I'm sure all our distinguished guests tonight would agree and we want to help make Miami Orchid Club and Orchid Magic the best. And get that trophy one more year."

Jen had leaned in close to Mark, "You should see Rachel! "Mark didn't dare look. "Cross your fingers she doesn't say anything." In fact it was Charlotte who spoke up. "Harry, forgive me for interrupting, but I've always wondered why doesn't the *club* put in an exhibit? Your own exhibit, Sun Corner's?" she asked innocently.

Harry was a little nonplused. "Well, you know Regina is so good at this sort of thing and we've always been rather a small society, affiliated with Miami, probably because so many of our members are snow birds."

"It would better serve the club, I would have thought, if you enter under your own name. Look at your membership, now! Look at your plant table! Some incredible specimens! And many of these will still be good for the show."

Harry looked across at Leonard. "It's a little late for this year," the President said, "but we'll need to bring it up at a future meeting."

"And look what happens," a member from the floor spoke up. "Look at Las Olas. We knew Edna and Will were going to be gone. Will had surgery scheduled. So some of our members never got pick up. They had plants ready and no pick up."

"But if everyone knew they were doing it for their own glory, their very own society, I think you'd find the level of anticipation and interest would be that much greater," Charlotte suggested gently. "There's all the difference in the world between helping someone else's projects, especially a large, successful commercial operation, or even another society and creating your own."

"A big topic," the President declared. "And right now, of course, we need to concentrate on this year's show. We have so much to do." Jen gave Mark another triumphant smile. "That's why Harry suggested scheduling a special meeting just for preparations for the Expo. There's a clipboard going round, no, two. Bert has kindly helped with getting us clear on reminders about categories for entries. Hallo, Bert! Forgot to include you at the start! And Pat and Jean once again need really definite maybes on the volunteers' sheet. This year we want to make sure we spread the load, so sign up, guys. OK, any more new business before the plant table? What, Ted? Sorry, any more *old* business before any more new business!"

Mark closed his eyes. There was a little pause. Larry was silent. There was the murmur of the ladies at the refreshment table, and the scrape of a chair as someone got up. It was no good looking at the clock. *Thank you so much for inviting me to conduct the plant table tonight...*

"Mr. President, we do have to remind members about the cups."

"Yes, Please remember to take care of trash. Yes, I know, Rosemary, we haven't got the recycling bin yet but it's no good leaving the cups on the counter. The custodian doesn't realize that, he just thinks we're being careless."

"We could bring in our own box. Take them home."

"Yes, sure," said the President patiently, "the old story: who's going to do it? I don't want to give Jean and the refreshment team any more work. Any volunteers for being in charge of recycling?" There was a pause. "There you are."

"There's some new material they're using," Larry, making one last valiant effort, thought Mark, feeling sick. "I think it's from Italy, maybe Japan. Tough as nails, looks like Wedgewood but bio-degrades in minutes. Won't harm pets. You can put the stuff, the cups, right in with your orange peel and old lettuce leaves. If anyone's interested, give me a call. Or you could fax. Or email. Hang on. Ken, do you remember the fax? Did we change our email?"

The President for the moment appeared to give up on reining in Larry. He had walked over and started talking to a couple in the front row. Mark said to Jen, "I'd better make my way over to Charlotte, though I don't know what good it'll do me." Jen tried to look encouraging: "Good luck."

Larry, having made three laborious mistakes with his email, and two on the fax, for the moment had fallen silent again. Charlotte, sitting alongside him, looked sunny and totally unconcerned. "Ah, there you are, dear boy!" She swivelled her chair so Mark could squeeze past. Ken moved up one and looked at his face, "Hey, cheer up!"

"*What* am I supposed to do?" Mark muttered.

"About what?" asked Charlotte. I swear, thought Mark, it's going to be a marvel if before I leave I don't cause Charlotte grievous bodily harm. "Just let things develop," Charlotte said quietly. "I would have told you but you were off hobnobbing with Jen. Glenda is here and that awful creature who tags along. But for tonight, perfect. Changes the equation. You'll see."

The President came back to the front. "OK, Harry, we're ready to go. Plant table and what a one tonight. And we want to invite our special speaker, here all the way from the good old UK to take us along. Interesting to hear what is new for him and some insights." Now there was real applause, and Larry hadn't even started it. Harry waited for Mark to join him at the end of the table.

"Wait up! Number one, that's my no name mutt! Harry! Leonard. I need to do this one!"

A wiry sunburnt woman had bobbed up at the front in a straight, short print dress and socks and sandals. Mark heard a muffled groan behind him and some shifting in chairs. "Yessir! I got this on the sales table at Sacred Heart bazaar. I always say you can get great plants anywhere. Don't need a fortune. Keep an open mind. There's that flea market in Hialeah where they always have good stuff.”

“Most of that's stolen.” Mark recognized Mike's deep voice.

“No, no, I get it from this old lady lives in a trailer over on 125th. Has to do *something* with that no-good husband of hers.”

“Right,” said Mike. “Stolen.” The wiry little woman shot a look of pure venom in Mike's direction. “Well, I looked it up!”

“Looks like an ordinary little *Oncidium* to me,” said Ken in a whisper. “Don't know why anyone would want to steal it. Could have probably got it out of a dumpster at the back of Home Depot.” Charlotte said quietly to Mark. “She doesn't know what the hell she's talking about but bless her, she's good for fifteen minutes. One time she disrupted the whole proceedings. You know, I bet she's been outside smoking with Cooper and he got her worked up, bless him.”

“This is Glenda?” whispered Mark. Larry had mentioned her as a potential treasure trove of lost minutes if she showed up. “No, her side kick. But like Glenda she scares the establishment. They don't know how to handle her.”

“Well,” said the President cautiously, “this may be a tough one for our guest-speaker but we've got all these professional orchidists here tonight. Probably a real chance to get the name straight.” He had said the wrong thing. “Well, I looked this one *up!*” Glenda's friend stared at Mike again, sticking her chin out. If she had a pipe, thought Mark, she'd be Popeye the Sailor-man. There was a little pause. “*OK!*” came a loud voice from the floor,” Let's all move on!”

Sounded like Arthur, thought Mark.

“Well, I think the members who brought their orchids in, they should introduce them. Otherwise Glenda when she comes, she usually does.”

Glenda must be the solemn-faced woman with the tight curls and dusty glasses holding on for dear life to the large plastic purse in her lap. She was in a row all by herself and no wonder, thought Mark. Glenda made him think of those women who sat down randomly at café tables in London, speaking firmly and relentlessly to the empty chair opposite. “According to Larry, they've paid their dues,” Charlotte murmured. “And you can't be thrown out for being bizarre. Ha!

If they threw people out of orchid societies for being bizarre!"

Mark could not believe his luck. He wasn't sure how long this could go on, before Arthur led a revolution from the floor and the President regained control, but for the moment Glenda and her friend were all set to eat up time. Glenda slowly moved along her row of chairs holding her bag in both hands.

"Come on Glenda! And you'll be next. This one's yours!" A little white, standard commercial *Phalaenopsis*. "I could almost have done that one!" Mark thought. The President was talking quietly to Harry. Some of the members too, had started talking in low voices.

Ken said. "The President will try and wind them down but it will take a while. They usually don't want to push them too soon or they both start crying."

"Did Larry invent them for tonight?" asked Mark dryly. Larry was sitting watching them both with a beatific expression. "I think my work is done," he said simply.

"Which reminds me—" Mark was about to thank Larry profusely for all his disruptions in their race to speed the clock when there was a commotion outside the door and someone exclaimed "Oh! *Regina!* Regina is here!"

17

Orchid Talk: Part 2

Regina stood framed in the doorway, caught at that moment when the weary traveler reaches a safe haven, can toss their head back and start to focus on their hair again. Business-like as usual in her military-crisp khaki slacks, wearing a cream silk blouse, she paused till every head had turned and the last innocent voice had trailed into silence and then protested, *"Please* don't let me interrupt!"

Regina had halted proceedings so efficiently, in fact, Mark saw her suddenly as an ally as much as a threat and Larry, he could sense, was ready to start clapping again. She was accompanied by Tony who followed two steps behind, a precise two steps behind: close enough to function as escort but distant enough to acknowledge he was a lesser breed.

Scanning the room, Regina registered Mike, Rachel, Charlotte and Mark, Jen, Larry and Ken. She embraced them all with a flashing smile, checking the battle array and deployment of the enemy. Mark looked at the clock: eight fifteen. Regina planted a kiss on the President's cheek and waved to Harry.

"Regina needs no introduction!" declared the President and Larry began a wild and hectic clapping, soldiering on alone for a whole thirty seconds after everyone else had stopped. Jean of the refreshments came forward with another member and in loud, reverberating whispers asked what Regina would like to eat and drink but she was shaking her head. Obviously no chocolate chip cookies and cranberry apple juice. "Oh, Please! Don't let me interrupt!" Regina repeated as she walked to the front to address the club. The President, no doubt grateful for a force stronger than Glenda and her friend, followed to announce, "I know Regina wants to say a few words."

"I *had* to come to say Thank-you, thank-you for all your help and hard work at Las Olas that got us so *many* wonderful and well deserved awards and here we are ready for Miami! And I see so *many* wonderful plants displayed here tonight! This is great news. Tony can coordinate pick up with Harry. I know we missed out on a few prize plants for Las Olas because of that. And I am so glad to be in time for the plant table and the talk given by *Mark*, our wonderful speaker from England! You know, it was my idea to bring him here tonight and I know you're just going to enjoy and benefit from his knowledge."

Here Larry started clapping hard at the mention of Mark's name and for a moment as Regina raised her voice to compete, they raced along together. "*So before Mark starts* I do just need to once more remind you it's that time again to pitch in, work together, and make miracles happen!" Larry clapped hard and long again but there were few takers. Mark missed having Jen next to him. He looked around. She was not only in the lee of Mike, standing close to him, but laughing at something he had just said. "*Wonderful* display tonight," Regina was repeating, ("Here! here!" cried Larry) "and you know, we always need your wonderful support. It's what we are all about—participating, working together as orchidists, sharing our treasures." Larry resumed clapping to celebrate these impeccable sentiments and Regina shot him a look that would have destroyed a lesser man.

Mark was willing Regina to go on; those cadences and emotional pauses mopped up the minutes too. And it was up to her now. Glenda and friend, having dominated the scene, had shrunk back into two minor, timid eccentrics. Mark had the feeling it was because they recognized underneath that silk scarf and Coral Gables facial, Regina was as street hardened as they were.

"I felt it would be *so* great to have Mark here tonight. In fact he's the main reason I put up with rush hour and beyond! I have heard he's a treasure trove of knowledge with a brilliant mind."

"Well!" Charlotte steered herself forward, raising her voice a little. "Mark, I'm sure, would hesitate to describe himself in such glowing terms. He's always been particularly averse to the grandstanding and rampant self-promotion that can go on in the orchid world, as indeed, in any other field where commerce and private passions meet. I know I speak for Mark when I say he'd feel like getting another ten years under his belt before he dared to stand up before such a knowledgeable crowd." Charlotte nodded towards Glenda and the wiry lady in sandals. "And indeed before the very President of the Miami Orchid Club, with so many years' experience under *her* belt, as it were."

Larry started clapping once again, ferociously and Ken, Charlotte, Jen, Mike and Rachel and finally Mark, joined in leading the membership in a little display of appreciation. Mark caught sight of Bert standing on the opposite side of the room from the plant table, looking apprehensive. "Bert always hates it when we're up to something," Charlotte had noted with satisfaction on their way up in the van.

Leaning over to Mark, Larry commented, "See how Regina's smiling the big smile but look carefully, it doesn't reach her *eyes!*"

Regina waited till all was quiet and said coolly, "But having brought Mark here all this way unfortunately we have only one chance to hear him and that's tonight!"

"Right!" said Harry. There was a murmur of agreement. Several members turned to look at the cause of all this debate. Larry, this time, did not start clapping. There was a little silence. Mark stood up. He pushed through the light metal chairs towards the orchid table ahead. He looked blindly at the plants and then focused on something, something familiar enough as he walked along. "Well, if I may be allowed to pick one." A member jumped up, saying shyly, "I bought it three years ago, just a pup at the Miami Expo. Didn't do anything for me, at first."

"But look at it now!" said Mark. "A wonderful, large *Oncidium*, a real specimen. You know, all one can say is keep on doing whatever you're doing, obviously exactly the right culture! And pretty soon you'll have an animal ready to rival Regina's which I call, rather facetiously, I'm afraid, The Great Big Yellow One!' You all must have seen the magnificent specimen from Orchid Magic used in the Las Olas show. Of course, here they can grow so large, almost like weeds compared to the UK."

"Indeed," Charlotte picked up. "This *Oncidium sphacelatum* is very common, as Mark says, grows like a weed here given the right conditions. A vigorous, attractive pot plant but, as in Regina's case, it is the size alone which makes these worthy of attention and as everyone knows here, veterans of Las Olas and other shows, *so* useful for filling up space in those grandiose exhibits! When you take on five-hundred square feet you have to shove everything in but the kitchen sink, as we say."

The President had retired to the side and was leaning against the wall, arms folded. The clock said eight thirty. Harry came over to have a word with the President.

"Oh, Mark! Now that one, there! the *Tetramica,* very nice!" Charlotte was definitely picking up the ball. "Not really suitable for your talents, Mark, more a subject for our Rachel at Bios or Mike, or Regina. A little known, very warm growing species but I know *you* have a great deal of expertise, Regina, having been so many years at this."

"Unfortunately, I had no time to check out the plant table. We mustn't lose sight of the fact that what he, what Mark, *really* has been invited here for is the talk! In fact, I must say I was surprised the plant table had not been finished with." Regina's comments had come out with increasing speed. Some of the older members were asking each other what she'd said. "I know the members would hate for him to have to cut short his presentation," Regina added, glancing at the clock.

The President detached himself from Harry and held up his hands. "How far have we got? Only up to Jean's *Brassia*? How many to go, Harry? What time is it? Nearly eight forty?" He pushed his head forward and scratched the back of his neck. He came over to Charlotte. "Mark, Charlotte, hate to do this but Regina's right. We are running a little late and it seems unfair to pressure Mark to race through the plant table, some unfamiliar, no doubt. And a great number. Charlotte, why don't we let you finish off so we can get on and let Mark have a moment to get his breath for the talk? Sorry, Mark, tonight things got away from us a bit."

"Well, what a treasure trove indeed!" Charlotte was maneuvering her chair to the front of the plant table. "Almost every *one* of these should be submitted for individual ribbons and even AOS consideration at Miami! Go for the gold! As Regina tells us what's so heart warming is co-operation among members but what we must remember too is the chance for individual achievement. And what better way to advertise your great orchid society than ribbons and dare I say AOS recognition? Go for it!"

Larry gave a whoop and clapped wildly. The President looked startled. "And on that stirring note, the clarion call to action," Charlotte proclaimed, "let's race through these bearing in mind their potential and, of course, Mark, add any information you think relevant, any insights you may have from a European perspective." Larry, no doubt in awe of Charlotte's apparent ability to run out the clock, had ceased for the moment to applaud. "We are indeed lucky to have real experts in their field with us. Rachel, of course, of whom we are extremely proud. Some of you may have heard her speak on micro-propagation but her interests range far and wide especially in connection with preservation and reproduction in the lab of endangered and rare species and the programs to reintroduce them to nature. Ah, forgive me! Forgive me!" Charlotte, the wily old bird, thought Mark, saw she had pushed Regina to the very edge and the President was stirring. "Yes, we must get on! And Mike, of course needs no introduction," Charlotte announced serenely, proceeding to introduce him while giving Regina's smile right back to her. Round one, thought Mark, to Charlotte.

Charlotte wheeled her chair along, picking up orchids, defining their characteristics, from *Doritis* to a large cane *Dendrobium* that nearly keeled over into her lap; from the one that looked like a parrot to the virginal *Paphiopedilum*. Mark was proud of her. She was careful to keep up an appearance of speed and bustle, so Leonard, the President, would not call a halt to the proceedings and was always ready to defer to Regina's extensive knowledge when Regina seemed to be getting restive. There were references to the new temperature tolerant *Oncidinae*, the breeding of short day plants to long day, the fact that cattleyas were still judged as corsages, and the need to work on the strengthening of their stems; the beauty of odontoglossums, so big in England and what a joy that the intergeneric breeding was creating temperature tolerant varieties for Florida. But the theme stated and restated was: almost everything on the plant table was worthy of *individual* entry at the upcoming Miami Expo.

And then would come the cry: "Whose is this? Betty! Betty! *My dear!* This is glorious! I don't see why a bloom like this on such a stout inflorescence should not garner at least an HCC at Miami! Go for it!"

"Well I think a lot of members feel our first obligation should be to Regina and the MOC," Harry had announced apologetically after one or two of these exclamations. Charlotte had swung her chair around. "Absolutely! But she would be the first one to want to give Sun Corner its due! She, like the rest of us visitors here tonight, had no idea of the riches you members had! Hiding your light under a bushel indeed! And unfair to all the hard work Leonard, Harry and the others put in! And our Jeanie and the gals at the back! Believe you me, that's where the sterling work gets done!" This, said Mark to himself, from the gin and taco chip lady.

"Surely it should be left for individual members..." Regina began. But how could Regina talk down the plants? It was true that any orchid could be picked out from a display for consideration but how could she insist in the face of Charlotte's lavish praise they were only fit to be part of *her* exhibit, or the Society's? Not worthy of individual entry? Of going for the gold? Regina, the inspirational speaker, the patron saint of orchid societies?

"And the crowd is going wild!" Larry whispered to Mark. "Charlotte sees a prize in everyone's future!" Charlotte had wheeled her way to the end of the plant table, having found something to praise in the least Cirrhopetalum as well as the most extravagant *Brassolaeliocattleya.* "Wonderful performance!" Larry remarked as he burst into applause. He stood up, clapping and some members stood up too, smiling, saluting Charlotte. Mark could sense a feeling had swept through the members, that this would be the last time, perhaps, Charlotte would come all this way to a monthly meeting. Suddenly everyone was on their feet, applauding hard. Some male voice was even booming "Yeah!" Maybe Arthur. Mark could hardly see Regina through the heads and shoulders of the members but there she was. *"Wonderful!"*

Larry whispered. "She's *got* to clap! Oh, that *has* to hurt!"

It had indeed been a bravura performance by Charlotte but when Mark looked at the clock it was only nine twenty. There was still almost three quarters of an hour to go.

With everyone standing, there was a natural break. People were stretching, moving out of the rows. This has got to be worth at least ten minutes, Mark prayed. The President and Harry were talking with Regina. Leonard had his hand on her arm. Poor Tony had wandered over to the plant table, waiting to be summoned.

"Hey! You were great!" It was Jen.

"You've got to be kidding," Mark said.

"No! Who said you didn't know anything? You were rattling along like a pro!"

"Another minute I'd have been running on empty."

"Well, this is a meeting for the ages!" exulted Larry, "And it ain't over yet!"

Mark winced. "Don't rub it in." He saw Rachel bending over Charlotte's chair, laughing as Harry started raising his voice and calling for order.

Jen was saying "Well, Charlotte has really come through for you."

"Yes, but she does love to leave me hanging. And now what? What slides?" Mark shook his head. "I am still deep in it."

"Sure, but it's almost nine thirty and the whole atmosphere is a little crazy. Hey, I know it's going to be fine. Break a leg!" Jen straightened up and left.

Rachel, raising her head from talking to Charlotte caught Mark's eye and grinned, giving him a thumbs up. Everyone looked happy, thought Mark. No-one else seemed to be worrying about the next half an hour except him. *Thank-you so much for inviting me here tonight.* What was it all supposed to be about? Orchids in the British Isles? Orchids I have known and grown?

"You got your slides?" Harry had come over. "The projector's ready. Oh, and whatever it is, keep the technicals down. Our members like to be entertained."

"Let me go and check with Charlotte," Mark said. The members were settling down. A few had left. Mark couldn't help feeling a little hurt at this. Couldn't stop to hear the speaker from the UK, then? The brilliant Brit speaker? Glenda and the wiry woman had disappeared. They might have been useful, thought Mark with a pang. He saw Jen over near the plant table talking to Mike again and felt another pang. Feeling a little light-headed, he almost said aloud, "Hey! I didn't mean it when I said a trade!" Jen was laughing *again* at something Mike had just said. Come on! Mike was a miserable sod. Everyone knew that. *He* was the one who made Jen laugh. The famous British sense of humor, well, he'd need it tonight.

Almost everyone had sat back down. It was an audience all right. Regina suddenly appeared in front of him, holding out her hand. She had a heavy gold ring on the right middle finger, with a large diamond cluster. Really big. Give someone a backhander with that, Mark decided and you could do some serious damage. "Mark! *Finally!* I have been *so* looking forward to this!" Regina smiled her big, empty scarlet smile. "Don't let me down!"

Mark was desperate to ask Charlotte, What's the subject? What on earth did you tell them? But she was deep in conversation with Harry and the President. Mark slid back for one more moment next to Larry and Ken. Now he saw Rachel and Jen laughing together. With Mike! No-one was giving a damn about him! "Everyone has stayed!" commented Ken. "Congratulations. You're obviously the star attraction."

"No, that has to be Larry. They're all waiting to see what he'll do next," Mark said.

"I will applaud for every slide," Larry promised solemnly.

"Until the President throws him out," added Ken.

"I still don't even know what slides they are!"

"You're *kidding!*" Larry was loving it. "That's our Charlotte! *Un-*believable! Don't you *love* her?"

"Don't ask me that right now," Mark said.

"Right!" said the President and paused a fraction, waiting for whatever new interruption, outburst, applause or protest might erupt. "Well, finally time for our speaker. Saving the best for last! As you all know by now, Mark has come all the way from England to be with us. He is, of course, Charlotte's nephew and doubly welcome for that! And he will be speaking on...Harry? No, Harry doesn't know either! Folks! We still don't know and somehow that seems all a part of this evening; lots of surprises yet to come! Charlotte gave us just a brief bio of this young man and I'll keep it brief because time is running low on us: Mark, a life long botanist and horticulturist, kept in close touch with his aunt all these years from her various orchid chasing adventures round the world. A whole list of countries here, folks. Some I can't pronounce... Obviously inspired by her, began his own collection, er, own collection of cool-loving English terrestrials. Showed annually at the county fairs (which of course would be like our state fairs.) Has worked closely with Kew. Has donated his collection recently to the herbarium at Todders? Tottle's Green?—The prestigious London high school where Mark currently teaches and so please welcome *Mark!*"

Mark stood up and made his way to the front. Larry led the applause once more which appeared genuine and in Larry's case, prolonged. It was nearly nine thirty-five; still more than enough time for him to make a fool of himself. In fact, if it was a question of finding out how little he knew, then, as he'd discovered at Las Olas, all that was needed was two minutes and a snotty twelve year old. Mark's mouth was so dry he didn't even think he could manage *Thank you so much for inviting me here tonight.* And after the whole last hour or so, that simple line seemed to belong to a more ordered and distant time. Harry was there in the seat on the other side of the aisle, ready to work the projector. A man in the back row jumped up and switched off the lights.

Thank you so much for inviting me to come here tonight. He'd already said that. Mark was about to try, "It's a great honor to be invited by Sun Corner to speak here tonight" when the first slide appeared, some kind of scene upside down. Members started to turn their heads sideways; so did Mark. The slide was righted and there were a few exclamations. Christ, it was Kew. Of course, he was supposed to be Our Man from Kew. Then Mark realized it was not Kew but the entrance to the Chelsea Flower Show. There was a buzz among the members. For a moment Mark thought wildly *do they even have orchids at Chelsea?* "Chelsea? No, Kew!" someone murmured.

"Chelsea!" Charlotte announced in the dark, "the Chelsea Flower Show. We thought you'd like to see something a little different. I know from talking to members over the years that it is a really wonderful experience, so we thought we'd give you a little preview but let Mark introduce it."

"Right. Well—"

"But Charlotte—just a moment." It was Larry. "Is it true it's the *only* horticultural event the Queen goes to? In fact, the only time she's ever really exposed to orchids?"

"Oh, no, dear boy, the Queen is always having to attend horticultural county shows and the like. Poor woman! Luckily she does love the horses."

Someone murmured, "Does the Queen *ever* go, then?"

"Oh indeed, yes," exclaimed Mark, surprised. "The Chelsea Flower Show? Oh, every year! It's absolutely a tradition."

"And does she take those little dogs with her?" queried Larry.

"They are cute!" someone murmured.

"Well, actually, corgis are nasty!" Larry again. "There are lots of stories of how they've bitten visitors, bishops, ambassadors. Of course, you can't really say anything when it's the Queen!" There was a ripple of laughter.

"Oh, but we must leave the dogs behind, amusing as these little stories might be." It would have been obvious to everyone even in the dark that this was the voice of Regina. "We need to get on to *orchids!* What time of the year is the show and what orchids are displayed? How do they conduct the judging? And what awards were given out last year? We'd all be interested to know which orchid was the grand champion." There was a little silence as people tried to absorb all Regina's questions, delivered at a brisk clip.

"Oh, absolutely," said Mark, "but just to concur with Larry. Yes, corgis can be quite vicious. But I'm sure the Queen takes them. In fact, I heard on good authority that at the last Chelsea Show they did their business on one of the prize exhibits. Luckily, *not* an orchid."

There was a burst of laughter. Harry grinned but had his head on one side, looking enquiringly at Mark, ready for the next slide. Someone at the back murmured something and another wave of laughter engulfed the last two rows.

"We are all primarily *orchidists* here," it was Regina again, "and I think we are entitled to some kind of material on *orchids!*" There was an uncomfortable silence. It was not the shortcomings of Mark as orchidist that were being registered but the anger in the voice of the President of the Miami Orchid Club. "Hang on," said Harry, "we've got another slide in wrong, upside down again." Another moment of silence and then from the side of the room, among the chairs, there came a strangled cry, a half muffled but tortured sound, an almost death rattle deep in the throat and then a gasp. "No! No! Ken, I'll—" and another chilling sound. Larry, Larry having an attack There was the wholesale scraping of chairs, a gust of worried cries and murmurs, a couple of 'Oh, my Gods' and someone at the back rushed for the lights.

Mark looked at the clock. Nine forty. And there was Ken, distraught, Larry, head back, eyes blinking hard in the harsh light; the screen gone blank in deference to the crisis. Two of the ladies had their hands across their hearts, two, hands across their mouths. And how clever, Mark noted: Larry was stuck firmly in his row, determined to be No Trouble; just needed to be left alone, not hurried out to the rest room or the cool of the car park, so Regina could call for the meeting to come to order and proceedings to proceed: *("I am sure Larry would have wanted us to go on.")* No, Larry was stuck, gasping now right on cue like a stranded fish, right in the middle of the kind, concerned members of Sun Corner Orchid Society.

Someone was murmuring, "You know we should have seen it coming. Look how he's been all the evening. Anyone could see something was wrong."

"Well I hope it's not his heart, after what he said to Arthur."

"Is he on medication?"

"There should be enough pills among this crowd."

Mark dared to look in the direction of Regina. Her expression, he supposed, could charitably be considered an expression of thunder-struck concern, though if one just came upon it with no preconceptions one might interpret it rather more readily as an expression of barely suppressed rage. Larry was taking a glass of water from Jean. Larry had his head back, then between his knees but no, he wouldn't budge, because he was going to be All Right. His face had gone bright red, but that flush was slowly subsiding. Mark wondered suddenly if they all really should be worrying. Maybe this *was* some attack. As the member had said, Larry had certainly been hectic all evening. Mark looked at Ken. Ken, quiet, low key Ken was elaborately and loudly worried so Mark knew Larry was indeed All Right. He made his way over with everyone else.

Charlotte was shaking her head. "Larry doesn't take care of himself enough!" she declared to the room at large.

"And when you're a worry wart," added Jean, sympathetically.

They hadn't had to sabotage the electricity after all, Mark thought, remembering the council of war convened at Orchid Empire. But with Larry's color returning, the President was saying "If Ken really doesn't want us to call an ambulance—Ken, any one of us could drive to St Jarvis Emergency. It's only three blocks away."

"No, no!" said Larry. "Let me just sit here quietly and so sorry folks, so sorry *Mark!* Stealing the limelight, like this! I'll be fine and I'll really be better just sitting, if you don't mind."

His eyes strayed to the clock. Mark hoped Larry wouldn't ask too brightly what time it was, though recovering from an attack of that magnitude, it would be more in keeping to ask what day it was, or, with Larry's dramatic flair, what his own name was.

"I wonder what it can have been! What caused it!" one of the lady members was asking of nobody in particular. "You know, it's only been chocolate chip cookies or angel cake! Nothing with mayo."

"Yes, *indeed*," said Regina. "Well, there's still time for those of us who've waited this long. Just turn the lights out, will you?"

"Right, Bill, lights out! No, hang on! The projector's not on. No, it's not working! Bill! Lights on!"

"Now what?"

"Oh, boy, someone screwed up!" Harry was sighing. "Someone turned off the projector! Burned out the bulb!" A groan went up from the technically proficient.

"Oh dear," a small voice, Jen, owning up. "Oh dear, that was me. I was just thinking to pause everything when Larry got sick. What have I done?"

"No, no, not your fault, honey," Harry said. "You just can't do that with a projector," he explained gently, "that's not how it works. They have to cool down. You never just switch them off!"

Jen was devastated. "Oh boy, Mark, I'm so sorry!" She bit her lip and glanced at the clock. Nine forty-five. "So there's nothing we can do?"

"'Fraid not, folks!"

"Doesn't anyone live near, isn't there *another* projector somewhere in this place?" Regina's tone seemed a little out of place what with a distraught Jen and sick Larry.

"Well, there's the storage room."

"No there's only an extra extension cord," that was Harry, "and often that goes missing."

"It just seems," Regina stopped to take a deep breath. Members were looking at her. "Well, for those of us who came to hear a *talk*." Regina's annoyance seemed, in the circumstances, out of place. "*I think the main question to be asked now is 'How is Larry?'*" someone said reprovingly and there was a murmur of agreement.

"I think in light of the long evening and Larry's indisposition we should just round off the evening in a gentler way. We still have a few minutes to go! And I see you were all so interested in Chelsea!" Charlotte's voice came loud and strong. "Of course I think when it comes to Chelsea, I really have more stories to tell than young Mark! There was a lot more fun in the old days."

"With due respect to Charlotte," Regina began, "I think we can hear reminiscences from that quarter another time, whereas Mark, I believe, is due to leave soon." Well," said Charlotte serenely, "talking of dogs sabotaging prize exhibits at Chelsea! Oh, this will only take a moment, Regina! Now, this is not known by anyone outside the diplomatic service, mind. My good friend Dottie knew all these tales.

Well, the old King that would be …George the Sixth, Queen Elizabeth's father, had a whole raft of brothers; Duke of Windsor of course you know, Mrs Simpson! And there was oh, Duke of York, Duke of Gloucester. And there was a slightly dotty one, somewhere. Anyway, it might have been the Duke of York and at one Chelsea you know, going round on a private showing he was caught answering the call of nature in a bed of begonias! Said he'd been at some damn reception for the French ambassador and couldn't get to find the lavs! Oh, that must have been back in the thirties. And the funniest thing was, he was surprised by one of the young girls, a horticultural student, watering the beds and there she is with her watering can and there's the Duke; well, say no more! What a photo op they'd say nowadays! What, Harry? No, No, No! No, never made the papers! Well, you know how reverential we all were back then! Changed now! Look at the way they treat the royal family! The Kennedys get an easier ride, by far!" A mix of argument and agreement erupted. Mark saw it was nearly ten to ten.

"But why does she wear those hats?"

"The Queen? Yes, they *are* awful but the problem is protocol! They've got to wear the damn things but they mustn't shade the face: the subjects must be able to see their monarch! And as you know the only smart hats are the ones that shade the face, saucy brim and so on! So the poor woman is stuck before she starts."

"But look at Jackie Kennedy," Jen said.

"Never thought about it before, but that proves my point!" exclaimed Charlotte. "Those little pork pie thingies, you could always see her face! Well, we always say the Kennedys are your royalty and I think that proves it!"

"If we could stop" Regina paused, realizing perhaps the battle was almost lost and then rallied. "I *did* want to ask Mark what he thinks the trends in orchids *are* now in England and Europe. We don't hear too much here so caught up in our busy South Florida."

"Um, pretty much the same problem as here," Mark started. It was ten to ten and he didn't care. "Domination of phals, cymbidiums, of course and for the orchid society people, cool loving paphs are always big though, as Charlotte will tell you, they are not even considered orchids any more! But there are only a few really dedicated people," he nodded to Rachel and Mike, "yes, like Rachel or Mike. Regina, you may well know more about the commercial aspects of European production than we do. I know you must be, well, probably the biggest importer among the small commercial orchid businesses in South Florida. I know Orchid Magic does a lot of importing from Thailand and Hawaii and Taiwan now, but haven't seen anything from Holland. Do you think that's in South Florida's future?"

There was a pause. Everyone looked at Regina. Larry had raised his head and was gently regaining his strength. Mark hoped he wouldn't start clapping vigorously: "Let's hear it for Holland!" The pause lengthened. We have won! Mark clenched his fists. Regina slowly stood up. In a very little while it would be five to ten. Time to put the chairs on the tables. The mood was a little of disappointment. As Larry said later, they had all just started to have fun. "I did not come here tonight for *this,* Leonard, Harry." Regina was hitting the wrong note again. She was implying the evening was a disaster and a shambles but the President and Harry had held everything together: business had been got through, rough patches and problems overcome. The President did not look happy. Mark saw Charlotte give a small, private smile which she turned into a pursing of lips, a judicial review of the evening. Regina, having stood up, having expressed her displeasure, really had no option but to sweep out the door, a public relations disaster for the Queen of the always brilliant smile and warm Christian heart. Tony could do nothing but trail after his boss, eyes to the floor, another unfortunate image. There was a general scraping of chairs. Voices were subdued. Several orchid society ladies were raising their eyebrows and shaking their heads. Members were coming over to Mark to say goodnight. "Gee, we really enjoyed listening to you! Sorry for the upsets." "Hey! How's Larry?" Leonard, the President was raising his voice to be heard over the movements of chairs and the departure of members. "Hey, lie low, buddy! Keep it cool for a bit, OK? Take care!"

"Charlotte continues to amaze." It was Jen. "What a life! I hadn't realized she'd been back to England."

"She's not been back at all," Mark murmured. "She just makes it all up."

"You're kidding."

"No way."

Leonard, the President, came over, declaring this had been one of the wackiest evenings in a long time. "Mark, we must apologize, we lost your presentation."

"Well, frankly, Leonard, you and the members have been spared!" Charlotte had wheeled over to say goodnight. "Mark's forte is really the higher reaches of theory! When he gets the bit between his teeth it's only the most advanced taxonomist or orchid scholar who can follow him!"

"Get that woman out of here!" Mark muttered to Larry and Ken.

"Good luck and see you all at Miami and don't forget! Next year your *own* entry, Sun Corner will reach the heights and Regina will bless you for it! Another beautiful exhibit for her Expo!" Charlotte was exhorting to the last, buzzing steadily out into the dark towards Bert's van.

Jen had waited behind in the now empty room. "Glad it all went off alright. Told you it would be OK."

Mark wanted to ask Jen what Mike had said that was so funny. "And Jen, thank you, thank you for helping save my bacon. But maybe you didn't know about projectors."

"Nothing much. Only that the bulb burns out if you switch them off too soon," Jen said dryly. They were quiet for a moment among the chairs.

" Still here? Oh, good!" It was Jean coming across the empty floor carrying a box. "Arthur forgot to take the cookies home! I've got them in here! Do you guys want some cookies?"

"No thanks," Jen said.

"I've never seen Charlotte eat a cookie, actually," Mark said. "What about Bert, Jen?"

"I've no idea."

"Well, hold this a moment would you, Mark, and let's turn these last lights off. What an evening! I'm afraid you'll get a rather odd picture of our society! Mind the door! It swings back rather hard. Oh, thank you, Mark. Do you think Larry will be OK? He's going to have to be careful. Charlotte's in the van? Of course! The chair! Well, let me just come over and say goodnight. She was so brilliant tonight! Left some of us behind, I'm afraid. Charlotte! I've brought Mark out with me! You were just so precious to come all this way and I don't have to tell you how much we enjoyed having you and Mark here. Mark, in you get and I'll close the door. Bert! Mark's got some cookies in the box! Oh, goodnight, hon. Mark's just helping Bert get Charlotte's chair fixed firm. I'll tell him you said goodnight."

18

Valentine's Day at the Mall

"It might be better if we were parked in front of the rest rooms," Rachel said. "At least we'd get some traffic." Facing their display tables an empty window announced: "OPENING SOON! Ready to Go Totes and Accessories." Beyond that was an entrance to Sears, open to a broad aisle of dishwashers and kitchen stoves.

They were in a row down the center of the Pelican Mall: Orchid Empire, Bios Orchids, No Limit Orchids, (Larry and Ken) and Hanson's, (Bert); anchored at the Sears end by a cart festooned with silk flowers and at the other by two silent Iranian brothers in a kiosk selling watches. Above them dangled and drifted fat, heart-shaped, pink balloons, nosing and bumping the girders overhead gently like fish in an aquarium.

"I'm sorry. Larry, everyone, it was a dumb idea."

"Rachel! It seemed a good idea *at the time*. God! Is *that* the story of my life!"

They had to stay till nine in the evening, when the mall closed. It was so empty voices echoed as though they were in a large indoor swimming pool. "Did we actually see this advertised anywhere?" queried Ken. "You usually get at least a few orchid people wandering in."

"But the watch guys aren't doing any better."

"Well, the management better be careful with Iranians!" Larry said. "We were selling next to some Iranians at a Home Show on Miami Beach once. It turned out to be a scam, no promotion! No-one was there! Rather like today! Anyway the phony promoters threatened to sue any vendor who left. The guys start rolling up their carpets. And Ken goes over: 'Didn't the guy threaten you?' And the Iranian says

221

'Yes, he threatened me and I said 'Don't threaten me. I am Iranian. I can have you killed for fifty dollars!' Of course," added Larry, "that *was* a few years ago. It might cost a bit more now."

"So what happened?" asked Mark.

"Oh, we all packed up and left!"

"Well, maybe we could try that here," Rachel said.

"If the guys selling watches know the right people."

"The problem is Valentine's day isn't on a Friday or weekend, this year," Bert said.

"I think we'd do better outside at the traffic lights," Rachel muttered, "like the people with the bunches of flowers."

"And whose bright idea was it to let that silk flower woman in?" demanded Larry. "Here we all are with living plants and there's that woman with whole floral centerpieces and dinner table settings and the care sheet for them all is one word: *Dust.* Though let me tell you, with fancy designs like those, that can be a pain too."

The management of Pelican Mall had offered good terms: reduced rent for tables, no extra display required and just the one day, February 14, Valentine's Day. And they'd called Rachel of all people. "Someone must have got my number at Las Olas." After the trek up there it was so close, Rachel said, it had sounded almost fun; just friends, the old gang and business had been a little slow and the Miami Expo was still at least two weeks away. But they were not even in the middle of the mall, they were stranded up at the north end where it was so empty Bert didn't even ask anyone to keep an eye on his orchids while he popped into Sears to get some bits for his drill.

"Talking about shop lifting, did you hear what happened at Las Olas?" Rachel asked. "The old woman with the golfing umbrella? Alvin said she was tipping small orchids off the display tables into the top." Rachel was the most talkative Mark had ever seen her, so apologetic she'd got everyone into "this *mess!*"

"No, not your fault" Bert said mildly. "Valentine's *should* be good. And now we've got Secretary's Day," he added. "That was the floral people."

"And Grandma's Day and Mother-in-Law's Day," said Ken. "I can just see Mother-in-law's Day in this mall."

Now it was afternoon they were getting some teenagers out of school; the young mothers with toddlers were gone. There were still some old men on the seats enjoying the air conditioning, as serenely indifferent to the pull of the market place as the pensioners warming up in municipal public libraries in England. "Hey, let's cheer up!" Larry said. "Let's talk about *The Talk!*"

"Now we have to watch out for Miami," Rachel warned. "We've pissed off Regina so totally there's going to be even more venom let loose."

"Whatever happens it was worth it," Larry announced. "Watching Regina self-destruct in front of the faithful. Even the loyal Harry registered that." A couple had stopped in front of No Limit's table. Larry drifted back "Hi! Can I help you with anything?" They started to back away, wide eyed and silent. Larry returned. "It's a good job I know I'm adorable or this whole day would be very traumatic."

At least, Mark said, there was no demand in the mall for orchid knowledge or expertise. Not that it would matter now everyone present knew he didn't know anything. "But you did very well at Sun Corner," Ken protested.

"Did you plan all that with Charlotte?" Rachel asked. "And the whole Chelsea Flower Show bit?"

"No. It was all made up as we went along. Charlotte says the way not to stammer and screw up is just to throw yourself in, cold. Of course, I thought she was just sadistically playing with me, the old cat and mouse routine."

"Oh, believe you me," said Larry. "That too. That's Charlotte."

"You make Charlotte sound so mean," Rachel protested.

"It's her survival technique, Rachel," Larry said.

Rachel was in a bright pink T-shirt, indigo blue jeans and brand new tennis shoes. Her hair was cut somehow that, short as it was, it could still swing forward to be tucked back again and again. Her nails were still bitten down; the fingers in fact quite stubby. Rachel was certainly much more friendly and open now, now that it didn't matter any more. If you were talking the language of flowers, Mark reflected, you'd say my feelings have dwindled to the small, brown, *Encyclia* size, the ones here which aren't selling at fourteen-fifty though fragrant. Steadfast but just friendly. What Larry would call a very English kind of love.

"Thank God you had your fit when you did, Larry," Mark said, "because apparently the next slide was the Horse Guards Parade. And then some hotel in Kenya. Charlotte had just grabbed a few odd slides she had from the couple who live on their boat in the Keys."

By six Ken declared they had broken some kind of record. The whole bunch between them had sold only eight orchids and three of those had been Bert's little pink Phalaenopsis. Mark had sold nothing at all.

Rachel was surprised her Calanthes hadn't moved. "Did you guys know there's a new *Phaius Calanthe* intergeneric hybrid? A '*Phaio-calanthe*'? It's so neat because the very *first* orchid hybrid was a *Calanthe* and one of the earliest intergenerics was a *Phaiocalanthe* registered in the nineteenth century, in England, way early, in the eighteen fifties or close."

"Well, Mark, there's a conversation piece for you," said Larry.

"How long are you here for?" Bert asked.

"I'll have about another ten days after the Expo."

"I'm afraid we haven't been taking you round," Ken apologized.

"We've all been busy," Mark said. "Show season! That's why I was here in the first place."

By now it was dark outside. The only passers by who showed any interest in Orchid Empire were two teenage girls in tight black T-shirts and jeans, lips outlined in black. They were as dark as Indian or Pakistani teenagers from Totters Green, bursting with the promise of young motherhood.

"Hi," said Mark cautiously. "Can I interest you in anything?" They found this so funny they had to bury their laughter in each others' shoulders.

"You're Mark, aren't you?" said the girl who'd spoken, lifting her head.

"Yes?" said Mark even more cautiously.

"You're from Inglan,' right?"

"Yes?"

"You know Carlos Vicente?"

"Yes!"

"He's my Dad!"

"Wow," said Mark.

Carlos' daughter was sobering up. She nodded her head. "Uh Huh. So how's it going?"

"You can tell your Dad it's a good job we didn't pack up many plants."

The girls were already getting restless, their eyes looking everywhere, not catching his. "Jus' wannid say Hi."

"Well, um, nice to meet you. I'll certainly tell Carlos, your *Dad*, I saw you."

"Don' tell him when! I gotta be in by siss dirty." By now it was seven fifteen. Carlos' daughter giggled and nodded at her friend. "I'm over her house right now studying!" Peals of laughter and they leaned against each other for support. "OK! Bye!" and they moved off, heads together, looking back at him and flashing grins.

"What was all that about?" Larry had come over.

"Carlos' daughter. And a friend," said Mark, still a little bemused.

"No kidding! Well, that's it: second generation! Story of America, Mark."

"Story of everywhere, now," said Mark.

"Hi, guys! Doesn't look like you've sold much!" It was Jen.

"Oh, you didn't have to come!" Rachel was returning from a walk down to J C Penney's and back. "You should have called Larry. Didn't I give you his cell? There's nothing doing. It's absolutely dead."

"Oh, that's OK. It's on the way home."

"Hi, Jen! You want to wander round the mall a bit? There's nothing doing here," Larry said. "You could catch up with Ken, maybe. He's gone to check out dress shirts on sale. Bert says there's a sale on power drills in Sears."

"Well, maybe one of *you* wants to—I mean go round the mall," said Jen. "I can keep an eye on things. Or would anyone like a coffee, something to eat or drink?"

"No. Everyone's fine."

"That's all we've been doing all day it's been so slow," Rachel said. Jen was standing in front of the tables, holding her briefcase. "You might as well go on home." Jen hesitated. Mark said, "Come and sit down for a bit anyway. You can watch the parade of non-buyers stroll by."

"I didn't realize it would be this bad." Jen slid in between the tables and Mark took the cash box off the other chair.

"You're looking very nice."

"Whenever you say something like that you always sound really surprised." Jen was wearing the light, peach colored suit Mark remembered from Las Olas that made her look warm and dark, almost Latin, and shiny peach lipstick. And she'd done something to her hair. Whatever it was, it looked much better than before, and if he didn't jump in with another subject, Mark knew he'd probably tell Jen exactly that. "Why are malls so depressing?"

Jen raised her eyebrows and shrugged. "I suppose as an economist I should say they pack a lot of economic punch."

"Except this one."

"Well, it's getting a little rainy but it is Valentine's. Maybe it's this end of the mall."

"Anyone send you a Valentine at the office, Jen?" Larry called over. "Oh, *right!*"

"Well, why not?" asked Mark gallantly to make up for his earlier remark. Jen gave him a quick look. "Well, guys," she'd caught sight of Ken, "you either brought in a truck load of stuff or you haven't sold much."

"No, but between us and the public we've managed to break some flower spikes."

"It seems a shame for you just to wait around till the mall closes," Mark said.

"You want me to go?"

"No, of course not. It's just I always think of you as doing heavy duty stuff down town while we kind of mess around in the sweaty end of the county like today. It looks like you've brought homework back with you." Mark nodded to Jen's briefcase. It was so full she had to lean it against a table leg. Jen nodded with a half smile but didn't say more. The talking had died down. Jen had missed all the best moments, thought Mark. Everyone had got tired, tired of not selling, tired of talking to pass the time and just wanted to go home.

"Maybe I'll just look around for a while," Jen got up. "It's OK if I leave the brief case here?"

"Of course! Don't hurry. We're all here till nine."

"Jen! You're still here!" Ken exclaimed. "You've got your car, right?" It was a quarter to nine and Jen had just reappeared. It didn't look as though she had bought anything. People were making their way to the exits. "Finally we have some action!" said Larry dryly.

"Let me help" Jen said, in front of Orchid Empire's table. "Where are you parked?"

"No, that's OK. There's not much." Mark realized he'd said the wrong thing. Jen had stayed around in the mall, keeping out of the way but in order to offer help at the end, just like one of the shows. "Well, actually, thanks. If you could stay here with this lot and I'll take these. But what about Rachel?"

"Ken took an extra load out for her. She's gone." It looked like they were the last ones. There was the standard, broad black man with a bunch of keys holding open the heavy glass door. The great expanse of car park was emptying, dark but shining. It had been raining. There was the Volvo, solid and patient, and what must have been Jen's car, in the distance. The security man held the door for Mark again, and for Jen. Mark was sagging under the weight of her brief case which he'd hung on one arm, under a tray of plants. "God, What have you go in here? End of the year tax stuff?"

"Something like that." They filled up the Volvo in the dark. Away in the dark were the lights of US1. The air was damp from the rain. A weak cold front; what was snow up in New York or even Kentucky, was a wet car park shining in South Dade. "I should escort you to your car, off in the middle distance. God, these car parks are so big."

"It was silly of me to come," Jen remarked quietly, more to herself than Mark.

"Well, I think it's starting to rain again. Um, have you eaten?" Mark asked cautiously.

"That's all right," Jen said, "you've been eating all day."

"Well, I would die for a beer. Isn't there a pub anywhere? Maybe we could find somewhere on US1?" A pick up truck appeared, wheeling round the corner of the mall and heading towards them. Mark thought if it's someone after the day's take, then anyone who'd been checking out Orchid Empire in the mall would be more likely to slip him a sympathetic dollar than ask for the cash box. But he didn't like the way it was heading straight for them.

Jen exclaimed, "It's Coop!" Cooper stopped alongside with a jerk. "I came to see how you guys were doing but forgot the mall winds down at nine." He hopped out of the cab and stood there, hands tucked in his windcheater. "So how did it go?" Balancing lightly on the balls of his feet, Cooper looked ready to settle down for a chat in the dark in a light drizzle.

"Cooper! It's raining," Jen said. "Do you know where we could get a beer?"

"I was going to this Thai restaurant. They've modified the dishes too much but they do use peanut oil."

Screw the peanut oil, thought Mark. "Do they serve beer?"

"Of course," said Cooper. "Follow me."

"I come here all the time." Cooper had settled them into a crimson vinyl booth with large, red menus, half the size of the table. The lighting was bright enough to meet the requirements of the Royal College of Surgeons. Overhead hung elaborate scarlet and gold lanterns and golden dragons. Framed models of gilt temples hung against the walls and golden gondolas sat on the window sills. There was a lot of detailed workmanship on display and, thought Mark, there was certainly the light to see it by. It was a shock to face Cooper close up, in such a bright light. For someone who preferred the shadows, Mark decided, it was certainly not the case when he ate. His hair was still pulled back into a neat, short pigtail and he looked healthy enough, sporting a solid, all season tan. If Cooper only came out after dark, how come he was so sunburnt? Well, he had to look after his orchids.

Mark was thinking the only time he had actually seen Cooper was Christmas Eve. He was in the usual T-shirt but there was no message on it, only rather disconcertingly, right in the middle, a large painted eye. Cooper suggested at such a late hour, just soup and rolls.

"Just beer," said Mark. "Jen, beer's OK for you?"

"So I hear Mark is not the orchid man," Cooper began, in his soft, Southern voice.

"No," said Jen, "but he managed an orchid talk! You should have been there, Coop."

"I was. Glenda and her friend are an interesting pair."

"So you heard all about Regina and Charlotte and Larry's fit."

"Rachel told me. Regina is learning that all existence is suffering," stated Cooper. Mark wasn't sure if he was joking.

"And, hopefully," said Jen, "what goes around comes around—right, Coop?"

Cooper looked towards the window and focused for a longtime on the car lights moving on US1. After a while Mark thought probably the Buddhist part of the conversation had ended and said, "This beer isn't bad."

Cooper turned his eyes back to the table. "So Mark, you are not one of us? An orchidist?"

"Only by royal decree from Charlotte."

Cooper smiled gently. "Well, that should do it for most places." The soup arrived and Cooper spoke to the waiter.

"So you know Thai?" Jen said.

"Oh, he doesn't understand Thai," Cooper said, slowly stirring his soup. Before Mark and Jen could ask more, Cooper remarked, "So everyone's getting ready for the Expo."

"Starting to run round in circles again," Jen said. "You're well out of it, Coop. Though," she added, "everyone's lucky to have you; all those orchids you just lend out."

"My interest is just more long term, especially with vandas. Breeding for fragrance. Watch people. You take a flower. You say 'How beautiful.' You bring it forward to your face, your nose. Quite instinctive. A painting? A necklace? You say 'How beautiful,' and you hold it *away* to view. Well, I seek the fragrance and I seek the sublime. Rachel and Charlotte are welcome to the rest." Mark wondered if Cooper were independently wealthy. "Oh, Charlotte always gives me something for them," Cooper added as though he'd read Mark's mind. "Sometimes too much. And Rachel does my bottles, my lab work, so it all rolls along."

That could be why Rachel was always worried about money, too, thought Mark. So much of her lab work was Cooper's. Maybe, in fact, she wasn't getting such a fair deal after all but more likely she, like Cooper, was so interested in all these crosses, she couldn't resist making more. "She's a clever girl," Charlotte had said. "Investment of time and labor! A few years down the road, what with Coop's new crosses, and the more sophisticated market plus all the lab remakes of species you can no longer get, she should be sitting pretty."

"And Rachel says you're making your escape, "Cooper turned to Jen.

"Yes, out from among the bottles."

Cooper shook his head. "Rachel was real lucky with you." His voice was so soft and low you had to really listen. Maybe that was all part of his Buddhism: the Zen of really listening, thought Mark.

"Mark and I think Rachel and Charlotte should get together, Cooper. You know, pool resources." Cooper looked down at his empty soup plate. He started thinking about this and stayed thinking about it so long that Mark had asked Jen in a low voice if she'd like another beer and they'd decided no and checked their watches, so by the time Cooper finally said, "Yes, good idea," they'd almost forgotten what the idea was.

"Anyway, Rachel is feeling better in spite of the whole Expo thing," commented Jen, "the way we zapped Regina."

"Regina still wants to fight, to control," Cooper suddenly grinned. "Not interested yet in setting herself free of passion."

"You can say that again!" Mark laughed. "Cooper's right. I've decided passion is overrated. Better have a cat and watch football, right Jen?"

Jen started to smile and then changed her mind. "It's getting late, everyone. Sorry, Mark, I should have taken my car."

Mark drove the Volvo back to the dark, empty wasteland of the mall car park. The windscreen wipers scraped and clunked in the silence. Jen, so lively with Cooper, had stopped talking. Mark wanted to say, needed to say, Hey I'm so *over* Rachel! Like a bloody Californian teenager: *She is SO yesterday!* Christ, then there was the whole daft lesbian thing. *And* New Year's Eve. With the orchid talk Jen had been so mellow, supportive. Mark needed a pub. A noisy pub. Even without Cooper present, a surgically bright Thai restaurant didn't cut it. With Jen silent beside him, staring ahead, tonight obviously wasn't the night. But the Expo was coming right up. And anyway, he'd call before then. Jen opened the door of the Volvo, car keys already in her hand. "Well, happy Valentine's Day."

"God, yes! How could I forget?"

"Good night." The rain was coming down harder. Jen was walking away fast on the passenger side. Bloody great car park. No way to say, let's pop into a pub. Such great spaces. Jen was already starting her car. Mark suddenly had a vision of being in a classic, noisy pub with her. The public bar, someone playing darts behind them, some old guy grinning at them both, the noise, that odd mix of openness and privacy, the shoulders, the sexy smell of coats coming in from the rain, up close, and suddenly, so close, as you tried to get a pint, it was closer than dancing with someone. He sat watching the lights of Jen's car receding across the empty, wet car park. Saw her taillights braking red as she slowed down approaching US1, the turn signal blinking and flickering in the rain as she drew out into the line of traffic and disappeared.

19

The Beginning of the End

"So one more orchid show and you'll be gone. I'll miss you." Althea was in the kitchen with Mark, having tea. Charlotte was resting after having been 'pulled about.'

"I'll miss *you* Althea but you wouldn't be coming much longer, anyway."

"No. I'd just visit for my tea." Althea gave one of her big laughs. "You should stick around. I think South Florida suits you. Find yourself a nice girl."

"What about you, Althea?"

Althea smiled. "You keep on like that I'm going to scare you one day, I'll say yes."

"Actually," Mark admitted, "that would scare me a bit."

Althea gave another gust of laughter. "Would be quite a trip though!"

What am I doing NOW? Mark asked himself. *I go nuts over one girl and immediately sleep with her friend. Despite the evidence arising from aforesaid episode I decide both are lesbians. I ignore repeated overtures from said friend until realizing I'm starting to have serious feelings in that direction I immediately propose marriage to an African American therapist who is taller than me.* "How's Charlotte really, Althea? She's going to be alright to be on her own again?"

"It's real good having Ruby come more. For Ruby, too."

"Well, we were all hoping we could get Charlotte and Rachel together, combine the two orchid businesses. Have Rachel live here but that's a lot to be worked out."

"Rachel, she's the blonde? Haven't seen her but once. She's a bit...

know what I mean... full of herself?"

"Preoccupied. Another orchid person."

"Like the one we had the run in with at New Year? How's that all playing out? Charlotte says you must make her as dust beneath your chariot wheels! She can sound like Ruby when she wants."

"Yes, Charlotte may not believe in anything but she can certainly put the fear of God in you. When it comes to the President of the orchid society we've been thinking up crazy scenarios, like tying up a goat in her exhibit the night before judging, you know to eat all the prize blooms."

"Need to find yourself a Haitian, someone from the islands. You know I bet security is all black and half Caribbean. You could swing it!"

"You know anyone?"

"No, but Cubans are deep into sacrifices and stuff too. They've got shrines at home and the whole thing. I've seen a goat's *head* by the side of the road, before now. You could try putting a spell on the woman! Get an Orisha! —One of their gods! And it's all African! Charlotte could tell you."

"That's West Africa, Charlotte says. She was East."

"Maybe but she's got one of those gods round here somewhere. Try the Florida room. Ruby found something. I know because she was telling Charlotte to put her faith in the Lord and not graven images! And it spooked Ruby, it's got razor blades sticking up in the head."

"You're kidding."

"No, and the one with the blades I know. Two of my girls on the team, Cuban, were joking around about the most powerful god to have in your corner—just before regionals. It seems this one has the knives to show his power: God of the Crossroads!"

"Where on earth would he come from? Charlotte doesn't seem to know any Cubans."

"Maybe Florida City Swap Meet. Before Andrew that was a great place. Folks would come from Homestead Air Force Base, selling stuff. Before shipping out, I guess. That old spear may come from there. Charlotte said she used to go sometimes, like when she was looking for stuff before a show." Althea finished her tea. "*OK!* You got to get that god out and dust him down and give him some offerings, that's what my girls said. A little rum, maybe, some coins. Maybe as this is all orchid business, an orchid flower or a bunch. You need to cook up something *real* strong." Althea was having a good time now. "And hey, can't do any harm and maybe not a good idea to leave a god like that too dusty and overlooked. Know what I mean? We all got enough bad luck in our life without encouraging more."

Intrigued, Mark went looking for the God of the Crossroads. It was on the floor, behind the pot of bull-rushes. Maybe Ruby had put it out of sight there. Not big, but quite a weight, looked like concrete, about four inches high, two old razor blades embedded in the top along with two small feathers. And when Mark turned it round, there was a startling, striking face; the eyes, nostrils and mouth made of cow-rie shells which mimicked the openings in the skull: the shells stuck in vertically for the ears. The eyes, like the eyes of Regina's Buddha, almost closed as the cowrie shells were almost closed. Mark brought him into the kitchen. "Here he is. Where should we put him?"

"I don't think we want him facing up to Ruby. Or Charlotte with her jokes. You ever hear about the mumbo jumbo affair? One after-noon Charlotte called Ruby's church-going *mumbo jumbo!* I tell you, it was almost the end right there! I had to follow Ruby out. She had marched through the dogs and was in her car turning the key."

"What happened? Did Charlotte apologize?"

"Yea. And Ruby wanted a real one. No half way. I think, deep down, she sees Charlotte ready to turn. Salvation down the road."

"Wow," said Mark." Ruby sees further than the rest of us."

"Hey, I gotta go. Thanks as *always* for the tea. And remember, for *you* Doctor Gibson is always *in!*" And there was that special whack of the wooden screen door swinging back against the door jamb, the sharp little red Mazda spitting out the gravel from the back tires and Althea was gone so quickly the dogs didn't even bother to bark.

Carlos had dismantled the ramp and Charlotte had begun to walk herself carefully down the porch steps every morning, leaning hard on her heavy black African walking stick. She said Mark and Carlos had been 'consistently over-watering' but that was a common mistake, one she was sometimes guilty of herself. And Mark knew that was as close as Charlotte would ever get of saying Thank-you, thank-you for keeping Orchid Empire going.

Charlotte had not been at all surprised they had sold nothing at the mall. "Don't know what she was thinking of! Rachel of all people. Maybe the lab work has fallen off; certainly I haven't been getting much material over to her and, of course, she has to shoulder all the expenses now Jen's gone."

"*Gone?*" They were on the porch as usual, in the late afternoon. "Where's she gone?"

"According to Rachel, California somewhere. Got a job interview, seeing friends. Given in her notice but actually quit, as they say, last week, right after Valentine's Day."

"She's not coming back?"

"Well, she was never intending to be a permanent fixture. She was here getting over some man, that cruise job was never meant to be a career. We'll certainly miss her. Especially Rachel, of course. Oh, and according to Larry, our Mike."

"When's she coming back? I mean to get her stuff?"

"*I* don't know." Charlotte looked over the top of the *Herald's* Business section at Mark for a moment but said nothing. Though after a while she remarked, apparently at random, "Rachel might have a number."

"I don't know" said Rachel. "You called her, right? Didn't she get back to you? She's seeing friends, hanging out. Lucky her! How's Charlotte? How's it looking for the Expo? Are the brassias holding? And the angraecums? And—hey, let me have a word with Charlotte."

"So now you're interested in Jen?" Charlotte had commented, having watched Mark scramble for the phone. "Always a day late and a dollar short! I thought you were all cows' eyes over Rachel."

"I was," Mark said simply, thinking it better to get it over with. What had Larry said? "Jen's salt of the earth. Attractive, just not a lot of oomph, know what I mean?" Being interested in someone like Jen was a private thing. But Jen had consistently seen him make cows' eyes, as Charlotte put it, over Rachel, close up. Jen was in California now, about as far away as she could get. People went to California all the time and never came back.

Jen had been there right under his nose and he'd just looked over her and round her, searching for his magic moments. Always ready to put his head on one side in other peoples' houses, checking the titles of their books, sizing them up. Ever since New Year Mark had given the repeated message to Jen, that patronizing, *Oh, well, thanks for everything.* What was the best he could do? *Oh! You look nice!* Was that one better than: *Oh, you smell nice?* And Jen had actually come on Valentine's Day, no less, stayed behind. Stayed to help, when there was nothing to do. And then there was Cooper arriving and off they'd gone on damn orchid stuff again and to that restaurant, battling those massive menus and nattering on about Thai food.

In fact, it was Cooper who had said the nicest thing to Jen. Sitting in the restaurant, he had suddenly out of the blue commended her on her auspicious name, saying how it suited her. "Confucianism sees man as bound to man, social man, by *jen,* virtuousness, human sympathy. So you see what a name to have! And you are the right person so to be called."

And now Jen was in California surrounded not by certified Florida orchid nuts like Mike and Cooper but bright, high tech graduates who had taken *courses* on sensitivity and women's issues, who had the easy smiles and lighter, golden tans of the West Coast. While he would have to leave the country soon, unemployed, his visa expired. It had been Jen who said an extension was no problem. In fact, if it were, he could always get in touch with Carlos. Carlos had a relative for everything: the aunts for catering, an Uncle Victor for cars, and for paper work, a distant cousin, a plumber, who forged documents in his spare time.

Well, Mark had chosen to ignore Jen. Choices. The God of the Crossroads, the concrete head there down behind the bull-rushes. "So he's a good god to have around?" Mark had asked Althea. And Althea had said, "Not good or bad. But the most powerful, they say. He's the god of possibilities. Know what I'm saying? It depends on your choices."

Crunching through the last of the falling leaves to pick up the

Herald every morning, Mark reflected how perfect the elegiac, autumnal mood was. In England the crocus and celandines, the winter aconites and forsythia on the bare branches, had been struggling out and opening, everything starting to tremble with the fragile, lemony touch of Spring. Here leaves had been withering and falling since the freeze. In South Florida, Charlotte said, it was in spring that the branches went bare. It was the end of something, not the beginning, as though the brilliant South Florida sun in winter, the fruit and flowers, all those orchids, had been nothing but a vivid dream and now were all dead and gone. It was all over.

20

Preparations for the Miami Expo

Charlotte was going to be there for the Miami Expo. Not with the zooming, mechanized chair, but the light, fold up one that could go in the back of the Volvo. "Wouldn't miss this for the world. And in fact, dear boy, you'll need an extra bod Tuesday when they give out the greenery, make sure no-one pinches our palms accidentally on purpose. Carlos can push me around. He'll like that. Give him a chance to see what's going on."

"Any news of what Regina's up to?

"Someone's sending out press releases with wildly inflated numbers. Apparently the Expo had forty thousand through the doors last year. Ken said only if they all just marched through non stop like filing past Lenin's tomb."

"You don't let Regina get away with much, do you?" Mark observed.

"Dear boy, it's because she gets away with *everything* we, the few, the precious few, feel the need at least to record some of the worst excesses of her rule! Bad news on the Sun Corner front. Harry's caved in. They're going to hand their orchids over to Regina and her cohorts. We can only hope Glenda and her side kick insist on taking an aggressive part in the process, with their flea market specials."

"Why did they *do* that?"

"What? Give in? Tilly says Regina kept calling Harry and Leonard, the President and oh, at least half the members. Well, look how *you* caved in! Who's got the energy? She probably doesn't even *need*

238

Sun Corner's damn plants! It's all control. Still, Leonard said next year they *will* have a vote on it and there's some new blood coming into that society so there's hope. I really can't worry about it all any more. No, I've decided at this late stage, ignore the woman! She thrives on confrontation. She's a street fighter. I'm going to listen to Coop. He wraps it all up in Buddhist mumbo jumbo but basically it's like bull-fighting or Judo: turn aggressive energy against itself! Leave your enemy charging an empty space!"

That's what it would be with him, thought Mark. He would be leaving and however pissed off Regina was, however much she held a grudge, he'd be gone, an empty space. Gone like the whiny kids departing Disney-world in Orlando, getting off stiff-legged in the morning at Heathrow with a tan and a coloring book courtesy of British Air or Virgin Atlantic.

"Jen? No idea, dear boy. Rachel hasn't heard a thing and I don't think Jen left a number."

The theme of the Miami Orchid Expo was to be 'Orchid Fantasy.' "Right," said Charlotte, "two garden chairs and a bird bath. We'll be doing two hundred square feet again and everything's in bloom; makes it's harder to do a small exhibit, to make choices. Takes longer to pack a small bag than a big one! Time to get out the clip board and look around! Of course, not a snowball's chance in hell of awards but we want to put on a show. Always good exposure for Rachel."

"And then, when I leave—You're going to be OK on your own?"

But even as he said it, Mark knew Charlotte wasn't really on her own. Still, what if she fell at night? "What if you fell again?"

"I'm not going up any more ladders!"

"No, I mean just fell."

"Then if I can't get to the phone I'll lie there till Carlos and Rosita come in the morning! Don't you go worrying your mother about me! By the way have you called her? Does she know when you're coming? When to put a hot water bottle in the bed?"

Mark realized he was not the person to bring up the whole question of Rachel and Charlotte combining forces. He was not an orchid person, he was family, as Larry said. When he talked about Orchid Empire and Bios Orchids merging, it was with the image of an old woman and sturdy young one sharing grocery bills, an elderly relative getting past it, not a leading orchidist joining forces with a rising star.

Certainly Orchid Empire was ready for a show. Suddenly the greenhouse was full of blooms; Mark's favorite, a beautiful, imperial purple *Vanda* that he hardly dared drag the hose near, for fear of marring its velvet face.

"Traditionally there's always been breeding done, of course, precisely so that orchids will hit at show time," Charlotte said. "But there's still plenty of time for freeze, flood, Act of God and what happens inside the van when you jam on the brakes on the way to the hall. Well, you're an old hand now, after *Las Olas*. And then, it's off you go!"

The *Cattleya lueddemanniana* that kept falling over at Las Olas had faded, worn out being a star for four days on its milk crate throne. But the *Cattleya guatemalensis* had hit it right: at least eleven beautiful orange flower spikes. In addition there was *Cattleya mossiae* and *skinneri*. A shame, thought Mark, making the list, the men discovering all these exotic, gorgeous orchids had such humdrum names. A whole bank of orchids was in bloom outside the green houses now, the stems climbing out of their old plastic pots with "seasonal exuberance" as Charlotte put it, up to fifteen feet high, in a riot of pink like rambling roses. "*Vanda* Miss Agnes Joachim, the national flower of Singapore —'*Joe-ah-Kim*,' though everyone is so used to Spanish here they all say '*Miss Wah keem*,' and there's my favorite, the tough old local, the orange and scarlet *Epidendrum radicans*. User friendly! Survives dogs and kids! Not to be put in unless we're desperate."

That might even happen, thought Mark as Charlotte had no more commercial white and pink *Phalaenopsis*. She had sold them cheap to a needy florist, even before Valentines, as though already gearing up for the stern, high standards of Rachel. But for the Miami Expo she had held onto half a dozen creamy yellow ones and a cluster of oncidiums. Some of the little brown and lemon fragrant encyclias had survived their day in the mall, ready to grace the more appreciative venue of the Expo. And two more fragrant cattleyas had come into bloom, big shouldered and broad, their flowers magnificently pinned on to their fronts, like ladies in their heyday on Miami Beach.

Rachel didn't have much flowering material; she'd be providing mostly seedlings. In that way, thought Mark, it was obvious Bios and Orchid Empire already worked together as a viable partnership. Larry and Ken were lending one or two of their 'pets' to Bert but promised Rachel and Charlotte two gems: a *Phalaenopsis schilleriana* and a *Phalaenopsis stuartiana.* "*Phalaenopsis* species for the purist!" Charlotte declared. "And Rachel has sib crossed each of them, and has seedlings to sell. I only hope Cooper doesn't forget about the *Renanthera* for the Expo. That thing anywhere else would get an AM, Award of Merit. *Renanthera elongata,* great *gorgeous,* branching scarlet inflorescence, tiny flowers but up to one hundred ninety on *one* stem. But Coop seems to have disappeared. Off with Mike apparently. They've been thick as thieves the last few days."

"We'll put it on the garden chair," suggested Mark.

"You know, dear boy, this is going to be the show when we have so much good stuff, so many stars, we won't have enough chairs. What we need is some elevation for display. It's a shame. So much in bloom and it's Miami, the Expo, Regina's call."

"*Orchid Fantasy... Orchid Fantasy.*" Mark was brooding about what they would call their exhibit; all those wonderful blooms engulfing a bird bath and two old iron chairs with the paint flaking off. Mark thought what was fantastic were just the orchids themselves: flowers like faces, faces that were all whiskers or lips, orchids like insects, spiders, moths, testicles, pudenda, pigtails and buckets. Lips like tongues, like shovels, brilliant little shovels or coal scuttles, Dutch clogs and frilly cravats, just the most sexy of flowers as Larry said, with those trumpet entrances and velvet caves for waddling bugs. "Examples of what Darwin's treatise calls: '*The Various Contrivances by Which Orchids are Fertilized by Insects,*'"Charlotte said. "You should read at least that. Had it somewhere but, same old story, lent it to some student judge."

"By the way, Charlotte, Larry called, he was wondering what was going to be your *Fantasy?*" Larry had been laughing: "Charlotte's two garden chairs! How *fantastic!*"

"Who cares? Two garden chairs and a bird bath," she said firmly. "It's only two hundred square feet, for God's sake! It's not the bloody cricket ground at Lords! I tell you," said Charlotte one more time, "you put in what you've got. No soul searching required."

242

21

Monday: The Sand

Monday was finding the exhibit spot and the allocation of sand; Tuesday allocation of palms and greenery and Wednesday "You trundle in the plants and get cracking." Wednesday was Putting in the Exhibit, the day Rachel would rent the U haul. Monday morning after they finished the watering, Mark and Carlos laid two shovels in the back of the Volvo and took off for Miami and the Expo hall.

They arrived about ten and marched across the parking lot with their shovels. Carlos had slung his over his shoulder where it rode along like a rifle or the traditional implement of the working man. Mark, too self conscious for this classic pose, discovered that grasping a shovel in one hand for any distance was not easy. After banging his shins repeatedly and then briefly holding the thing aloft with two hands like the standard bearer for the Municipal Grave-Diggers Union, for the last few yards he swung it over his shoulder like Carlos and they arrived at the Expo entrance looking like a pair ready to work for bread and soup and a night in the hayloft.

Rachel had said she would meet them there, on their show spot; to make sure, Mark thought, he wasn't duped out of Orchid Empire's ration of sand. He and Carlos plunged into the Expo with their shovels. It was huge, light and airy, the sort of place where they held boat shows and towed in sail boats complete with masts. Workmen were setting up towering palms, tall as masts themselves, in the central area. There were no shovels or spades but front loaders and hydraulic platforms moving boulders of coral rock. And around this central oasis with its palmettos and ferns were the exhibition spaces and beyond

243

those, circling the perimeter, would be the booths of the nurseries exhibiting and then furthest out, beyond those, the people selling Orchid Fantasy T-shirts, baskets and painted plates.

Rachel and Charlotte had agreed that of course Orchid Empire would be allocated a bad spot even though the whole process was supposed to be by lottery. "The President always gets the best spot for Orchid Magic," Charlotte explained. "Well, it's traditional, it dates all the way back to that historic moment when Regina became President." Mark didn't have the floor plan with him. Charlotte thought she must have mislaid it. "Rachel will be there. Someone will know, or go to the office. Or just look for the worst spot; that'll be us!"

Mark and Carlos started marching round the periphery with their shovels, along the rows of chalked outlines on the floor, each with the name of the exhibitor, a few already with sand. Mark couldn't see the name Orchid Empire anywhere and there was no one to ask. He saw only workmen and a few nursery people. Then he caught sight of Bert and his two workers who nodded to Carlos as Bert came over. "Try and keep Rachel from doing anything silly," he said. Before Mark had time to digest this, Alvin emerged from behind an impressive heap of sand. He walked over, grinning. "You're in for some fun," he said. "Your girl friend is mad and on the loose! Well, this time, I don't blame her."

Mark felt the first thing he should do was put down his shovel. But Charlotte had said you don't leave anything around the first day. There's no security; it'll get pinched. And Mark didn't feel like giving it to Carlos to hold, along with his: *Here, my good man! Hold my shovel!* The thing to do was to keep on trudging with Carlos and look for Rachel or, according to Alvin and Bert, listen for raised voices and breaking glass.

"Mark!" It was Rachel behind him. "Mark! They've screwed us over totally. They're saying we don't have a spot at all! Something about having sent a letter, and someone calling. *Bull*-shit! Hard for me to lodge a protest because I'm not Orchid Empire or not officially here really till the judging. You'll have to do it on behalf of Charlotte!"

Carlos had put down his shovel, smiling benignly at Rachel till hearing her tone of voice, averted his eyes and gazed discreetly off into the middle distance. Rachel was wearing crisp blue jeans and a tight, white T-shirt. Her hair was pulled back, sleek and shining, held with tortoiseshell clips, no stringy shoe lace or piece of rag. It was a shame, thought Mark; Rachel had come ready to be professional, keep a low profile. Without this crisis she would have been as cool and crisp as a standard white, professionally elegant *Phalaenopsis*. "OK. Where am I supposed to go and what am I supposed to say?"

"*Where* is our space, our two hundred square feet! And let's hurry before all the sand goes! Near the main entrance! On the left. The office is there."

"Well, try and keep it cool. I'm sure we can work this out." Still not wanting to play boss, Mark nearly handed over his shovel to Rachel rather than Carlos but looking at her face, thought better of it. A small front loader was grinding about, weaving through the scattered workers, shoveling in sand and dumping it in piles, each pile a show spot. The Miami Orchid Expo was a big operation. Amidst the noise of machinery, the shouting and hammering, Mark felt pretty insignificant and thought maybe he should have held on to his shovel. But he was there to play it cool, not to storm in, not even to lodge a complaint but just to ask nicely, where were they supposed to be; where was Orchid Empire's spot.

To the left of the main entrance was a trestle table with a scattering of the inevitable clip boards and three metal chairs. Just behind, a passageway made a right angled turn and stopped in front of two doors; one closed said No Admittance the other, General Office, was ajar. Mark stood in the little passage way. Behind him he could hear shouts and the whine of machinery and after listening for a moment, suddenly a cough, and voices. He knocked on the General Office door with his knuckles. But with the noise behind him, after three tries, said "Hallo!" and cautiously put his head round the door.

Mark was not sure what he'd been expecting. He'd been in America long enough to take for granted at least an automatic appearance of openness and warmth, an ease in social relations if not always the genuine good cheer of those solid orchid ladies with the clipboards. Regina herself was not present but as he emerged from behind the door Mark felt a chill, almost a hard freeze. There were three people; the two behind desks were a plump young man and a smart, silver-haired woman, and the third one, apparently visiting, Marjorie. Mark waited a moment for Marjorie to introduce him but she said nothing. None of the trio did. They just looked at him. In that moment Mark realized how, to some extent, even though Rachel was out of the Expo, even though he'd seen Regina in action, he had never really believed all the stuff about her. It had all seemed on some level a little trivial like enjoying having a favorite teacher to hate. But here it was; there was no doubt these people were not just Regina's spear carriers as Larry called them, these were, for whatever reason, fully paid up party members. "Hi. I'm not sure where our spot is. I'm here for Orchid Empire. I'm afraid I'm rather new at this, and probably it's all quite obvious..."

"Didn't Rachel tell you?"

"No. What?"

"Letters were sent, quite a while ago."

"What letters?"

"Didn't Orchid Empire get the phone calls?"

"No. Nothing."

"Charlotte *was* called."

"Unfortunately as no one at Orchid Empire answered the letters. Or the phone calls—"

"Well, no one expected an answer. Everyone knew Charlotte's been sick." There was a silence.

"So you're saying there is *no* spot for us, for Orchid Empire?" Mark began slowly, after a moment. The plump young man heaved a sigh. "Nothing *we* can do. I can't understand why no one told you. Well, Charlotte has been sick. Hard for her to keep up with everything."

"A blessing, really," said the silver-haired woman. "Charlotte doesn't need all this." No, indeed, thought Mark. Marjorie said nothing

"What am I, are we supposed to do?" Mark asked, in a tone of wonder. It was obviously, as Rachel said, bullshit.

"Well, no one else is here. We are just here to make sure the sand is given out."

"Charlotte was planning to come tomorrow," Mark began slowly.

246

"Is that going to be too late to sort all this out? Or should I call her now?" It was ten to eleven.

"We can't do anything, I'm afraid. We are just—"

"Doing the sand," said Mark.

"Right!"

The trio looked at him. Marjorie couldn't suppress a little smile. Mark wondered if he should go home for Charlotte. Ruby would be getting lunch. "So you are saying definitively there is no spot, no space for Orchid Empire, our two hundred square feet?" Mark began again.

They were not definitively going to say anything. They were going to say what they'd said before and if Mark needed more clarification they would obligingly say it all again. They knew nothing. Though for people who knew nothing, only sand, they certainly seemed to have followed closely the steps by which Charlotte and Orchid Empire would be exiled from the Expo. Mark sent up a silent apology. Charlotte might like a fight and Larry might get a little paranoid but here it was: these two behind the desks and Marjorie, were primed. They knew what they were supposed to say and they said it. "Will Regina be here tomorrow? Early?"

"Hard to say."

"Do you have a number where she can be reached?"

"Why do you want to talk to the President? Decisions were made by the Show Committee."

"So where's the Committee?"

"Monday? Not around, at all," the plump young man said, looking at his watch. "Tuesday? I really couldn't say. There's so much happening. Definitely Wednesday. Definitely."

"Wednesday's a little late, isn't it?"

He shrugged. "Well, it's not up to us. We're just doing the sand."

Even Charlotte seemed a little stunned when Mark called. "No place, no spot at all, eh?"

There was a pause. "Who was telling you all this? Marjorie? Interesting! Gone over to the other side! The other two, I've no idea. Mark, have you received any calls in the past weeks about this?"

"No, certainly not."

"I'm going to make some phone calls. Get back to me in an hour. Take Rachel off for brunch. And Carlos. No, let him hang out in the hall. He's going to know half the nursery guys there."

"Two versions of events" Charlotte began slowly, when Mark called back. "Two *misunderstandings*: everyone thought, no, *knew* I would not be doing the Expo this year. I have been so sick, confined to a wheelchair, a bed, a coffin. Not withstanding the fact we did Las Olas and trundled out to Sun Corner that night. So they were kindly going to refund my money and send a wreath to my funeral. *Misunderstanding* number two: someone thought Orchid Empire entered one hundred square feet, and now, if we need two hundred they only have this spot they can try and enlarge especially for us so we must say 'Thank you. How kind!'"

"Well, anyway, good," said Mark. "I thought it must be just a mistake but that pair in the office and Marjorie were acting like total—"

"You kidding?" cried Charlotte. "What do you think I've been doing? I've been on the phone to my lawyer! Now listen. By now Regina will have got back to her foot soldiers. You go back to the office and find out where our spot is. Never mind how bad! We need our spot. We need our sand."

"You're saying Charlotte didn't care *how* bad the spot was?" Rachel demanded.

"She wants us to get the sand." They were standing in a dead end, past a small square designated for the North Florida Amateur Orchid Species Preservation Club. Ahead, some feet in front of them, was a fire hydrant and three chest high, dark green plastic bins marked TRASH DO NOT REMOVE. To the right a small arrow pointed helpfully round the corner to the emergency exit. Along the wall above was a series of pipes, one above the other, part of the entrails of the Expo. "Well, if we want to sabotage the Expo, we're probably in the right place!" Mark joked. "Or tap into the lights for extra lighting..." his voice trailed off.

"Mark! We can't stay here!" Rachel was almost yelling. "You can't be serious!"

"Charlotte's coming tomorrow. Let's see what she says."

"Be too late to change it then!"

"Well, it's too late now," said Mark. "No one's going to give up their spot. And we have no bargaining power. This is obviously the pits but you know Charlotte! She may well use that fact as a bargaining chip. We've only got this far because of her lawyer. And we *are* getting our sand!" Mark said doggedly, while wondering if the front loader could even make it round the corner. It somehow seemed if they got their sand it would legitimize their claim. Get the sand. That's what Charlotte had said.

"Why even bother?"

"You bet we'll get the sand. We've been carting these bloody shovels round all day, right Carlos?"

Carlos smiled his sweet, general purpose smile. There's another word, thought Mark. God knows what the Spanish for shovel is. "So, Rachel! Who do we see about the sand? Oh, of course, that pair in the office. I bet they'll say we're too late or something."

"We're not going back to that office!"

Looking at Rachel Mark realized it didn't matter they were late trying to get sand. Send a Rachel into a group of construction workers and she could come back with anything she wanted; probably Orchid Empire's own personal front loader, probably her own squad of guys to shift the sand. And thinking along those lines, he heard himself asking: "Any word from Jen?"

Rachel was puzzled. "No?"

"By the way, is the ginger cat still around?"

"What? The cat? Haven't seen it for a few days. Since Jen left, in fact."

She'd taken the cat. If Jen had taken the cat she was not coming back.

22

Tuesday: The Palms

Mark wheeled Charlotte into the Expo hall Tuesday morning. She had on Bob's Bait and Tackle baseball cap, the cancelled check for the booth rental in her hand and her lawyer's phone number. "Business as usual at the Miami Expo!" she announced. Mark hadn't seen Charlotte so lively for a long time. There was a sparkle in her eye now and color in her cheeks that Cooper's Buddhist principles had failed to bring forth. "You'll never nail a woman like Regina with Cooper's approach. You need lawyers. When a lawyer asks a question you tend to get an answer."

The answer Charlotte's lawyer got was yes, the Miami Orchid Society had cashed Orchid Empire's check but that was way before Charlotte's accident and, yes, due to a clerical error there had not yet been a refund. However, there had been an understanding that Charlotte would not, could not, do the Expo. No, maybe nothing had surfaced in writing but it had been, "This is rich!" said Charlotte, 'a gentleman's agreement!'" And apparently the President herself had been in communication with a Dr. Gibson who was acting as Charlotte's spokesperson.

"So it's agreed that *Dr. Gibson* is the real culprit in all this. A Doctor who does not exist! How convenient! I told the lawyer pure fabrication! Not known at the hospital but supposedly in charge of my life! Have you ever heard of this person?"

"It sounds crazy to me," said Mark.

"Show me our spot!" Charlotte had commanded on arrival, "Let's see what the damage is." All around people were landscaping their chalked out squares: trundling in their rationed allocation of palms and greenery, the background for their Orchid Fantasies. Mark pushed

250

Charlotte's chair on and on, through the broad walkway between the central landscaped display and the exhibition spaces and on to the north end, past the future booth areas and on, beyond the North Florida Species Club Preservation Society who had still not arrived, stopping in front of the three trash cans and the wall busy with pipes, the sand just roughly spread out over Orchid Empire's one hundred square feet.

Mark could tell even Charlotte, always ready for the worst where Regina was concerned, was stunned. The dead end with the looming wall, the red light to the left: EMERGENCY EXIT, the trio of giant trash cans. "And this time we had so much good material. Would have been a wonderful display...We can sue them, they can refund money, but right now there's no way we can *make* them give us a decent space."

"I suppose we'll get the spin off from the North Florida Species Preservation Society," said Mark dryly. "Do you think anyone's going to make it out here?"

"We'll make damn sure everybody does!" Charlotte declared, rousing herself. 'If we can't make them give us a proper space by the same token they can't make us go away *if* we accept this spot!"

Rachel had not yet arrived. Mark had heard Charlotte on the phone with her the night before, telling her not to rush in, the lawyers would sort it out: this is America! And it's their job anyway.

"I wonder how much of the general Miami Orchid Society's funds go into Regina's legal defenses, to pay her lawyers?" Charlotte had mused. "For such a caring Christian woman it's remarkable how many law suits and legal spats she's been in! With any luck, she'll get someone to manhandle us out of the hall, me in a wheel chair! And she'll have another one! Maybe that's what our 'Dr. Gibson' was worried about!"

When Carlos appeared, having parked the Volvo, Charlotte told Mark to hang around keeping an eye on their space while she had Carlos wheel her over to the office. "Show I'm alive and well and cause them some grief; demand our *real* two hundred square feet. And make sure we get our palms and foliage, our *allocation* for two hundred square feet! All part of the package, Mark! Stay here in case they appear. Take whatever they've got."

It was certainly a quiet spot. The shouts and bangs from the central area sounded far away. No palms, fig trees, rubber plants or large ferns or anything else had appeared next door either; maybe Regina had invented the North Florida lot too, thought Mark, to cut Orchid Empire's space in half. And the exhibitors beyond North Florida, back towards the center, were erecting some sort of palisade, some background for their exhibit which was effectively going to cut off Orchid Empire from view. There was no traffic even to the bins.

When Charlotte reappeared with Carlos her color was still up and she looked fresh as a daisy. "One of Regina's little helpers was all ready to refund Orchid Empire's entry fee! Fancy! Who would have thought she'd have the authorization all by herself, early on a Tuesday morning? Oh, and the placing of show spots is all done by secret ballot—ask any committee member. *But* unfortunately, due to the pressure of the popularity of the show, and extra applications this year, there was the chance that some vendors would not get the choice spot they wished for!"

"Did you see Regina?" asked Mark.

"Course not! She's lying low. She knows no-one buys this rubbish. Well, here comes our greenery." A small fork lift ground into sight, bearing a six foot palm tree and a large straggly philodendron. "There'll be another palm and more greenery coming." Charlotte seemed to be going ahead, treating this bizarre corner as though it were a legitimate space. Mark wondered, not for the first time, that maybe stress and age were turning her 'doodle ally' as she called it. After the forklift returned with the second palm and two raggedy rubber trees Charlotte got Mark and Carlos to set the palms in place, one at each end of their space so they appeared to be framing the wall and the three trash cans. Maybe, thought Mark, maybe Charlotte's going to leave it like that and when the ladies come around with the clipboards, announce that yes, this is the exhibit and it's called, "Regina's Revenge.'

"Where's Rachel?" asked the young man operating the fork lift.

"Be here soon," said Charlotte, "I'll send her over." She sat back in her chair, on the edge of the sand, looking up at the wall between the palms.

"What do we do now?" Mark asked.

"I think it's going to be alright," Charlotte announced. "...Oh, *do?* You or Carlos got your Swiss army knife? You need to mark these damn palms, just a little cross. And wouldn't hurt to do the philodendrons. If these disappear over night we'll check every damn bit of greenery in the place. She wants war she can have it!"

Mark decided it was time to go for coffee. He started the long trek back. Behind him, Charlotte with the wheels of her chair on the edge of the sand, sat and stared at the wall, their very own dead end.

"You can see the wall in the distance from the center!" Mark said as he handed out the coffee. "I could certainly find my way. This is definitely the full stop, if we weren't so damn far out."

Charlotte, sipping her coffee began half muttering, half singing: "With a pair of steps and glasses, you could see to 'ackney marshes, if it wasn't for the 'ouses in between! Old music hall song!"

"...Right," said Mark, warily.

"Looking back, you can see the center from here, right?" It was true, beyond the tufts of allocated palms dotting the line of exhibits, stretching away to the center there, plainly in view, was the sudden central extravagance of landscaping, with its towering Royal palms. "You see," said Charlotte, "there *are* no ''ouses in between.' So, contrariwise, everyone in the center should be able to see *us*, right?"

"Only if we were up in a cherry picker or on a very tall ladder."

"Exactly! Are those pipes hot?" Charlotte asked suddenly.

"Not the ones I can reach," said Mark.

"And the emergency exit is round the corner! We'll need lots of wire, the rolls of chicken wire. We'll get them off the porch. Start a list, dear boy. All the blue wire cutters, small and long S hooks, wire hangers, the roll of tie wire. And WD40." Charlotte was gazing again at the wall with its pipes and metal bars. "Good, no switches, no breaker boxes, no terminals," she was saying dreamily. "The technique will be Cairo greengrocers!"

Cairo greengrocers. Cairo greengrocers? Mark reminded himself he was, most of the time at Orchid Empire, after all, just a mid level, Anglo Saxon version of Carlos and in that concept lay sanity. Just stand pretty much upright, answer when spoken to and move objects around when asked and don't think, don't listen to anything and don't try to work anything out. For example, even if you forgot the bit about Cairo greengrocers, why were the two palm trees set up like a pair of goal posts with the philodendrons between them, in a line, a straight line along the edge of the narrow walk way in front of the wall and bins? If they were intended to block the view they were laughable. And Charlotte hadn't wanted the sand landscaped, no heights and depths, no Liliputian mountain-tops for different members of the orchid family. The front loader had nudged it about and Carlos and Mark had flattened and evened it out with their shovels and that, said Charlotte placidly, was fine. "On we go, uninterrupted! Far from the madding crowd! The only other thing we have to do now," she said, "is move the trash cans!"

"Can't be done," said Mark. "They're chained to each other and the wall."

"When Rachel comes," said Charlotte, "we get the bolt-cutters."

"Charlotte! Hi, Mark! Glad to see you again! Charlotte, everyone thinks you're AWOL! Gone missing! What are you doing poked away back here?" It was Harry from Sun Corner Orchid Society. There certainly wasn't going to be much hugging and 'How's it going?' like the Las Olas show, thought Mark. Orchid Empire was just too far off the beaten track.

"What do you think, Harry? Offended the powers that be! And you saw us do it, that night at Sun Corner! And all in vain. I hear you are throwing in your lot with the Miamians and Orchid Magic, anyway."

Harry looked uncomfortable. "Old story, when push came to shove not enough volunteers and Regina's got a lot of old friends at Sun Corner. You know, have bought things from her and feel a little obligated to lend them back."

"How has Regina managed to convince people that if they buy something from her they haven't really bought it but merely rented ?" asked Charlotte innocently. "Not to worry, Harry! Not to worry! So what's the theme you're all working on over there with Orchid Magic and the Miami lot?"

"Don't really know yet. Regina keeps going off on committee stuff and you know Regina, she still wants to be in charge. And Leonard can't make it till six tomorrow, so tomorrow going's to be a late one. And you know what happens, someone new arrives and they always want to change plants around in the exhibit."

"And put their pet one in! Well, give our greetings to Regina, when she emerges," said Charlotte. "Tell her we're so happy her lawyer managed to squeeze us in."

It was getting on for noon. Mark wondered where Rachel was.

"I told her not to rush in. Not a lot she can do here now. Tomorrow will be her big day. And of course, she hasn't had Jen to help."

"Any word from California?"

"Rachel says Jen sounds like she's having a very pleasant time. And making some good contacts."

"Everyone will miss her with the Expo."

"Some more than others. Ah, here's Rachel."

Rachel looked not at all ready to work up a sweat with sand and foliage. She was wearing a tight pink T-shirt above tight, faded jeans and her hair, swinging free and falling forward, was no more mysterious *alba* but Veronica Lake blonde.

"Ah! Rachel, dear! Welcome to our humble spot! No, don't fret! It's all going to be fine and you're looking perfect!"

"Regina's gone too far this time!" It was Alvin. Suddenly Orchid Empire seemed to be back on the map. "Heard you were back here and found it hard to believe. What have you done *this* year?" Alvin nodded to the wall and the trash cans. "Been put in the corner again?"

"Same old, same old, right, Alvin?" said Rachel.

Alvin shook his head. "You gotta raise a stink this time, Charlotte!"

"With whom?" asked Charlotte.

Alvin shrugged.

"We need a peasants' revolt!" Charlotte announced.

"Well, don't look at me," said Alvin.

"What about booth space, though?" Rachel suddenly asked.

"The Committee must have been so sure I'd clear out in a huff, they didn't bother to deny there's more than enough space at the end of the central row. Regina's missed the chance to absorb Orchid Empire's booth space as Orchid Magic has done with out-of-favor vendors in the past! Selling will not be much more than the usual hassle and 'end of the central row' is not bad at all. Now, how's Cathy and the children, Alvin?" Charlotte it seemed wanted to keep any further plans to herself. "I don't see her here."

"She's like the rest of us, had enough of all this but she's lucky she can stay home."

"She paid her dues all those years, Alvin! Well, tell her if she wants any of the marmalade oranges this year give a call. They escaped the freeze and I can't convince Mark here to make use of them! We could bring them in to the show."

"How's the pack of hounds?"

"Daft as ever, daft as ever."

"Better get back before they bring the front loader round again and bulldoze out my palms. Good to see you back on the circuit, Charlotte! Been missing your sharp tongue though Rachel's taken over that department. She's losing her boyfriend? Just when she took my advice and got her hair done! You're going home, right?" Alvin turned to Mark. "So it's Ta, Ta old fruit!"

By two o clock Bert had come over, worried and then bemused by a quiet, almost mellow Charlotte who kept returning her gaze to the trash cans and wall with something that seemed almost like affection. "Tomorrow we'll get visitors," Charlotte announced. "Word will have spread that we *are* here after all."

Rachel had seemed calmer too; in fact was happy to leave early but not before she'd run some errand for Charlotte. "Chuck will be coming over just to make sure," she said when she got back, "but he says OK, no problem. Nothing vital here and they'll have it ready for us any time we want it."

"Tomorrow morning will be fine. No need to signal our intentions ahead of time."

"You cooking up something, Charlotte?" asked Mark

"What me, dear boy? This little old lady in a wheelchair? You know, I think we can go now, too. Don't forget the clip board! Right, Carlos, we're off! Home, James, and don't spare the horses!"

23

Wednesday: Putting in the Exhibit

"We are very lucky," Charlotte observed as they arrived on Wednesday morning. "The emergency exit sign is well over to the side. And there are no complications among the pipes."

They had moved smartly through the hall, Mark pushing Charlotte's chair, a box of wire cutters, pliers and other tools on her lap. Carlos walked behind with two bales of chicken wire in his arms. Their palms and greenery were still there, like a little frieze at the base of the bare back wall. Mark and Carlos went straight to the emergency exit, pushing the heavy door open and wedging one of the bales of wire in the doorway. Mark started the long trek back through the Expo hall out to the Volvo and drove it round the giant car park, till he found the open doorway. A little while later Rachel pulled up in the U haul truck, having cruised round the exhibition hall looking for an exit wedged open with a bale of chicken wire. With their own private entrance just a few yards away, they were unloaded in minutes, ranging the big exhibition vandas, cattleyas and specimen plants, the trays and crates, on the sand.

Having got Mark and Carlos to check the spacing between pipes, Charlotte set them to work, measuring and cutting the chicken wire into strips and squares. Rachel, dressed that morning in a skimpy red T-shirt and the faded blue jeans too tight to kneel in, had disappeared. Charlotte said no, she'd not gone for coffee but if Mark wanted to, that would be a very good idea. It took a long time to go through the hall. For every "Hey, Mark, how's it going?" there were two, "What on earth happened? Where *are* you guys?"

"Don't encourage anyone to come back and see us," Charlotte had instructed, "we need to work as fast and unobserved as possible." Luckily, the other exhibitors, without the benefit of their own private emergency exit, were still unloading. There was still no sign of the North Florida Preservation people but as Mark rounded the North Carolinian's palisade with the coffee he saw a small, narrow cherry picker, a hydraulic lift, parked by the bins.

"Chuck says he or one of the boys can be here about an hour after lunch," Rachel was telling Charlotte. "Can't be more, but after that they can probably get us a ladder."

"" What?" said Charlotte, seeing the look on Mark's face. "You didn't think we could do all this with just the long handled fruit picker did you, dear boy? Oh, and Rachel has got the bolt cutters. Let's get those bins."

In a daze Mark, after some false starts, cut through the chains and moved the bins around the corner out of sight towards the emergency exit. He was suddenly seeing with awful clarity where all this was leading. Just as he was telling himself not to be ridiculous Charlotte declared,

"Alright! A plain canvass! We're going vertical! The wall is ours!"

So that was the meaning of the chicken wire, the baling wire, the hooks, stripping off all the Spanish moss from the trees at Orchid Empire. Not just a little trellis, a pitiful attempt to draw attention away from the dead bare wall; Orchid Empire was going vertical, going to attach the orchids to the sheer wall, or rather the pipes. That's why Charlotte loved the pipes. "The hanging gardens of Babylon! At least thirty feet! And we've got a hell of a lot to do. And fast! No second guessing! Well, *they're* breaking every rule of civilized show conduct, then we'll break all the damn rules too. Cairo greengrocers! Greengrocers in Cairo! Everyone only has a little space, bang on the street so they go vertical! Not just a few trays outside the front but inside, up to the ceiling, everything piled high! Oranges, olives, pomegranates, carrots, crocodile tails, vertical! You want something, they get it down with a long pole and a hook. They are miracles of brilliance, organization and compactness. You see them at night from across the street and they look wonderful. Ha! They'd all get first prize: Best 50 square feet! Only problem *here,* every orchid needs a hook or some tie wire, some Spanish moss to hide the basket or those damn ugly plastic pots. Spanish moss is the thing; it drapes and holds. Sphagnum will just fall off. And we all need to know the master plan."

Charlotte turned her chair towards the sand and using Beemers' Supplies yard stick, drew a rough rectangle. "Well, the master plan is, if Cooper doesn't let me down, his *Renanthera* in pride of place, that means center, a great burst of scarlet but delicate. It needs reds and oranges under and round it, not to follow the rules but to be *seen!* Across the heads of the competition, above all their tiddly tufts of palms! All the way to the Expo center! Then underneath, like a sun burst, the cattleyas; Gold-digger front and center and the aurantiacums, then the scarlet and orange ascocendas radiating out, anything that's gold and yellow. We have two *Oncidium* spendidums, bright yellow and your old friends the golden shower, Mark, luckily in plastic pots, light on the chicken wire. Oh, and the *Cattleya guatemalensis* peachy orange. There's no bigger one anywhere and that will rest on the next set of pipes below. I've never brought it in to a show but it'll be too high up for any one to pinch the pollen! And if the AOS judges don't recognize it as the biggest they've ever seen then they've no right to be in a judging hall! And *this* will be our 'Orchid Fantasy!'" Charlotte cackled.

"No place for the garden chairs, then?" asked Mark, still in a daze.

"We may put them in the sand in front, contemplating the mirage before them!"

"You could say it's Mayan," Rachel suggested. "Celebrating the sun. Charlotte's thinking it's going to be totally stylized, something like an oriental rug," she told Mark. "Or a mosaic. Isn't it wild?"

"Ferns will be used only to outline the exhibition plants, to make them stand out *not* fit in. And it will be *all* color breaks!" Charlotte was having fun, rewriting the rules for orchid exhibits. "Color breaks, properly done, draw the eye. That's what we need. Over the heads of all the other exhibitors."

"Isn't it wild?" Rachel said again. "We'll stick the lilac-purple catts, the *skinneri* and *lueddemanniana*, in the two top corners and run a border of blue vandas across the top and put the two big pink vandas bang in the middle."

"Can we put the big purple *Vanda* in the middle down below? Just above Cooper's scarlet one? Like the gem in the turban of the Sultan?"

"Now you're getting the idea, dear boy!"

And that really is how vandas should be shown, thought Mark. It was no good trying to fit them in among ferns; just as they certainly couldn't sit on a rich matron's bosom, like a *Cattleya*. "Problem is, though, when they're in the eight inch basket, even the six, Charlotte, even with the Spanish moss, the basket is going to stick out so far."

"That's why I love this wall! See the big pipes? See how they're spaced? There *should* be enough space to slide the baskets in, angle them in. And the very fact that Orchid Empire's prize plants are all grossly overgrown and in *desperate* need of resetting is perfect—basket and pot still fit the pipes but the plants themselves overflow magnificently! The only problem is we may have to raise some of the flower heads up a little, need to do it very gently with the soft wire."

"She was figuring all this out while sitting here yesterday" Mark muttered to Rachel. "But Charlotte, what's Regina going to do?"

"We are not blocking access to walkways or emergency exits," Charlotte proclaimed. "We are not obscuring or covering vital electrical doodads or fire hydrants. We *have* removed three bins for safe keeping and are ready to reimburse the Expo hall for cost of chains. Though I think we send the bill to the Miami Orchid Expo Committee. We certainly are being totally outrageous but word around the Expo of course, is that, as even Alvin said, this time Regina has gone too far. No way can she play any of this as an accident, an oversight, a mistake. She's usually a lot smarter. My gut feeling is she's going to be very cautious about zapping us further, hounding this old woman in her wheel chair, out of her last show! *And,*" Charlotte concluded, "we are utilizing the space provided by the Miami Expo Show Committee for the display of our plants to delight and educate the public. As for being outrageous, my lawyer says being outrageous is not grounds for breach of contract. And he should know, I've been his client for years."

Rachel was showing Mark how to fit each orchid with its wire and hook, ready for placement. It made Mark think of the 'We are one world' Christmas pageant; fixing the chorus of angels, going down the row attaching wire wings between their shoulder blades. "How did you get the guy to come with the cherry picker?" Mark asked. "I mean, I can see they like Rachel..."

Charlotte, over with Carlos cutting wire, gave a cackle. "These construction guys, they're the permanent Expo workers. They don't answer to Regina and her show committee. And she's had run ins with all of them! Apparently they call her something totally unmentionable. In English *and* Spanish."

Mark felt he should keep on worrying; that someone should be aware this was all totally nuts. And if one of them realized it was totally nuts, they would be forgiven; somehow they'd be allowed to get away with it. "Well, OK but what about security? Night watchmen? When *they* see all this?"

Charlotte grinned again. "All those gentlemen? Believe you me, most individuals who work nights are pretty independent souls and don't want to be messed with. That's why they've signed on for nights. Chuck says none of them can stand Regina either."

"What about names?" Rachel asked. "The orchid names."

"I think a piece of the black board in front of the exhibit with the names listed according to their place on the wall, like a diagram, should suffice." Charlotte was making it all sound like a rational enterprise. "OK! Line up the blues and the two catts so when Chuck comes we'll be ready!"

Chuck arrived just about two, tanned, wiry and short. He looked a perfect size for the cherry picker bucket but as Charlotte had explained he was perfect in another way: "Short men tend to have short fuses! Chuck has a low tolerance thresh-hold for Regina."

Chuck had got something out of the cherry picker, a bright yellow hard hat for Rachel. She stepped in the bucket, clutching not the sides but the big *Cattleya skinneri,* with its two dozen stalks of lilac blooms. Inching up the left side of the wall, Chuck was taking it very slowly; Rachel finding the right spot on the pipe, Charlotte yelling "*Yes!*" from below, Rachel leaning out, Mark holding his breath. If the basket couldn't be wedged somehow between the two pipes then the whole plan would be ruined, the project would collapse. Rachel leant forward, fumbling with the wire and then "OK!" she was calling down. "It's OK! OK, Chuck! I'll get quicker!"

Chuck lowered the bucket halfway. Carlos hooked a big blue *Vanda* up on the end of the fruit picker and swung it up to Rachel. Rachel turned, going back up, managing to get it wedged right away, the big tessellated blooms reaching out. She gave a yell and raised her arms in triumph. The yell turned into a squeal as Chuck lowered her down fast to the ground.

"Chuck's not got long," explained Charlotte. "The fact that we're always a day late and a dollar short with staking is perfect! The blooms are swooping forward, leaning down a little, showing the flowers to perfection for those down below!"

Rachel was right; she was getting quicker. Filling in the gaps with Bert's ferns, in fifteen minutes Rachel had done the top frame: a row of purple and light purple vandas, with Charlotte's brilliant *Vanda coerulea*, the true blue, and the big cattleyas on the left. To the right, the *skinneri* and *lueddemanniana*. From down below and far away, they would look like rosettes in the corners of the carpet.

Chuck was good. Rachel only had to give a shout, or sometimes, when she misjudged her balance, a squeal, for him to be maneuvering exactly to the right spot. Getting a crick in his neck gazing up, Mark was waiting no longer merely for a Regina or the plump young man from the General Office, but someone in uniform pulling out a notebook if not a gun, writing up a citation, a fine. But Rachel completed the row with no interruption and was lowered to the ground. She handed over the wire cutters, the gloves and the circle of wire to Mark, grinning and breathing hard. She also handed over the yellow hat. Mark shook his head. He already knew he was probably going to look pretty inept up there. In that thing he'd look about as dashing as Prince Charles touring a building site.

"Put it on!" roared Chuck. "Let's go!"

Mark had never liked heights. Some of his most vivid memories of childhood shame and self loathing involved stranding himself up high, panic-stricken in trees or on seaside cliffs. He looked at the narrow, rather shallow bucket; he thought fleetingly of the chariot race in *Ben Hur.* He wondered where was a man in uniform, any man, to call a halt to all this and ask him calmly to step out and away from the bucket, please.

"Get a move on!" cried Charlotte "We've only got Chuck for an hour!"

Mark told himself he wasn't even going up so high as Rachel. He prayed he wouldn't drop anything. It had been decided he would alternate with Rachel, fixing the chicken wire rolls in between the pipes. The wire would provide the backing to hang the small plastic pots of orchids and ferns and any orchids on drift wood, while the big baskets, the specimens perched between the pipes. Mark was just about to settle himself in and say "Right, Chuck!" and he found he was going up.

Don't look down! Don't drop anything! If you screw up Carlos will take over and your manhood will be totally down the tubes. Mark could feel the length of chicken wire in the bucket quietly curling up round his legs. On the end there was Carlos' loop of wire ready to tie on to the pipe under the first orchid, the big shaggy *Cattleya.* Just hook over and twist with the wire cutters, that was all. Straighten the strip of chicken wire, fiddle like Rachel, fiddle under the *Cattleya* basket trying to get behind the roots, find the bloody pipe. At least the bucket was fairly rigid, not swaying like something at a fair. There didn't see to be many cobwebs around but a thick layer of greasy dust on the pipe wasn't helping. The chicken wire wouldn't stay flat; now in mid air it curled in lazily and persistently towards the bucket. Mark wanted to yell down "This is harder than it looks, guys!" But he was pretty sure he was making it look quite hard enough. Everyone was watching; Rachel, Charlotte and Carlos, Chuck of course. He wished they'd all settle down with Ruby's fried chicken and corn bread, fix their eyes somewhere else; that is, all except Chuck. "Right, Chuck!" Mark had spoken too soon. He lurched forward and back "Whoa! Sorry!" He had to ask Chuck to edge back so he could have another go. At least the wire hadn't fallen, just rolled down in a lazy curl, holding by one hook of wire. Chuck, he knew, was checking his watch. Mark made the mistake of looking straight down and for a moment had to close his eyes.

Charlotte's voice floated up: "You know, I'm finally having fun putting in an exhibit!"

Chuck yelled "Ready?" and moved back a few feet. Miraculously the first hooked section of wire held and Mark was able to hang the next, the fork lift bucket slowly moving back so he could straighten it out, one more time. Mark, suddenly in some rapt state, fingers black, found himself able to do it: hook the wire loops under the baskets Rachel had fixed, the top row, and then over the pipes! And on we go! Don't think! Don't look down! The Zen of chicken wire hanging. Three more places along the pipe and Chuck zoomed him down.

From the ground it looked a little wavy but "covered in Spanish moss and orchids, who will know?" said Charlotte bracingly. Mark's arms ached. He felt like taking off for a few beers to celebrate not dropping the wire cutters but the whole thing had only just begun.

Rachel was bouncing on the balls of her feet like a boxer, "Let's *go!*"

They'd lined up whites next: standard *Phalaenopsis* they'd begged from Bert, to intersperse with the green of Bert's ferns and the two *Phalaenopsis* species from Cooper, Rachel's favorites: the *schilleriana* with branching sprays of little apple blossom pink blooms for the left and on the right, the *stuartiana*, its sprays white and creamy brown. Rachel took up the *schilleriana* and got it in one. Carlos passed up the pots of phals one by one but quickly and Rachel just did it, covering Mark's stretch of chicken wire in ferns with white phals round the *stuartiana*, pink ones round the *schilleriana*.

"We're nailing it! cried Rachel draping Spanish moss over the plastic pots. The moss was perfect, hanging down in a lacy mist, gently catching the currents of air. They were down to the second set of horizontal pipes but Chuck said in ten minutes he had to go and Cooper had not arrived with the center piece, the *Renanthera*. If Chuck left, they'd still need some kind of special, very tall ladder. It was three o clock. Really, thought Mark, if you compared what they accomplished vertically in an hour and a bit it was pretty impressive; elsewhere on the ground vendors would be starting their exhibition dance. Couldn't be into that with Chuck. That would be the answer to the pair who couldn't decide and started all over in the evening: put them in a cherry picker, with Chuck in charge and they'd be finished in an hour.

For all that they had decided this was going to be the dramatic statement, their maverick brilliance shining across the Expo hall, it seemed to be passing unnoticed. The top third of the wall was done, the purples, blues and now most of the whites and light pinks and no one had raced around the corner, with exclamations of shock or wonder. "They've all got their eyes down among the sphagnum and mulch!" Charlotte chortled. "Have you forgotten so soon, dear boy? As Rachel says about this time everyone's starting to fall to their knees in front of their creations. Well, we have a legitimate tea break, awaiting Cooper and a ladder. So far so good!"

Chuck, apologizing profusely, mostly to Rachel, wished them well, adding a few choice comments on the Miami Orchid Club, its President and elected officials which were greatly appreciated, and whirred off with his machine. Rachel started off in the same direction; it was her job now to scrounge a ladder. Mark could not suppress the feeling of imminent doom. Though if he thought about it, that had been his fairly constant state whenever he was near Charlotte in the thick of the South Florida orchid scene. This was just the latest most bizarre example, and the last. The fitting finale: climbing up a wall with prize orchids. Why? Because of a feud, because of orchid politics: *What's the latest from Miami?*

"Oh my heavens! Oh *my!*" Tilly had arrived, coming round the corner with her clipboard and shorts and ready to ask, "Anything for individuals?" Tilly looked up, from left to right and down to Charlotte, Mark, and Carlos who was marching to and fro on a section of chicken wire to flatten it. She looked up again. "But you won't be able to enter any of these for individuals!"

"This is more fun, Tilly!" Charlotte exclaimed. "And speaking of fun, what about Regina, our President?"

"Well, I saw her come out of the committee office with a face like thunder, though, of course," added Tilly dryly, "these shows do take their toll." Tilly couldn't drag her eyes off the orchids already suspended on the wall. "I heard you were tucked away in the corner and until I saw all this, I was going to ask you if you decided on a quiet life for once?"

"Tilly, my dear, I won't gossip till after the show so you can turn that nice little face to Regina and be full of innocent surprise."

"What fun!" said Tilly. "Well, if you change your mind about individuals, tell Rachel to look for me."

"Looks like Rachel hasn't been able to get anywhere with the construction people. Chuck said for a ladder she'll probably have better luck with maintenance, one of the electricians," said Charlotte.

"I wonder why Regina's not put in an appearance yet." Mark said, worried.

"Calling her lawyers! Maybe they can't find that this is against the law; taking your extra hundred feet vertical! It's a first! She's certainly not got much satisfaction or she'd have been here by now. We've got maintenance on our side, security. I suppose she could get the Fire Marshall but how can this be hazardous? Non-flammable plant material. No way for the public to be standing directly underneath in case of faulty hanging and if they're after hazardous materials then he'd have to check half the exhibits round the hall with their standard crop of cardboard walls and plastic grottos. And this is a weight bearing wall! If *this* wall won't support a few flowering plants then we'd all better get out of this building right now!"

It was four thirty. There was still no Rachel, no equipment, no ladder. Carlos had been sent for sodas and had been gone for twenty minutes. "Got talking to his pals," Charlotte sounded tired. Looking up at the orchids hanging in space half way up the wall, she muttered "And how the hell we're going to keep them watered? Need a hose." This time Mark had remembered the little sprayer but that wouldn't do much good. "And where's Carlos got to?" Charlotte sat back in her chair, surrounded by orchids and closed her eyes. It was at those moments Mark realized how old she really was. The noises from the center of the Expo arrived muted, like street sounds registering faintly over some old high brick wall in an English garden. Mark pulled up one of the narrow garden chairs and sat down facing the wall. Even if they had to tear it all down he hoped they could finish it first; at least take some pictures. Have some spectators, some of the orchid people see it; Charlotte's swan song, Charlotte going out with a bang. Orchid Empire's last hurrah, Orchid Empire's 'Orchid Fantasy.'

There were voices behind them and laughter, sounded like Rachel. Carlos appeared, grinning broadly. He was holding the front end of a ladder so long it was a moment before the other end of it appeared with the man holding it. Security, thought Mark; the standard large, black man complete with name tag and bunch of keys. And walking beside him, talking and laughing, Rachel. "Hi, guys! We caught sight of Carlos just when we needed him!" They set the ladder up. Shaped like an A, it was free standing. Mark had seen a similar one in a grove near Orchid Empire, designed to nose up into top branches like a giraffe. The maintenance man, maybe an electrician, looked up at the orchids on the wall, grinned and shook his head. He came over to Charlotte. "Now if push comes to shove, you don't know me and I don't know you. Know what I mean? Unless I got me an emergency you're alright. Rachel and your guy knows where this needs to go."

"As Ruby would say, 'Great will be your reward in heaven,' but maybe you'd like an orchid or two here on earth to take home?"

"Well, I'm more into having a beer or two on the way home, know what I mean?"

"I think you should have both," declared Charlotte, leaning forward to read the name tag, "...Theodore."

"Call me Ted but don't call me anything till the ladder's back, hear what I'm saying?"

Rachel had been sorry to see the cherry picker go but Mark was happier with a traditional ladder, however high. There was no Chuck in charge, waiting to jerk him along to another section of pipe. And no mandatory wearing of the Prince Charles shiny yellow helmet. It wasn't so far up any more; they were already below the purples and blues, about six feet nearer the ground. And right on cue, just as Ted had gone and the ladder was in place, Cooper appeared round the corner of the wooden palisade, past the bare space reserved for the North Florida Preservation Society. He was gazing upwards. He didn't seem surprised. He shook his head and smiled slowly.

"Charlotte, Charlotte— You are creating a mandala!"

"Cooper! You're *absolutely* right!"

Rachel wanted to know what Cooper was talking about. "Mandala," said Mark "I always think of them as circular, but basically it's a geometric design, symbolic of the power of the universe. A device for meditation, for Buddhists and Hindus. Created with great devotion and labor and then destroyed."

"Ha! Cooper! I've just realized something!" Charlotte exclaimed. "*All* orchid exhibits are mandalas!"

"This is just Orchid Empire's attempt in the crass market place to give some serenity and inner peace to the scene," Mark joked.

"It seems Orchid Magic is after the same darn thing," said Cooper dryly. "They appear to be creating a temple scene. Certainly have a lot of Thai objects."

"Like the Thai restaurant," said Mark.

"Yes," Cooper smiled slowly. "That's about it."

"Yes, all well and good, but *where's* the *Renanthera?*" Charlotte interrupted. "Coop don't tell me you dropped it."

"No. I just left it in the cab till I was sure I'd found out where you were. You decided on a retreat? What are you doing in this corner?"

"Cooper! Need you ask?"

It always seemed strange to see Cooper in daylight, Mark thought but it was getting on for evening. This time his T-shirt just said Save The Planet. "Well, that narrows it down a bit," said Charlotte.

"I'm going for the *Renanthera,*" Cooper said.

"Don't trip over anything," said Charlotte. "No! Coop, listen! We'll open the exit here again. Drive around till you see some chicken wire."

"We've used it all up," said Rachel.

"In that case drive round till you see a large trash bin wedged in a door."

Rachel and Carlos had started filling in low key encyclias and epidendrums as an edging down both sides while waiting for Cooper. When he arrived Mark realized why Charlotte had been waiting. The *Renanthera* was like a miniature tree, a tree with one magnificent arm, a canopy of tiny crimson flowers on a long, multi-branching stem.

"Wait till we've put the yellows and oranges round it," Rachel said, "we'll light the sucker up!"

"It's killer," said Charlotte, calling up to Rachel on the ladder. "You and Coop need to breed this to everything but the family dog! Whether it ever gets an award or not!"

"Speaking of breeding, said Cooper "I've got my two tricolors here and new *denisoniana* hybrids. So you'll have fragrance too."

"Glorious things for the true orchid lovers who make the pilgrimage back here!" declared Charlotte. "I think we could ask Carlos to hunt up those sodas now."

"Could we make it beer?' asked Mark. "We *are* getting nearer the ground."

Charlotte said "I should send you off to Tilly, Coop. That *Renanthera* really should be entered into individuals. It's a crime to have it here where it won't even be nominated."

"No," said Cooper softly, "I consider this the place. High above the orchid scene, center of a mandala. What's an AOS award compared to this?"

Orchid Empire's exhibit space was, in Charlotte's phrase, "accidentally on purpose" obscured, cut off from the general traffic. Back towards the Expo center, beyond the no-man's land of the North Florida Species Preservation Society's one hundred square feet, there rose up the palisade, the backside of the last exhibit in the mainstream: three hundred square feet allocated to Fountain Farm of North Carolina. No one had come across to introduce themselves; "not even to borrow a cup of sugar" as Charlotte put it. "They've never been here before. And it's a little unusual for an out-of-state firm to hazard three hundred square feet straight off the bat. I have the feeling they're Regina imports for the occasion."

But Orchid Empire's obscurity had turned out to be a blessing. Though they were, as Rachel joked, "Definitely rising above it all," they were off the beaten track and with most of the exhibitors still on their knees among the mulch had been able to work with an uninterrupted, and with Rachel setting the pace, a furious concentration. Now Mark felt, short of a SWAT team, they could make it: finish the whole wall, take back the ladder, take pictures; show the whole crazy creation off and let the lawyers take over tomorrow. They were all waiting now, though no-one admitted it, for the arrival of Larry and Ken. Especially Larry, Larry, who was still expecting nothing more fantastic than Charlotte's garden chairs.

"We haven't even checked how it all looks from the center!" Rachel cried. "No time!"

It couldn't be too impressive, thought Mark, or there would have been a surge of wondering townspeople flooding round the Fountain Farm palisade.

"No, it is like a mirage," Charlotte announced firmly. "No one can believe it! Even if they see it. People see what they expect to see." As long as Charlotte's feeling positive, Mark told himself, that's the main thing. Rachel, to Mark's amazement, had begged to be the one on the ladder. But even she was starting to flag." It's 'beer o clock'" she wailed, "but I don't want to fall off the ladder."

Charlotte had vetoed beer earlier. Now it was well after six but she said "Let's wait for Larry and Ken."

Carlos was still quietly wiring ferns and orchids, smiling when someone made a joke, attentive to Rachel on high. When he was asked how he thought it was all looking, he said, "Very good." When Mark asked him how he was doing, he said, "Very good." And when Charlotte reminded him he'd be home rather late Carlos said, "Thassokay." Rachel had got down to the last ten feet. Above, the oranges, reds and yellows had burst out in a ring round the *Renanthera*.

"Now, lower down we can have the intricacies to be seen from the ground: the brassavolas, angraecums, diacriums, all my odds and sods," Charlotte declared.

"My God, Charlotte! My GOD!" Larry and Ken had arrived,

carrying a cooler and a large pizza box. After a minute or two Larry's voice was heard above the others: "Charlotte! Just because I kidded you about your garden chairs..."

"Did you see us from the center?" Charlotte demanded.

"Yes! You see it as you come in, for God's sake! You're looking at the central display and there in the corner of your eye is this strange blaze, these colors to the right. You turn and there it is rising above everything like the Times Square New Year Apple! No! Rachel is right—like a quilt, a Persian rug. We should have known it was you! Well, Ken did say he recognized the *skinneri* but most of the vendors still think you're kicked out! Where on earth did you get the idea?"

"Cairo greengrocers," said Mark.

"I was going to grab my extra square feet where-ever I could find them."

"You mean Cairo, Egypt? The pyramids? No, you're thinking Babylon, the hanging gardens. But Egypt? That's very Art Deco! Very South Beach!"

"Humble green-grocers, Larry, dear boy. Though I must say, Cairenes are hot on flowers, so many street vendors selling cut flowers, all sorts. They get a lot of them in from Alexandria. You and Ken ought to go, Larry, you'd love it!"

"You know me, Charlotte. It's a stretch to get up to West Palm."

"We were going to ask what can we do?" said Ken

"Go for beer!" Mark and Rachel cried.

"Oh, that's all taken care of," said Larry. "But first, anything we can *do?* I see no sheet sphagnum moss. And no color co-ordination! Wicked! So, speaking of outrageous, what's the fallout been?"

"We're waiting for the royal visit. I think Regina is a bit stunned by events."

"Aren't we all," said Ken.

Rachel had reached the five to six foot level. Carlos and Mark moved the ladder to one side and Ken and Larry were able to start helping: there were the gold and orange laeliocattleyas, the delicate white brassavolas, Charlotte's angraecums and the *Diacrium bicornutum*, its flowers like small white stars. Mark, relieved of high level operations, busied himself moving the tall pinks in their sturdy plastic pots along the sand, the *Vanda* Miss Agnes Joachims, the orange *radicans* and the *Arachnis*, the pale yellow spider orchid. Charlotte had brought them in after all, why not? All the tubs from the front of the green house, the open air, survivors from the freeze, take what nature gives you, brigade.

"Where are Cooper and Mike?" asked Ken.

"Haven't seen Mike at all. There's Coop's *Renanthera*."

"Looks like you don't need anything more from us."

"Somehow everything of Charlotte's hit right!" Rachel was triumphant. "*And* mine and Cooper's! Have you seen Bert's display? My God, we totally forgot about him."

"He's toddling along. Nothing fantastic there! Has he seen what you're up to? He'll have a fit."

"So where is our dear President in all this?" asked Ken. "Has she come to gasp and wonder, too?"

"Before all this we had the dance of the lawyers on Monday," Charlotte said. "Legal standing, liability, lost income; Rachel and Mark having found we had *no* spot at all. My lawyer reminded the Miami Expo's lawyer, who just happens to be Regina's, that in light of some of the unpleasantness that has taken place at earlier shows they might be grateful for an amicable outcome to this whole unfortunate episode. And since Monday afternoon, so far...nothing!"

Larry looked thoughtful. Mark could see he considered that a bad sign. He himself had been wondering where the other ladies with clip boards were, some kind of official acknowledgment, apart from Tilly, that they were there. "But maybe Regina's misjudged this one," Mark suggested. "You can see her ploy is to lie low, hide behind the committee, till the dirty work is done or it's too late. Well, maybe this time she waited too long. I mean, if she wants to stop this now it's a bit late today, or rather, tonight, for lawyers. I'd think it's a bit late for the fire-marshal. And now it's night staff, not her people anyway."

" I think Mark's got something," said Ken. "Regina didn't want to have a confrontation, all the exhibitors crowding round, worried for the frail old lady in the chair."

"Of course, everyone knows it's Charlotte," Larry was grinning.

"Sure, that's just it," said Ken. "She knew Charlotte wouldn't go quietly."

"Oh, she can sue me, she can take me off in shackles Sunday evening. She can hang, draw and quarter me just so long as it's not before Sunday night. And it doesn't even matter if she does take me to court! The way things work in this country, it all takes years. I'll be long dead and gone."

Looking at Charlotte hunkered down in her chair like Churchill ready for Stalin, Mark could see she was looking forward to one last good fight, mandala or no mandala. This would be her last show and she was ready to go out with a bang. "Cooper's got to understand. Sometimes you can't let old Buddha get in the way of a good fight!"

"So what about a name?" Larry asked. It was only seven thirty. They were all tired and amazed: they had almost finished.

"Don't let's take the ladder back just yet," Rachel said. "I'm afraid something's going to come crashing down and we'll have to reset it." She was sitting on one of the ladder's steps, Mark on a crate, Charlotte in her chair, Ken and Larry on the garden chairs and Carlos on another crate, a discreet foot or two further away. Larry was handing out beers from the cooler.

"When I realized Charlotte was going to make something of this corner I thought 'She dwelt among the untrodden ways' was the perfect line," Mark said, "but the whole thing has got too wild for that."

"If nothing better comes up, then obviously The Magic Carpet," said Ken.

"No! 'Up Against The Wall!'" said Rachel, back on ground and already looking for another beer.

They were sitting in what had become their work area; the space designated for the North Florida Preservation of Orchid Species Club who had never appeared. They were facing the hundred square feet of sand and then Orchid Empire's wall, the tapestry of orchids.

"It's obviously 'Orchid Oasis'" said Charlotte "and a mirage, a dream of paradise! That's why I held back on these orchids, Rachel's and my tiny species. The final thing we do is nestle these in the dunes; windblown, wind bitten, struggling little devils in the sand, holding on, battening down in a hostile environment. Ain't *that* the truth, here!"

They were all impressed, not to say dumbfounded. Here was Charlotte, the arch despiser of orchid themes and scenes, and she had contrived this: a drift of sand to the frieze of green foliage, the two palm trees framing the orchids above, the magic carpet mirage. Mark was reminded of the label on the box of dates his mother used to get every Christmas: the two palms on either side and a camel ambling across the lid between them. And then the flowers, the orchids, climbing up to heaven; a vision, a mirage, brilliant, exotic, fragrant, the Moslem garden of delights, paradise.

"Much as I despise all the plumbing at these events," Charlotte was saying, "we could have done with the sound of running water; *that's* the sound of Moslem paradise."

"Well, with all these pipes..." Larry joked.

"And back down on the sand, the most inhospitable environment, the desert!" A reminder, back to Mark's first days, when Charlotte would emphasize how orchids were canny survivors, closest to cacti, growing slowly where nothing else could grow at all. "*The whole essence of becoming epiphytes—air growing plants—is to escape from the enemy, fungus. Fungus likes to be moist. So orchids have learned how to be dry. Dryness is the important factor in growing all orchids: not what moisture your plant needs but how much dry it can tolerate!*"

"And they can tolerate a damn lot," Charlotte had said. "We ordered some plants from Java once and the damn man sent them surface! *Seven* weeks parcel post! And those orchids were still alive! Not looking good but alive. Can you imagine another plant managing that? Can you imagine reviving your pansies or Michaelmas daisies after seven weeks in a box? With only a few damp pages of the *Java Evening News* for company?"

Larry couldn't resist. He was asking Charlotte, "So where're you going to put the garden chairs?"

"Well, tonight," said Charlotte, "Cooper and Carlos will be sitting in them, just keeping an eye on things."

"We'd sure hate for the whole thing somehow to fall apart because of *faulty workmanship*," Rachel announced. "Know what I mean?"

"Speaking of which, let's get the ladder back to Ted— Theodore. We can settle up with him tomorrow."

After Mark and Carlos returned the ladder, Larry went on an expedition to Fountain Farm land, round the front of the palisade. "Visiting the neighbors! They were offered their space just a month ago," he reported. "That would make it just after the Las Olas show. Apparently Regina said, 'Oh, just take this for now but I think the actual Expo week we'll be able to offer you an extra hundred.' They don't have enough material for *two* hundred! And they were told to spill into this space! But they said yesterday one of the Reginistas came round and told them not to venture back here! Not to fraternize! Poor things," said Larry. "They're a nice bunch. We had a chat across the garden fence. They're a little bit disconcerted by the atmosphere. I told them not to worry. If they hear raised voices or gun fire just to keep their heads down below the palisade. It's just *Miami!*"

24

Thursday: Judgement Day

Judges were all required to be at the Miami Expo by 8.30 sharp on Thursday morning for coffee and donuts and the assignment of teams. First came ribbon judging, the "biggest turnip in the village stuff" as Charlotte called it, and then American Orchid Society judging, the process that "gets your turnip into the history books, so to speak and can turn it into the most *expensive* turnip in the village. Hence Regina's personal interest."

Charlotte and Mark were on the road by seven, already into rush hour traffic. Rachel had left even earlier, making sure she would be on time. Student judges, Charlotte said, had to toe the line. "Next step, probationary. Takes seven years, like being a vet! Regina only made it by jumping regions. Judging is a very decorous affair. Pinning ancient members in the corner to vote for your plants, not done! Had to take her winning ways to another region. But once you're an AOS judge you can judge anywhere. So we are blessed with Regina, President of the Miami Orchid Club, organizer of the Miami Expo, making sure the judging teams are put together in such a way nothing disturbs Orchid Magic's winning streak."

This time the judging was the least of Charlotte's preoccupations. She just had to be there, at the Expo, whether to accept rave reviews, praise from colleagues, injunctions or citations issued by Regina's lawyers or face the wrecking balls to destroy their magic carpet, no one knew. "You can do a Carlos, be the silent observer just pushing my chair," she told Mark. "Rachel needs to be free for clerking. Very important part of her student training. Regina can't interfere with that."

The giant hall was almost deserted and almost silent. The Expo would not be open to the general public till Friday. Mark had to wheel Charlotte in the main entrance but she had told Mark to keep on walking; ignore the group drinking coffee, the judges, just wave and keep moving. The two of them would be intent first on making their way right to the back of the hall, eyes raised and fixed on their creation, their exhibit: Orchid Empire's 'Magic Carpet.'

Mark was marveling that neither of them had, in fact, really seen their exhibit in its entirety as the public would; from the first glimpse inside the main entrance, the tapestry of orchids rising up beyond the Royal palms, then gradually closer as they walked past the standard exhibits, ignoring the orchid studded grottoes and mini mountains, eyes raised to that far wall. And that seemed all part of the craziness. That not one minute had been spent the day before on moving backwards and forwards in the exhibition dance and no-one had really stood back, right back and narrowed their eyes and pronounced the 'Magic Carpet,' the mirage in the desert, *OK!* Not even Larry, when he went visiting the North Carolinians. They'd all just fixed the last orchids and tidied up the night before and left. Mark had paused only to collect the empty cans and bottles for recyclables in silent tribute to Jen. They had all slipped away, out of their own private door, the emergency exit, into the car park away from any possible confrontation or ultimatum, leaving Carlos and Cooper settled into the garden chairs.

"Carlos will just smile at everyone in Spanish and Coop? He'll be even more out of reach," Charlotte had declared. "It will take more than a lawyer's clerk on overtime or a nervous Nellie of a security guard to tap into Cooper's world when he's decided to remove himself mentally from the hurly burly. And of course, Coop's always happiest after dark, probably knows half the night people working here."

Mark had been surprised at how few people were gathered by the judges' coffee and donuts, how quiet it was. But when he got further away from the center and closer to the Fountain Farm's three hundred feet there was a hum of voices and as Mark pushed Charlotte's chair round the palisade into the North Florida's Preservation of Orchid Species empty space, they discovered where the judges were. Holding coffee cups, some with donuts in their hands, they were gazing up at

Orchid Empire's Magic Carpet. Close to, Mark thought it was more like a heavy, sumptuous quilt, rich and bumpy with stitched in treasures. Miraculously none of the big specimen orchids were sagging or had pulled free. Nothing, not even a humble fern, had dropped off. Mark wondered how on earth they'd done it. Everyone was turning, exclaiming when they caught sight of them, crowding in. But all Mark could do was smile and shake his head. The whole thing was crazy, so crazy neither he nor Charlotte said a word.

Most of the group of judges looked well over fifty; several, in fact, looked like they should be in wheel chairs themselves. Mark only recognized John, the *Cattleya* man and a pair from the New Year's party Larry had pointed out: an ancient figure leaning on a cane and a slightly younger man in a Panama hat: "Doctor Cartwright still goes to judging, Rachel says. They're trying to bump him up to judge emeritus. Totally past it but no-one likes to say. That's young Jim in the straw hat. Everyone calls him young Jim because he's the son of the son of the guy who started Orchids of Dade, one of the old originals till Andrew."

Suddenly the Major appeared round the corner. Apparently Regina had not arrived and it was the Major from Las Olas who called the judges to order, herding them back from the far reaches of Orchid Empire's exhibit, back to the central point, to the coffee machine and cups, the clipboards and two late arrivals among the student judges, frantic they'd mistaken the time and the place.

Mark was kept busy introducing himself and being introduced by Charlotte—the nephew who would be back in England very soon— glad to note there was no more mention of his expertise at Kew, the Chelsea Flower Show or anywhere else. Charlotte had grander preoccupations than putting her nephew on the spot. And nothing that morning could compete with the subject of Orchid Empire's wall of orchids, Charlotte's contribution to the Expo theme: Orchid Fantasy. "The judges are mostly a very orthodox bunch," Charlotte predicted. "There'll be a lot of shock and upset but no support." And she was right. A lot of heads were shaking, less, it seemed, at Regina's behavior, more at Charlotte's wild defiance. At this rate, thought Mark, Regina would be home and dry again: what the poor, long-suffering President had to endure with this maverick, quarrelsome old woman. And as Charlotte had said, judges were there from other judging centers. How could they be expected to sort out what was going on? *Hey, this is Miami!*

Charlotte was explaining to the judges that she was much, much better. The chair was just so convenient when there was so much standing to do. "But holla if I'm blocking the view!" Swept up in a tide of shocked and excited judges, Charlotte had not had a chance to say anything to Mark except "Make sure you get a donut, dear boy! This is going to be a long morning!"

When Mark first saw Rachel he hardly recognized her. She was wearing a charcoal grey suit with a loose, boxy jacket and her hair was pulled back hard, no tendrils allowed, as though by a vindictive Matron at Totter's Green. Her black leather shoes had little heels, the sort of shoes no longer seen in the real world but only in photos of the candidate's wife. Rachel didn't come over, just smiled demurely, deep in conversation with two spry old male orchidists.

Mark was about to pour himself some more coffee and choose a second donut when there was a flutter on the edge of the group and Regina burst through. The President of the Miami Orchid Club was in her trademark tan slacks and, fittingly enough, a blood red blouse. Her hair was so black, the mouth so red, that Mark thought Regina looked a good deal less sophisticated than Carlos' teenage daughter and friend trying out *sexi* looks in the Pelican Mall. At moments like these Mark's head was liable to swirl with irrelevant thoughts. As Regina ploughed through the greetings from orchid judges and old friends, making a beeline for Mark and Charlotte, he was thinking: *Put a bunch of bananas on her head and she could be Carmen Miranda. Actually, any woman of a certain age now in heavy make up, looks like Carmen Miranda, or rather a man in drag. Hey! I bet Carmen Miranda WAS a man in drag.* "I won't allow you to make a travesty of *my show!*" Regina was staring down at Charlotte, breathing hard. "Defacing county property! This ...*mess* must come down immediately! I will not have it! And *you!*" Regina raised her face to Mark, "are you a judge?

Who gave *you* permission to be here?" Far from looking like Carmen Miranda Regina had snapped her mouth so tight shut it had shrunk until, in Charlotte's delicate phrase recalling the scene later, it looked more like a rabbit's backside. Heads were turning. Mark looked down on Charlotte sitting in the chair, her innocent pink scalp and white curls, head bowed forward a little, like the Pope's. Clever! Let Regina rant. Let everyone see Regina in action. As Cooper would say, Let the energy of the enemy turn against itself.

"Oh, dear!" Charlotte was murmuring in her cucumber sandwich voice. "Oh, dear! Mark was merely helping me, pushing the chair! Quite happy to be merely a passive spectator."

"He is *nothing* to do with the orchid scene here! *Nothing!*" It was as though all the pent up frustration in the face of 'Dr. Gibson's' bland rebuffs, Mark's visit to Orchid Magic, the defiance of Las Olas, the orchid talk at Sun Corner, maybe right back to the New Year's debacle, the freeze which emptied the party of almost everyone but lachrymose Cubans, had all been driven through Regina's tight rabbit backside of a mouth. "Leave! I want you out of here *right* now!"

Perfect! thought Mark, though a little stunned. He could see embarrassment and consternation, even annoyance, on the faces of the judges. They stood there with their donuts and coffee wanting only a quiet life, a glaze of gentility on the orchid scene, the sort of smoothly organized event that Regina could usually deliver. Mark saw the Major looking very troubled and decided Regina had, for the moment certainly done all she could to look bad. He spoke up sadly.

"I am so sorry, everyone! I had no idea! But I wonder how Charlotte will be able to manage?"

As Mark regretfully let go of the fragile chair, its slight canvas and light metal frame so innocent and frail, almost unanimously every judge said "Oh, I can push Charlotte! No problem!"

It was a collective whack on the knuckles for Regina. She was obviously starting to realize, still breathing hard, how difficult it was going to be to return to the role of gracious and warm President and hostess of the Miami Orchid Expo.

"You are all being so kind!" Mark tried to keep from catching

Rachel's eye. "Charlotte, I'm leaving you in good hands. And, um, well, everyone... have a great judging!"

Apparently he could have demanded to stay, Charlotte said afterwards, but congratulated Mark on playing it right. The fact that the Major insisted on pushing frail old Charlotte round was a constant visual reminder of how Regina, as Rachel said, 'had gone ballistic."

Mark, having crept modestly away and fortified by coffee and doughnuts, felt like a child let out of school early. In fact, free to wander around the whole Miami Expo, the displays and exhibits mint fresh, the walk ways swept clean, Mark started to feel even more like a journalist or VIP. It was being the Queen going round Chelsea the night before, everything perfect and dew fresh like the creation of the world, the Garden of Eden. And facing the main entrance, across the Expo hall, in the distance on the far wall there was The Magic Carpet, Orchid Empire's extravaganza. And all around were the other banked up extravaganzas of orchids, the exhibits, poised and perfect. Charlotte always said she was mystified how exhibitors got so rapt over their exhibits, how much they'd sacrifice in time and effort, how they'd lay their most beautiful orchids at the altar of commerce and the quirky prejudices of the judging system. Mark suddenly saw it as religious ritual: nothing less. Mandalas maybe but these were all rites of spring, ceremonies of rebirth and renewal.

Mark found he was checking out the displays, if not like an old hand, as Charlotte had said, at least with an exhibitor's eye. Looking for 'Orchid Fantasies' Mark could see the exhibitors, like Charlotte at any other time, had decided to stick with what they knew and what they had: the grottoes, the trellises, a few tiny bridges to nowhere and only one cardboard wall. Orchids by Ed had a very nice effect; gauzy, draped muslin, a dreamlike feel, billowing over the plants but unfortunately already drooping here and there and snagging top flowers. Most exhibits seemed to have at least one big old specimen plant eating up space. "You can't blame the big commercial people for going with the quick and easy stuff but who now is going to keep these sacrificial wonders in their greenhouses?" Charlotte had grumbled even about her magnificent *Cattleya guatemalensis.* "Takes up a quarter of a hundred square foot exhibit for three days *if* it's in bloom and a magnificent section of my bench *all year.*"

It was Bert who had lamented the fact that when the old firms died out, with them went so many of the great orchids, the perennial one of a kind stars and 'pets,' like Larry and Ken's *lamellata*, the great *Vanda* by the pool.

There were the tiny gravel paths and mulch strewn nooks, the neat sign-posted names in gold or silver on black; the traditional white and pink and now yellow and new colors of the *Phalaenopsis*, the orchid exhibitors' friend, everybody's friend. Down in the front of exhibits were the delicate clumps of orchids like hare bells and tiny irises, or milk maids and violets among the moss and paphiopedilums, the slipper orchids that made Mark think of garden gnomes. Bert said they used to be called 'toads' but maybe no longer as the standard mottled greens and browns seemed to be losing ground to fancy pinks and iridescent purples. But the traditional purples and lavender blues of Charlotte's cattleyas and vandas were still everywhere, the big blue vandas rising up like delphiniums or hollyhocks.

The sun was shining through the glass doors, the whole place empty of people and so quiet, the occasional voice of a cleaner or worker came as low as though they were in church. All the banked up flowers, thought Mark, like a big church, a cathedral, ready for a great wedding or a funeral. Certainly Rachel had been dressed formally. Mark realized how long ago it was that he'd ached for even a sight of Rachel. Now he looked to Rachel for news of Jen. And she was totally useless, so preoccupied, especially this week. Jen could have been packing up those gloomy earthenware plates, unplugging the TV and Rachel would not have noticed. And it was a shock how quickly and completely all links with Jen seemed to have been broken.

"Charlotte, when you hear from Jen ask her to call. If I'm gone remind her it's UK time, five hours on. She can leave a number with my mother."

"Rachel, don't you have an email address for Jen? Well, that one, she's not responding."

"Charlotte, could you get me Jen's number from Rachel when she calls, if she calls, wherever she calls from, when she comes back, if she comes back..." '

Mark was feeling chilly as he always did inside buildings in South Florida, even though he'd worn his long sleeved shirt for the judging. He wanted to go out into the sun. In a week he'd be back in the uncertain North London weather of early March. The sun was shining away, wasting itself beyond the glass doors but Mark was not sure with this reverential empty, hushed hall, whether he'd be allowed back in or whether, with the orchid judging going on, there'd be anyone at the doors. He thought wistfully of Orchid Empire's private entrance round the back, the emergency exit, but inaccessible now, the bale of chicken wire gone.

Mark decided it would be a good moment to see Regina's triumph; Orchid Magic's exhibit and quickly, before any of her people were around. And there it was, five hundred square feet, a tribute as Larry said to all the people Regina had intimidated over the years, full of their beautiful specimen plants. Mark wondered how many of them were from Sun Corner members, or were borrowed, wheedled, bamboozled, or extracted from probate. He certainly had not seen much evidence of these when he'd visited Orchid Magic. As for the theme, stuck among the plants on Orchid Magic's trademark gently rounded hill ('Regina's burial mound' as Larry called it), there appeared to be the contents of Cooper's Thai restaurant. Red and gold lanterns sat among the phals and gilt dragons poked their snouts out of the ferns. Decorated golden boats like jewel encrusted gondolas nosed into clumps of epidendrums and oncidiums while on the summit of the little hill a soft spotlight played on a miniature pagoda and in the center of the pagoda was what looked like the Buddha, the Buddha from Orchid Magic.

Mark thought of the crazy idea they'd had of tethering a goat in the midst of Regina's exhibit. In fact, of course, it would just eat every one's contributions, their own prize orchids, not Regina's. Certainly, at the moment, it seemed no sabotage was needed. Socially, at least, with the judges, Regina had sabotaged herself. Mark could tell Althea how well the God of the Crossroads had done: Regina had made so many bad choices. He took another turn of the hall, almost in a dreamlike state with the heady flowers, hushed voices, high ceilings. There was the sound of birds high up and then the cooing of doves. Birds, way up, inside, far above the Magic Carpet, far above the reach of the cherry pickers and fork lifts, above the little woods and hillsides and gardens created below. And for all the silly titles, the little gimmicks, it did seem for a moment, with the fresh sparkle and velvety brilliance, a kind of still life paradise, a Rousseau; the trickle of running water, those orchid plumbers at work, the dream gardens and tiny grottoes and forest glades. It was as though a lion's head could poke out with little round ears through the greenery, a wolf lie down with the lamb in the middle of the phals, kittens and puppies among the angraecums, with lambs nibbling round the paphs along the front, their hooves deep in the jewel orchids, while behind, a massive *Epidendrum* would cascade down like a weeping willow beside a haughty wading bird.

Here Mark was on his own in this vast arena, no-one wondering how much he knew. It didn't matter if he couldn't tell a *spathulatum* from a *Brassolaeliocattleya,* an early hybrid or a late mistake, an award winner or a dog, or whether it was a Mr. Hooker or Mr. Watson who discovered this or that orchid or a Glenda Snodgrass had been the orchid judge named for that unfortunate *Oncidium*. The beauty was just laid out before him or rather, as Mark well knew, stuck in, tied down, staked, hammered, cursed and pleaded with.

There was a surge of voices behind him and Mark saw bearing down groups of threes and fours, fours and fives, the orchid judges. Suddenly a group disappeared, plunging into an exhibit. What had Charlotte said? Starting with ribbon judging, orchids were nominated among those entered for individuals, the best of those Tilly and the other ladies of the clip boards had registered, but then the teams chosen would go round the hall to see if they wanted to pull out any *other* orchids from exhibits for scoring too. Mark moved further on, towards the sale booths. He saw Charlotte with another group, the gallant Major still pushing her chair. No sign of Regina. After the ribbons were awarded the serious judging began, the American Orchid Society judging that would go into the record books. Each AOS judge could also pull an orchid from a display and present it to the team, Charlotte said: "An *Oncidium* for the *Oncidium* team, and so on and all the judges vote on the AOS show trophy. As Regina hand picks her team to judge for the Best Exhibit, usually her First Place ribbon is waving in the breeze by the time the AOS judges come round and it takes a hardy soul to stand back and decide maybe it's *not* the best display in the show after all." So there were these groups stepping into the enchanted forests; little forays hunting down the elusive, the prize flowers, making that orchid dance, the steps forward to view and the steps back. Some of the teams were jostling in front of the same exhibit, the student judges with the clip boards and the reference books, keeping score. Mark couldn't see Rachel. She must have been on another team, going the other way.

Mark moved further on, between the booths, the hutches for all the *vendors;* that would be himself and Rachel, tomorrow, Friday morning. They were supposed to be bringing material in that afternoon, set up the booth and then stay for the party. Rounding the curve Mark found himself back to the pride of place where Regina's exhibit was, the central five-hundred square feet. It looked like he'd been forestalled. A judging group had got there before him, must have come the other way.

As Mark grew closer he saw the group in front of Orchid Magic's exhibit was composed of Cooper and Mike and three men, two with brief cases, all in suits. This was it. Regina had pulled out all the stops. Could it be a federal offence to take your exhibit up the wall? Or maybe it was USDA or the State of Florida sales tax people. No telling what laws and rules Charlotte had broken. Regina was out to get her any way she could. The birds were still twittering far above. One of the men was talking into a cell phone. The fact that Mike and even Cooper were in suits gave the whole scene a chilling, nightmarish quality. It was Cooper who spotted Mark first. "Hi, Mark! In fact, right here is the gentleman who first alerted me to the concrete evidence. Mark, I believe you visited Orchid Magic back in early January? Yes? These gentlemen are interested in the fact that there was a small statue of a Buddha there and the proprietor intimated to you that it was a genuine Buddha, that is a statue from a temple, right?"

"Um... Yes."

The oldest man in the group, asked, "And, sir, would you say this is the same one?"

"Well, I'm not very close, of course. It's certainly approximately the same size. It looks the same. In fact, when I first saw it here I thought maybe it was a copy, I mean because it *did* look the same. And well, a copy because, Regina did say it was very precious, so I wouldn't have thought it was actually *here*. But I was told that there were other artifacts there...so may be this is one of them..." Mark, annoyed with himself for rattling on, couldn't stop from adding, "Oh, though I know the security is very good." Mark had the sudden chill feeling, this was something very serious indeed. He wanted to ask Mike or Cooper what on earth was happening but didn't even want to catch their eye, to look like he was trying to slip mental messages across the space, like an illicit note through the bars.

There was a moment of judicial silence. The oldest man was flexing his jaw, staring hard at a *Cattleya lueddemanniana*. Someone was jingling change in their pocket. Mike was looking at the exhibit over the man's shoulder; even at this moment, thought Mark, probably checking out the number of frivolous *Phalaenopsis* or the mislabeling of cool loving bulbophyllums.

"Well, there we are, gentlemen. And you've given all the paper work, that was all the paper work that came through?"

"Yes," said Cooper. "And all the contact numbers are there. There's a time difference but we can catch up with my sources tomorrow, no, tonight."

Mark realized these guys are cops. This is not anything to do with the American Orchid Society, the top Expo people. This has nothing to do with security, or Dade County ordinances or, what had Bert said sometimes happened? The USDA spraying for bugs. A group of judges came into view, in a soft swirl of voices. One, more dominant than the others was heard to repeat *Oncidinae*...Mark watched them drift closer, the *Oncidium* alliance group.

"I am sorry, ma'am, sir. I am afraid this exhibit, this area must be off limits at the present time." The group slowed to a halt; voices grew louder. "Now if you wouldn't mind just moving on…"

Mark wondered if they would put the yellow tape there: Crime Scene DO NOT CROSS THIS LINE. Christ. His heart thumping, he stared at the ground, definitely not wanting to catch Cooper or Mike's eye. Thank God Charlotte always just shoved in two garden chairs and a bird bath. Maybe her spear in the Florida room was the property of a chief, the assagai: "Though a word of Berber origins, in fact a missile of the South African tribes." Well, they raided nurseries now for anything, especially orchid nurseries: evidence of smuggling, of robbery, undocumented aliens, dealing in endangered species. There was another quiet moment as though these men really were mourning something, the moment before landing Regina with the big one. The group of judges drifted away, murmuring, looking over their shoulders and another group hove into view. There was the Major still pushing Charlotte. Now they were doing *Vandaceous* and angraecums.

"Sorry people. If you wouldn't mind just omitting this exhibit here. Thank-you. What? Sir, we'll be holding a conference shortly to let everyone know what's happening." The speaker, the man with the poker face, turned to Mike and Cooper. "And where is the proprietor, the owner of this firm?"

"She's got to be right here," Cooper said, "the member of another team."

The man in charge obviously didn't think it appropriate to go on waiting for every group to drift into sight. "Well I suggest we go look for her and let's call security and post someone here. Has Metro Dade or Miami been informed?"

"Right, sir," he turned to Mark. "You are resident here?"

"Actually I'm from England. I was going home in a week."

"We may have to ask you to stay or to return. This investigation is still in its early stages."

Suddenly Regina seemed too unimportant for all this. Mark had been thinking of joking with Althea, joking that the God of the Crossroads certainly came through for us; of course, the rum we were giving him was first class. Charlotte had a stockpile of excellent rum.

Everyone from the islands brought it up as a present but she couldn't be shifted from her beloved gin. But this was not the thing for jokes yet. This was like a traffic accident. Mike and Cooper moved off with the officials. Charlotte had disappeared, propelled out of sight by the Major who, true to old instincts, was clearing the area of civilians.

Birds could still be heard high overhead in the upper reaches of the Expo. Mark felt a little weak at the knees and went to sit down on a bench between two litter bins. No more groups hove into sight. Perhaps everything had ground to a halt. Mark could hear a murmur, maybe distant traffic, maybe a little fountain in one of the exhibits. Well, he had been summoned to Miami, South Florida, to save his aunt from the machinations of orchid predators, to whit, as Charlotte would say, the Queen, the President of the Miami Orchid Club and her cohorts, and in a slightly unintentional, off center kind of a way that looked like exactly what Mark had done.

25

The End

The Major had gathered the judges together on Thursday morning and the vendors and exhibitors in the afternoon, pleading with them not to get involved talking and trying to explain the whole thing to the general public: "They would, unfortunately, be reading about it all soon enough in the papers." He had taken over in the vacuum left by Regina's removal. All possible rivals or independent thinkers in the Miami Orchid Club having been long since eliminated or exiled there was no one left. The handpicked vice-president had totally gone to pieces on hearing that Regina was no longer with them. Regina herself had disappeared: taken into custody, under arrest, held at the Dade Correctional Institute demanding softer sheets or just forbidden to leave Orchid Magic premises, no one was quite sure and there was no Mike or Cooper around to ask. The ribbon judging had gone on and the American Orchid Society judging but in such a lopsided, weepy atmosphere that for the first time in Miami Orchid Club history the judges actually gave out a total of fifteen American Orchid Society awards.

"Unheard of!" Charlotte said. "More orchids grown here than anywhere else in the US and apart from Regina's hoard we are usually the stingiest region for awards."

Regina's entries might have swept the board in the traumatic atmosphere surrounding her removal but the Major ruled that it was neither seemly nor maybe even legal in the present state of affairs to submit Orchid Magic's plants for competition and anyway, they were sequestered behind the yellow line. So the Major and team leaders had led the shaken judges right past the central five hundred square foot crime scene exhibit and in the ruins of Regina's empire they had discovered many neglected gems. Cooper's *Renanthera* was awarded an FCC, a First Class Certificate, even though it was suspended above the judges' heads. To be suspended over the heads of judges seemed, after seeing the yellow crime tape, the policemen at the main entrance, quite an innocent digression from the norm.

One of Rachel's own crosses, a first bloom seedling, took an AM, an Award of Merit. She also received two CHMs, Certificates of Horticultural Merit, and Bert won second place in the two-hundred square foot division for Best Exhibit and several ribbons. And Hank with the dynamic Las Olas Orchid Club won first place, three hundred square feet *and* the AOS show trophy. At the conclusion Charlotte was also presented with a lifetime achievement award which she said seemed to have been invented on the spot or more likely, had been intended for Regina.

The gala party was always held on Thursday evening. As it had been decided there was no way to cancel the food or the arrival of the guests, most of whom had no idea what had gone on that morning, the party went ahead. In any other circumstance Mark and Charlotte would have driven back from the judging in the early afternoon and that would have been it. After getting orchids ready for the booth on Friday morning, Mark would have retired to the porch where Charlotte would have joined him following her nap. Mindful of having to be on the road again by seven the next morning, Mark would have had two less beers than usual, fed the dogs, rehashed the stories and gossip and gone to bed early. But such was the adrenalin flowing and the tension in the air that it was accepted even though they hadn't got home till three in the afternoon, Mark would be driving the Volvo straight back with Charlotte no later than six.

After feeding the dogs, pouring a quick Scotch and a gin and lime for Charlotte, Mark started back to Miami, going much too fast down Quail Roost Drive. "Trying to get there before the Volvo realizes it has problems" as Charlotte said. They were both afraid of "Missing any of the good stuff" though they weren't quite sure what the good stuff might be. Perhaps some presentation by one of the serious men in suits, appearing in front of Fredz Kloze Out Grecian urns, laying forth the intricacies of the plot before the assembled company or giving a short but eloquent speech about crime not paying.

What Mark and Charlotte had almost forgotten about was the impact of Orchid Empire's contribution to the Expo: their tapestry on the wall, their magic carpet, their *Orchid Fantasy*. It dominated the hall even more at night, there beyond the buffet tables and banks of flowers and ferns, glowing above the Royal palms. Someone, perhaps Ted or Chuck and the boys, had set up a spotlight, paying their own tribute to Orchid Empire's rebellious enterprise, and it lit up, in the center of the far wall, the crimson cascade of the *Renanthera*. Down below every guest, colleague, vendor, exhibitor, old acquaintance or friend was congratulating Charlotte. And, sweetest of all, as she told Mark on the way home, it was the most conservative, the most genteel, the most hidebound "pain in the necks" who were the most grateful; grateful for a counter attraction to the yellow tape crime scene.

Charlotte, the disruptive member of the Miami Orchid Club, the local thorn in the side of the respectable orchid world, had become its salvation, leading the reporters, the journalists and gossip mongers to a counter attraction, a crazy, eye-stopping departure from the norm. Making light of her new found celebrity, Charlotte announced credit where credit was due: to Rachel of Bios orchids for her dynamic energy in bringing Charlotte's vision to fruition; to Regina, "Who did, so to speak, drive us *all* up the wall!" and above all to the unsung genius of Cairo greengrocers, who, as she pointed out to her puzzled listeners, "From now on will no longer be unsung!"

The story going round was that Regina had been caught as importer of forbidden art artifacts from Thailand, of theft of Thailand's national treasures. Many more were expected to be discovered at her house or on the premises of Orchid Magic. There'd been a tip off apparently, and some clever electronic communications between Bangkok and Miami and verification, still awaiting official confirmation, had taken place the very morning of the judging. More facts were coming out. There was also a faint rumor, spread by a desperate *Reginista,* said

Larry, that someone had planted stolen property in Regina's exhibit. That *was* plausible, said Rachel: as so much in her exhibit wasn't really hers anyway, how would she know? But old stories were surfacing too, stuff about involvement in drug smuggling long ago.

They were all together for the evening, Larry and Ken in lightweight dinner jackets, Larry a pale blue, Ken white, looking, with their smooth tans, very out of reach, glamorously American. Rachel was sparkling in a short, strapless emerald green dress. Charlotte had draped some exotic shawl over her standard slacks and was wearing a beaded black top that glinted and caught the light. "Haven't worn it for years, probably all perished," she was telling everyone, "so if the threads break, pick up at least the larger beads. This is all pure jet."

Mark once again had his one good shirt on but it was much warmer than New Year.

"Not so much that it's March," said Ken, "but at a show they need to keep the orchids feeling comfortable."

"No Mike, no Cooper," observed Charlotte. "It's almost as though they've been taken into custody themselves."

"Maybe," said Rachel, "they've both been told they shouldn't say much at this stage."

"You know," said Mark, "mentioning the Buddha being at Orchid Magic, I never gave it a second thought."

"Mark, the modest Brit!" Larry raised his glass. "The man, the hero behind it all! The dragon slayer and never even knew it! And now what? Back to chilly old England."

"You're sounding like Alvin."

"Ouch! Seriously, Mark, there's going to be real gap when you go. Got to get Charlotte to have you back."

"With all this business, the boy may be back sooner than you think."

"—So are you coming or going?" Charlotte had asked Mark on the way to the party. "You're welcome to stay!"

"They're supposed to let me know. I've told them when my flight leaves. I can't help feeling bad in a way. I mean I'm glad Regina's out,

out of power and can't influence people, you know cause trouble, hurt people like you and Rachel but it all seems rather drastic."

"Don't you worry!" Larry was saying that evening: "This is America! We look after our own! The worst that will happen is she'll land up in some minimum security place, learn to cheat more on her taxes and improve her golf swing."

"Shame she wasn't on one of her trips to Thailand, and got caught *there!*" Charlotte said with one of her wicked grins. "Then it might be legitimate to feel a little sorry. Don't take yourself too seriously, my boy! Larry's right. Regina will get a smart defense lawyer and they'll bugger about with all this. But the main thing in practical terms is she's out of the AOS and Miami scene. Can never be President again. Orchid societies don't like scandal. Ironically that's why Regina survived for so long. Members prefer to ignore low level skulduggery rather than draw attention to themselves by making a fuss."

"Someone must have raided the cellars!" Larry nodded over to the buffet where two young bar men were pouring out wine non stop. "This is not Regina's style at all. This proves once and for all the old regime is dead! Who's for a refill?"

The dinner plates were a generous size and plastic, not paper; Mark needed no Jen to organize him. No one had mentioned Jen. Bert was always pretty quiet about everything but here were Larry and Ken, Rachel and Charlotte, and himself and it was as though Jen had sunk without trace. So this was the famed short attention span of Americans, their shallow, transitory attachments, easily broken across these vast distances. Mark felt sad and disappointed in these people he considered personal friends, forgetting entirely that, brooding about her in private, he had not mentioned Jen either.

The Miami Expo's Orchid Fantasy opened to the public on Friday morning. At the pleading of the Major and the Expo committee the yellow crime tape had been removed but flagging tape looped between the standard metal chairs had been considered not official or solid enough and the maintenance people had been called in to create a real barrier of saw horses and planks around Regina's exhibit. Bereft of extra lights, its center piece was shadowed and forlorn. Crowning the gentle hill rising in the center of the exhibit, the little golden pagoda-like trellis that had housed the Buddha, looked drab and cheap, the niche dark and empty. Mark thought of the garden of Gethsemane, dark and bleak on Maundy Thursday, though if the atmosphere had been more joyful, it would have been more like Easter morning, with the tomb thrown open and Christ gone.

It had been a futile hope that, if anyone asked, word could be spread that Regina was sick, worn out by the pressures of the Expo and her multitudinous duties and there it was in Friday's *Herald: This Year's Miami Orchid Expo Opens In Face of Scandal. The President of the Miami Orchid Club and Chairman of the Miami Orchid Expo was detained Thursday morning at the Expo Center on suspicion of trafficking in stolen Thai artifacts. A police spokesperson in Miami Dade declined to comment, stating this was a Federal investigation in co-operation with Interpol. A lawyer for Orchid Magic, the nursery currently owned and operated by the suspect, declined to comment. A source close to the investigation who declined to be identified stated that some sources both in Thailand and South Florida say this maybe the 'tip of the iceberg.' Local orchid enthusiasts and fellow growers expressed shock and surprise but said the show will go on. Hours today and Saturday will be 9:00 AM to 9:00 PM: Sunday 10:00 till 6:00 PM. Admission $12. Children under 12 free.*

Well, as Larry was to say, reflecting later on the record breaking attendance at the Expo,

"What a trooper! We always knew Regina would do anything to get the Expo on the front page. She's done it again!"

Six fifteen Friday morning: trudging through the dogs to push trays of plants into the back of the Volvo. Pulling them out at six twenty because they've not been watered. Pushing them back in, wondering what seedlings will sell, fitting in as many flowering ones as possible in on the passenger seat, pushing the seat back for a tall *Encyclia*. Taking along the cash box; Rachel always says you get the float. Sales book, pens, pencils, extra tags, price dots, cardboard for extra signs and heavy black pen in case she hasn't done them on the computer: *Clones 2 @ 20 each, three for fifty*. Seedlings: different prices. The extra five minutes Mark took to make a pot of tea and let it stand, meant ten minutes stuck in the queue for the toll plaza. But once there, at the Expo, driving right across the car park to leave the Volvo outside their own private emergency exit door. Then racing back to the *front* entrance, past the exhibits, the vendors: (not "How's it going?" this show but "Did you *hear?*" and "Anything new?") all the way to the back and The Magic Carpet. Round the corner, past the three trash bins, wedge open the emergency exit and unload the Volvo. Help Rachel unload, carting everything back towards the center and the sales booth, to be ready for the doors opening at nine. And no problem this time, however far away their sales booth might be from their exhibit. All they had to say was "Look! Look up! See? There's the parent plant, the exempla–it's on the wall!"

On the road home at ten past nine Friday evening, home by ten. Carlos had fed the dogs. Fumbling for the light switch in the shade houses, checking in the back with the flashlight for two special orders, the plants forgotten that morning; replenishing the seedlings that had sold. More flowering stuff if it's been selling well and even if it hasn't. Saturday is a whole different day. Sometimes. True, though, Friday was the day for the botanicals, for the orchid society people and the best and cleanest of the commercial plants so the orchidists won't decide the nursery's going downhill and the spray program a total disaster. Saturday always mainstream but wait till Sunday to bring in the scratch and dents and the fully open, even fading so the Sunday afternoon bargain hunters can be allowed to beat you down, you with heart-rending reluctance, on price.

Charlotte sitting on the porch waiting for a report Friday evening so cut preparation for Saturday short, though that means getting up earlier still on Saturday morning. Stop just to estimate how much can be packed in with the back seat down; one large Cuban pig or a dozen six and eight inch flowering baskets and three or four trays of seedlings plus a few odds and sods. Drinking too many beers, feeling tired and deserving. Set the alarm for six, no, it's Saturday morning, no rush hour. Reset alarm for six thirty. Lie there remembering forgot to ask Charlotte about the special orders. "This woman says you had a lovely yellow *mini-catt* in your exhibit two years ago and promised her one." One of the friends of Charlotte. Wondering which person to offend more: Charlotte, waking her up at six on Saturday morning or the customer. No-brainer: *So sorry, Charlotte says those crosses are no longer available.*

Saturday: home by ten fifteen with plants Rachel decided not likely to sell on Sunday and not to be sold cheap, and a six pack from the closest gas station. Feeding the dogs by flashlight. Hunting around by flashlight again, anything coming into bloom, but they all need names. Reporting to Charlotte; all the compliments on The Magic Carpet, all the shock, horror, drama of the Regina debacle. Going like a bomb, though: *Any more seedlings of... ? Any more flowering stuff at all?* Making sure float is OK; shoving money and checks under the pillow. Friday and Saturday night, Charlotte saying "Just put it somewhere, dear boy." Battle report and battle strategy for Sunday: *how low to go with these, Charlotte?* "Low as you like, dear boy. Don't want to see these back here."

Sunday: the trays emptying, the culture sheets flying out but have to make decisions, decisions because it all has to come back Sunday night if it doesn't sell or unless you sell it cheap.

"Vendors, do not take anything out of your exhibit before six o' clock. Breakdown is not till six."

Breakdown: what an appropriate word, thought Mark, so tired his voice had almost disappeared. There was the booth to dismantle, the unsold flasks and compots to tray up and move out. But a lovely number of empty trays stacking up: that meant great sales. There was Rachel's prize-winning AM to collect from the display area, the first bloom seedling Mike had entered. And her prize. A very nice...was it a butter dish? ("I see you in twenty years, Rachel, surrounded by cut glass fruit bowls and butter dishes.") At least it wouldn't be ash trays. So many people to hug and say goodbye to. A lot of last words to share on the incredible Magic Carpet, Regina, Charlotte and Mark's departure. It was six forty before they had time to get to their wall and the whole thing to dismantle. The quilt of orchids had lasted but the top vandas had a definite droop.

There was still no Cooper or Mike but just as Rachel was saying wearily that it looked like Larry and Ken were helping Bert, they appeared, full of apologies. There had been a crisis with one of the cats. They were ready to help and had just checked with Bert on the way in who had his own faithful band of volunteers running to and fro, and would be out of the hall in no time. Mark got the fruit picker from the U Haul. They couldn't locate Chuck and the cherry picker but Rachel took Larry off to find Ted's tall, triangular ladder and with the wire cutters and Larry and Ken helping, they managed to unhook and disentangle all the orchids. Rachel happy up the ladder; the smaller orchids placed in the fruit picker for a quick swing down, the big cattleyas just dropped, like victims from a burning building, into the waiting hands below.

"Vandas dehydrated, definitely, "said Larry. "But wow! Can't really be sorry. The whole thing unbelievable! And what a triumph."

Rachel had backed up the U haul to their exit. "God bless our exit" she said wearily. Mark was filling the Volvo, the trays of smaller orchids from Charlotte's permanent collection, the cash box and trophies as Rachel insisted and the box of macadamia nut chocolates from one of the Hawaiians.

"There are so many ferns left," Rachel muttered, looking up at the chicken wire between the pipes. "But we can come in and finish Monday morning."

"I'll bring in Carlos," said Mark.

Mark pulled into Orchid Empire just after nine, the Volvo nosing through the dogs. Something else to do before a beer, thought Mark wearily, feed the dogs. Charlotte's voice came from the porch: "Just leave everything! Carlos will get the plants out early! Leave it all to the morning!"

"Hang on! Let me just feed the dogs!" Mark knew if he sat down first he would never get up again. Dropping down into the rocking chair five minutes later, Mark announced, "We did fine! You'll be pleased!" Though he felt too tired to go through it all; the great day Rachel had with her flasks and compots, the surprising sale of a strapping, mud-colored *Vanda* whose only claim on any one's dollar was that it had a second flower spike. Rachel had put a price on it of seventy-five for a joke, before the bargain hunters arrived, and someone had snapped it up.

Mark had brought in a cold beer and a spare from the fridge in the potting shed. Charlotte had been good; there was already corn bread and some of Ruby's fried chicken on the little bamboo stand. "Well, dear boy, thank you for manning the fort," she announced crisply. "We can talk about it all in the morning."

It was wonderful to sit back in the rocking chair with a cold beer, eyes closed and silent. The dogs had finished pushing their hub caps around. The night before, ladling out the chow, Mark had seen an owl gliding away under the branches of the mangoes. There was, as always, the engulfing, industrial strength, hot weather noise of the crickets or cicadas drilling through the dark among the big, tropical leaves. And the sounds of the bamboo, creaking and squealing as the stems rubbed together, sometimes making kissy noises.

Mark opened his second beer. He might do a Charlotte, just nod off and sleep on the porch. He couldn't decide if he was hungry or not. Rachel had opened a tin of cashew nuts sometime in the afternoon; no, that had been Saturday. There'd been those limp grapes that had been fresh on Friday. Rachel had been right: sign of a good show, no time to eat, no time to pee.

"I think Orchid Empire's done really well. Bios too. We aced it! Cooper's got his *Renanthera* back. Promised Rachel he's going to put a bunch of seed pods on it. Hard to believe, really." Mark shook his head. "Harry and the Sun Corner people took a bunch of pictures. A lot of people did. Rachel says she'll make sure you send me some. No one could believe it! I couldn't and I'd been up in the bloody cherry picker. It's a real shame—"*It's a real shame Jen wasn't there, wasn't there to see...Jen who always did so much.* Overhead a forty year old Royal palm suddenly shed a frond that hit the ground with a great *whomp* that started the dogs barking. The first time it happened Charlotte had cackled, "It's a falling *leaf!* A leaf that can block two lanes of traffic! Now *there's* the tropics for you!"

Mark would miss Charlotte's comments on the natural world and everything else. Like the whole world of ants: all the different sorts. When he said why are these big ones just milling about on the table, like they've got no plan? She'd said, "Oh they're called carpenter ants. Ever had to deal with carpenters?"

"I'll miss all the noises," Mark said sleepily. "When I'm at the computer at night, really strong thumps against the screen, those big lizards lunging after the moths. First time I thought it was someone outside trying to get my attention. Of course, Charlotte you're no friend of the lizards. If you don't put the lights on they're not going to get their moths. And they all seem to be pregnant. At least the pale ones. You can see the eggs inside as they run up the screen."

No word, no email, no number. And no one seems to know. She's disappeared. You could always extend your ticket, that was Jen. No word yet about staying on because of the whole Regina affair. Do the authorities pick up the tab? Maybe not, if you stay with relatives i.e. Charlotte. Have to face the fact Jen already said goodbye. Outside Pelican Mall in a steady drizzle. That bulging brief case, leaving the job. Hey, Happy Valentine's! Well, Thank-you and Goodnight!

"Lizards? Most are imports; ghekos, chameleons, chance arrivals from somewhere else," Charlotte was saying, "like the people. And here they don't freeze to death or go down into the drains they hop on a tree and find a sunny spot. Look at our group. Coop's the only one who's always been here, a Florida boy. Even Bert came from somewhere else as a child. The rest of us are typical; the *real* South Floridians, as Mike says, all transients and transplants. He and Rachel and Larry are all Mid-west. Ken, Ken's from New England I think."

"Larry's from the Mid-west, too? The outrageous teenager in some small place having to get out of town!"

"Well, I don't know about *that*. He's a dear boy but he's certainly a bit of a ham. Of course, Jen was the ultimate transient. What do they call them? An army brat!"

"I'm sorry Jen missed all the show, *The Magic Carpet*," Mark said. "She was always so good at shows, doing so much of the background work. And, Rachel says, the selling too."

"She called from California."

"What? When?"

"Rachel says apparently she's going to Bristol. She's got a job in Bristol."

"Oh... You hear Americans say all the time, 'He's going to Paris, France' and you think 'Of course, you fool! Where do you *think* Paris is?' We don't know there's a Paris in —what? Idaho or somewhere. So now it's *Bristol, California*. You see? Same thing." Mark stood up and for a moment felt he'd stood up a little too quickly. After only two beers! And *American* beers! The Miami Expo had taken a greater toll on him than he'd realized. But, as Ned always declared, it was precisely at these moments of stress, doubt and confusion, that you needed another one.

"Well, let's toast the new job, then!" Mark announced loudly and was off, zig zagging through the couches in the dim Florida room and into the kitchen. No tray, and to hell with tea towels, to hell with hygiene. He was heading back to Grungy Land. Grabbing the bottle of Scotch by the neck, he shoved the other hand, all sweaty thumb and fingers, into a pair of Charlotte's squat, solid glasses. Jen wants to mess around with these California types, that's her problem. How can anyone compete with California? That bourne from which no traveler returns.

"Apparently a good opening," Charlotte continued when Mark came back. "No, not for me, dear boy. The company headquarters are in California. Rachel says Jen may take a cut in salary but it's going to be something new, some kind of small, speciality shipping operation. They want someone to organize the paper work."

"Well then, cheers! Here's to Jen and the ships and the lizards and the moths! And wait a minute, why not throw in the hedgehogs while we're at it!"

"Young man, I think you need to go to bed. By the way, we're going to be planning a little get together, a little party before you leave. Larry and Ken are feeling guilty we never did anything for you while you were here. But we'll talk about it all in the morning. No, no pig! Only a little 'do.' We'll talk about it all in the morning."

26

The Last Party

"We've got you a week in a wonderful little hotel on South Beach. Well, you've got ten days left and Ken has all these good connections from his hotel management days so it's settled. And at least it will get you out of HOME-stead!"

Larry had remained resolutely unimpressed by the fact of the rodeo in Homestead, the availability of Stilton cheese and Mark's lyric account of the Martin Luther King Parade: the black and Latin Miami high school bands that had come down to march through the town, all spangles and smiles, white gloves and frowns, capes and flashing instruments. Mark wondered if something like that could ever come to Totters Green.

"I don't know if Ken's connection means free board and lodging," said Charlotte, "but I've got a check for you here. Nonsense! Can't send you back to north London without some sand in your shoes. I don't think your sister and mother realize how far we are from the sea. Typical of the old houses, of course, a healthy respect for hurricanes and storm surge not like this damn fool business now of building on the beach." Charlotte waved away thanks and protests. "You did better than I thought you would! I'll be sorry to see you go. Never thought I'd be saying that! And in fact one reason to ship you off to the beach right now is you're losing your room! Rachel will be coming!"

"When I heard how much Rachel was paying in *rent* on that place especially now Jen is gone! Ridiculous! Dead money! Well, we may very well fight, as my dear mother would say, like two wasps in a bottle but Coop will keep the peace, and Bert. So your send off will also be a little party, the inaugural bash for Bios Orchids and Orchid Empire.

Larry thought it up. Killing two birds with one stone! Haven't told Rachel about any party. She's scurrying about to get out of that place. If she can vacate in the next day or two then she avoids some kind of a penalty; they have a new renter they say, though I think they're rushing her out of spite. It'll be a bit of a shambles but at Orchid Empire that's par for the course. Ruby's been asked for her legendary corn bread and fried chicken and we provide the legendary drink. So I suggest you go off for it tonight because I need you to pick up a lottery ticket. When it hits twenty million," Charlotte said, "I buy a ticket. From that place on Krome."

Charlotte's lucky gas station, where Mark went for emergency milk and beer, was lit up in the twilight in the corner of a ploughed field on Krome Avenue. There was always a queue as the sun went down, men in jeans and work boots buying their beer, this night a long line for lottery tickets too. Mark thought of Ruby's neighbor, picking beans again. The farmers had replanted after the freeze, the *Herald* reported and with South Dade's climate were back in business.

"Just move the ashtrays off, dear boy and put out the glasses. In fact, let's get rid of those ashtrays altogether. Need to get Carlos to trim things back a little more. Some of the bottles from the lab will probably land up here and they'll need more light."

The Florida room was growing darker again as the foliage grew back. There were still staples in the screen frames from New Year's Eve, from the tacking up of that plastic. And now Rachel would be sleeping in the spare room. Mark thought he should warn her about the wardrobe door; it swung open in the middle of the night with a groan if you didn't wedge something against it. He wondered if she could do anything about the classic, indestructible spare room smell. Maybe bring in some of Coop's new fragrant hybrids. They'd have to put Ruby's stuff somewhere for safe keeping before the march of the bottles. Ruby wasn't coming; it was Althea who'd be bringing the corn bread and chicken.

"Your *Dr. Gibson!* Oh, *yes!* Althea thought I knew. You have crust, young man! Couldn't have done better myself. No word on the Queen's fortunes yet. Mike is off apparently pursuing some new Queenly transgression, some Royal misdemeanor, on his own account."

Mark tried to make Charlotte sit down. Unusual for her, she looked too hot, leaning heavily on her stick and starting to scowl. It wasn't the party Charlotte was worried about Mark realized but the advent of Rachel. "I'm fine! Mid March can have the hottest temperatures of the year, dry too. In the summer here, storms *drop* the temps. Up to ten degrees cooler! People forget that! Too busy whining."

"We came early!" Larry's voice carried over the barking of the dogs. He had his Edwardian whicker picnic basket and a bunch of bright, mixed flowers ("Relax! Not an orchid among them!") Ken followed, carrying straight on to the kitchen with a stack of containers.

Larry looked at Charlotte. "Mark, I think we should all sit down and have a nice cup of afternoon tea. Charlotte, what time did you tell everyone to come?"

"I said six to catch the light in the greenhouses but it's all over the place today. Everyone's helping Rachel. Bert's getting a load of plants in the van. Coop's got his pick up. Place was furnished so Rachel only has the orchid material to bother about. She prefers to do that bit by bit rather than stacking everything up in a U haul. Ah, that will be Bert."

"Park in the shade, Bert," Larry called. "Sit down and have some tea then we'll unload."

"Where's your covered dish, Bert?" asked Ken and Larry.

"Come on, boys," said Bert. "The gin's in the van."

"Did you see Coop over at Bios?"

Yes. He should be on his way."

"My God," Larry said. "You should be honored, Mark. This is not even twilight yet."

"Hey! *Cooper!*" It seemed whenever Cooper appeared in daylight he elicited a cheer.

"Rachel is coming over with a load." Cooper gave his nod and turned back down the porch steps. "I've got some things in the truck," he murmured. "I'll put them in the shed."

"Don't hide away on us, Coop!" Charlotte commanded. "Come straight back!"

"Did you see his shirt?" she asked the others. "What are we saving this week?"

Mark was thinking how Jen had joked on New Year's Eve that he should send Coop a hedgehog shirt from England.

"Pygmies and the rain forests."

"Fair enough!"

Bert left with Ken to get another load from Bios and Cooper followed in his truck. Charlotte was getting worried about space. "You've got rid of your phals," Larry said firmly. "And the pantry will be perfect for a little lab; put in an air conditioner. You never use it. And our Rachel won't change *that* scenario."

Larry went off to the kitchen with the tea tray and Charlotte said she'd go down to see how Carlos was coping. Someone else arrived. Mark went to look. The red Mazda; it was Althea with Ruby's chicken and cornbread.

"How you *doin*? I read about it all in the paper! You guys sure cooked up *something*.

What did you do? Kill a *cow?* I was sorry I couldn't get away to see the show! So what's happening with your president *now?* Wait. Let me get this to keep warm in the oven."

In the kitchen Mark introduced Althea to Larry. "Ah! Doctor *Gibson*, I presume!"

By five Bert and Ken were back with a van full of lab equipment and Coop with his truck. Larry had everything ready in the kitchen with help from Althea: ("No! All I'm doing with *this* man is *laugh!*") Charlotte was rested up and Mark had cleared out the historic remnants from the pantry: ("Charlotte, should guava jelly look this color?") They were only waiting for Rachel.

"Just a few more bottles, Charlotte!" Rachel was on the porch. "Where should Jen put lab stuff? Hey, what's going on?" Jen was behind Rachel, half hidden by the pile of boxes she was carrying.

"Didn't I tell you? Oh dear, that's what happens at my age," Charlotte said innocently. "Just a little get together. Mark hasn't left yet, a little delay to take in our celebration. And how lucky *Jen* should be back! Come on in, Jen! Don't just stand there!"

Jen, hair 'absolutely screaming for help' as Larry would put it, stood there, her faded cotton dress drooping unevenly above a pair of old flip flops. Maybe the ones left in the porch by the recyclables, Mark thought, even as he was telling himself *Jen is back*. Charlotte must have known. Why hadn't she said? Maybe on the same principle as the orchid talk; throw him into it so he wouldn't have time to prepare a statement, organize his thoughts and screw up.

"Put those boxes *down*," commanded Larry. "This is the Hail and Farewell party! Hail to Rachel at Orchid Empire, farewell to Mark and, in fact, Jen, for *you* it's both. Great timing! Where've you *been*? We had no news at all!"

Jen was still in the doorway, frozen, behind her pile of boxes. "I was just helping Rachel. No-one said anything about a party."

"No-one's dressed up!" said Larry comfortingly, though that wasn't true. For the first time Althea was not in her pale blue hospital garb, name tag dangling but a creamy, short sleeved summer suit. Rachel, as always, looked smooth and sun-kissed even in a dusty T-shirt and smudged shorts. Even Cooper looked quite sharp; his shirt not just brand new but, strange for a T-shirt, exactly the right size.

"That's working downtown, right, Jen?" Ken said. "Having to dress up every day. I was the same when I was in hotel management. Get home and it all comes off."

"Oh, I *wish* I had known you then!" Larry exclaimed.

"*I* think you look wonderful," Mark said loudly.

Jen shot him a look round the side of the boxes that was worthy of Regina. There was a brief pause.

"Well, good for you!" Larry filled the silence.

I've done it again! Mark told himself. *What did his sister say?* "*You know, you're not such a bastard with girls, like Ned—I mean you can talk them up but when it's serious you're a bad liar. And you always manage to say the wrong thing. You don't further your cause. Nina says it's kind of sweet but then she's not your sister.*"

Althea was helping with drinks. She and Larry were getting on like a house on fire.

"OK!" said Larry. "Let's call this meeting to order. Althea, does everyone have a drink? Coop, you are *not* allowed to slide off! Not yet!"

"—A question from the floor! Do we have enough for a quorum?" Ken asked. "Well, any Old Business? No treasurer's report, unless Charlotte and Rachel want to report how well they did at Miami. And Bert, too! Let's hear it for the commercial growers! And any news of our one time ruler, Coop?"

"The wheels of justice move slowly," Cooper rolled out the words.

"But you are smiling as you say it, Coop!" exclaimed Larry. "Folks, I have the feeling things are going well. And with reference to the Miami orchid scene's recent dramatic hit—*Fall Of A Titan*—does everyone know the saga of 'Dr Gibson?' Come on, Althea, take the floor!"

Jen was the only one who appeared not to be enjoying the tale. Mark could not catch her eye. Jen, who was always so good at seeing the joke, exchanging a glance, giving support; the face he'd home in on. The face across the crowded room. Not this time.

"Now, New Business: Mark will be off soon, Our man from Kew!"

"Shall I start the clapping?" Ken asked.

"This time let's wait and hear what he's got to say! Mark, a few words, as our distinguished guest."

"OK. I will keep this very brief. This is really the moment to be celebrating the union of two remarkable women, two remarkable *people,* who have worked so hard and achieved so much. I don't have to say more. Ladies and gentlemen, please raise your glasses to Orchid Empire and Bios Orchids, to Charlotte and Rachel!"

"Mark, you must say a few words about yourself before you sit down," Larry declared over the applause. "It's in the rules."

"OK," Mark started slowly. "I have learned much from living among you, no, not just the quaint customs of orchid vending. Though I must say, I have discovered you could sell an old boot if it has buds on it. But how many people here, let alone in North London or South Beach, for that matter, have cornered a possum in the kitchen armed only with a pair of oven mitts?" Jen was still looking down at the floor, her Rosita look. "I've also learned you can hose toad venom right out of a dog's mouth. You don't need the vet! On a more serious note. You know, I have come to realize I am very like my dear Aunt Charlotte. Larry, it's true! We both have a hard time expressing our emotions, the classic English problem." Jen was resolutely studying the floorboards at the back, perched on the corner of one of the old, extra long, imperial couches. "I've had such a great time here. I feel so fond of you all but you won't catch me saying it." There was a burst of laughter and everyone clapped.

Aren't there Americans like that, Jen? Up near Canada, in the colder parts? Cooper and Althea had moved further in. Jen now had a straight run for the porch. Mark was afraid she was going to slide out: 'Do a Coop' as they said, and just leave. Bert was being elected by voice vote to make the formal speech congratulating Charlotte and Rachel on their merger. Mark yielded the floor and made his way to the back of the room. He stood in the porch doorway, blocking Jen's escape route.

"—So you didn't take the cat?" Bert's voice was not very loud so Mark had to almost whisper.

"Rachel said the cat just disappeared when I left." Jen answered so softly it was almost a hiss. Looking at her expression Mark decided that was no accident.

"Where is it now?"

"Sitting by the front door. Seems it was waiting for me to come back."

"Weren't we all!" Mark meant to keep it light but sincere, but realized, once again with Jen, he had either said the wrong thing or said it the wrong way.

"Look, I'm going. I'm not *dressed* for this. I was just doing *one* trip to help Rachel with the last stuff before having a shower. I'm certainly *not* in the mood for a party or anything else and I've got a *lot* to do."

"When are you actually leaving?"

"Soon as I've sorted out everything here."

"Oh. What do you think of Rachel and Charlotte getting together?"

"Like we said. Seems like a good idea." The dogs started barking. Soon be time to feed them, Mark thought. He'd have to tell Rachel how much and not to worry if Bella hung back. Not that she was shy, just always on the look out for something better than the chow. "Excuse me!" Jen had got tired of Mark standing in the doorway. He followed her out to the porch. Behind them they could hear Bert raising a laugh. Jen turned round, keeping her voice low. "*Why* do you always have to say these dumb things?"

Mark wondered which dumb thing was that, realizing that where Jen was concerned there always seemed to be a number to choose from.

"Why did you say in front of everyone 'You look *wonderful!*' I *look like shit!* And it's none of your business anyway! What *is* it with you? Some silly British thing, your 'great sense of humor?' Are you like that with every girl? *Oh, you look nice! Oh, you smell nice! Sur-prise!* Sometimes it's just not funny. In fact, it's never really funny and I'm certainly not in the mood for it, now. OK?" Jen stopped and took a breath. "You know, after ... OK. I can't figure you out, that's all and I've giving up trying."

"Jen, I think you're going to have to put up with the fact that I will always say the wrong thing. I mean, I thought I'd never see you again and so when I saw you..." Mark trailed off.

Jen looked at him suspiciously, waiting for the punch-line, the smart remark, or, what seemed more likely, thought Mark, the smart remark gone wrong. "*Everyone* knew I was coming back! I had to get my things!"

"Well, no one told me," Mark mumbled.

"Come and eat everybody! It's all laid out in the kitchen!" They could hear Larry. "Just bring it through, *a la buffet.*"

"We'd better go eat," Jen said. "Otherwise it'll be a big deal."

Mark wished he had an appetite. Ruby's classic southern fried chicken and corn bread were balanced to perfection as Larry pointed out modestly by his deftly low-cal, multi-green salad, and the artichokes and salmon. Jen did not pile her plate high; she didn't even fill it. She was insisting to everyone she must go; there was just too much still to do.

"What?" Rachel exclaimed. "Jen, almost everything's out!" Just leaving *How to Improve Your Golf Swing* for the next tenant, Mark thought. He could see that dark green volume lasting through the years, unmoved on the shelf, like the Gideon bible.

Everyone had raised their voices in protest so Jen for the moment seemed to have given up the idea of making her getaway. She had begun talking earnestly to Bert. Maybe saying goodbye. Then she moved on to Larry and Ken. Larry was trying to make Jen laugh. Not succeeding. Not even *Larry*, Mark told himself. Althea now had turned to talk to the three of them. And Jen was smiling. Probably something about how daft he was. God, maybe about a proposal of marriage. If that was going the rounds, he might as well give up.

"Charlotte says you got the label program going quite well. You've got to show me." Rachel had sat down on the arm of Mark's couch. Just at that moment Jen looked their way. "So you're off to South Beach! That's cool! A break from all this."

"I'm really so pleased you and Charlotte are getting together," Mark said. "Apart from anything else, it will stop my mother from worrying."

"It's going to be great. Not just the financial side. I just think Charlotte is the bomb. And there's so much I can learn from her."

"You should run for President of the Miami Orchid Club."

"Ha! Wait till I'm an accredited judge!"

"Charlotte," Mark raised his voice," don't you think Rachel will make a great MOC President some day?"

Charlotte gave a cackle. "You bet! She'll upset some apple carts!"

"Won't suffer fools gladly?" Mark asked. Jen had gone. Just like that. Mark had just taken his eyes off her for a moment. She was not in the Florida room any more. Coop was gone too but that was standard. Maybe they were talking on the porch. Mark stood up. "Hey, Rachel. We'll check the label program later, OK?"

Jen was leaning on the porch rail close to Cooper. Not another complication, thought Mark. Cooper turned when he saw Mark. "Jen's been telling me her plans. It's all coming along, all blending together!" He gave his precise and gentle nod and made off down the steps. Maybe if you're into cosmic spaces and lofty contemplation, thought Mark. For the rest of us, California and the UK are a hell of a long way apart.

"Must be nice for Cooper, able to see the whole world as one like that," Mark said. "Did you notice? I've just realized, Cooper never makes the dogs bark." There was a burst of noise from inside. Mark could hear Althea's laugh. "So you're off to California...Congratulations."

"Who told you that?"

"Charlotte. Said you'd got this great job in Bristol."

"Yes, Bristol. Bristol, UK."

"You mean Bristol, England?"

"I don't think there *is* a Bristol in California."

"What?"

"I'd wanted to ask you about it, what you thought of the place, that evening in the mall, but—"

"But I was useless. As usual. I was really looking for a pub."

"Oh. How far is Bristol from London?"

"God, it's all Mickey Mouse distances after the US. Maybe two hours, less than Miami to Orlando, must be... Much less. I've never really checked it out." Silence. "Jen, I've been thinking you'd got some great job in California. Gone for ever."

"What happened to the whole idea of Rachel?"

"That's it exactly. It was just an idea. And, you know, Rachel has no real sense of humor."

"So the rest of us humble beings have a chance if we laugh in the right places?"

"Yes! *No!* Come *on!* Jen. It's obvious at critical moments I'll always say the wrong thing when I'm with you, drunk or sober. You're just going to have to accept it. It's a sign I'm serious. Actually, it's a very romantic thing. Ask my sister." Suddenly it hit Mark. Jen *would* be able to ask his sister: it was Bristol. *Bristol, England.* "Hang on. Christ, you'll meet Ned. No, I'll lock him up. You're going to meet my sister. She'll try and put you off me because that's what sisters do. She won't want to *further my cause.* Well, not till she's had some fun. Like Charlotte.

God! I'll have to keep you away from the family. You've already heard about Uncle Frank. Take no notice if he says he wants to drop a bomb on you. 'That's just his way,' as my dear mother says. Well, at least you can see where I get it from. No, in fact, I'm giving the wrong message again. I *should* be saying: *Will* you meet my family?

Isn't that what we're supposed to say to prove we're serious?...Jen? Jen, I don't think you can take the cat. I know we've got these heavy duty rules about dogs. You'll have to find a home for her here. No good at Orchid Empire now that Rachel is here with all her bottles. Shame. It would have been the right place. We've got rats, I know. And the dogs are useless. One ran past Tod the other night and he just looked. Waiting for his chow. Tod, I mean, though probably the rat too. Of course, Larry and Ken have those three ferocious Persians...Maybe Bert or what about Coop? A mellow environment. But he's a vegetarian. Vegetarian cat food—that's not fair on a cat."

"Sometimes you don't need to talk at all," said Jen quietly, beginning to smile. She had moved along the porch rail almost to the broken part with the chicken wire and was looking down into the leaves.

Mark thought about what Jen had just said for a moment. And what it might mean. "Trouble is, in the States there's such a distance between people," he started. He was recognizing, finally, a magic moment and knowing, no doubt, he was about to ruin it. "And if there's always going to be such a distance between us then I'm not sure *what* the outcome will be."

"But I told you I'm coming to England."

Mark looked at Jen's hands in the moonlight holding tight to the old porch rail about six feet away.

"No, actually," he said, "I meant right now."